PRAISE FOR ANTHONY SLAYTON

Slayton gets everything right—the fairly planted clues, plot twists and characters who are more than stereotypes. P.G. Wodehouse fans will want to have a look.

— PUBLISHER'S WEEKLY

Thanks to vivid writing, lively characters, and quietly snarky humor...this entertaining mystery hits all the right genre buttons in a fresh way. An English country house mystery infused with humor, verve, and plenty of surprises.

— KIRKUS REVIEWS

Reminiscent of the tone of classic mysteries which deliver suspects, clues, and questions around every corner...A Most Efficient Murder is clever, enjoyable, charming, and a must-read for all historical mystery lovers.

— READER'S FAVORITE

ALSO BY ANTHONY SLAYTON

A Quite Deadly Affair

A Most Efficient Murder

A RATHER DASTARDLY DEATH

A RATHER DASTARDLY DEATH

ANTHONY SLAYTON

Copyright © 2023 by Anthony Slayton

All rights reserved.

No part of this book may be reproduced in any form or by any electronic or mechanical means, including information storage and retrieval systems, without written permission from the author, except for the use of brief quotations in a book review.

For my mother, who always said I should write mysteries

DRAMATIS PERSONAE

Lord Edward Statham, *the 13th Earl of Unsworth*

Hon. Frances (Fanny) Statham, *His Niece*

Hon. Arthur Druce, *His Nephew*

Lady Constance, *His Elder Sister, and Arthur's Mother*

Mr. Quayle, *Lord Unsworth's Highly Efficient Secretary and Sometime-Sleuth*

Lady Rosaline Barrett De Marchi, *a Thrice-Widowed and Altogether Scandalous Figure*

Hon. Raymond Montague Barrett, *Her Son*

Hon. Genevieve (Vivi) Barrett, *His Wife*

Lord Clarence Weatherford, *an Influential Publisher and Newspaperman.*

Count Scarlioni, *an Italian Nobleman of Considerable Charm and Dubious Pedigree.*

Countess Scarlioni, *His Wife*

Herr Darvas, *the Elderly Curator of the Musée de Saint-Jean le Décapité*

Márta, *His Research Assistant and Daughter*

George Dabney, *an Amateur Sportsman Who Once Raced the Blue Train for a Bet*

Jean-Paul Léger, *a Noted Painter and Sculptor*

Anne-Marie, *His Wife and a Former Painter in Her Own Right.*

Joseph Hollins, *a Socialist and Aspiring Playwright*

Henry Carrodus, *a Distinguished Playwright in the Twilight of his Career*

Sir Julius Markham-Smythe, *an Aristocratic Socialite and Impoverished Journalist*

M. Tallier, *a Gentleman from the Sûreté*

M. Jarre, *the Juge d'Instruction or Examining Magistrate*

PROLOGUE

DEATH ON THE BLUE TRAIN

Afterwards, everyone agreed it was the soup that killed him. Although it must be said that even before his untimely demise, Lord Clarence Weatherford—owner and founder of the illustrious Weatherford Publishing House and onetime editor-in-chief of the *London Chronicle*—had not exactly been enjoying his dinner.

Well-known in certain circles—infamous even—for being a man of very particular gastronomical and dietary preferences, Lord Weatherford had recently been forced to limit his already narrow diet. His doctors were concerned about his weight, you see, or possibly his heart. But, as a spokesman for the Paris-Lyon-Méditerranée Railway Company later insisted, it was not the food itself which had spoiled His Lordship's appetite. Certainly not! The world-famous Blue Train was the absolute pinnacle of steam-powered luxury, and its dining car —resplendent with bone-white china and extravagant five-course meals—was more than capable of meeting His Lordship's exacting dietary requirements.

Indeed, in any other circumstance, Lord Weatherford might have allowed himself an audible sigh of satisfaction after that first spoonful. But not that night, alas! That night, he barely noticed the taste or the smell. Perhaps if he had paid closer attention, His Lordship might have caught the faint hint of almonds where no almonds should be.

Perhaps.

* * *

As the first course was served, Lord Weatherford noted absently that the waiter—a young man of Swiss extraction—had ignored all his careful instructions and that the dish in front of him, while no doubt deliciously rich and creamy, would not have been approved by a single one of His Lordship's over-priced doctors. Those fools!

Lord Weatherford scowled. He was fit as a fiddle! Healthier than many men half his age! Still, that was doctors for you—worriers, the lot of them. And Soupe à l'oignon Lyonnaise *was* a particular favorite of his.

Weatherford's first spoonful left a bitter aftertaste in his mouth, but he paid no heed. Having indulged himself in this one small rebellion against the tyranny of the medical profession, he soon turned his mind to other matters.

A newspaperman by training and inclination, Lord Weatherford amused himself by listening with half an ear to the low murmur of conversation around him. Most of what he overheard was in English, of course. The Riviera was *the* preferred playground for the wealthiest of Weatherford's countrymen, after all, but he also caught snippets of French and German and a few mutterings of Italian here and there.

From what Weatherford could tell, the favored topics of conversation appeared to be either the exploits of a gentleman thief known in France and beyond as La Chimère, or the newly christened "Trial of the Century"—the so-called Unsworth Murders.

Lord Weatherford scoffed into his napkin. *Trial of the Century, indeed!* In the past decade alone, no less than six different trials had earned that epithet, all forgotten now. In time, this one, too, would pass from memory, but until then, Weatherford could not help but feel a distant sort of sympathy for Lord Unsworth's plight.

The two men had never been close friends, but in their youth they had both shared one or two interests in common. So, when asked, Weatherford had done his best to accommodate Unsworth's secretary, a quiet, efficient little chap with an odd name—something to do with a bird, he thought—and had made sure the *London Chronicle* was comparatively gentle in its coverage. But only up to a point. People loved a good murder, after all.

It was funny, Weatherford reflected, how things turned out. Until recently, he hadn't thought about Unsworth for years, and now the man was everywhere—plastered across Weatherford's own headlines. It was as if all Lord Weatherford's old ghosts were gathering at once.

Even being here on the train brought back memories. Once a regular visitor, Weatherford hadn't travelled to the Riviera in years and, in truth, never thought he would again. But the summons had been urgent in its abruptness:

IN TROUBLE. STOP. NEED HELP. STOP. COME AT ONCE. STOP.

No one else on Earth could have dragged Lord Weatherford from house and home with such few words, but she had always been different. *Always.*

His Lordship sighed at the memory. Lady Rosaline Barrett De Marchi—the infamous Widow of Treville-sur-Mer—had been a penniless actress at some backwater theater when Lord Weatherford had first met her. But within a few short years, she had all but conquered the globe—dazzling audiences from West End to Broadway, from Salzburg to Paris. Until, suddenly, while still at the height of her success, she had abandoned the stage to embark upon an equally successful marital career—for a given definition of success.

Widowed thrice over since then, her trail of death, heartbreak, and scandal had been, at one time, the talk of Europe and fodder for countless headlines and gossip columns. Since then, her star had faded from public view, but unlike most of her former admirers, Lord Weatherford had never deserted her. Recently he had even agreed—against his better judgment—to publish her rather salacious memoirs. It was a prospect which had already caused a great deal of consternation in certain circles. Her old admirers may have forgotten her, but to their dismay, they discovered she had not forgotten them.

Indeed, not! Lord Weatherford had heard from several sources that Rosaline had begun sending out letters—hundreds and hundreds of them—to many of her former acquaintances, friends, and lovers, discreetly offering to either alter their names or remove them from her upcoming memoirs—all for a small fee, naturally.

Now, Weatherford had no personal qualms about blackmail. It came with the territory, but, in his opinion, Rosaline was being exceedingly reckless. After all, her old lovers weren't the only ones with skeletons in their cupboards, not by a long shot. Her past, too, was a briar patch full of stings and nettles, and no one knew that better than Weatherford.

Distractedly ladling another spoonful of soup with one hand, Lord Weatherford found the other reaching into his left breast pocket almost of its own accord. And as his fingers brushed against the crinkling yellow paper inside, he breathed a quiet sigh of relief.

Still secret. Still safe.

He had committed every word of that ancient letter to memory. Of course he had. Its contents had changed the trajectory of his life along with so many others. And it was proof that long, long ago, the future Lord Weatherford had done the soon-to-be Lady Rosaline a great and terrible service, and now he feared they might both pay the price.

Lord Weatherford frowned suddenly. Something was wrong! He could feel a strange pain stabbing into his side, and when he brought his napkin to his lips, it came away bloody.

"Garçon!" he cried out, but the waiter's back was turned. "Garçon—"

The words choked in Weatherford's throat, and he collapsed back in his chair, too woozy to think or speak. The dining car itself seemed to be spinning all around him, while the familiar clink of cutlery and tinkling of glasses echoed painfully in his mind, each noise sharp and dagger-like in his ears. And beneath it all came the constant rumbling of the train, thundering in time with the damnable pain in his chest.

He was dying, Lord Weatherford realized in an excruciating moment of clarity, and in those final moments, his hand made its slow, trembling way back towards his breast pocket and the letter within.

To have and to hold—

"Here, monsieur," said a waiter, looming out of the spinning, swirling confusion. "Let me help you."

* * *

Lord Weatherford's death somewhere between Cannes and Nice caused something of an uproar in the luxury dining car. Two Russian princesses, a count, and an elderly Bavarian knight all fainted in the excitement, but the head waiter moved with admirable speed and efficiency to reassure the other passengers. Smelling salts were acquired, drinks were poured, and suitably salutary words were spoken—first in French and then in increasing accented Italian, German, and English.

A doctor came aboard at Nice, accompanied by a Commissary of Police, who together made quick work of the investigation but proved considerably slower when it came to the paperwork.

Lord Weatherford was determined to be a gentleman of elderly persuasion with a known history of heart troubles and a cantankerous habit of ignoring sound medical advice. In light of these facts, the soup was quickly considered the most likely culprit. However, in deference to the Paris-Lyon-Méditerranée Railway Company, the offending dish did not appear on any official report, and the cause of death was listed as a heart attack.

In the interest of thoroughness, however, it should be mentioned that the Commissary *did*, in fact, note that a telegram had been found in Lord Weatherford's right jacket pocket. Its contents were dutifully transcribed by one of his deputies and filed in the appropriate manner. No mention was made of a letter, however, and when the jacket was returned to England—along with His Lordship's body—the pocket in question was found to be entirely empty.

It would be several long months, and at least two more bodies, before foul play was even remotely suspected.

And that would only be thanks to the largely unrelated efforts of a certain quiet, efficient little chap with an odd name.

Something to do with a bird.

PART I

THE WIDOW OF TREVILLE-SUR-MER

1

MR. QUAYLE ON THE RIVIERA

Mr. Quayle was not, he reflected sadly, enjoying his time on the Riviera—not in the least. Oh, it was beautiful, to be sure! The sun-drenched coast and achingly blue seas were as bewitching as promised. And Quayle longed with all his heart to wander the little fishing villages and towns, to practice his rusting, pidgin French at the varied stalls and markets, and, most of all, to lose himself amidst the oleander trees and olive groves. But, alas, such pleasures were not for him—not yet.

It had only been a little over a month since his employer, the Thirteenth Earl of Unsworth, had gathered what remained of the family and fled to the south of France, hoping to escape the scandal that threatened to consume them. It was a desperate hope, in Mr. Quayle's opinion, but he could hardly fault His Lordship for trying.

As Lord Unsworth's personal secretary, Quayle had gone far above and beyond the call of duty, doing his best to protect the family's reputation in the weeks and months leading up to the trial. But in the end, no matter what tricks Quayle employed or how he wriggled and connived, the truth was incontrovertible. After all, he had uncovered it himself. The family *had* been involved in the murders—involved up to their necks—and even in France, there was no escaping that fact.

Not that Mr. Quayle begrudged his labors on behalf of the family. After all, he owed Lord Unsworth a great deal—his livelihood, for one. After Quayle's rather ignominious departure from Whitehall two years ago, potential employers had been few and far between, but Lord Unsworth had accepted him with open arms and had never asked a single awkward question. His Lordship required discretion from his servants and retainers but was always willing to offer the same in return. Mr. Quayle appreciated that more than he could say, but it was to Lord Unsworth's *son*—to the lamented Lieutenant Colonel Theodore "Teddy" Statham—that his true debt was owed. And it was in Colonel Statham's memory Quayle had labored—solving not one but three murders, and doing his best to blunt the aftermath. But now he was tired, so very tired. He could feel it in his limbs and in his thoughts. Some nights, he was so tired he *dreamed* of sleep, and he had hoped their little French excursion would give him the time he needed to rest. But it was not to be!

Within a few days of their arrival, Lord Unsworth had asked Mr. Quayle to keep a quiet, watchful eye on His Lordship's nephew, the Hon. Arthur Druce, a task which soon proved as exasperating as ever. Having learned nothing from his brief stint as a murder suspect, Arthur had taken to frequenting the casinos at Monte Carlo and fallen in with a dubious set of gamblers, adventurers, and cardsharps. And so, following in Arthur's wake, Mr. Quayle had traded the fresh, pine-scented air and vast, stunning vistas for hazy, smoke-filled rooms.

Mr. Quayle glanced down to check his watch, though he could barely read it properly in the haze and gloom. It was nearly five o'clock. Two long tables dominated the center of the room, each ringed by an ever-present throng of gamblers and onlookers—widows and heiresses, politicians and princes—all pressed in close as they watched in rapt attention while fortunes were lost and won and lost again.

Arthur was seated in the far corner, away from the press of the crowd, enthusiastically trying his hand at baccarat as he had been these past few weeks. In fairness, Mr. Quayle was forced to admit that Arthur was not a *terrible* player, but he was an *inconsistent* one, much to the delight of his new friends, the mysterious Count and Countess Francesco and Lucia Scarlioni.

Naturally, Mr. Quayle had made it his business to discover all he could about them and what he had found did not fill him with confidence. There was something almost sinister about their interest in Arthur, and Quayle wouldn't trust them as far as he could throw them.

"Ah, Monsieur Quayle! I thought I might see you here!"

Mr. Quayle turned, startled, to find an owlish, well-dressed little Frenchman pushing his way toward him through the crowd.

"Monsieur Tallier," Quayle greeted. "This is a surprise."

"A pleasant one, I trust?"

"Naturally," Mr. Quayle replied, and meant it. The two men had struck up a casual acquaintance over the past few weeks—one of the trip's few bright spots in Mr. Quayle's estimation—and found they shared both a keen eye and a wry sense of humor.

It was curious, though. Despite only ever encountering the man at the casino, Mr. Quayle could not recall a single instance of Tallier trying his hand at any of the tables—not roulette, baccarat or even blackjack—and the Frenchman had also proven to be *remarkably* well-informed about the various personalities around them. Indeed, much of Mr. Quayle's information about Arthur's new friends had come from Tallier.

"I haven't seen you in a few days," Mr. Quayle said. "I was worried you might have gotten lost."

"Not at all. I simply had some business to take care of," Tallier replied.

"*Business?*" Mr. Quayle raised an eyebrow expectantly, but M. Tallier feigned not to notice.

"Keeping as close an eye as ever, I take it?" he said instead, glancing over at Arthur.

"Always." Mr. Quayle accepted the blatant sidestep without pursuing the matter. It was hardly the first time M. Tallier had avoided the topic, and on the Riviera, discretion was the rule rather than the exception. Ask me no questions and I'll tell you no lies, as the saying went.

"You're worried about him, non?" Tallier asked.

"Always," Mr. Quayle repeated with a wry smile. "Arthur has an amazing talent for landing himself in the most absurdly troublesome situations."

"Ah, oui, I might have read a thing or two in the paper," M. Tallier admitted. "Something about falling in love with his father's mistress and absconding out the window in the middle of a police investigation?"

Mr. Quayle frowned. It had been impossible to hide Arthur's stint as a fugitive—after all, there had been a countywide manhunt—but Quayle *had* managed to keep some of the more embarrassing details out of the papers. Even the attorneys at the trial had—after some gentle persuasion—been obligingly circumspect.

"Where did you hear about the window?" Mr. Quayle asked.

"I told you," M. Tallier replied. "I must have read about it somewhere."

"Mm. Perhaps." Despite enjoying the other man's

company, Mr. Quayle harbored no illusions that Tallier had approached him by mere happenstance. There was a purpose to the Frenchman's interest in him and in the Unsworth family, and while Mr. Quayle did not believe it to be malicious per se, it was undoubtedly pointed.

"They've offered him another loan," Mr. Quayle said, testing the waters. "Quite a substantial sum this time."

"The Count and Countess." It was not a question, and despite his best efforts, M. Tallier could not quite conceal his quickening interest, just as Mr. Quayle had hoped.

"Indeed." Mr. Quayle indicated the table, where Arthur—flanked on one side by the tall, austere figure of the Count and on the other by the Countess' striking, glamorous visage—was in the process of losing for the fourth time that hour. "That's *their* money he's squandering," Mr. Quayle said darkly.

"Have you spoken to the boy?"

"I've had a quiet word or two," Mr. Quayle admitted. "He said they were being *kind*."

"Those two are never kind, mon ami."

"No," Mr. Quayle agreed. "I wouldn't have thought so."

"What have you done, then?"

"Done?" Mr. Quayle shrugged. "Nothing. I work for the family, but I'm not one of them. And Arthur—Lord help us!—is a grown man. If he wants to consort with suspicious characters and accept dubious loans, that's his own affair. I'm not his mother."

"But you *could* inform his mother."

"What? And bring Lady Constance crashing down on his head every time he makes a mistake? Arthur would never trust me again." Besides, Quayle thought to himself, in this matter, he was acting on His Lordship's instructions, not Her Ladyship's, and he had no intention of being caught in the middle. Not if he could help it.

"So, instead, you're giving him enough rope to hang himself…"

"I was rather hoping to cut the rope *before* it comes to that."

"Be careful, mon ami." M. Tallier placed a warning hand on Quayle's arm. "The Count and Countess are not to be trifled with. You must have heard the rumors."

"Some of them."

"They are said to have fled Mussolini's Italy for…political reasons," M. Tallier whispered. "But there are those who believe they are suspiciously close to the Italian ambassador and that they might have a *different* role to play…"

"Spies, you mean." Mr. Quayle shot M. Tallier a quick, searching glance. Was that it, then? Was that M. Tallier's true identity—a spy catcher circling his prey? Mr. Quayle sighed. What had Arthur stumbled into this time?

"That's one possibility," M. Tallier agreed.

"But what would two Italian spies want with Arthur?" Mr. Quayle wondered.

"Je ne sai pas." M. Tallier shrugged. "Probably nothing, but there are *other* rumors about their activities."

"Ah, yes." Mr. Quayle had heard those rumors too, but surely a pair of charlatans and mountebanks could find a more promising victim than Arthur Druce! The man was all-but-bankrupt. Still, they *were* paying Arthur an inordinate amount of attention, going out of their way to make his acquaintance, and encouraging all his worst habits. But to what end?

There would be time enough to ponder their motives later, however. For now, he and Arthur had a more pressing engagement, and it was well past time they were on their way.

"If you will excuse me, M. Tallier," he said with a regretful tilt of the head, "I really should be collecting Arthur. We have a busy night ahead."

"Oh?"

"Yes." Mr. Quayle's lips twitched in what could have been a scowl. Like his employer, he was not particularly social at the best of times. "Lady Rosaline Barrett De Marchi is throwing a party tonight."

"Lady Rosaline! So, Arthur has merited an invitation from the Widow of Treville-sur-Mer, has he? Quite an honor."

"The whole family has," Mr. Quayle explained. "Even *I* was invited for some reason."

"Well, of course, mon ami." M. Tallier laughed outright. "You're quite the curiosity yourself—the secretary who solved Lord Unsworth's little murders."

"I didn't solve anything!" Mr. Quayle protested ingenuously but retreated in the face of M. Tallier's disbelieving stare. "That is to say, I may have assisted the police in their investigations, but I never—"

"You are too modest, monsieur." M. Tallier shook his head in mock disapproval. "Far too modest. It was *you* who discovered this Major's lies, non? Who ferreted the truth out of your war records?"

"I have no idea what you're talking about," Mr. Quayle lied. That was another piece of information he had deliberately kept out of the papers. Indeed, Quayle had done his utmost to downplay his own role in events, especially when it came to any *connections* he might have in the War Office. "And now, if you'll excuse me, monsieur—"

"Bien sûr!" M. Tallier waved him away. "The Widow's villa awaits. I hear she throws the most sumptuous parties."

"Mm." Mr. Quayle took his leave warily. Tallier had revealed a depth of knowledge in the past few minutes that was, frankly, concerning. Perhaps Quayle had been too quick to judge the Frenchman's purpose benign. But again, that was a problem for another time.

Straightening his shoulders, Mr. Quayle made his way

carefully through the press of humanity toward the baccarat table. He was not looking forward to extracting Arthur from the Count and Countess. Since coming to the Riviera, Arthur had regained much of his obstinate, reckless self—urged on, no doubt, by his two new benefactors—and was becoming harder and harder to manage.

But then, Mr. Quayle reflected, Arthur was not the only one retreating into old, familiar patterns.

2

THE GREAT ARTIST AND HIS WIFE

No one was watching as Fanny strode out to the edge of the cliff and stared down at the waters of the Mediterranean glistening far below. Standing there on the precipice with her eyes closed and her head thrown back, she took a moment to luxuriate in the warmth of the sun on her face, and listen to the sound of distant birds crying and circling overhead. It had been an eternity since Fanny had last felt so at peace with herself. Free from prying eyes and gossiping tongues. Free from the nagging voice whispering in her ear, from the endless self-recriminations, the judgment, the guilt, and—worst of all—from the *embarrassment*.

Fanny felt her cheeks, already warm from the sun, reddening at the shame of it. She had thought herself so clever, so discerning—not at all like dear Cousin Arthur—but in the end, Fanny had been no less fooled and no less foolish.

Since then, she had gone over events again and again in her mind searching for something—anything—that she might have missed, but to no avail. There was *nothing*, not a hint or a sign of the treachery to come. That should have made her feel better, but it hadn't. All it meant was that she was still blind, even with the benefit of hindsight. And Fanny refused to be blind any more, refused to be tricked a second time. Never again.

She opened her eyes with a sigh and, gazing down, turned towards the village of Treville-sur-Mer. A forest of masts and sails rose from the docks and quays, while brick rooves and painted houses—orange, pink, and blue—hugged the shoreline before sloping here and there upward into the hills and orchards above. It was a picturesque little town, almost from another century—serene and peaceful. But Fanny didn't want serenity. She wanted noise and distraction. She wanted an escape and she had found one—of a sort.

FANNY TURNED AWAY from the grand vista before her and back toward the house. She had absented herself from their little gathering for as long as she could without being churlish or impolite, but had no desire to be rude to her hosts—or at least not to her *hostess*.

The house itself was a charming little cottage nestled quietly amongst the trees, and in her short time on the Riviera, it had quickly become something of a home away from home for Fanny—moreso than the monstrosity her aunt and uncle had rented a few miles down the coast.

The cottage was home to the acclaimed French artist and sculptor, Jean-Paul Léger, and his wife, Anne-Marie. They had both—Anne-Marie especially—been quite welcoming, and Fanny had allowed herself to be drawn into the small group of writers, artists, and playwrights over which the famed couple presided. Although, it might be more accurate to say it was Jean-Paul Léger alone who presided—or rather, held court—while Madame Léger played the dutiful wife and hostess. It was a role to which she was long accustomed, her devotion seemingly undiminished by her husband's litany of rumored affairs or by his decades of towering self-aggrandizement.

That was the legend, at least, but it had not taken Fanny long to spot the cracks in the façade, and to her eyes, Madame Léger was more seething than devoted. Whatever patience the older woman might have once had was clearly running thin. Not that Fanny could blame her.

As she approached the cottage, Fanny saw Madame Léger coming down the garden path from her husband's studio—a cube-shaped outbuilding set away from the main house, where the Great Man could paint and sculpt to his heart's content.

Madame Léger was a brittle, dignified woman in her late forties or early fifties—Fanny had difficulty distinguishing the age of anyone over twenty-five—who still retained more than a trace of her youthful vivaciousness and attractiveness when she smiled.

She was not smiling now, however, and gave a little start when she noticed Fanny watching her.

"Fanny!" she cried, slipping a key into her pocket. "I thought you were inside with the others."

"I was," Fanny replied. "But I stepped out for some fresh air and thought I'd take a moment to enjoy the view."

"Yes," Madame Léger agreed, following her gaze out toward the sea. "It *is* breathtaking, isn't it? We bought this cottage nearly fifteen years ago now. Of course, in those days, we were still mostly living in Paris, but even after we moved here year-round—"

This time Madame Léger did smile, and her face was transformed into something bright, innocent and young.

"—Well," she continued, "they say familiarity breeds contempt, but that view, at least, never grows old."

"No, I imagine not." Fanny was trying to decide what did,

in fact, grow old when Madame Léger took her by the arm and led her toward the patio doors.

"Come along, dear," she said. "We shouldn't leave that young man of yours alone for too long."

"He's not *my* young man!" Fanny protested, perhaps a touch too loudly.

"Of course not, dear." Madame Léger patted her hand soothingly. "Of course not. But he'd like to be, non?"

Fanny opened her mouth, another denial ready on her lips, but Madame Léger's gaze was far too knowing. Unable to meet those merciless, teasing eyes, Fanny turned away, grumbling under her breath.

He wasn't her young man! She hadn't been lying when she'd said that. But she hadn't been telling the truth either and Madame Léger knew it. Damn her!

Madame Léger laughed and, murmuring something about 'young love' which made Fanny's blood boil, ushered them in through the back door.

* * *

INSIDE, the cottage was filled to bursting with the fruits of Jean-Paul Léger's career. Every wall was covered floor to ceiling in *his* paintings and sketches; every available surface was laden with *his* sculptures and an array of *his* preliminary models and maquettes.

Looking around, Fanny wondered—and not for the first time—what it must be like for Madame Léger to spend her days living in what amounted to a museum dedicated solely and exhaustively to *her husband's* greatness. It was not a pleasant thought.

The others—a motley group of artists, sculptors, writers, and various hangers-on—were gathered in the drawing room, listening intently as Léger expounded on the philosophical nature of art and railed quite vigorously against those upstart Cubists and Surrealists. His sermon on the settee was met with a sea of nodding heads, but Fanny couldn't help but notice one or two of them biting their tongues.

Perhaps the Great Man's grip on his disciples was not nearly as tight as he would have liked. Perhaps, at last, the world was beginning to pass him by! Although, Fanny reflected, if Léger was still referring to the Cubists as upstarts, perhaps the world had passed him by a long time ago. Certainly, he appeared far older than his wife, although only a scant few years separated them.

One of the acolytes separated himself from the others. A handsome young man with reddish hair and a hangdog expression, he approached Fanny eagerly.

"Where were you?" he asked, his tone a quiver shy of reproachful.

His name was Joseph Hollins, and he was decidedly *not* Fanny's young man, no matter what Madame Léger or, for that matter, Hollins himself chose to believe.

"I took a quick stroll in the garden," she replied and watched as Mr. Hollins clearly wanted to ask why she hadn't invited him along and then just as clearly thought better of it.

The poor man! He wasn't nearly as subtle as he thought he was. But these days, that very quality, more than anything, was what appealed to Fanny.

Hollins was an aspiring playwright and an avowed socialist without money or prospects. He had held a job once at one of Lord Weatherford's many newspapers but had quit, purportedly on political grounds, and run away to join the theater.

It was all quite romantic—at least in his own telling—but Hollins' political leanings had not, Fanny noted, prevented him from pursuing her—the Earl of Unsworth's distinctly *aristocratic* niece—or from idolizing Léger's one-time friend and neighbor, the celebrated but decidedly *bourgeoise* playwright Henry Carrodus.

No, as far as Fanny was concerned, Joseph Hollins was, at best, a grasping, moderately talented, and wholly hypocritical young man. Entirely unsuitable for the future Countess of Unsworth!

Of course, after the fiasco last year, such characteristics only made Hollins more perfect in Fanny's eyes. The Major, after all, had been *eminently* suitable, but he had turned out to be a liar and a murderer. And while Hollins might lack the courage of his convictions, he was hardly a killer. Besides, Hollins made her laugh, and laughter was supposedly the best medicine.

The clock on the wall struck the half-hour, jolting Fanny from her thoughts. It was about time they started making their excuses. Hollins met her gaze and nodded, having reached the same conclusion.

Fanny turned, searching for Madame Léger. Not wanting to offend, she preferred to have a quiet word in her hostess' ear. Hollins, however, chose a different tact.

"Fanny and I have been invited to Lady Rosaline's party this evening!" he explained, practically giddy with glee.

It was understandable, of course. Hollins had been trying to approach Lady Rosaline for months, desperately seeking her patronage, and tonight, at long last, he would have his chance. But the home of Jean-Paul Léger was not the ideal place for such a pronouncement.

Indeed, within a moment, the air—largely congenial, if a trifle stifling thus far—grew tense, almost threatening, and all eyes turned to Léger. Clutching a wine glass in his trembling hand, he rose to his still considerable height. Even stooped and arched, he towered over the room like some fading colossus and stared down at Hollins with fury in his eyes.

Watching, Fanny could only sigh. There was a reason she had tried to be discreet.

Like many artists of his generation, Léger owed much of his early success to Lady Rosaline's generous patronage. For decades he had painted only in the styles *she* had dictated, had art shows only in the galleries *she* had chosen, and had sold his pieces only to collectors *she* had approved, including his erstwhile rival for her affections—Lord Weatherford.

Her connections and her direction had, without a doubt, made Léger one of the wealthiest and most revered painters in Europe, but eventually, he came to be seen as Lady Rosaline's creature—her tame little artist.

And so, desperate to succeed on his own merits, Léger had broken with Lady Rosaline. Unfortunately, his reputation had plummeted in the years since, leading many to believe that he had owed more to her influence than anyone realized.

"Hah!" Léger barked a laugh, the sudden burst of threadbare humor doing nothing to ease the tension. "But of course, she's invited you, Fanny. And the whole family too, non?"

"Oui," Fanny answered carefully. "We're all invited. Hollins is coming as my guest."

"Naturellement." Léger's face cracked in a merciless, devil-may-care smile, but Fanny noticed the glass still shaking in his hand. "How could dear Lady Rosaline resist inviting the only residents in Treville-sur-Mer more notorious than herself? No, our Rosaline treasures her reputation for scandal far too much. Think of it—all those stories! She encourages them. How else would you explain the countless, meaningless duels fought over the right to escort her to *this* ball or *that* ball. Or poor Christophe Marchant, who drowned himself in the Seine when she rejected them. And he was hardly the only one. At least two other men threw themselves from the Blue Train because of her. The fools!" Léger shook his head in disgust.

"And then, after all that, she ran off and married a fascist and was accused of spying by the Italian government!" He scoffed. "No one knows how many of those stories are actually true, of course, and Lady Rosaline prefers it that way, but you—"

"—*we'll* be attending the party as well, of course," Madame Léger interrupted from the doorway, effectively undercutting her husband's scorn. "Lady Rosaline has kindly invited us, and my husband has gracefully set aside his pride and accepted. Forgiveness is a wonderous thing, non?"

No one dared disagree, although Madame Léger herself did not look particularly forgiving at the moment, and Fanny couldn't help but wonder who Madame Léger hated more—her husband or Lady Rosaline.

3

THE WIDOW OF
TREVILLE-SUR-MER

Lady Rosaline Barrett De Marchi, the Widow of Treville-sur-Mer, burst through the doorway and embraced the Earl of Unsworth and his sister, Lady Constance, in a terrifying explosion of exuberance and feathers.

"Oh, but it is wonderful to see you again, Eddy!" Lady Rosaline cried, opening her arms wide and pitching her voice so as to reach the furthermost seats of some imaginary theater. "Absolutely wonderful!"

Faced with such aggressive cheerfulness, Lord Unsworth could only smile and nod awkwardly. Quiet and retiring by nature, he found Lady Rosaline's extravagant gestures and assumed familiarity to be more than a little exhausting. *Eddy, indeed!*

His Lordship did not need to turn to see his sister's expression, not when he could practically hear her eyebrows raising like guillotines readying to strike.

It had been over twenty years since Lord Unsworth had last seen Lady Rosaline—or rather, Rosie Swanson, as she had been then—and, as far as he could see, she hadn't changed in the slightest.

Oh, that was not to say that time had not marched as steadily onwards for her as it had for him. Beneath the expertly applied powders, she had wrinkles and laugh lines aplenty—the marks of a life lived to the fullest—and yet she remained as beautiful and dazzling as ever.

Lord Unsworth had been, he supposed, one of Rosaline's earliest admirers, and he could still remember his first sight of her lighting up the stage as one of the ladies-in-waiting in some long-forgotten operetta. Constance had never liked her, though, and a quiet word in Father's ear soon put an end to any possible association. Under no circumstances could the future Earl of Unsworth be seen cavorting with a mere actress. And as for marriage, perish the thought!

They had been right, of course. Quite unsuitable. Although, as Lord Unsworth recalled, it had been a few months before he had stopped sulking and accepted the unhappy truth. God, had he ever truly been so young?

And yet here they all were again—apart from Father, naturally—and Lady Rosaline was oddly determined to renew their acquaintance and resume old familiarities, as if no time had passed at all, as if it hadn't been decades since they last set eyes on each other. It was, if Lord Unsworth was honest with himself, downright unsettling. Connie, no doubt, would use a different word—suspicious, perhaps, or conniving.

Lord Unsworth sighed. He should have torn up the invitation to Lady Rosaline's party. That would have been simpler all around. Or better still, he should have settled in a different part of the Riviera, somewhere the Widow of Treville-sur-Mer did not hold sway. But, in truth, Lord Unsworth had not spared Lady Rosaline so much as a single thought for over twenty years, and when he had asked Mr. Quayle to see to the travel arrangements, His Lordship had not known that Lady Rosaline had enthroned herself in this particular village.

"Are we early?" Constance asked, glancing around the cavernous entrance hall for any sign of the other guests.

"Early?" Lady Rosaline beamed at them. "Heavens, no! You're as punctual as ever, Constance. No, the other guests are all out mingling in the gardens. There was a slight contratemps with one of the orchestra conductors, but the music should be starting up soon. In the meantime—" Lady Rosaline hooked one arm through Lord Unsworth's, and then, in an even more Herculean feat, managed to capture Lady Constance's arm with the other. "—before we join them, I thought the three of us might have a chance to become reacquainted."

"I beg your pardon?" His Lordship asked quietly, trying not to feel alarmed.

"I've heard tell of your little trove, Eddy," Lady Rosaline said with a wink. "But I have something of a collection myself, and there's so much I want to show you—both of you. I just know you'll love it!"

* * *

THE VILLA BARRETT DE MARCHI had been designed by Lady Rosaline herself with the help of a rather famous architect—another one of her admirers, no doubt—who had been willing to indulge in her architectural fantasies. Courtyards and fountains abounded, while sudden staircases emerged out of the shadows in the oddest places, and a preponderance of halls and corridors twisted and turned, seemingly leading nowhere.

The entire structure was, in short, little more than a series of architectural cul de sacs, but every single corner and crevasse was filled with paintings, sculptures, and tapestries. Many of them had been gifts from her various friends and suitors, but some she had purchased in her own right, and

Lady Rosaline was clearly proud of her knowledge and taste. There was not, she soon demonstrated, a single item in her collection that she could not discuss at length.

As a renowned, albeit highly specialized collector himself, Lord Unsworth understood better than most the sheer time and effort Lady Rosaline must have expended, although he could not help but note that her selection of medieval tapestries and artifacts was riddled with errors. Not that he blamed Lady Rosaline, of course. Some of the pieces were genuinely impressive, if occasionally mistakenly labeled, and Lady Rosaline was an *amateur*, after all.

"And this," she finally declared, showing them into an antechamber which gazed out onto the gardens, "is the crowning jewel of my collection!"

Perched atop a pedestal in the center of the room rose a small bronze statuette. It had clearly been gilded at one point, but the gold coating had mostly chipped away over the years, leaving only a handful of gilt remnants to glint in the evening sun.

Perhaps thirteen centimeters high—not counting the pedestal—it depicted a young woman clearly caught in the grip of some religious or spiritual ecstasy. Lord Unsworth leaned in closer and could not resist a sigh of appreciation. The detail was exquisite, from the carved draperies protecting her modesty to the young woman's face, resting in her hands as she gazed inward toward some secret, divine knowledge. It was beautiful, but also familiar.

"Forgive me if I'm mistaken," His Lordship murmured thoughtfully. "Renaissance Italian sculpture is hardly my forte, but surely I've seen her somewhere before? In Italy, perhaps? At the—"

"—at the Cathedral in Siena," Lady Rosaline finished with obvious pleasure, gratified to have her prized treasure recognized, "in a little alcove beneath a marble arch."

"Yes." Lord Unsworth nodded. "That rings a bell, a distant, rusting bell. Siena, eh?"

He cast his mind back to his long ago grand tour of Europe. The trip had not been a roaring success. His companions had been far more interested in exploring the local nightlife than in seeing the sights, and their guide—a mincing little Oxford tutor who was now Vice-Chancellor of the university—had been a dyed-in-the wool classicist who believed that history ended with the fall of the Roman Empire. He had dismissed Lord Unsworth's beloved medieval period as the darkest of dark ages and had only acknowledged the Renaissance with the greatest of reluctance. Naturally, the two men had despised each other and maintained an enjoyably contentious correspondence to this day.

Nevertheless, his guide had ultimately managed to impart some small knowledge of the period, and they *had* visited the Cathedral in Siena where Lord Unsworth had seen a statue very much like this one, only larger and in marble.

"The original is a Bernini, is it not?" Lord Unsworth asked, peering down at the statuette.

"This *is* the original," Lady Rosaline said a trifle sharply, but quickly recovered herself. "That is to say that when His Holiness Pope Alexander VII commissioned a statue of Saint Mary Magdalene for the Chapel, Bernini made a number of preparatory sketches, drawings, *and*," she gestured proudly, "one, single full-body maquette. The only one in the world!"

"That is quite a find," Lord Unsworth said.

And it truly was. Even Lady Constance, who had worked long and hard to cultivate an utter disinterest in either art, history, or architecture—largely, Lord Unsworth was convinced, for the purpose of aggravating him—was reluctantly impressed.

"How did you come by it?" Lady Constance asked. It was the first time she had shown the slightest interest so far, and for a moment Lady Rosaline looked triumphant, as if she had won some game that no one else knew they were playing.

"The Marquis de Saint-Adelin left the statuette to me in his will."

"How generous of him," Lady Constance murmured.

"I had admired it many times at his chateau, and he knew that I've always felt a particular affinity for Mary Magdalene."

"Have you, indeed?" Lady Constance's voice, while sharp and pointed as ever, was so quiet that Lord Unsworth barely heard her. "I *can't* imagine why."

For her part, Lady Rosaline gave no sign that she had heard anything amiss. Circling the statuette until she was across from Lord Unsworth and Lady Constance, and flanked on either side by two large windows that opened like doors into the gardens, Lady Rosaline reached out and gently caressed the statuette's face.

"We keep each other's secrets," she said softly. "Mary and I."

Lord Unsworth wasn't quite sure what to make of that, but he was saved from having to respond when Lady Rosaline continued.

"Herr Darvas—the curator of the Musée de Saint-Jean le Décapité—authenticated the Bernini himself," she said. "So kind of him. But then, he is a very great friend of mine and has visited many times. In fact, he *personally* helped catalogue my collection," she revealed with a grand wave of her hand.

"Did he?" His Lordship had never visited the Musée de Saint-Jean le Décapité in Paris, nor, if what he had seen so far was any indication, did he intend to. Whatever this Herr Darvas' virtues were when it came to Renaissance painting or Baroque sculpture, his knowledge of the medieval period was noticeably lacking.

"In return," Lady Rosaline continued, thankfully unaware of Lord Unsworth's thoughts, "I loan certain items to the museum on a rolling basis so they can be enjoyed by the public."

"How philanthropic of you," Constance replied. It was not a compliment, but Lady Rosaline could hardly be expected to discern that.

"When I die," Lady Rosaline divulged, leaning in close to whisper. Lord Unsworth caught a whiff of her perfume, and for a moment had trouble breathing. "When I die," Lady Rosaline repeated solemnly, once His Lordship's coughing had subsided, "I intend to donate the bulk of my collection to the museum." She smiled beauteously. "It is my dearest wish to be remembered first and foremost as a devoted patron of the arts."

This time Lord Unsworth could not resist a darting glance towards his sister. Poor Connie's face was contorted in a strange sort of grimace from the sheer effort of biting her tongue, but before she could say anything—or more likely burst a blood vessel—Constance was saved by a most timely distraction.

A rotund, jolly gentleman reeking of cigar smoke and whiskey came charging into the room. "Ah! There you are, Rosey! I've been looking for you everywhere," he cried.

"Julius, how lovely to see you!" Lady Rosaline rose onto her tippiest toes and planted a kiss on each of his cheeks. More than capable of matching Lady Rosaline in exuberance if not decorum, Julius replied by engulfing her in a hug which all but lifted Lady Rosaline from the ground.

"Forgive me, darling," she said, once she had been deposited. "I didn't realize you had arrived—"

"—Not to worry," Julius said warmly. "Raymond and Vivi were more than welcoming in your absence."

Lord Unsworth turned and noticed for the first time the young couple lurking aimlessly in the doorway, their arrival having been overshadowed by the twirling Sir Julius. The young man was in his early twenties and had sharp, familiar features, a vaguely military bearing, and an expression that could curdle milk. He did not, in short, appear particularly welcoming. In fairness, the young woman glittering on his arm was attempting to compensate, but her smile was a little too strained to be wholly believable.

"Oh!" Lady Rosaline clapped her hands together in a theatrical burst of glee. "I don't believe you've been introduced." She summoned the young couple with an imperious wave of her hand—one which she had to repeat thrice over when the young man proved reluctant to obey.

"This is my son, Raymond—" she said with pride, while beside her, the young man's expression worsened—if that were possible—and Lady Rosaline rolled her eyes. "—I mean the *Honorable* Raymond Montague Barrett, and his wife Genevieve—although everyone calls her Vivi."

Lady Rosaline smiled broadly. "And this, Raymond, is my old friend, the Earl of Unsworth and his sister, Lady Constance Druce."

Connie's lips thinned dangerously at the unwelcome reminder of her husband, but Lord Unsworth intervened as deftly as he was able.

"A pleasure, Mr. Barrett," he said with a polite nod, one which the Hon. Raymond Montague Barrett begrudgingly returned, but only following a subtle jab in the ribs from his wife.

"No, no! You simply must call him Raymond," Lady Rosaline insisted. "After all, we're practically family."

Lord Unsworth raised his eyebrows. He did not, as it happened, feel as though they were all *practically family*, and by the looks of him, neither did Raymond.

Lady Rosaline, of course, was blithely oblivious, or, perhaps more accurately, blithely unconcerned. "And this," she continued, "is Sir Julius Markham-Smythe. Lord Weatherford introduced us years ago—long before the knighthood. In fact, he was something of a protegee."

"You're too kind." Sir Julius and Lady Rosaline shared a roguish grin for a moment, but unlike the rest, Sir Julius proved himself capable of greeting Lord Unsworth and Lady Constance with all due protocol and deference.

As soon as he was done, however, he turned back to Lady Rosaline. There was a familiar, adoring look in his eyes, which Lord Unsworth remembered from his own reflection some thirty years before, but there was also a hint—a soupçon—of desperation.

"Might I have a word, Rosey?" he asked. "It's rather urgent."

"O-o-oh?" Lady Rosaline looked positively delighted. "How intriguing." She graced Lord Unsworth and Lady Constance with a dramatically apologetic glance. "If you would excuse us for a moment?"

"Of course." Lord Unsworth bowed his head, relieved to have a reprieve, however brief. It was exhausting being the object of that woman's attention.

"I'm sure you can all amuse yourselves without me," Lady Rosaline said with a mischievous curl of the lips. "Try not to miss me too deeply, darlings!"

And with a playful a wriggle of her fingers, she was gone, leading Sir Julius by the arm through the open doors and out into the garden, and leaving Lord Unsworth and the others alone with the artwork.

* * *

BEREFT OF LADY ROSALINE'S glistening, overbearing presence, the unexpected quartet found themselves united in an awkward, uncomfortable silence. As Lady Rosaline's son and daughter-in-law, Raymond and Vivi might have been expected to keep the conversation flowing with a little light, trifling banter—something to do with the weather, perhaps. But Raymond was far more interested in glaring down into the garden, where his mother and Sir Julius were engaged in hushed, if not entirely friendly, conversation. Meanwhile, his wife, Vivi, seemed at least moderately aware of her duties and kept glancing over apologetically. But she, too, was preoccupied, as the bulk of her energies seemed to be spent in soothing Raymond's seething anger.

As for Lady Constance, she was seething herself, albeit for different reasons, which left Lord Unsworth to break the ice. Unfortunately, His Lordship would be the first to admit that small talk was not one of his more prized talents—his repertoire of informative asides and obscure historical witticisms seldom having elicited the desired effect.

It was Raymond, however, who unexpectedly broke the silence, and in so doing unknowingly saved the others from a rather torturous pun that would have required both a working knowledge of Middle English and a more-than-passing familiarity with Chaucer if they were to find it even remotely comprehensible.

His Lordship, of course, was rather proud of the quip, and had once deployed it with great success in the back corner of the Reading Room at the British Museum. The resulting laughter had seen both himself and a visiting professor politely but firmly removed from the premises. But in truth, Lord Unsworth was not displeased to find his pun no longer needed.

"He's asking her for money," Raymond said, his lips curling in a disgusted sneer.

For a moment, Lord Unsworth found the young man's pronouncement as indecipherable as he, no doubt, would have found His Lordship's pun, but the confusion soon passed. Not even Lord Unsworth could miss the target and nature of Raymond's ire. And, sure enough, Sir Julius appeared to be earnestly and vehemently attempting to convince Lady Rosaline of something.

"But how can you be so sure it's money he's after?" Lord Unsworth asked.

Raymond started, obviously unaware that he had spoken out loud, but recovered quickly and regarded Lord Unsworth with an incredulous, withering stare.

"Because, Lord Unsworth," he explained, "Weatherford was more than Sir Julius' mentor. He was his patron and employer."

"Employer?"

"Oh, yes. Sir Julius writes for the society pages, you see, although his career mainly involves attending lavish parties and spending other people's money. But now that Old Moneybags Weatherford is dead, Sir Julius finds himself in need of a new...benefactor. Enter my mother, stage left." Raymond scoffed. "Besides, his ilk are *always* after money. See!"

He pointed back toward the garden where Lady Rosaline and Sir Julius had been joined by a tall, elderly gentleman with stooped shoulders and shock-white hair.

"That's Henry Carrodus," Raymond explained. "Mother's favorite playwright. She funded all his plays for decades, and now she pays him a little stipend to do God knows what." He frowned. "Whatever it is, she keeps him close. He lives in one of the old convent buildings on the grounds."

"That's very generous of her," Lord Unsworth.

"Isn't it, though? But that's never enough, is it? Because all her gentlemen are the same in the end—pathetic old men panting after my mother, desperate for scraps from her table."

Raymond's pointed glance made it abundantly clear that he included Lord Unsworth in his indictment.

His Lordship was taken aback. It had been a long time

since anyone—excepting Constance, of course—had dared insult him to his face so brazenly. Even now with his family besieged by scandal, most people still had the common courtesy to whisper their slurs behind his back.

Lord Unsworth scowled. He could feel Constance rearing up behind him, preparing to spit fire and brimstone, and he could think of a few choice words of his own. But before he could defend himself or Lady Constance could berate Raymond for his intolerable rudeness, the young man stormed off, disgusted by the spectacle in the garden, leaving his wife to apologize on his behalf.

Deprived of her target, Constance wheeled on Vivi, who had the good grace to at least appear embarrassed.

"Please forgive Raymond," Vivi said softly, somehow managing to withstand the full force of Constance's glare without collapsing. "Living in his mother's shadow all these years has been...difficult for him."

"I'm sure it has." Constance had never approved of Rosaline and was only too willing to believe the worst of her parenting. "But as I recall, his father, General Alexander Montague Barrett, was not the most sterling role model himself."

Vivi's eyes widened. "I wouldn't let Raymond hear you say that. He barely remembers him, but Raymond idolizes his father, mostly for being everything his mother is not."

"Does he, indeed?"

Judging by her tone, Constance was distinctly unimpressed. And so, for that matter, was Lord Unsworth.

4

THE CALM BEFORE THE STORM

Wandering along the outskirts of the party with a blandly polite smile firmly affixed to his face, Mr. Quayle should have felt pleased with himself. Only a few minutes ago, he had successfully delivered Arthur back into Lady Constance's loving talons and in recompense he had been released for the evening to mingle and enjoy himself. Freedom, at last! It was not quite how he would have chosen to spend his evening, of course, but the prospect of a few hours to himself without any duties or responsibilities was more than welcome. And the drinks were quite strong—*wonderfully* strong. And yet, for some reason, Mr. Quayle remained stubbornly, frustratingly on edge. Perhaps it was because the last time he had been present at a garden party, a young woman had been found murdered. Or perhaps it was because Mr. Quayle was not sure what he was doing there, rubbing shoulders with the great and the good.

Indeed, everywhere he turned, the villa was overrun with guests. They heaved and swelled through the gardens in great waves of coats and dresses. Anyone who was anyone in Treville-sur-Mer had answered Lady Rosaline's summons.

There were numerous lords and ladies, viscounts and barons, several titans of industry, one or two stars and starlets, the usual gang of writers and artists, and then there was *Mr. Quayle*.

It was unnerving, especially since it soon became apparent that, like M. Tallier at the casino, Lady Rosaline was far better informed than she had any right to be.

Emerging suddenly from behind a row of hydrangeas, the Widow of Treville-sur-Mer herself fixed him with an assessing, judging eye, as if she could peer into his soul, if only she looked deep enough.

"Good evening, Mr. Quayle," she said, the gimlet gaze giving way at last to a charming, devil-may-care smile. "I must admit you're not quite as I imagined you."

Although taken completely by surprise, Mr. Quayle managed to limit himself to a single raised eyebrow in response. "I apologize if I'm a disappointment, Lady Rosaline," he replied evenly. "But, in all honesty, I'm not sure why you bothered imagining me at all."

"Oh, such modesty! How delicious!" She clapped her hands delightedly. "But you mustn't think yourself a disappointment. Oh, no. How could I be disappointed by the Unsworth's savior?"

Mr. Quayle tilted his head as he considered whether he was being mocked. Lady Rosaline's affected manner and air of assumed intimacy made her frustratingly opaque. Certainly, she was showing him an unusual amount of attention, and she must have been aware of the curious eyes watching them from every corner of the garden.

"Your Ladyship is remarkably well informed," Mr. Quayle said. "Although, calling me their 'savior' is, perhaps, a trifle exaggerated."

"Spare me the false humility, young man," Lady Rosaline scolded. "It doesn't become you. And as for my information

—" she smiled sharply, showing a row of glistening teeth, "—surely, you didn't think that you were the only one with friends in high places?"

"I wasn't aware that I had *any* friends in high places, Lady Rosaline."

"Not even Whitehall's Grand Inquisitor? Oh dear! I'm sure Mr. Finch would be heartbroken to hear that."

Mr. Quayle started. That was not a name he had expected to hear bandied about on the French Riviera and by Lady Rosaline, no less.

"Oh, yes." Her grin turned sly as she reveled in his surprise. "Your Mr. Finch and I have had our share of dealings."

"Indeed?" Mr. Finch was something of an institution in Whitehall. His official title was as nondescript as his person, but his actual function—or at least the one with which Quayle was most familiar—was as the government's spy catcher extraordinaire, their so-called Grand Inquisitor.

And Mr. Quayle belatedly remembered that Lady Rosaline was rumored to have been expelled from Italy on suspicion of espionage. Perhaps, against all odds, there was some truth to those stories, or perhaps her dealings with Mr. Finch had been more *domestic* than foreign.

Over the years, quite a few ministers and members of parliament were whispered to have been involved with Lady Rosaline, and if even half of those stories were true, then Quayle could only imagine what indiscretions Mr. Finch might have been called upon to sweep under the carpet.

Lady Rosaline shook her head almost coquettishly. "And you see," she continued in a voice like a whisper, "there was a time, Mr. Quayle, when your employer and I were quite close. Quite close, indeed. So, when I opened my newspaper one morning and discovered that there had been a murder on his estate, I naturally made sure to keep abreast of developments.

And having, as I do, some small experience in these matters —scandal that is, not murder—I couldn't help but notice a few traces here and there of someone's hand guiding the family through troubled waters."

"I see." Mr. Quayle was unconvinced. Lady Rosaline was keen to present her interest as natural curiosity, but she hadn't seemed curious. She'd been *digging*—then and now—ferreting out every stray scrap of scandal she could find. But for what purpose?

"Please don't mistake me," Lady Rosaline said, lowering her voice further, forcing Mr. Quayle to lean in closer. "It was all very deftly done, and avoiding the spotlight can't have been easy, considering how central you were to events, but I'm afraid your role is quite obvious if one knows where to look."

"So I'm learning," Mr. Quayle murmured, to Lady Rosaline's amusement, but he was thinking instead of M. Tallier.

She grinned. "In any case, Mr. Quayle, whatever you did, you're clearly someone worth keeping an eye on."

"How kind of you to say so," he replied, but it wasn't, not even remotely. In fact, to Mr. Quayle's ears, it had sounded almost ominous.

"Kind?" Lady Rosaline shook her head. "Well, there's something I've seldom been accused of," she said. "Such a flatterer you are!"

"And that's something *I've* seldom been accused of, Lady Rosaline," Mr. Quayle replied. "So, I suppose we're even."

Lady Rosaline threw her head back and laughed. "Very good!" she said. "Very good indeed! I'm pleased to see that Lord Unsworth's little gamble is working out so well."

"Gamble?"

"Why, hiring you, of course."

"I'm not sure I—"

"—Oh, come now!" Lady Rosaline laid a teasing hand on Mr. Quayle's arm. "Surely you're not about to pretend that hiring you wasn't a risk on Edward's part? Not when there are such delicious rumors circling about you in Whitehall—something about misplaced documents, I believe, and a cabinet minister's dead mistress..."

Mr. Quayle was prepared this time and did not react in the slightest. He could feel the weight of Lady Rosaline's attention, hungry for the slightest hint of shock or surprise. This was how she entertained herself, he realized. She hunted out people's secrets and then dangled her knowledge in front of them like a cat playing with its food. But did she do more than play? Blackmail, after all, was but a hop, skip, and a jump away from her current amusements.

Deprived of the reaction she had hoped for, Lady Rosaline merely shrugged at Mr. Quayle's stoicism. "Of course," she continued, her expression deceptively innocent, "you already knew the family, didn't you? I understand you were close to the son, Teddy—"

"—Colonel Statham, yes," Mr. Quayle interrupted sharply. "He was my commanding officer."

If Lady Rosaline was bothered by his tone, she gave no sign. "I gather you were there when he died," she said instead, offering a sympathetic little smile. "Such a tragedy that was. No wonder his father welcomed you with open arms."

Mr. Quayle's face hardened. There was something dangerous in her voice, something pointed and barbed, but before he could respond, he spied Lord Unsworth looming over Lady Rosaline's shoulder with a face like thunder. His Lordship had clearly overheard her last few comments and was not best pleased.

Following Mr. Quayle's gaze, Lady Rosaline frowned, and something almost like regret passed across her face. She had miscalculated, and she knew it.

"Eddy?" Lady Rosaline asked. "I'm sorry. I didn't see you there. Is everything alright?"

"Everything is perfectly alright," Lord Unsworth replied coldly. "But if you would excuse us, I need to speak with Mr. Quayle."

"Of course, of course." Lady Rosaline nodded, then hesitated for a moment, clearly weighing her options. "But first, I was rather hoping that you and I might have a word, Eddy."

"A word?" His Lordship frowned. "We've exchanged quite a few words, Rosaline. Less than an hour ago, you were showing us around your collection and, honestly, I—"

"—Yes, I know," Lady Rosaline interrupted in the first outright show of impatience Mr. Quayle had seen from her, the first true crack in the facade. "But I'd prefer to have a word in private. Without your sister...or your secretary."

"And what," Lord Unsworth asked, "would be the point of that?"

"The point?" she smiled sadly. "Oh Eddy. After all these years, don't you think it's finally time we cleared the air, you and I? Don't you think you owe me that much?"

"Do I?" Despite his words earlier, His Lordship was not alright. In fact, he was positively fuming—in his own quiet, particular sort of way.

Lord Unsworth had only agreed to attend the party in the first place, against Constance's advice, out of a congealed mixture of curiosity and barely remembered sentiment—compelled by the weight of might-have-been. And, in fairness, the evening had started well enough. There had been a few odd moments here and there, of course, but it had been pleasant, if a little awkward, to wander through Rosaline's collection. She had truly become quite knowledgeable over the years, and that Bernini statuette truly was an incredible find. No, the real trouble had started after they had joined the others, when, for reasons of her own, Rosaline insisted on personally introducing Lord Unsworth and his family to every single one of her guests.

An exceedingly private person, His Lordship despised being the center of attention at the best of times and these were not the best of times. Worse, with each new introduction, each tedious exchange of useless pleasantries, he began to feel more and more like another object in Lady Rosaline's collection—a curio to be paraded around for other discerning collectors to admire, as if he was some performing monkey and not the Thirteenth Earl of Unsworth!

But that had always been Rosaline's way, and, despite what Constance believed, Lord Unsworth could detect no true malice in it. Not even, once his temper had cooled slightly, in her mention of Teddy. Rosaline simply gave no thought to the consequences, to the unintended effect her words could have on others. That, too, was her way.

The real question, though, was why Rosaline had invited him. *What was she after? What, all these years later, could she possibly want from him?* And here was the opportunity to find out and sate his curiosity once and for all. In the end, how could he refuse?

"Excellent!" Lady Rosaline grinned, taking Lord Unsworth by the arm. "I've been trying to get you alone all evening."

And as they headed down towards the outer gardens, the eyes of the party following their every move, His Lordship hoped beyond hope that he had not just made a terrible, terrible mistake.

5

VEILED WARNINGS

To her surprise and delight, Fanny found Henry Carrodus, celebrated playwright, award-winning director, and world-renowned man of letters, to be really quite charming. Indeed, he reminded her slightly of her uncle, that is, if Lord Unsworth had possessed a modicum of ambition or any literary talent beyond the dry recitation of facts. Having witnessed Jean-Paul Léger's bitter, self-aggrandizing behavior, she had expected much the same from his rival. After all, although one was an artist and the other a writer, they had both spent their lives in the same trenches squabbling over scraps from Lady Rosaline's table.

But instead, Carrodus seemed genuinely eager to speak with her and Hollins, and Fanny was pleased that with Carrodus' gentle encouragement, Hollins was returning to his more usual self. She knew that Hollins had been looking forward to attending Lady Rosaline's party. Indeed, he had spoken of little else for the past few days, but since they arrived, the poor man had not made a very good showing of himself.

Hollins' initial efforts to ingratiate himself with the family had been embarrassing at best, even before Fanny had been forced to rescue him—*and herself*—from Aunt Constance's ire. But she had been expecting that much. Fanny might not have known Hollins for long, but she had a firm grasp of his quirks and foibles, or, at least, she thought she had. He was a follower by nature, forever desperate for attention. It was endearing in a sad, puppy dog sort of way, but more importantly, it was understandable.

Since they had arrived at the party, however, he had been acting strangely—painfully eager to attract Lady Rosaline's attention and positively sulking when she had ignored him in favor of Quayle.

Fanny was well aware, of course, that Lady Rosaline's patronage could make or break an artist or writer's career. One could not spend more than five minutes in Léger's company without learning that particular lesson. But there was more to Hollins' desperation. Fanny was sure of that. Indeed, if she hadn't known better, Fanny would have almost thought Hollins in love with the older woman.

He wouldn't be the only one, of course, although Fanny herself did not quite understand the appeal. Lady Rosaline's manner had struck her as painfully staged and outright rude at times, but even Carrodus was clearly besotted with their erstwhile hostess. Fanny could hear it in his voice when he mentioned Lady Rosaline's name, which he did often, and see it in the way his gaze kept seeking her out, even as he listened attentively to Hollins' gushing compliments and blatant, fawning hero-worship.

"You're very kind, Mr. Hollins," Carrodus said. "Although I'm afraid that of late, my work has fallen somewhat out of favor."

"I can't believe that," Hollins protested. "You're still highly regarded."

"Yes," Carrodus agreed with a wry smile. "Highly regarded *but* seldom performed." He chuckled. "What a fine epitaph that will make one day. It'll even have the distinction of being true."

"Sir?" Hollins glanced at Fanny uncertainly, but she could only shrug. "Are you—"

"Oh, don't mind me, Mr. Hollins," Carrodus replied easily, waving their concerns aside. "I'm just an old writer feeling sorry for himself." He sighed mournfully. "Times change, of course," he continued. "Tastes change, but in the end, it was the War that drove the final nail into my coffin."

"The War?" Fanny frowned. "But how? Surely the theaters—"

"No, no," Carrodus shook his head. "Nothing so prosaic, my dear. But after all that death and horror, there was little appetite for my tired old tragedies. Rosaline saw it coming, of course. That woman knows how to read an audience. She suggested I write a comedy, something light and airy to take people's minds off their sorrows, but no matter how I tried, everything I wrote turned sour and sad. It's hard, I've learned, to find humor in the midst of grief."

Fanny averted her gaze for a moment, allowing the old playwright to compose himself. "Who did you lose?" she finally asked.

"Am I so obvious?"

"Not at all," Fanny promised. "But I know that look."

"Yes, I rather think you do." Carrodus nodded. "You're right, of course. I lost my favorite, no, my *only* nephew. Simon was barely twenty-one when he died, and the cruel irony of it is that he almost made it to the end safe and sound. That poor boy spent three years in the trenches, digging through the mud, but he survived the worst of it. Until one day, he was sent out on a routine patrol and never returned. Missing, presumed dead."

"I'm sorry," Fanny said sincerely. "I lost my parents when I was young, and I was still a child when my cousin was killed at Ypres. Grief has accompanied me for as long as I can recall—practically since I could crawl—and I've never been sure if it was a blessing or a curse that I can't remember the times before."

"It's made you stronger, I think," Carrodus suggested. "Your whole generation, those who've learned to laugh and dance and *live* in the shadow of so much pain. But whether that's a blessing or not, I'm afraid is beyond me."

Hollins glanced between them, clearly at a loss for what to say. "I was too young to serve in the War," he admitted. "And while everyone I know, it seems, has lost someone—fathers, brothers, sisters and cousins, even mothers—I never had any of those to lose. In fact," he cleared his throat awkwardly, "I used to be jealous, as awful as that sounds, of other people's losses, as if I'd been left behind somehow." He paused a moment, then added, "But my guardian passed away recently, and I don't feel jealous anymore."

"Of course not." Fanny squeezed his hand tightly. Hollins hadn't mentioned any of this to her before, and she recognized, as the faint stirrings of guilt pressed against her chest, that it was her fault. Until this moment, she had not spared so much as a single thought for Hollins' troubles. Instead, she had used him as a convenient escape from her own cares and woes. It was a sobering realization.

"We were never particularly close," Hollins admitted. "He wanted me to enter politics, so I became a communist out of spite, and when that wasn't enough to drive him away, I ran off to join the theater. Now that he's dead, though, I...I—" Hollins' fell silent.

"You must have been very fond of him," Fanny said.

"Yes." Hollins' eyes widened in surprise. "Isn't that strange?"

"No," Carrodus interjected. "I don't find that strange at all."

Hollins looked up and managed a small chuckle. "Well, of course not, sir," he said. "Fathers and sons—or guardians, I suppose—only realizing they loved each other when the other has died? That's the ending to practically every play you've ever written."

"Ha, so it is!" A moment later, however, Carrodus' face darkened and an infectious bark of laughter died in his throat. Curious, Fanny turned to follow his gaze and couldn't quite restrain her own surprise at what she saw.

Lady Rosaline was walking arm-in-arm with Lord Unsworth, whispering softly in his ear as she led him a merry dance through the flower beds and among the topiaries. All together, it made for an oddly intimate sight, or would have, if not for the countless eyes watching them from every corner of the garden and the countless tongues poised to wag and scorn. Lady Rosaline had arranged it that way. Fanny was sure of it. The Widow of Treville-sur-Mer was deliberately parading her clandestine assignation in front of all and sundry.

Unlike the rest of the impromptu audience, however, Fanny knew her uncle quite well and recognized the signs. His back was ramrod straight, his movements stiff, and while she could not see his face, she could well imagine his expression. Uncle Edward was ill at ease and decidedly uncomfortable, perhaps even angry.

A few moments later, Lady Rosaline and Lord Unsworth disappeared around a hedge, heading towards the gardens on the other side of the house, where they would be safe at last from prying eyes. Immediately, the low murmur among the onlookers erupted into a cacophony of raised voices, and Fanny caught more than a few sneers and notes of confusion. *Why him?* the people of Treville-sur-Mer asked one another. Of all people, why him? Fanny would have been insulted on her uncle's behalf if the thought hadn't occurred to her as well, along with one that no one else had probably thought to ask: why her? Why Lady Rosaline?

Fanny caught a glimpse of Léger by the fountain further down in the garden. Unlike the others, he was not indulging in idle chitchat or gossip. Instead, the painter was glaring with such hatred at the spot where Lady Rosaline and Lord Unsworth had walked only moments before. Léger, it seemed, had abandoned his wife, not that Madame Léger appeared to mind. She was standing by the fountain talking to a young woman wearing spectacles and a pinched expression.

"It would appear that your uncle has been anointed the new favorite," Carrodus observed.

"What is that supposed to mean?" Fanny demanded with a frown.

Carrodus no longer seemed particularly friendly. "I did wonder," he mused, "why she was so insistent on personally introducing him to everyone."

"I can assure you," Fanny replied primly, "that Uncle Edward has no intention of being anyone's...favorite."

"No?" Carrodus did not appear convinced, but after a moment, he reconsidered. "Perhaps you're right," he admitted. "But he may have little say in the matter. Our Rosaline usually has her way in the end."

"Is that so?"

"Yes." Carrodus pursed his lips, and Fanny could practically see his mind racing. "I will admit, though, that Lord Unsworth *is* an unusual choice for her. These days she tends to prefer them younger and more...athletic. Is he—"

"Yes?" Fanny glared up at him. "Is he what?" she challenged.

Carrodus, at least, had the good manners to grimace apologetically, but continued, nevertheless. "Would you consider your uncle," he asked, "to be particularly competent?"

"He can be," Fanny allowed slowly. "In his own sphere."

"Hmm." Carrodus narrowed his eyes, seemingly deep in thought. "And wasn't there something about a murder a while back? Quite the scandal, I heard."

"I'd rather not discuss it."

"No, I'd imagine not. But His Lordship *does* appear to have steered you all through it relatively unscathed. I wonder…"

"Yes?"

"Never mind," Carrodus' friendly smile returned. "I'm sure they're just reminiscing about old times."

Of course, neither of them believed that for a moment, and Fanny was left with the distinct feeling that Carrodus knew more than he was saying.

"But now!" Carrodus slapped Hollins on the back heartily, sending the younger man stumbling forward half a step. "On to happier things! Weren't you going to tell me all about this play of yours?"

"My play? Oh, yes," Hollins beamed hesitantly. "M-my play! Well, I…um…are you sure you really want to—?"

"Of course! New blood. Exactly what the theater needs, young man."

As Hollins geared himself up, preparing to launch into a, no doubt, enthusiastic recitation of his play, Fanny took her chance and coughed delicately.

She had read Hollins' magnum opus weeks ago and alas, had found it to be painfully, earnestly horrible. Somewhere between a three-door farce and the Communist Manifesto, it was full of slamming doors and extravagant disguises when it wasn't spouting socialist dogma. Despite, or perhaps because of all that, Fanny found the whole thing endearing, although whether the distinguished playwright Carrodus would share her views remained to be seen.

"If you don't mind," she said, "I think I'll leave you to it."

"Of course, of course." Hollins was already lost in the world of acts and scenes, and, smiling at the sight, Fanny left him and Carrodus deep in conversation.

* * *

She had not taken more than a few steps, however, before her smile disappeared. Until recently, Fanny had believed herself an excellent judge of character, and she still prided herself on her ability to sense the mood and temper of a place. Standing here in Lady Rosaline's garden listening to the dueling bands play their waltzes and their jazz, what Fanny felt, more than anything, was a creeping sense of unease. Old Carrodus had been so friendly at first, if a little melancholy, but had briefly turned ugly in his jealousy of her uncle. They were all like that, Fanny realized. Léger had simply never turned back, caught instead like amber in his own envy and bitterness.

Fanny sighed. The Riviera was meant to be a place of freedom for her and her family, a place of escape, and yet wafting on the breeze, she could almost hear the distant clang of the iron bars shutting them all in their cages. But who then were the jailers, and who the inmates?

Lady Rosaline had built a stage for herself, and was determined to imprison all who came into her orbit within it, casting them in whatever role she saw fit or seating them in her audience willingly or otherwise. But her own role had been chosen for her long ago—the Widow of Treville-sur-Mer—and Fanny wondered if Lady Rosaline ever rattled at the bars of her own cage. Idle thoughts, perhaps, but disquieting ones, and there was one thought more disquieting than all the rest, a question which that kept churning about in Fanny's brain. What role exactly did Lady Rosaline have in mind for Uncle Edward?

Mr. Quayle would know, or have a better sense, at least. He had spoken to the Widow, after all, and for such a quiet, retiring man, he had an unexpectedly sharp nose for these matters. Even Aunt Constance had come to rely on him of late, and if that was not a sign that the end of days was upon them, then nothing was. Glancing around the party, however, Fanny was confronted with various scenes of gaiety—the wine had been flowing quite freely all evening—but no Mr. Quayle.

A gust of laughter blew in on the breeze, and Fanny turned to stare in frank astonishment. She had seen Madame Léger smile before and had heard her laugh only this afternoon, but there had always been a shadow accompanying her mirth. Anne-Marie Léger, after all, had a cage of her own.

Now, though, she was practically giddy, as if relieved of a great burden. This, Fanny reflected, was her first true glimpse of Anne-Marie poking out from behind the mask.

"Ah, Fanny!" Madame Léger waved her over with a smile, her voice still echoing with glee. "I don't believe you know Márta, do you? She rarely attends our little soirees."

"I believe we were introduced briefly the other day," Fanny replied, nodding to the bespectacled woman beside Madame Léger, who, after the briefest of hesitations, returned the gesture curtly. "Your father works at a museum, I understand? Forgive me. I didn't quite catch the name."

"My father does not merely *work* at a museum," Márta replied. "He is the curator at the Musée de Saint-Jean le Décapité."

Fanny blinked at the strident tone. "I apologize if I offended you," she said. "That was not my intention."

"Mmm." Márta studied her for a moment, and Fanny felt as though she was being judged, although 'appraised,' perhaps, would be more apt, and her intentions weighed according to some scale or criteria all Márta's own. "Very well, I shall accept your apology. My father, you see, he is not always respected as he should be in this country."

"I'm sorry, I had no idea." Fanny attempted a sympathetic smile, but Márta was unmoved.

"That is why," she continued, "Lady Rosaline's support is so important to him. Without her influence, he would have merely 'worked,' as you say, at the museum, rather than curated, as is his due."

"I see," Fanny murmured. "I believe my uncle mentioned that he also helped Lady Rosaline with her collection?"

"That is so." Márta's lips thinned dangerously. "Like all of us, my father must sing for his supper. Your uncle, he too will learn this soon."

"And do you also sing for your supper?" It was an impertinent question, but Fanny's hackles had been raised. There was something insinuating in Márta's voice, something ugly and knowing and sharp. Fanny had heard similar notes earlier during Carrodus' brief bout of jealousy. Uncle Edward hadn't yet returned from his walk, and already the knives were coming out in unexpected places.

"But, of course," Márta sneered. "I have had the honor, at times, of assisting my father in his work, but recently with Lady Rosaline's backing, I have also established a small art gallery in Paris. Naturally, most of my offerings are from artists in her circle, but I do occasionally showcase a few pieces of my own choosing." She glanced at Madame Léger, who had shed veritable decades in her excitement.

"May I?" Madame Léger asked Márta.

"It's your secret to tell."

Madame Léger grinned. "Márta has arranged a showing for me in a few months! And apparently, she has already found a few interested buyers!"

"Congratulations!" Fanny exclaimed but was unable to

hide her confusion. "Although, forgive me, I wasn't aware you were...painting."

"No." A rather unladylike giggle escaped Madame Léger's lips. "Neither is my husband. And I would prefer to keep it that way."

"He won't hear anything from me," Fanny promised, only too happy to conspire in pulling the wool over Léger's eyes.

"Thank you." Madame Léger nodded. "I knew I could count on you."

"Glady! But I still don't—" Fanny fell silent, belatedly realizing she was in danger of becoming rude. Why should Madame Léger having an art showing in Paris be so surprising?

Something of her thoughts must have shown on her face because Madame Léger graced her with an understanding smile. "Despite what you may have heard," she said quietly, "I am not unskilled with a paintbrush. I've even done a little sculpting now and then."

"She's being modest," Márta explained, squeezing her friend's arm reassuringly. "There was a time when Anne-Marie was considered one of France's most promising young artists. Even Lady Rosaline said so! But then—"

"But then, I married Jean-Paul," Madame Léger finished. "And it soon became clear that there was only room under our roof for *one* great painter, and between them, my husband and Lady Rosaline decided who it would be. He was her great discovery, you see. Rosaline plucked Jean-Paul from obscurity, paid his way through art school, and ultimately anointed him the Greatest Artist of His Generation."

"Until *he* stopped singing for his supper," Márta added.

"Yes." Madame Léger's pleasure was not so innocent this time. "Rosaline likes her gentlemen to be appropriately grateful, and when they fail to acknowledge her contributions or escape the roles she's assigned them, well..."

"Vengeance is mine, sayeth the Lady," Fanny suggested lightly, but neither of the other women were laughing.

"Exactement." Madame Léger nodded gravely, and Fanny realized that she, and by extension, her entire family, was being warned. It was a different warning than Márta's, but a warning all the same. "And it is not just her gentlemen, non," Madame Léger continued. "We all of us have our roles to play. Mine was the selfless, devoted wife, and I, at least, have done my best, despite Jean-Paul's absurd pretentions or his litany of...other offenses."

Fanny followed Madame Léger's gaze and found the man himself, stumbling through the crowd and fawning after a blatantly disgusted Genevieve Barrett. Jean-Paul Léger's mood had not improved any since Lady Rosaline and Uncle Edward had gone off together, and while the drink in his hand had not proved the distraction he had expected, it seemed he had higher hopes for his hostess' daughter-in-law.

The sight left a foul taste in Fanny's mouth, and she felt a sudden jolt of sympathy for Madame Léger. Fanny herself had been forced to fend off her share of Léger's advances, half-hearted though most of them had been, and had come to the conclusion that he had once been a reasonably successful lothario before bitterness and drink had dulled whatever attractions he might once have possessed, leaving him a bewildered, slightly pathetic, but regrettably persistent figure.

Obviously Vivi agreed with that assessment and did not find Léger's advances even remotely welcome. Nor did her husband, who emerged suddenly from the crowd like an avenging, slightly underwhelming angel, and within moments he and Léger were in each other's faces, shouting threats and obscenities. Léger was taller, with a bruiser's build and a drunkard's unsteadiness, but Raymond was younger, and his hatred fresher.

Both men, for the moment at least, were more bark than

bite, but even in bark, they were more or less evenly matched. So, it was ultimately Vivi herself who turned the tide. The words themselves were lost. Unlike Madame Léger and her husband, Vivi did not stoop to shouting, but her tone was unmistakable—sharp and unyielding.

Before the entire party's watchful eyes, Léger stumbled back as if struck and retreated almost forlornly into the hedges. Triumphant, Vivi took her husband's arm, and together she and Raymond marched towards the villa, her with a palpable bounce in her step.

It was only once the domestic altercation was over that Fanny remembered with dawning embarrassment that she had observed the entire scene while standing beside Léger's own wife. Risking a glance over, she struggled not to shiver. The expression on Madame Léger's face required little interpretation. Indeed, Fanny had recently seen not one but two murderers with less hatred in their eyes.

"And this is why everyone adores Rosaline's parties," Madame Léger spat. "There's always someone storming off into the shrubbery. Dinner and a show!" she sneered.

"Are you alright?" Fanny asked, immediately cursing herself for such a foolish question. Of course, the woman wasn't all right. How could she be?

"I'm fine, my dear." Madame Léger's smile was jagged enough to draw blood. "Never better. But now, if you'll excuse me, I believe it's my turn to make an exit."

"Anne-Marie, are you sure—?"

"I said I'm *fine*," Madame Léger said firmly, and then without moving so much as a muscle, appeared to crumple in on herself, not physically so much as spiritually, as if weighed down by an old, familiar load. It was hard to remember how happy and carefree she'd been only minutes before. "Thank you, Márta," she said at last. "And you too, Fanny. I appreciate your concern, but if you don't mind, I'd like a moment or two for myself."

"Of course." Fanny and Márta agreed.

And then, with her head held high, Madame Anne-Marie Léger strode towards the villa, the party crowd parting before her silently as she made her exit with more dignity than either Lady Rosaline or her son had been able to muster.

* * *

"Poor Anne-Marie," Márta said. "She doesn't deserve this… this constant lifetime of humiliation. Sometimes, I think about dragging Léger by what's left of his hair down to the sea and—"

"Yes?"

Márta shook her head, but her eyes told their own tale. "She's not like the rest of us, you know," she said instead.

"Pardon?"

"Anne-Marie's father was the Marquis de Saint-Adelin," Márta explained.

"I see." Now that Fanny thought about at, Madam Léger did have a familiar grace about her, a deportment born of wealth and breeding. "And her mother?"

"A rich heiress, I believe. The family made their money in perfumes, but Anne-Marie turned her back on them years ago. She hated society life. The balls, the parties—"

"I can understand that."

"Yes. I believe you can." Márta's lips quirked in a wry, knowing smirk. "So, she ran away to become an artist. Her mother was furious, of course. She wanted Anne-Marie to marry and marry well—to be the good wife—but her father was more indulgent…at least at first."

This was all sounding more and more familiar for Fanny. Only instead of a father, she had an indulgent uncle, and in place of a furious mother, she had a furious aunt. But the shape was much the same.

"So, what happened?"

"What do you think happened?" Márta snorted. "You heard her! She married Léger and became everything her mother raised her to be—the very best of wives. Devoted, self-sacrificing, and willfully blind."

"Is that why you're helping her?"

"Da." Márta nodded. "Although, please don't misunderstand. Anne-Marie is a rather talented artist in her own right. I am simply reopening a door for her that has been closed for far too long. There was a moment not so long ago, when I thought she had gathered her courage and found a little happiness of her own, but it was not to be. Even so, I would see her free of that man if I could."

"A noble pursuit." Fanny studied Márta for a moment. "You're a lot nicer than I thought you were," she said.

Márta's grin was all teeth. "Don't be fooled," she said, peering over her spectacles. "I'm only nice to people I like, and those are few and far between. But Anne-Marie seems fond of you, and, if I am honest, there are precious few of us in Lady Rosaline's circle."

"Us?"

"Women," Márta explained. "Lady Rosaline prefers her gentlemen to be unencumbered by wives, sisters, daughters...nieces."

Raising her eyebrows, Fanny pondered Márta's words. It was a warning again, her second of the conversation, but friendlier this time.

"I suppose in that case," Fanny said, "we should probably look out for each other."

"In certain matters, at least."

6

MR. QUAYLE BEGINS TO WORRY

"Well?" Lady Constance demanded, cornering Mr. Quayle and manhandling him into a distant corner of the shrubbery. Her eyes were sharp and keen, and her fingers dug into him like talons. "What was all that nonsense about, Quayle? You must have seen my brother and Rosaline practically prancing through the garden just now. Everyone else did!"

Mr. Quayle straightened his tie protectively. "Lady Rosaline expressed an interest in speaking with Lord Unsworth privately," he revealed.

"And Eddy agreed to that?"

"Reluctantly, yes."

"Reluctantly? Pah!" Lady Constance's face was caught between a scowl and a laugh. "He's always had trouble refusing that woman anything, and nothing has changed, it appears, not even all these years later. I dread to think what nonsense she's dragging him into as we speak."

Mr. Quayle held his tongue. Lady Constance was showing him a degree of trust that would have been unthinkable only six months ago, but it would not do for him to overstep his mark.

"I knew we shouldn't have come," she grumbled. "Edward insisted on being polite, but I've been wondering why she invited us."

"Forgive me, Lady Constance, if this is a little self-centered of me," Mr. Quayle hesitantly interjected, "but, on a similar note, I've been wondering why I was invited."

"You?" Lady Constance blinked. "I hadn't thought of that."

"There's no reason you should have, but when Lady Rosaline and I spoke—"

"You spoke to Rosaline?"

"For a few minutes, yes, right before Lord Unsworth joined us. I had the distinct impression that she had sought me out deliberately."

Lady Constance's gaze narrowed. "Why?"

Mr. Quayle chose his words carefully, partially because his own thoughts and impressions had not yet fully solidified and partially because there were some aspects of his conversation with Lady Rosaline that he did not wish to share. "I'm not sure exactly," he said. "But Lady Rosaline appeared to be aware of certain particulars regarding my past, specifically my role in last year's unfortunate…incident."

"Particulars?"

Mr. Quayle grimaced. Despite all his precautions, family secrets had leaked out into the world, and it was hard not to see that as a failure on his part. "I don't know how much she knows for sure," he admitted, "or how much she merely suspects, but Lady Rosaline referenced several details which I am quite sure were not included in any newspaper report."

"Are you suggesting that Rosaline has been spying on us?" Lady Constance was livid. "The gall! How dare she!"

"All I'm saying, Lady Constance," Mr. Quayle answered,

"is that Lady Rosaline knows more than she should about your family's affairs and that she used me to ensure the family knew it."

"For what purpose, Quayle?"

"She was somewhat opaque on that point, but personally, I can think of several reasons."

"So can I," Lady Constance murmured. "You weren't here earlier, Quayle, but she was parading Edward and I around like animals at the zoo. And whenever one of the other guests recognized us or connected our names to the trial, she didn't even try to hide her smug little smile. She was enjoying it."

"You think she invited you here to gloat?"

"I think that woman enjoys causing trouble and tearing down her betters! As you said, now that she has all of us in her clutches, she wants us to know it." Lady Constance sneered, "Not that she has any right to gloat. Look at that son of hers. And that business with her first husband. Time, I think she'll find, does not heal all wounds."

"Perhaps," nodded Quayle. He had no doubt Lady Rosaline was quite capable of the malice Lady Constance described, but there was more at work here than merely settling old scores, even if whatever history lay between His Lordship, Lady Constance, and the Widow of Treville-sur-Mer clearly went far deeper than Mr. Quayle had realized. The dangers, old wounds and old debts lurking beneath the surface were almost tangible. Wheels within wheels within wheels, all threatening to spin out of control.

"Where's Arthur?" Quayle asked, glancing around. "I thought I left him with you."

"Don't talk to me about Arthur," Lady Constance's scowl deepened at the thought of her son. "That boy is impossible! Fanny was introducing me to that ridiculous young man of hers—" she stopped for a moment and eyed Quayle sharply as another thought occurred to her. "Incidentally," she hissed,

"Edward needs to have a word with her about him. This Hollins is wholly unsuitable, even worse than her previous strays and vagabonds. Some sort of writer, I gather?"

"I believe so, yes."

"You *believe*?" Lady Constance raised her eyebrows pointedly. "Don't be coy with me, Quayle. I'm sure you can do more than believe."

"Yes, well." Mr. Quayle coughed delicately. As Lord Unsworth's secretary, one of his more delicate obligations involved auditing Fanny's various friends and suitors. It was a distasteful duty, to be sure, but one which his predecessor had neglected with tragic and fatal consequences. "I have been a trifle preoccupied lately, but I may have made a few inquiries."

"And?"

"I understand that, until recently, Mr. Hollins has been touring Europe with a repertory company."

"Another actor?" Lady Constance scoffed. "Like our hostess?"

"A playwright, apparently," Mr. Quayle answered. "But I gather that he is also..."

"Yes? Spit it out, Quayle!"

"Something of a socialist, Lady Constance."

Lady Constance wrinkled her nose. "And Edward's allowing this? A penniless writer is bad enough, but a socialist? Fanny is the future Countess of Unsworth, not some... some..." She sputtered into silence and glared at Quayle expectantly.

"It's not my place to speak for His Lordship," he began, but Lady Constance was having none of it.

"Tell me," she demanded.

"I was under the impression that after recent events, His Lordship does not quite feel able to criticize Fanny's choice of companion."

"No? Well, I do."

"Forgive me, Lady Constance," Mr. Quayle interjected cautiously, afraid for a moment that she was about to march over to Fanny there and then, "but what does this have to do with Arthur?"

"I was talking to Fanny," she explained, "when he wandered off into the crowd. Heaven knows where he is now."

"I see."

Arthur had clearly chosen his moment well, waiting until Lady Constance was at her most distracted, but then, Quayle reflected, Arthur had a lifetime's worth of experience wriggling out from under his mother's clutches. It was a damned nuisance, though!

"Find him, Quayle," Lady Constance commanded, just as Quayle had known she would. "Drag him back here by his ears, if necessary!"

"As you wish, Lady Constance."

Mr. Quayle did not relish the task. He had noted a few familiar faces from the casino milling about in the crowd, and had a sinking feeling, almost a premonition that although he had seen no sign of the Count or Countess, they might be making an appearance sooner rather than later.

7

AN INNOCENT GAME OF CARDS

Arthur placed his cards down with a flourish. Four of a kind! He glanced around the table expectantly, trying and failing not to smirk as he was met with an audible groan and a chorus of largely good-natured grumbles. It had been a good night for him thus far—an exceptionally good night. For once, it seemed, the Goddess of Fortune, Luck, and Degenerate Gamblers was smiling down on him.

Across the table, the Italian, Count Scarlioni, leaned back in his chair and regarded Arthur through narrow, lidded eyes. Lean and quick with a faint scar bisecting one eyebrow—a souvenir from a would-be thief in Rome, or so he claimed—and an ever-present smile that lingered mockingly on his lips, the Italian made for a charming, vaguely threatening figure at times. But he was not smiling now, mockingly or otherwise.

Arthur was confused. He had thought they were friends... or friendly, at least. The man had loaned him a not-insubstantial sum of money, after all. But then, Arthur supposed, the Count did have reason to be a little miffed, since it was Scarlioni who had suggested a friendly game of cards in the first place.

The Count had been well prepared for Lady Rosaline's party, bringing along his own bespoke poker box for the occasion. It was a beautiful thing, crafted from finely polished mahogany and glistening despite the dim glow in Lady Rosaline's little-used gaming room. And from out of its depths, Scarlioni had produced all the necessary accoutrements—both playing cards and poker chips—to a resounding cheer. But in the hour or so since, Arthur had won almost every game.

"Darling." The Countess placed a delicate hand on her husband's shoulder. She had accepted her defeat with good grace and a wry smile, and when Arthur eyed her cards, he found that she had managed a highly respectable full house. No doubt, she had expected to win this hand, but, alas for her, it was not to be.

"Mmm?" The Count relaxed slightly at her touch and a moment later, he was all smiles again. "Well done," he said, nodding to Arthur. "You win again. Soon, perhaps, you will be able to pay me back, yes? And with my own money, no less!"

He appeared amused by the irony, but Arthur had not forgotten the dark look in the Count's eye, and a faint sliver of unease pierced his excitement. Arthur was not, as it happened, quite the fool his mother believed him to be. Oh, he could be foolish, of that there was no doubt, but he was not *entirely* empty between his ears. He had always possessed a nose for trouble. Whether he would listen to himself was another matter.

"Just lucky, I suppose," Arthur replied with a less-than-modest shrug as he reached over to pull the chips toward him.

"Humph." Further down the table, a rotund, deceptively baby-faced gentleman grunted to himself. Sir Julius Markham-Smythe was Lady Rosaline's resident court jester— a latter-day Falstaff resplendent in a slightly thread-worn coat and tails. Armed with a laughing face and a relentlessly jolly disposition, Sir Julius lived on the indulgences of others, paying his way with wits and charm.

"Could use some of that luck, myself," he murmured. "That is, if you wouldn't mind sharing, Mr. Druce? You seem to have plenty to spare."

There was no malice in his words, only disappointment. It was Sir Julius who had groaned earlier when Arthur first revealed his hand, and it was Sir Julius who had lost the most tonight. Luck had abandoned him of late both here and at Monte Carlo, where Arthur remembered seeing the older man spinning the wheel fruitlessly on the roulette tables.

"Perhaps you should call it a night, Sir Julius," the Countess suggested from behind her husband. "Tomorrow is another day, and you may find your luck improved on the morrow."

Sir Julius frowned for a moment, but his good humor quickly reasserted itself. "Oh, what a kind lady," he beamed. "A marvelous lady—"

"A prudent lady," added the woman in question.

"But not to worry, my dear." Sir Julius grinned, benevolent in his optimism. "The night is young. Our Mr. Druce has had his turn, but I can feel the winds of favor shifting once more! And so, first, I shall avail myself of Rosaline's excellent libations, renew my prayers to the goddess of fortune, and then we shall see what we shall see. *Fortuna audaces iuvat*, no? Fortune favors the bold!"

Sir Julius rose and made his way through the darkened, smoke-filled room over to the drinks cupboard pressed against the far wall and poured himself a liberal portion of whiskey, then downed it in a single gulp. Watching, Arthur wondered if Sir Julius' disposition would be quite so jolly without the aid of such libations.

"If that were true," the Count pointed out, "if Fortune

truly did favor the bold, then Mr. Dabney here would never lose. And yet..." he trailed off suggestively.

It was not a friendly remark, even accompanied as it was by a smile, but for his part, Dabney only shrugged. A fair-haired young man with a sportsman's demeanor and build, he accepted his losses easily enough. He could afford them, for one, and, for another, he had never been one to hold grudges.

"I say, Dabney!" Arthur exclaimed, cocking an eyebrow at Dabney's discarded cards. "A pair of nines? What on earth were you playing at?"

"*Fortuna audaces iuvat*, as Sir Julius says." Dabney shrugged again, and Arthur caught a glint of amusement in his old friend's eyes—amusement and something else. "I was rather hoping for a straight, but the cards were in your favor."

"Risky."

"Risk is my business, Druce. You know that."

And he did. George Dabney, Esq. was the only one of his current companions Arthur had known for longer than a fortnight. They had been at school together, in fact, and while they had never been bosom companions, they had nonetheless shared a love of fast cars and fast horses and had together once shared joint custody of an impressively large collection of racing programs. In the years since, Arthur's interest had remained purely academic, while Dabney had made a name for himself in the racing world, winning five tournaments in the past year alone.

"Risk, eh?" Sir Julius said, rejoining them at the table. "Isn't there some story about you floating around, Dabney? Something about the Blue Train?"

"Ah," Dabney scowled into his glass. "*That*."

"What's this?" Arthur leaned forward.

"Oh, nothing much," Dabney attempted to wave the topic aside, but to no avail.

"Nothing much?" the Count exclaimed. "It was splashed across half the front pages on the coast."

"That does sound like something," Arthur agreed. It wasn't often that he saw Dabney embarrassed.

"Yes, well." Dabney sighed resignedly. "A few months ago, I may have attempted to race the Blue Train from Treville-sur-Mer to Paris."

"Race...the Blue Train to Paris?" Arthur was incredulous, but after a moment his expression cleared as he understood. "For a bet, I assume?" he asked knowingly.

"Naturally! Anything worth doing, is worth doing for a bet. And I thought there was a good chance, too. The train has to make all those stops and then spends a good hour circling around the outskirts of Paris. Whereas, with the right roads and the right motor, I should have been able to drive straight there. And I *did* have the right motor!"

"And yet," Sir Julius offered, his face all innocence, "remind me, how much did you lose, again, Dabney? Raymond was strutting around the place for days after."

"Oh, the money doesn't matter." Dabney was almost annoyed at the suggestion. "Raymond was welcome to it. I just wanted to...to feel the wind in my hair and the engine roaring beneath my feet and to know—*know!*—that I had outpaced the train. The worst of it is that I got close. Damn close!" He slammed his fist down on the table. "It would have been glorious!"

"So, what happened?" Arthur asked.

"The bloody French arrested me just outside Paris."

"For what?"

"For reckless driving. Can you believe that?"

"Mmm." Arthur *could* believe it—quite easily, in fact—but this was not the best moment to say as much. "Well, I'm not sure I—"

Dabney rolled his eyes. "Same old Druce," he said. "Still a spoilsport, I see."

"Apparently," Arthur shook his head with a laugh. "Although no one in my family would believe for a single moment that of the two of us, I'm the sensible one."

"Sensible? I'm not sure I'd go that far, old boy."

"Maybe not," Arthur allowed, "but then I haven't gone around racing any locomotives recently."

"Of course not," Dabney grinned. "As I said, you're a spoilsport."

Even as they fell back into their old familiar banter, however, Dabney's grin could not quite mask the lingering disappointment. It wasn't often that Dabney was challenged on his own ground and failed. That loss had hurt far more than any card game ever would.

"I thought you were absolutely dashing," the Countess soothed. "And I'm sure Rosaline thought so too."

Arthur blinked in surprise at the effect her words seemed to have. Was Dabney blushing? It was difficult to tell. Together the dim lights and drawn curtains conspired to shroud the room in darkness, a lingering gloom that made it all but impossible to see beyond the faces around the table, and even those were half-hidden behind the great clouds of tobacco smoke that glowered over the proceedings like a stormfront.

Into this gathering gloom burst the distracted figure of a distinguished elderly gentleman, who, having erupted onto the scene, immediately grew shy and hesitated briefly in the doorway.

"Ah, Carrodus!" Sir Julius greeted with all the appearance of friendliness. "How kind of you to join us."

So, *this* was Carrodus. Personally, Arthur was not of a particularly theatrical bent, but he had been dragged to more than his fair share of plays over the years—by his mother, or his cousin, or whichever overly optimistic young lady had been attempting to "improve" him at the time—and he had found them all eminently boring—Carrodus' plays more than most. Still, it was nice to put a face to the name, and Arthur had heard an awful lot of the name lately.

"Sorry I'm late," Carrodus said. "I was delayed by a Mr. Hollins. Delightful fellow. Delightful!"

"What he means to say," Sir Julius informed Arthur in a sotto voice, "is that this Hollins flattered him outrageously."

Arthur nodded. Hollins had made no secret of his admiration for Carrodus. In fact, apart from Lady Rosaline, Carrodus had been the other man's main topic of conversation the few times they had spoken.

"As it happens, he was quite complimentary," Carrodus said, eying them balefully. "Quite complimentary, indeed."

"Naturally. And then, no doubt, he asked you to cast an eye over his magnum opus, whatever that might be. I've found that young writers are always immensely complimentary when they want something in return."

Carrodus was not dismayed by Sir Julius' biting commentary. Instead, he fixed him with a gaze that carried the faintest suggestion of pistols at dawn.

"That has been my experience as well," the great playwright replied, deploying irony in place of a gunshot. "In fact, as I recall, Sir Julius, you once professed yourself a devotee of my work. Right before begging me to glance over your own modest scribblings." He smirked, a hint of triumph showing itself on his face.

"Just so," Sir Julius nodded. "And, as I recall, you were not exactly complimentary. Something about my having a 'tolerable talent for witticism but no understanding of either plot or character.' You suggested, I believe, that I might have a future in writing obituaries or holiday cards."

"Did I say that?" Carrodus let out an unrepentant chuckle.

"Verbatim."

"My, my, my," Carrodus folded himself into one of the chairs with a creak. "How rude of me. But then, you *do* write obituaries, don't you, Sir Julius? Something of that sort, anyway. I'm sure I've heard—"

"I write, or rather wrote, a rather highly regarded column for the society pages of the *London Chronicle*," Sir Julius replied plainly. "As well you know."

"Do I?" Carrodus frowned in exaggerated thoughtfulness. "Why would I know that?"

"Well, you ought to," Sir Julius said. "After all, you're the one who introduced me to dear old Weatherford, whose patronage and generosity kept me in vittles and gin for many a year."

"Ah, yes, Weatherford always did have a talent for spotting diamonds in the rough."

Arthur stifled a grin. Watching these two old warhorses politely bash away at each other was the most fun he'd had in ages, and a quick glance confirmed that he was not the only one enjoying the fireworks. The Count and Countess were exchanging hushed, excited whispers, and even Dabney, who seemed the most uncomfortable with the verbal sparring, couldn't resist a slight smile here and there when one of the combatants landed a particularly cutting blow.

"Are you calling me a diamond in the rough? Goodness, your opinion of me improves by leaps and bounds!"

"I really couldn't say," Carrodus said. "To be honest, Sir Julius, I haven't paid your career much attention. At least not until you reemerged over the summer, foisting your attentions onto Lady Rosaline."

"I assure you," Sir Julius replied smugly, "Rosaline has never complained about my...attentions."

If Sir Julius had hoped that remark would elicit some jealousy in his opponent, he was sadly disappointed. Instead, Carrodus was almost gleeful, as if Sir Julius had given him the opening he was looking for.

"Oh, she would never," Carrodus admitted. "Not in so many words, of course. But you will soon find that with a handful of exceptions, namely Weatherford and myself, Rosaline's affections can be quite fickle indeed. In fact, while you've been in here, helping yourself to her gin and losing what I'm sure must be her money, Rosaline has been promenading through the gardens with that new favorite of hers—Lord Whatshisname. Unsworth, isn't it? He's an Earl, I believe, while you're merely a Baronet, aren't you, Sir Julius?"

"Promenading through the gardens?" Sir Julius was thunderstruck, and he was not the only one. "But she promised me he was just an old friend."

"Whatever their history," Carrodus replied, "in the here and now, Rosaline seems rather determined to renew His Lordship's acquaintance."

"I'm sorry?" Arthur gaped in dawning horror. "Surely, you're not suggesting that Lady Rosaline is...*pursuing* Lord Unsworth? You can't be!"

"Forgive me," Carrodus frowned, "but who are you, exactly?"

"Arthur Druce," he introduced himself, then added the more pertinent information. "Lord Unsworth is my uncle."

"Oh, of course! The nephew!" Carrodus was effusive in his greeting. "I was speaking to your charming cousin, Fanny, only a few moments ago, before she slipped away. I gathered that she had heard all she could stand of her Mr. Hollins' play. Not that I blame her. Delightful fellow, extraordinarily enthusiastic, but a trifle...didactic in his politics."

Arthur was decidedly uninterested in either Hollins' play or his politics. "Fanny," he asked. "Did she see—?"

"Oh, my dear fellow, absolutely everyone saw." For the first time, Carrodus sounded genuinely sympathetic. "I'm afraid Rosaline is never one to miss an opportunity. All the world's her stage, after all, and all of us men and women merely her players, or, failing that, her audience. But to answer your question: yes. I rather think Rosaline is pursuing your uncle, Mr. Druce, although to what end I can't imagine."

"Pardon me." Sir Julius stood abruptly. "I believe I..." He paused, groping fruitlessly for an excuse. "Well, I—"

Abandoning the pretense, he made a short, apologetic little bow before turning and barreling out of the room as fast as his legs could carry him, in search, no doubt, of Lady Rosaline.

"I thought the winds of fortune were changing," the Count called after him. "Fortune favors the bold, wasn't it?"

But Sir Julius paid no heed, the game of cards forgotten as the door slammed shut behind him with a thud.

"Someone's not best pleased," the Count said with a smirk.

"Indeed not," the Countess agreed. She was far too gracious to smirk openly, but there was something decidedly sly about the amused crinkle around her eyes. "Why, I do believe Sir Julius thought that *he* was Rosaline's new favorite."

"Indubitably," her husband nodded. "And I dare say that he was not the only one." Across the table, Dabney shifted uncomfortably under the Count's knowing stare. "But now I think it's time for another game, wouldn't you say? Will you be joining us, Carrodus?"

"But of course. Wouldn't miss it for the world." Carrodus was all amiable smiles now that Sir Julius had beaten a hasty retreat.

"Dabney?" the Count turned.

"Hmm?" The sportsman frowned distractedly. "Oh, yes. Deal me in."

"Excellent. And I'm sure there's no need to ask you, Arthur. Not with the run of luck you've been having."

Arthur forced himself to nod, but his heart wasn't in it. He was too busy shuddering at the thought of Lady Rosaline and Uncle Edward. She was a handsome enough woman, he supposed, and her eyes had a certain sparkle to them, but—for goodness sake—she had to be near sixty at the least. And Uncle Edward was no spring chicken himself. Naturally, he deserved every happiness, but why Rosaline? Arthur shuddered again. The very idea of the two of them...

The sound of the cards shuffling in the Count's practiced hands mercifully broke through Arthur's thoughts. As he began to deal, however, the Countess demurred, placing a hand against her head.

"If you don't mind, I'll sit this one out, darling," she said. "I appear to have developed a bit of a headache."

Immediately, the Count was all solicitous, loving concern. "Perhaps you should take a walk outside," he suggested. "It's quite smokey in here, and the fresh air might do you good."

"Nonsense, darling." The Countess waved his concerns aside. "There's no need to fuss. I'm sure I'll be fine in a moment or two. Best if I just stay here and watch you play. You can show me how it's done." She grinned teasingly. "Or perhaps Arthur can."

Arthur acknowledged the compliment with a wane smile and accepted his cards, grateful for the distraction. But he couldn't escape the feeling that something was terribly wrong. The earlier laughing, congenial atmosphere had faded, leaving in its place raw nerves and suspicious glances. Carrodus' announcement had left everyone on edge, Arthur included.

After a moment, he snorted at the direction his thoughts had taken. He had never seen himself as a contemplative sort before, yet here he was, scrutinizing his fellow players.

Quayle's influence, perhaps? Or was he growing up? Maturing. Perish the thought!

Next, he'd be spouting opinions about the state of the empire, or the by-elections, or the price of tea in China. Oh yes! Arthur could see it now, a lifetime of serious suits and stifling collars complete with a *proper* job in the city, with the Financial Times in place of the Racing Times and stocks and bonds in place of horses and hounds. All very proper and correct.

Mother would be pleased, of course, and so would Father from his prison cell. They had spent a lifetime trying to beat or cajole some sense into their son's head. But what did they know, eh? What did they know? Mother had spent so much time berating Arthur for his failings that she had missed her husband's. And in the end, the father had proved to be just as much a fool as the son, just as much a gambler. And a crook besides!

No, Arthur decided, he preferred the horses and hounds. They were more honest. A man knew where he stood with a horse. He could check its teeth and learn its pedigree, and he could watch as it sent the dirt flying beneath its hooves. What were stocks compared to that? Just numbers and dreams.

Better a silly, honest fool, in the end, then a somber, dishonest one.

"Well?" the Count demanded. "Are you playing or not?"

Arthur shook his head and managed a slight smile, belatedly realizing that everyone else had their cards in hand. "Of course," he said. "Play on!"

But what game were they playing, exactly? And whose?

8

LADY ROSALINE'S REQUEST

Lord Unsworth had not particularly desired to accompany Lady Rosaline, and his misgivings only grew the further she led him from the party. Her villa had been built on the grounds of an old seventeenth century convent—a fact which was of great amusement to the local wits—and extended out to a cliff before descending all the way down to the water's edge. She had her own private dock there, large enough for a whole fleet, although Lord Unsworth could only spy a single yacht swaying and rocking with the tide.

Away from her varyingly adoring and scornful public, Lady Rosaline seemed somehow smaller, not diminished exactly, but certainly less at ease. Sadder, perhaps, and almost *frightened*. As if she had finally decided or felt comfortable enough to put aside her mask and her props and give him—and him alone—a peek behind the curtain. Such trust all but demanded intimacy, and Lord Unsworth felt a sudden jolt of protectiveness—a sort of tenderness he had not felt in years—and yet he found himself wondering if this too was a performance.

It was an unkind thought and one which sat uncomfortably in his mind. Lord Unsworth had always preferred to take people on their own terms, an attitude which had served him well and made him few enemies. Recent events, however, had taught him suspicion and it was not a lesson he would soon forget.

"Do you ever wonder?" Lady Rosaline asked, her voice unusually pensive.

"About what?"

"About us," Lady Rosaline said. "If we would have been happy."

"Ah." Lord Unsworth found to his surprise that he had been expecting the question all evening. Why else would she have invited him, and why else would he have come, if not to rake over old wounds?

"Do *you*?" he asked, dreading her answer as much as he dreaded his own.

"Sometimes," Lady Rosaline smiled wistfully. "You may think it presumptuous of me, but I think I would have enjoyed being the Countess of Unsworth. The parties, the dresses, the castle. You were always so proud, so passionate about the castle. We could have made a home there together —you and I."

That thought was far less presumptuous then it might have been. Certainly not as presumptuous as Constance would have wished. Lord Unsworth had, in fact, strongly considered the possibility of marriage once upon a dream. But he had woken up years—decades—ago, and of all his old dreams, this one struck him as the most childish.

"We would have been miserable," he replied, not ungently or unkindly but firmly, nonetheless. "Even if my father had miraculously agreed to such a match, you would have grown tired of me soon enough, and in the end, I would have retreated to my books and my histories and left you to indulge yourself in...other ways." He shook his head. "I'm not blind, Rosey, or deaf. I've heard the stories. Your hobbies would have bankrupted the estate and your activities would have made me a laughingstock."

"My activities?" Taken aback by his quiet vehemence, Rosaline stared at him, as if seeing him for the first time as he truly was and not as she remembered him.

Her gaze was frank and searching, and more than a little hurt, but underneath it all she seemed more puzzled than anything. His Lordship let her stare in silence. She would find the answer on her own soon enough. Whatever she was hoping to find, there was room enough in his heart for only one great sadness, one towering regret, and that space was long since full.

"I was wrong," Lady Rosaline said in a wondering tone. "You *have* changed after all."

"Yes," Lord Unsworth agreed. "I have."

"But do you truly think so little of me, Eddy?" she pleaded. "You were fond of me once, after all. I remember you wrote me a rather sweet, ardent letter."

It was Lord Unsworth's turn to be taken aback. Why mention the letter? "That was a long time ago," he said. "We were both different people then."

"Was it your—" she hesitated before continuing. "Was it marrying your wife that changed you?"

"No." Lord Unsworth's answer was immediate. "Oh, it was a brilliant match as far as my father was concerned. Mary's grandfather was a duke and her mother a viscountess. But Mary and I were never particularly happy together. She, too, tired of me quite quickly, perhaps even quicker than you would have." Lord Unsworth sighed. "But then we had Teddy, and that changed everything."

"Teddy." Lady Rosaline grimaced and had the good grace to look moderately ashamed. "I suppose that was...thoughtless of me, mentioning him like that. I should have known better, but I..." She shook her head, banishing whatever she might have said with a frown. "Whatever else happens," she said instead, "for what it's worth, I *am* sorry about your son, Eddy. Truly, I am."

Lord Unsworth believed her, but still couldn't quite bring himself to either accept or reject her apology. But as the minutes ticked by and the silence became almost companionable, he realized that they had come to a kind of détente after all.

"You are right, though," Lady Rosaline admitted. "I would have destroyed our marriage in the end. I wouldn't have been able to help myself." She laughed softly. It was not a kind sound. "In those days I was forever chasing excitement—skating on the edge of ruin for the sake of a few laughs. But now that I'm older, I've found that I crave stability more than anything. And I have no idea where to find it."

Lord Unsworth had nothing to say to that.

"All my friends are fading away," she continued. "Léger betrayed me years ago, but now suddenly he's come crawling back, desperate for forgiveness yet still whispering his poison when he thinks I can't hear. The nerve!" She sighed. "But the worst part is that he's right. I probably will forgive him in the end."

"Why?"

"Because I always do," she snapped. "I forgive all of them sooner or later. My boys, my useless boys! Even Carrodus is no help. He used to be such a fiery, passionate man, but time has made him jealous and far too dependent for his own good. That's why I let him live on the grounds. The poor man can't be trusted on his own. Not anymore."

"And Sir Julius?" Lord Unsworth asked, morbidly curious despite himself.

"Ah," Lady Rosaline grinned. "My darling flatterer. Raymond is right about him, of course. Sir Julius is after my money, and he asks for a little more each time. Always another sob story, as if I haven't seen his ilk a thousand times." She snorted. "All of them circling, all of them desperate. It's a familiar dance, but I can't help but feel there's something different this time."

"Oh?" Lord Unsworth sensed that they were approaching at last the heart of the matter. "What do you mean?"

"I'm not sure, exactly, but lately there have been a number of incidents at the villa—objects being moved, paintings disturbed, papers and letters not quite where I left them. I thought I was going mad at first, but now I'm not so sure. That's why I sent for Weatherford."

Lord Unsworth remembered Weatherford well enough, although they hadn't spoken in years. They had never been friends, not exactly, but Lord Unsworth had admired the newspaperman's forthright intelligence and had, for a time, been jealous of his closeness with Rosaline. Water under the bridge, now, and Lord Unsworth had been truly sorry to hear of his death.

"Weatherford was the only one I could trust to be on my side," Lady Rosaline said, "the only one who never demanded anything in return. And now that he's gone, I'd hoped that *you*..." Lady Rosaline trailed into silence, unable to finish the thought. "Never mind." She shook her head regretfully. "It was a silly thought."

"No," Lord Unsworth disagreed. "Not silly, but you must know that it was never going to happen."

"Yes, I see that now. I'd thought, perhaps, for old time's sake, but as you say, we were very different people then." She laughed suddenly. It was a rueful, brittle sound. "I kept your letter, you know. That last one, before—"

"—before my father brought me to my senses."

"Oh?" Her voice was teasing now, regaining its former gaiety. "Is that what he did?"

"Perhaps." Lord Unsworth snorted. "Although I didn't see it that way at the time."

"No, I imagine not. Strange, isn't it? How our wounds and memories fade? I suppose that's why I keep them—all my old letters—to remind me."

"Remind you of what?"

"I'm not sure. Of myself, perhaps?" Lady Rosaline shrugged helplessly. "I'm sorry, Eddy. I had no right to ask anything of you. I know you have enough troubles of your own."

"Yes, I suppose I do." Lord Unsworth was not pleased at the reminder. "But not as much as there might have been."

"Yes." There was a considering glint in her eyes. "Your Mr. Quayle must be quite helpful in that regard."

"He has his uses," Lord Unsworth answered warily. "Why?"

"Oh, no reason," Lady Rosaline waved her hand dismissively. "I was simply wondering if I might borrow him for a spell?"

"Borrow him?" Lord Unsworth scowled. "What exactly do you mean by 'borrow him'?"

This was it—the moment of truth, the moment Rosaline had been working towards all evening in her own particular way. And so, after one final, hesitant flourish, she began to explain. It was a simple enough tale in the end, for all her trappings and embellishments, but a concerning one nonetheless. And the more he listened, the more worried Lord Unsworth became.

Something was wrong here. Something was terribly, terribly wrong, although whether the trouble lay with Treville-sur-Mer or with Rosaline herself, he could not say. In either case, though, His Lordship wanted no part in it. The past, as he had been vividly reminded tonight, was the past, and anything he might have felt for her once had long since faded, leaving only echoes behind, nothing more. And he owed such echoes nothing.

No. Lady Rosaline was not—could not—be his concern. No matter what she had hoped, he was not her knight in shining armor, not her savior.

And neither was Mr. Quayle.

9

AT PARTY'S END

Lingering for a moment in the doorway of one of the villa's interminable rooms, Mr. Quayle allowed himself the luxury of a brief, frustrated sigh. It was times such as these, he reflected, that were sent to try men's souls, specifically his own. It had been nearly an hour now, and thus far his search for Arthur had been a complete and utter failure. Further proof that a lifetime spent under his mother's tyrannical eye had, if nothing else, given Arthur a thorough appreciation for the fine art of making himself scarce. It would have been impressive, if it wasn't so irritating, and to make matters worse, Mr. Quayle's own talent for unobtrusiveness had seemingly deserted him tonight.

While wandering the gardens on the hunt for Arthur, he had been accosted by any number of lords, ladies, viscounts, and barons, as well as several titans of industry and one or two starlets, all strangely eager to make Mr. Quayle's acquaintance. Not for his own sake, of course. Not entirely. But Lady Rosaline had been observed to single him out for a private, albeit brief audience, and not long after that she had absconded into the bushes with Quayle's employer. Naturally, this had aroused a great deal of curiosity and no little suspicion amongst the partygoers, and in Lord Unsworth's absence, Quayle was left to bear the brunt of their attentions.

None of this, of course, had helped in his search for Arthur, although Mr. Quayle had heard that Count Scarlioni had been granted Lady Rosaline's blessing and was arranging a poker game somewhere in the villa. The Billiards Room, perhaps? Hearing this, Mr. Quayle was immediately convinced. Where else would Arthur have slunk off to? Of course, the fool was gambling again! And with the Count, no less.

M. Tallier's vague warnings earlier had only confirmed Quayle's suspicions about the Italian's friendship with Arthur. Scarlioni was circling, insinuating himself into Arthur's life, but for what purpose Quayle could not be sure. Just another danger lurking over the horizon, another motive he couldn't quite grasp. He was becoming increasingly frustrated with his own slowness, with the creeping sense that he was missing something—more than one somethings. People, a few of them, at least, somehow knew more about him then he knew about them, and that was not a feeling he enjoyed. Not in the slightest. There were too many questions crowding his mind and not enough answers. The most pertinent question at the moment being: where exactly *was* the bloody Billiards Room?

Turning down yet another corridor he came to a sudden, stumbling halt. Mr. Quayle could see at once that something was wrong. At the center of the room was a small, raised platform where a pedestal had clearly stood, but that pedestal had fallen and cracked against the floor, shedding shards of stone. And that was not the only thing amiss.

The paintings and sketchings which dotted the walls, including two Bernini drawings and a Degas, were all of them askew. It was easy enough to overlook, just the slightest cant to the side, but leaning in closer, Mr. Quayle saw at once that he was correct. Someone had carefully lifted each of the paintings and then almost as carefully returned them to their moorings.

If not for the fallen marble, he might have believed it the result of one of the servants being a trifle overzealous in their dusting, but instead Quayle felt an unfortunately familiar sense of dread creeping up his legs and his thoughts.

And that was when he saw it—saw her—lying prone and motionless beside the shattered remains of the pedestal.

With his heart thundering in his chest, Mr. Quayle hurriedly knelt down and placed his fingers gently against her neck, feeling in vain for a pulse. But he saw at once that it was no use. She had been struck on the side of her head; her left temple smashed in quite brutally. He had seen such blows before on the battlefield and in the trenches, and he knew from intimate experience just how much force, how much desperation and anger was required. This was no accident, no mistake. No! Lady Rosaline Barrett De Marchi had been murdered.

Deliberately and viciously murdered.

As Mr. Quayle rose to his feet with a tired, remorseful sigh, a single thought pounded through his mind, drowning out all other considerations.

Well, he thought to himself, here we go again.

PART II

MR. QUAYLE TAKES THE CASE

10

ANOTHER FINE MESS!

Another murder! Another potential scandal! Another fine mess! At least this time—thank heavens for small mercies—the victim had been kind enough to be killed in her own home. But even so, this was all in danger of becoming something of a habit, and Mr. Quayle did not appreciate it, not one tiny bit. Recent events notwithstanding, murder was not his forte. He was a secretary, not a detective, and Lady Rosaline's death, while undoubtedly tragic, was none of his concern.

Or was it?

Almost against his will, Mr. Quayle could feel the cogs and gears begin to churn inside his head. Lady Rosaline had been playing games all evening, circling Lord Unsworth and the rest of them like some socialite spider spinning her web, and now that she was dead, Mr. Quayle had a terrible feeling that she had somehow succeeded in ensnaring them from beyond the grave.

Certainly, the police were full of questions and Quayle had been forced to tell his story several times, first to a constable, then a sergeant, and finally to two plain-clothed detectives—

Inspectors Duvot and Barras—who had regarded his answers, if not with outright suspicion, then certainly with a degree of well-earned skepticism. After all, not only had Mr. Quayle found the body but, by all accounts, Lord Unsworth was the last person to have seen Lady Rosaline alive.

After nearly two hours, however, Mr. Quayle was released from purgatory and ushered into the Billiards Room, of all places, where the Unsworth family had been left to wait, although what precisely they were waiting for remained unclear. Lord Unsworth was pacing nervously when Mr. Quayle arrived. His Lordship's head was bent, and his gaze fixed firmly on the ground as he marched up and down the length of the room, occasionally muttering to himself. But he turned at once at the sound of the door and let out a joyful cry.

"Ah! There you are, Quayle!" he exclaimed. "Capital!"

Lord Unsworth was positively relieved to see him, Mr. Quayle realized with a frown. And His Lordship wasn't the only one. Fanny and her elusive Mr. Hollins had taken up residence by the windows, and, having pulled back the curtains, were amusing themselves by spying on the police on the front lawn. Such distractions were soon forgotten, however, and Fanny turned to greet Quayle with a smile and a massive sigh of relief. For his part, Mr. Hollins was not quite as welcoming, although he seemed more preoccupied than hostile.

Even Lady Constance relaxed her iron grip on Arthur's arm and ceased berating him long enough to send Quayle a quick, assessing glance.

"Took you long enough!" she snapped. "Edward was getting worried." Her glare relaxed a fraction of an inch. "We all were."

"Thank you," Mr. Quayle said, somewhat taken aback. "I must say I'm surprised and rather touched by your concern, Lady Constance."

"Nonsense," she huffed and hurriedly clarified. "I may not be particularly fond of you, Quayle, but in the past year you've proved your loyalty and your usefulness several times over, and I will not allow a faithful family retainer to be detained by...by...foreigners!"

"Of course not." Mr. Quayle was relieved that Lady Constance had not turned suddenly sentimental. The night had been filled with enough surprises. "But thankfully, no one's been accused of anything, let alone arrested, as of yet."

"Then what are we still doing here?" Lord Unsworth demanded. "Do you know?"

"I'm afraid not, sir," Mr. Quayle replied. "The police seem to be waiting for something," he frowned as a new thought occurred to him, "or someone."

"I don't care what they're waiting for. This is intolerable!" Lady Constance spat with all the considerable outrage she could muster. "How dare they keep us penned up in here as if we were...involved?"

"But we are involved, Connie," Lord Unsworth said tiredly as he placed a placating hand on his sister's shoulder. "At least for the moment."

"No, I won't have it," Lady Constance declared. "One murder was quite enough for this family. Two starts to look like carelessness. And what happens when it's three? Or four?"

Lord Unsworth's efforts to calm his sister having been rebuffed, His Lordship sent Mr. Quayle a pleading glance over her shoulder.

"I promise you, Lady Constance, that it won't come to that," Mr. Quayle said with considerably more confidence than he felt. "Our involvement in this...unpleasantness is purely a matter of happenstance, a quirk of timing, nothing more. His Lordship happened to be the last person to see Lady Rosaline alive, and I happened to find her body.

Together these facts may seem suggestive, but they are entirely circumstantial, and I've little doubt the police will realize that soon enough."

"Will they?" Lady Constance was not convinced, and Mr. Quayle acknowledged her point with a reluctant nod.

"Perhaps not right away," he allowed. "But Lady Rosaline did not strike me as a universally loved figure, not even within her own circle, and if we scratch the surface, I'm sure that more than a few motives will come crawling out of the woodwork and turn the police's attention in a more deserving direction."

Or so he hoped.

"You had better be right, Quayle," Lady Constance said. "For your sake." And then, without another word, she marched over to the windows, where Arthur had ineffectively hidden himself, leaving Mr. Quayle alone with His Lordship.

Neither of them seemed to be in any particular hurry to break the silence, however, and Quayle could feel the oppressive weight of the unsaid building with each passing moment. Lord Unsworth obviously had something he wanted to get off his chest. That need was etched onto every line on his face, written in the stiffness of his back and stoop of his shoulders. Yet still, he held his tongue, preferring instead to look at anything and everything apart from his loyal and efficient secretary.

Well, so be it! It was not Mr. Quayle's place to pry. He thought he had earned Lord Unsworth's trust after last year's debacle, but in the end, either His Lordship trusted him, or he did not.

In the meantime, Mr. Quayle busied himself examining the elusive Billiards Room. For all its size, it had a dark, almost claustrophobic atmosphere, with its wood paneling and dim lights, and everywhere he turned, he found signs of Arthur's game. The smell of alcohol, sweat, and tobacco lingered in the air, but the great wafts of shrouding smoke were all but gone, revealing cards, chips, and half-empty glasses strewn across the table, abandoned in the aftermath of Lady Rosaline's death.

Quayle counted six glasses, but only four card-hands, and noted the impressively large pile of chips in front of a chair with Arthur's coat still hanging over the back of it. By the looks of things, it had been a good night for at least one person.

Aware of someone's eyes watching him, Mr. Quayle glanced over to find Lord Unsworth regarding him with a reluctantly determined expression.

His Lordship, it appeared, was, at last, ready to talk.

* * *

"I was in love with her, I suppose," Lord Unsworth began. His voice was low and melancholy, as though he was speaking from a long way away. "At least, I *thought* I was in love with her at the time. Looking back, it was probably more of an infatuation, but she could be quite...bewitching, as you can imagine." Lord Unsworth shot Quayle a shrewd glance. "Does that surprise you?" he asked. "The thought of dry, dusty old Unsworth in love with an actress?" His Lordship laughed. "Well, I wasn't quite so old then. None of us were."

"No, sir," Mr. Quayle answered truthfully. "It doesn't surprise me. We, all of us, contain multitudes, and love is but one of them. Besides," he shrugged, "she told me."

"Rosaline did?"

"Yes," Mr. Quayle nodded. "She mentioned that the two of you had been 'quite close' at one time."

"Oh?" Lord Unsworth's voice was unexpectedly sharp. "Well, we were, although not nearly so close as my father feared. Rosaline was much too canny for that."

Mr. Quayle kept his expression unchanged and His Lordship did not deign to elaborate, instead resuming his story-cum-confession.

"We were her earliest admirers," Lord Unsworth said. "Myself, Weatherford, and her future husband, General Alexander Montague Barrett." Lord Unsworth's lips thinned, unable to disguise his distaste and, for a moment, he was the spitting image of his sister. "Weatherford was a nobody in those days," he explained, "and could never have kept her in the style she desired, and as for me," His Lordship shrugged, "my father and Constance quickly conspired to remove me from the picture. They shipped me away on a Grand Tour of Europe, and I returned to the sound of wedding bells. My marriage had been arranged in my absence, you see, and I did my duty and forgot all about Rosaline. In fact, I hadn't even thought of her in years, not until we came to the Riviera."

If Mr. Quayle had any doubts about the neatness of Lord Unsworth's story, he kept them close to his chest. It was better that way, and he had a sinking feeling that Lord Unsworth's history with Lady Rosaline would prove full of snares and pitfalls if examined too closely. Besides, Quayle was more concerned with why Lord Unsworth had chosen to share this story. His Lordship was extremely private, and he would not have told Quayle a single word of it unless he had an excellent reason.

"Have you told the police any of this?" Mr. Quayle asked.

"Not yet," Lord Unsworth replied. "And not ever, if I have my way. I'm only telling you this much because of what happened to her and because of what she said."

"When you were alone in the gardens?"

Lord Unsworth sighed. "We spoke of the past mostly. After all, we had little else in common anymore, and she told me that...that..." He took a deep breath. "She told me that she regretted not marrying me and that she had thought of me often over the years."

Mr. Quayle hesitated for a moment, then decided to take the plunge. "Did you believe her?" he asked.

Lord Unsworth did not answer for nearly half a minute. "It was always hard to be sure where Rosaline was concerned," he finally admitted, "but yes, I think she was telling the truth, or parts of it at least. But..."

"Yes?"

"She wanted something from me, Quayle, and she chose the truth most likely to achieve her ends. That was her way, even when we were young. Rosaline would never tell a lie if the truth could do the job just as well."

"And what did she want, sir, may I ask?" Neither Mr. Quayle's manner nor his voice betrayed more than polite interest, but inside he was dying to hear the answer.

"I'm not sure," Lord Unsworth said, unknowingly crushing his secretary's hopes. "Rosaline wouldn't give me all the details, but it was clear that something had frightened her badly. She felt persecuted, besieged and, I think she was genuinely starting to worry that she might be losing her mind."

"Forgive me, Lord Unsworth, but in such circumstances, why—"

"—would she come to me for help?" His Lordship finished. "Yes, I wondered that myself, but I got the sense that she didn't trust her companions here—Carrodus, Léger, and the others—and she made no mention of her son."

Mr. Quayle was not surprised by that. Raymond had proven utterly useless following his mother's death, barely managing to give a brief, halting announcement before disappearing into the bowels of the house and leaving his wife to make a doomed effort before retreating herself. Hardly the first person one would turn to in a crisis.

"Of course, if Weatherford was still alive," Lord Unsworth said, "Rosaline would have turned to him immediately, but with him gone, an old friend, someone with no designs or ulterior motives, must have seemed the safest option. But as it turned out, it wasn't my help Rosaline was after. It was yours."

"Mine?"

"Yours," Lord Unsworth repeated. "She knew all about your efforts on our behalf last year, and she wanted to...well, borrow your talents."

Mr. Quayle supposed he should feel gratified that Lady Rosaline had wanted to poach him, that she had gone to so much trouble on his behalf, but instead he felt hunted and ever so slightly insulted. Just once, he would like to be in demand for his secretarial skills. "Did you agree?" he asked hesitantly.

His Lordship shook his head. "I would never have done so without discussing the matter with you first," he said, "and besides, I didn't feel as though I owed her anything, least of all your services. But now she's dead." His whole face crumpled for a moment. "Do you understand, Quayle? I turned her away. She came to me for help, I turned her away, and not an hour later, she was found murdered."

"It's not your fault, sir."

"I know that," Lord Unsworth said, "but I can't help but feel responsible in some way. Now, I have no desire to put you in an uncomfortable position, Quayle, or to ask more of you than I have already, but—" he paused, seemingly too embarrassed to finish.

"Are you asking me to investigate a murder, Lord Unsworth?" Mr. Quayle asked. "*Again?*"

"Ah, yes...well, I...um..." His Lordship floundered for a moment, then looked away.

Mr. Quayle was not floundering, however, and did not

look away. Only a few minutes ago, he had thought of Lady Rosaline as a spider spinning her web, and there was still some truth to that, but she had also been a rattled, desperate woman. Desperate enough to turn to a man she had not seen in over twenty years, and there, at last, was an answer to the very first riddle, or at least the beginnings of one.

Lady Rosaline had not, as it turned out, pursued Lord Unsworth so vigorously merely to renew their old acquaintance or to gloat or any of the other motives the family and guests had bandied about. No. She had wanted his help and had gone about getting it in the only way she knew how—by spinning her web and trying to lure him in. What a waste! Had she truly been so twisted up inside, so insecure, that she couldn't just ask an old friend for aid?

And as for Quayle, he had not been invited to a party but rather to an audition. Lady Rosaline had referred to him outright as the Unsworth's "Savior" and had plainly hoped to cast him as hers as well. But savior from what? A few minor incidents, a vague sense of malice, a creeping fear that she might be losing her mind? Those were little more than parlor games—smoke and mirrors. For all her theatrics, though, it seems Lady Rosaline had been right to worry. Her murder showed that much, if nothing else.

Mr. Quayle sighed heavily. That was it, then. He may not have been particularly keen on the woman when she was alive, and he wasn't sure he liked her much more now that she was dead, but when Lady Rosaline was in danger, she had thought of Lord Unsworth and, more importantly, of his private sleuth-cum-secretary. And Mr. Quayle knew himself well enough to know that he was not immune to such appeals to his vanity or his conscience.

"If I agree to do what you still haven't quite asked me to do," Mr. Quayle began, not quite believing the words coming out of his mouth, "then the same rules as before will apply. I will follow the evidence wherever it may lead, and I will not be held responsible for the outcome."

"Understood," His Lordship agreed readily enough.

"And this time, Lord Unsworth, there must be no secrets. You'll have to tell me everything, including whatever you're still holding back."

"Ah." Lord Unsworth's face contorted into an embarrassed sort of grimace. "Now that you mention it, there was something else. I didn't think much of it at first, but Constance believes..."

"Yes?"

"There was this letter, you see," His Lordship said, refusing to meet Quayle's eyes. "I barely even remember writing the wretched thing. It was thirty-odd years ago, after all. But Rosaline claimed she'd kept it, that she kept all her old letters, and something about the way she said that—"

"You think she was attempting to blackmail you?"

"Constance does," Lord Unsworth said. "She's absolutely sure of it, but there's hardly anything scandalous about a thirty-year-old love letter." His Lordship frowned again. "Apart from my dreadful poetry, perhaps."

"Even so, in the current circumstances, the very existence of such a letter could be considered suspect."

"I am aware of the danger," Lord Unsworth said quietly, his eyes glinting sharply. "What I can't figure out is why Rosaline would bother. It's not as though she needed the money."

"Hmm." Mr. Quayle had come to recognize the telltale signs of someone living beyond their means, desperate to keep up appearances. Lady Rosaline's party may have been a sparkling, glittering spectacle, but away from the bright lights and the sound of music, the villa appeared to be crumbling around the edges.

"I say!" Arthur cried. "I wonder who that could be?"

Interrupted, Mr. Quayle and Lord Unsworth both started and rushed toward the window where the rest of the family had gathered.

A rather important-looking black car had just pulled up outside the house, and as Mr. Quayle and the others watched, a small, owlish, well-dressed gentleman emerged. When he saw his face, Mr. Quayle cursed himself for a fool.

It was M. Tallier.

11

THE GENTLEMAN FROM THE SÛRETÉ

Officially, of course, Detective Chief Inspector Jean-Baptiste Tallier of the Sûreté in Paris was on vacation, not that anyone believed him for a moment. His niece, who had been staying with him and his wife for the past few months, had laughed in his face when Tallier told her he was planning to spend a few relaxing weeks in the South of France. And Tallier's Superintendent had glared at Tallier over the rim of his spectacles, not even trying to hide his disbelief. But all the paperwork had been in order, and Tallier *was* owed a holiday, so the Superintendent had confined himself to a disapproving grumble and signed on the appropriate line.

In Treville-sur-Mer, meanwhile, Tallier's old friend, Judge Jarre, had not even acknowledged the fiction, simply pouring him a generous glass of calvados before calmly but firmly demanding the truth. Even Tallier's newfound acquaintance, Mr. Quayle, had seen through the charade, although, unlike the others, he had been ignorant of Tallier's true intentions. The Englishman was clever, though, and had almost certainly pieced some of it together, even before this evening's debacle.

Debacle? *Disaster* might be a more appropriate word. And everything had been going so well too! After months and months of hard work and long nights, at long last, the greatest gamble of his career had been about to pay off, but pride, as they say, goeth before the fall. And Lady Rosaline's death had changed everything.

Perhaps if he had been more careful, more alert, she would still be alive. But such thoughts were merely another species of conceit, so he locked them away in a strongbox at the furthest reaches of his mind. Neither Tallier's guilt nor his pride—two sides of the same coin—had any place in this investigation going forward. They would only distract him, and he had made enough mistakes already.

Both here and in Paris.

* * *

"Well, Chief Inspector, have you arrested him yet?"

Tallier tilted his head, studying the other man. Every murder was a tragedy to someone, if only to the deceased, but Raymond Montague Barrett did not appear overly saddened by his mother's untimely demise. Instead, he had chosen anger—an understandable, if inconvenient, response.

They were on the second floor in the family's private wing, a far less gaudy and extravagant setting than the one Tallier had seen downstairs. It was still richly furnished, of course, but there was dust on the mantlepiece and an empty space on the adjacent wall where a rather large painting had clearly hung quite recently.

"Arrested who, monsieur?"

"Why, that man, of course! Quayle."

"Monsieur Quayle is assisting us with our inquiries," Tallier replied cautiously. "But I'm afraid that no one has been arrested at this time."

"Why ever not? I heard he was caught red-handed, standing over my mother's body, no less. Sounds pretty conclusive to me." Raymond turned to his wife for support, which she gave, somewhat half-heartedly, in Tallier's opinion. "Now, far be it for me to tell you your business, Chief Inspector, but—"

"Discovering her body, monsieur, is not quite the same as being caught red-handed." Tallier's tone was gentle but firm. "You are understandably eager to see your mother's killer found and arrested. C'est naturel, *très naturel*—" Tallier's English, like his German, and, to a lesser extent, his Italian was far better than he usually let on, especially in the face of angry foreigners. "—but it would be unwise to leap to conclusions, non?"

Raymond sputtered and grumbled but ultimately agreed. "I suppose you know what you're doing," he muttered begrudgingly.

"Merci," the Chief Inspector smiled, deliberately ignoring Raymond's tone. "Now, was there anything else before we—"

"Yes." Rekindled in less than a heartbeat, Raymond's anger sparked to new and sudden life. "I would greatly appreciate it, Chief Inspector, if you removed that rabble down there." He pointed an imperious finger towards the window, which offered a commanding view of the village, the sea, and, most importantly, the gardens.

"Rabble? Do you mean your guests, monsieur?" Peering down, Tallier could see a few remaining people—the last leavings of Lady Rosaline's party, huddled together in varying states of agitation."

"My mother's guests," Raymond corrected. "But yes, I want them off my mother's property—my property—starting with him."

Tallier followed Raymond's finger with some interest and was only mildly surprised to learn that Jean-Paul Léger was the target of his ire. The Chief Inspector had been to several of Léger's showings in Paris and had greatly admired his work, but in person, the artist had proved to be an unpleasant, aging bruiser who had spent nearly twenty minutes in his interview earlier extolling Lady Rosaline's many virtues and declaring himself—not entirely convincingly—to be her oldest, dearest, and most bereaved friend.

And now, perhaps in a misguided effort to prove his claims, he had apparently decided to embark upon an impromptu funeral oration. Perched atop one of the abandoned chairs in the garden, he was repeating much of what he had told Tallier but to a larger and less forgiving audience.

"The audacity," Raymond growled. "The absolute audacity. That jealous little bastard hated my mother when she was alive, but now that she's dead, he's suddenly singing her praises." He scoffed. "If Léger insists on trying to rewrite history, he can do it in his own bloody house!"

Raymond was not the only one who objected to Léger's little speech, however, and as Tallier watched from above, the playwright, Carrodus, emerged from the crowd with an angry cry and dragged Léger from his perch, his shouts mixing with tears as he threw a series of sharp but inexperienced punches.

His opponent was a trifle unsteady on his feet, but Léger had a boxer's build, and his fists knew their business. A hard, sudden blow sent the taller man stumbling back, but a moment later, Carrodus was back for more.

At long last, two young plain-clothed detectives burst through the crowd and, after a brief moment of confusion, leapt into action, pulling the older men apart, a feat that was easier said than done. Afterwards, the two fighters retreated to their respective corners with what dignity they could muster. Léger's wife, Tallier noted, made no move to comfort or tend her husband.

Interesting.

"You see, Inspector," said Raymond. "I was right—a rabble. Nothing more and nothing less!"

Tallier frowned. There was a great deal to parse in Raymond's little outburst, but the Chief Inspector preferred to ease his way into that particular tangle of resentment and rage. The angry, possibly grieving son would need to be handled with care.

"Do they live nearby?" Tallier asked.

"Yes," Raymond replied. "Léger's house is about a quarter of a mile along the cliff, and my mother allowed Carrodus the use of a little cottage on the estate...although I suppose it's probably his cottage now."

"*His* cottage?" Tallier raised his eyebrows. A new avenue for resentment had just opened before him, and yet Raymond did not seem nearly as spiteful, although in this case, spite was relative. "You are suggesting Lady Rosaline may have left it to him in her will?"

"Let's just say I wouldn't be surprised."

"But you don't know for sure?"

Raymond's wife reached out for him, and Raymond clasped her hand gratefully. "No, Chief Inspector," he said, "my mother and I never discussed the matter, but I have always assumed that, artwork notwithstanding, the bulk of her estate would come to me as her only living relative." He waved his hand vaguely. "Minus a few minor bequests and the like."

"Such as Carrodus' cottage?"

"For example." Raymond's eyes flashed, although whether that was at the thought of Carrodus, Tallier couldn't say. "It all depends on how generous she felt at the time and when she last updated her will. My mother, you see, adored writing wills."

"And the artwork?" Tallier had not intended to broach Lady Rosaline's last will and testament quite so soon, but

Raymond appeared willing enough, and Inspector Tallier often found what people chose to tell him as interesting as what they avoided sharing. Which, naturally, begged the question: what was Raymond avoiding?

"My mother made no secret of her desire to leave her collection to that pet curator of hers, Herr Darvas, and his interminable museum. I expect the good curator will come mincing around sooner or later to measure the drapes. Or should I say the statues and canvases?"

"One of those statues has been stolen, I understand."

"Yes," Raymond frowned. "Her Mary Magdalene, her pride and joy. A Da Vinci, I think. Or a Michelangelo, or—"

Inspector Duvot coughed. "Herr Darvas has identified it as a Bernini, sir."

"There, you see!" Raymond exclaimed. "I told you Darvas would come mincing over to make himself indispensable. Somehow that man is always turning up underfoot."

"And did you resent that, monsieur?"

"What? Darvas being under my feet?"

"No, Darvas inheriting your mother's collection."

"Oh, that," Raymond scoffed. "Not at all. Mother's artistic pretensions were her own affair."

"But the collection *is* worth a great deal of money, non?"

"One would assume so, yes," Raymond replied. "Although it's never been formally appraised."

"Never?"

"Not to my knowledge, but I'm sure the ever-helpful Herr Darvas could supply you with a rough estimate. His kind always know the price of things."

Inspector Tallier held his tongue but watched in interest as Raymond's wife gave his arm a warning nudge. Madame Genevieve Montague Barrett had not uttered so much as a single word thus far, but she had been listening quite intently, and Raymond's eyes kept seeking her out, as if looking for approval. Lady Rosaline, by all accounts, had been a veritable force of nature and, no doubt, an extraordinarily overbearing parent. In the end, Tallier wondered, had Raymond merely traded a controlling mother for a controlling wife?

"But even if the collection is worth a fortune," Raymond continued, unaware of Tallier's musings, "it would hardly matter to me. I have a fortune of my own, you see, so I hardly need to bump my mother off for the inheritance."

"Is that so?" It was true that a man with a fortune was seldom in need of another, but most people would probably consider two fortunes better than one.

Something of Tallier's thoughts must have shown on his face because Raymond was unusually hurried in his response. "My father's will was quite specific, Chief Inspector," he explained. "His estate was held in trust until my 21st birthday, and then all General Alexander Montague Barrett's assets, which were considerable, passed directly to me, his eldest son."

"And Lady Rosaline?"

"My mother was only permitted a small stipend, just enough to live on but hardly enough to keep her in the lifestyle to which she had become accustomed. Her later husbands were less prudent, of course, but that's neither here nor there as far as I'm concerned. No, Chief Inspector, if you're searching for a financial motive, then you had best look outside the family." Raymond sneered. "You'll find no shortage of vultures and leeches to choose from among her admirers."

"Do you have anyone specific in mind?"

"Hah!" Raymond snorted. "Take your pick. Léger? Carrodus? Sir Julius Markham Smythe? Between them, they'd stretched my mother's generosity rather thin. And then there's the new arrival, Lord Unsworth. He and my mother looked thick as thieves when they ran off into the shrubbery together, but Unsworth was alone when he returned. Now there's a dark horse for you, Inspector."

Lord Unsworth, eh? Chief Inspector Tallier clicked his tongue thoughtfully. How interesting.

"Was Count Scarlioni ever one of your mother's...admirers?" he asked.

Raymond was caught unawares by the sudden change in topic. "No, I don't believe so," he answered carefully. "At least, not to my knowledge. I wouldn't have put it past him to try his luck, though. Everyone knows that Scarlioni has a very particular taste in mistresses—rich, cultured, and, not to put too fine a point on it, old. But as far as I could see, my mother and he were barely even friends. All they had in common were the cards. Although—" He turned to his wife. "—now that I think about it, there was a rumor going around, wasn't there?"

"Concerning Lady Rosaline and the Count?"

"No." It was Genevieve Montague Barrett who spoke. "Concerning the Count and Captain De Marchi."

"My mother's final husband," Raymond explained. "Nasty little fascist! Supposedly, he and the Count were involved in a contretemps in Milan a few years ago, but I'm afraid I couldn't tell you much more than that. My mother and I were not on speaking terms at the time. If I'm honest, we rarely were."

"Oh?"

"Yes," Raymond chuckled bitterly. "Our present reconciliation was a rather recent development." He spared his wife a brief, surprisingly tender smile. "Actually, it was Vivi's idea."

"May I ask why, Madame Barrett?"

"Please, call me Vivi." Faced with police questioning, she was the very picture of demure, feminine modesty, but when she replied, it was in a clear, well-enunciated voice. "There's no great mystery, Chief Inspector," she said. "I was close to my own mother growing up, and I thought it was important for Raymond to give his mother another chance before it was too late."

"And did you?" Tallier asked, turning his attention back to Raymond.

"I did my best," he answered. "And I suppose, in her own way, so did she." Raymond's eyes glazed over. "If nothing else, she was more honest than she'd ever been."

"Well," Tallier said, "thank you, Monsieur et Madame Barrett, for your time. And I promise you that as soon as the...rabble have finished making their statements, my men will see them on their way."

"Merci, Chief Inspector." Raymond managed a grateful smile.

"But one more question before I go," Chief Inspector Tallier said with a small smile, "could you tell me, please, where you both were at the time of the murder."

Raymond frowned. "But we've already made our statements."

"I'm sure you have." Tallier held out his hands placatingly. "Just as I am sure that Inspectors Duvot and Barras are both commendably thorough." And they were, Tallier noted, having each taken pages and pages of notes during this conversation alone. "But I would prefer to hear your accounts, Monsieur Barrett, in your own words and your own voices. S'il vous plait."

"Of course. Anything to help. I...um—"

"We were here, Chief Inspector," Vivi cut in firmly. "Alone."

"Avoiding your mother-in-law's guests?"

Vivi grimaced. It was the first sign of outright distaste she had allowed herself. "One of them, yes," she answered. Tallier raised his eyebrows but said nothing. There was no need. "It was Léger," Vivi said after a long pause, answering the unspoken question. "We were avoiding Léger."

"Pourquoi?"

"Because Léger was making unwanted advances to my wife," Raymond spat. "And naturally, I took offense to that."

"And that was quite chivalrous of you, darling," Vivi said evenly, "but you know I'm more than capable of handling myself."

"Yes, of course, you are, but I-I...I just..." Raymond fell silent, his face a paroxysm of aborted rage.

"Léger has something of a reputation as a skirt chaser, Chief Inspector," Vivi explained. "And I believe he was annoyed at the sight of Lady Rosaline and Lord Unsworth."

Raymond scoffed. "Not that he was the only one."

"No," Vivi agreed. "He wasn't. Anyway, a few minutes later, Léger...approached me, at which point my husband emerged to defend my honor."

"And how, precisely, did you defend her honor?"

"Léger and I exchanged words."

"Only words?" Tallier pressed. Apparently, Raymond had more than one reason to hate the artist.

"Well," Raymond admitted, "I very much wanted to hit him in the face, but—"

"But I thought it might be best if Raymond and I withdrew for a while," Vivi said. "Give tempers time to cool."

From what he had seen of the two men, Tallier agreed that had probably been for the best. But something was bothering him about Vivi. The more she spoke, the more familiar her voice sounded, and he was sure he'd seen her somewhere before. But where? The image of a stage, of Vivi bowing to the crowd with flowers in her hand, flashed suddenly across his mind. Was Genevieve Montague Barrett an actress, then, like her mother-in-law? How peculiar.

But the name was different, Tallier was sure of that. Her maiden name, perhaps, or a stage name? Tallier's wife would know. She was a devoted theatergoer and avid collector of magazines and playbills, and had dragged Tallier to all manner of plays over the years. Yes, Tallier nodded to himself. She would know.

"So, you came up here immediately?" he asked, showing not a hint of his inner thoughts.

"Oui."

"Did anyone see you? The servants?"

"No." Vivi shook her head. "They were all helping with the party."

"And you stayed up here the whole time?"

Raymond and Vivi both nodded. "We had a few drinks and talked for a bit," she said. "And then, just when we were about ready to come down—"

"That's when we heard the commotion." Raymond took up the story, only the faintest tremble audible in his voice. "That's when we heard that my mother...that she..."

"Of course." Tallier nodded. "Merci. I thank you for your time, monsieur et madame. We shall have further questions, but for now, I leave you to your grief." He and Inspectors Duvot and Barras rose to take their leave.

"Wait!" Raymond called after him. "You will find him, won't you, Chief Inspector? The man who killed my mother?"

"Oui, monsieur," Tallier replied with a decisive nod. "Certainement."

It was a promise.

12

A MEETING OF MINDS

Mr. Quayle studied the Frenchman cautiously from across the table. M. Tallier had burst into the Billiards Room a few minutes earlier, flanked on either side by Duvot and Barras, and embarked on what could only be considered a charm offensive. The wry, somewhat retiring man who Quayle had encountered over the past few weeks had transformed into the very image—almost a caricature—of the genial, voluble Frenchman. Even Tallier's accent seemed more pronounced as he greeted Lord Unsworth and Lady Constance with the appropriate decorum and invited the family to sit.

It was all a ploy, no doubt, a well-honed tactic designed to disarm and confuse, but for the moment it appeared to have succeeded quite well in Quayle's estimation. Indeed, Lady Constance, who had been visibly readying herself for a monumental explosion, had quickly found her rage stymied, cut off at the pass, by M. Tallier's onslaught. It wouldn't last, of course, but then it was not meant to last. The Frenchman had deliberately set out to bemuse and befuddle, but that was only the first move in his game, and Mr. Quayle could see Tallier watching them closely even as he smiled.

The billiard table was the only place large enough to accommodate the entire family, so they all took their seats amidst the cards, glasses, and poker chips, much to Lady Constance's disgust. Curiously, though, Tallier took a moment as they sat to congratulate Monsieur Arthur on his winnings that night, and against such able opponents.

Arthur, of course, accepted the praise at face value, but Lady Constance's eyes narrowed protectively while His Lordship sent Mr. Quayle a quick, questioning glance, but he had no answers to offer.

Seemingly unaware of the confusion on the other side of the table, M. Tallier made a great show of preparing himself. He had been carrying a leather-bound briefcase when he arrived, and from its depths emerged several folders, a notebook, a fountain pen, and an ink well, all of which he arranged with careful and exacting precision. Everything had to be just so. And then, at last, he produced a pair of wire-rim reading glasses, which he perched precariously on the end of his nose. It made for a rather comical sight, but the eyes were shrewd and cunning.

"Mesdames et Messieurs," Tallier began once he had everyone's attention. "Please allow me to introduce myself. As I said earlier, my name is Chief Inspector Tallier from the Sûreté, and I have been asked to oversee this inquiry—"

"—Begging your pardon, monsieur, but I don't much care about your credentials," Lady Constance interrupted, having recovered her rage. "We have been kept waiting for almost two hours now, and I, for one, do not appreciate being treated in this manner. Comprenez vous?"

"Bien sûr, madame." Tallier held out his hands placatingly. "And I do apologize for any inconvenience you might have suffered. It has been a long night for all of us, but a woman has been murdered, non?" And with that, Tallier's tone began to change. His voice lost none of its earlier geniality, but there was a warning note of steel in it now. Just one note, but that was enough. "A woman," he continued, "who I understood you all to know quite well."

"I wouldn't say that," Lady Constance replied curtly. "I wouldn't say that at all."

"No?" Chief Inspector Tallier turned to Lord Unsworth with an innocently raised eyebrow. "And would Your Lordship also say that you didn't know the deceased well?"

Ah, Mr. Quayle thought to himself, there's the sting in the trap.

"It has been some thirty years, Inspector, since I could claim to know Rosaline well," Lord Unsworth answered. "Indeed, it has been quite some time since I knew her at all."

"And yet she invited you here?" Tallier pressed. "Pourquoi? To rekindle la passion? L'amour?"

"Whatever her reasons, I assure you they had nothing to do with l'amour," Lord Unsworth said. "As I have already explained to your colleagues more than once."

"Oui, that is true." At a stroke, Tallier's smile was benign and amiable again. "Unfortunately, my presence here has necessitated a certain...duplication of processes, but I have read over your statements. In fact, I have them right here." He tapped the folder in front of him lightly. "And everything appears to be in order."

"I'm pleased to hear it," Lord Unsworth said cautiously. "But, in that case, what are we still doing here?"

"As I said, monsieur, a slight duplication of processes. My colleagues felt it important that I should speak to you myself."

"And now that you have?" Lord Unsworth demanded.

"There's just one final piece of business to attend to," Tallier replied. "If you would all take a moment, s'il vous plait, to read and sign your statements, and once that is done, Lord Unsworth, you and your family are free to go."

Inspectors Duvot and Barras were visibly startled, Mr. Quayle noticed, and none too pleased. They had separated the Unsworths from the other guests for a reason and had clearly expected more from Tallier, but the Chief Inspector was playing a longer game, and in Quayle's eyes, that made him far more dangerous.

Duvot and Barras had already done their best, hammering at Lord Unsworth and Mr. Quayle's stories for over an hour but to little avail, and Tallier was far too clever to mount the same assault twice. No! The man was sly. He would watch, gauge, and adjust.

"Merci," Inspector Tallier said once they had all signed and graced Lord Unsworth and the others with a pleased, beatific little smile. "I must thank you again for your patience and forbearance." Lady Constance snorted audibly. "And now, mesdames et messieurs, I must bid you adieu. Inspectors Duvot and Barras will see you out."

"So, that's it?" Lady Constance demanded. "We're free to go?"

"Oui, madame," Tallier agreed. "For the time being. Although..." he held up a hand as the family rose to its feet, "before you take your leave, might I borrow Monsieur Quayle for a few minutes?"

"Excuse me?" Lady Constance looked about ready to spit poison, and Lord Unsworth was not far behind, but Mr. Quayle nodded. Tallier might be clever and dangerous, but so was Quayle, and he wanted to know what game the Frenchman was playing.

"Of course," Mr. Quayle said. "I'm always happy to help the police with their inquiries, Chief Inspector."

"Are you sure, Quayle?" asked Lord Unsworth.

"Quite sure, sir." Mr. Quayle's eyes never left Chief

Inspector Tallier. "After all, I have a few questions of my own."

* * *

Neither of them spoke for nearly half a minute as each man regarded the other carefully, like a pair of well-matched duelists gaging their opponent, alert for any sign of weakness, or for any hint of the other's true thoughts.

"You hid it rather well," Tallier said, breaking the silence. "I was impressed."

"And what would that be?"

"Your surprise, Monsieur Quayle. After all, you must have been quite shocked to see me. Unless, of course, I was expected?"

"No." Mr. Quayle shook his head. "I wasn't expecting you at all. You see, Chief Inspector, until you arrived, I was half convinced that you were working for French Intelligence."

"Intelligence?"

"But instead, you've turned out to be a policeman. From the Sûreté in Paris, no less."

"I never lied to you, mon ami," Tallier replied. "Although I may have sometimes...avoided the question."

"So I noticed." Mr. Quayle narrowed his eyes. "But surely Treville-sur-Mer is a trifle outside your jurisdiction, Chief Inspector?"

"More than a trifle."

"Then, forgive me, but why exactly would a local magistrate invite you to lead this investigation?"

"That is a good question," Inspector Tallier acknowledged.

"Mhm." Mr. Quayle smiled. "And you've no intention of answering it, do you?"

"Not at the moment."

"Well then," Quayle continued, "all I can say is that this magistrate of yours must have been quite pleased to learn that such a distinguished detective just so happened to be in the neighborhood."

"A distinguished detective? How very flattering of you, mon ami, but what makes you say that?"

"Oh, nothing at all, Chief Inspector." Mr. Quayle was all innocence. "It's just that soon after you arrived, I had a rather enlightening conversation with the constable watching our door. Apparently you have something of a reputation."

"I have had a few successes in my career," Inspector Tallier allowed, rubbing the back of his neck sheepishly. "And it's true they have given me a certain degree of...notoriety. But what is that depressing English saying? The higher the rise, the harder the fall?"

"And have you fallen, Chief Inspector?"

"Mmm." Tallier pursed his lips but did not answer. "Let us merely say that while you may have managed to keep your exploits out of the papers, Monsieur Quayle, I have not always been so lucky."

"I see." That was a less than subtle reminder that while Quayle may have leveled the playing field slightly, the Chief Inspector still knew much more about him than he knew about the Frenchman. A small victory was better than none, however. "But now, as much as I enjoy your company, His Lordship is waiting for me, and since I doubt that any of this is what you wanted to discuss, perhaps it's time we got down to business."

"Very well," Chief Inspector Tallier agreed. "Then I was wondering, mon ami, if you might do me one little favor."

"What sort of favor?" Mr. Quayle asked with no small amount of caution.

"Oh, there's no need to look so alarmed," Tallier waved his hands as if to brush any of Quayle's concerns aside. "I was simply hoping you would accompany me while I examine the body."

"While you *examine the body*?" That felt like a trap. "Tell me, why precisely would you want me to do that?"

"To help me with my inquiries." Tallier's face was all innocence. "You did discover Lady Rosaline, did you not?"

"I did. And you can read all about it in that statement I just finished signing."

"I could," Tallier admitted, "but I prefer the personal touch. Reports can be quite dry, non?"

"If you say so."

"I do." The Chief Inspector's tone was polite but unyielding.

"Then," Mr. Quayle said, matching Tallier's tone, "I suppose I'm only too happy to help."

"Excellent! Shall we?"

"After you, Chief Inspector."

"No, no," Chief Inspector Tallier insisted. "After *you*, monsieur."

13

CARDS ON THE TABLE

And so once again, Mr. Quayle found himself gazing down at Lady Rosaline's lifeless body, this time with the newly revealed Chief Inspector by his side. It made for a cruel tableau—the Great Widow laid low like some ancient Egyptian Pharaoh, surrounded by all her treasures. What did that make him, Quayle wondered? An archeologist, perhaps? Or a grave robber rattling about in her tomb?

Lady Rosaline had apparently stumbled back under the assault and collapsed in a sprawling tangle of limbs and blood. The poor woman, that former actress and ever-poised grand dame, would have found the staging deplorable. And yet, even in death, she managed to maintain a few stray scraps of her dignity. There was nothing defeated about her, nothing scared or broken. Apart from her skull, of course, but that was only her body.

Chief Inspector Tallier crouched down beside Quayle. The Frenchman had withdrawn into himself as soon as they arrived, but his eyes had taken in every last detail as he made his way around the room, pausing to examine each painting with the air of a historian at a museum or a penitent in a church, before circling back to the body. And behind that watchful silence, Quayle could detect the telltale signs of a mind whirling with thoughts and suspicions. It was almost like looking into a mirror.

"The angle of the blow indicates that she was facing her attacker when they struck," Tallier said.

"Yes," Mr. Quayle agreed. "And they must have been standing quite close."

"Oui," Chief Inspector Tallier nodded. "D'accord. Which indicates...?"

"Indicates? Are you testing me, Chief Inspector?"

"Non! I am merely soliciting suggestions."

"In that case, I would say it indicates Lady Rosaline knew her murderer quite well. Certainly well enough to let them get rather close."

"A crime of passion, then," Tallier suggested. "Un crime passionnel!"

"Possibly. Lady Rosaline had a talent for eliciting all kinds of passions, for better and for worse."

"What makes you say that, mon ami?"

Mr. Quayle eyed Tallier cautiously. "Nothing in particular," he answered. "But watching her guests flock around her tonight, I doubt that any of them were neutral regarding Lady Rosaline."

"Love her or hate her."

"Precisely," Quayle nodded. "With little in between."

"And what did *you* think of her, Monsieur Quayle?"

Mr. Quayle frowned. He felt as though he was on dangerous ground suddenly, but why? The Frenchman was probing again, but his purpose remained stubbornly elusive. For the moment, therefore, Mr. Quayle judged honesty to be the best policy—within reason, of course—and let the chips fall where they may.

"I found her to be quite charming," he admitted,

"although I only spoke to her the once. She had a gift for making you feel as if you were the only other person in the world, at least for a moment or two."

"But?"

Mr. Quayle paused to choose his next words carefully. He had no desire to obstruct the police, of course, but nor did he wish to share Lord Unsworth's confidences unless absolutely necessary. "I'm not sure," he responded. "Not exactly, but there was something else about her, something…calculated."

"Interesting." Tallier clearly knew that Quayle was keeping secrets, but then, so was Tallier.

"Have you found the murder weapon?" Quayle asked.

"No," Tallier replied with a queer look in his eye. "We haven't found the murder weapon."

There was something odd about that statement, but before Quayle could delve any deeper, the Chief Inspector nodded to the coroner, whose assistants carefully lifted the body and bore Lady Rosaline away on a stretcher, covered in a pale white shroud. And then, in a moment, she was gone.

Rising and brushing off his trousers, Mr. Quayle glanced around, and could not help but reflect on how quickly the character of a place could change, not just this room but all the other halls and galleries as well, brimming with their paintings and tapestries.

He had stood in much the same place only an hour or so before and passed among the same paintings and statues. They had seemed almost alive then—vibrant—as if animated by some underlying spirit. But Lady Rosaline's death had cast an immediate shadow. What was once a living, almost breathing collection, now in her absence felt more akin to a mausoleum—lifeless and inert.

"Any thoughts, monsieur?" Tallier asked, interrupting his musings.

Mr. Quayle turned. "Do you want me to have thoughts?"

"Mais oui." Tallier smiled encouragingly. "But of course!"

"Very well, then." Mr. Quayle gathered himself. "Two points immediately spring to mind. Firstly, where did the murderer come from? The house or the gardens?"

"That would narrow down the list of suspects considerably, non?" Tallier agreed.

"Considerably." Mr. Quayle glanced over at the twin doors, still open to the night— or possibly early morning— air. "I don't suppose you know where those lead?" he asked.

"Naturellement," Tallier replied. "Out into one of the flower gardens and then down to the cliffs." He eyed Mr. Quayle slyly. "But I understand there is also a path that winds along the side of the house to where the party was being held."

"So, whomever-it-was could have excused themselves from the festivities and crept in this way."

"C'est possible," Tallier nodded. "We are checking for footprints now. There are traces of mud on the floor, but unfortunately, quite a few servants and guests have admitted to passing this way."

"Not particularly helpful."

"Indeed. And your second point?"

"My second point? Oh, yes!" Mr. Quayle rubbed his eyes tiredly. "How exactly did the murderer know Lady Rosaline would be here? A secret rendezvous? She did have something of a reputation."

"Perhaps," Tallier shrugged. "Although, in that case, your Lord Unsworth would be a prime candidate." Mr. Quayle opened his mouth to protest, but Tallier waved his objections aside. "Or," he continued, "perhaps Lady Rosaline's presence was entirely unexpected. Perhaps, instead, they were after something else, something our killer knew for certain would be here."

"The Bernini?"

"Précisément." Tallier was watching Quayle closely now like a hawk. "It is missing, after all."

Mr. Quayle frowned. "Earlier, you said you hadn't found the murder weapon."

"That is what I said."

"You think she was killed with the statuette." It was not a question.

"Judging by the wounds, she was struck by a large, heavy object."

"Mmm." Mr. Quayle removed his glasses and regarded Tallier for a moment. There was more to it than that. There had to be. The Frenchman seemed absolutely certain that the statuette was at the heart of all this, far more confident than he had any right to be.

"What am I doing here, Chief Inspector?" Quayle asked finally.

Tallier blinked in exaggerated confusion. "I told you," he replied. "You're helping me with my inquiries."

"But what sort of help did you have in mind, I wonder?"

"Monsieur?"

"You asked me for my thoughts on the case. Well, I have one more for you, if you would care to listen?"

"Bien sûr."

Mr. Quayle smiled thinly. "You are not here on the Riviera, Chief Inspector Tallier, by mere happenstance. Nor is it a coincidence that the local magistrate asked you to take charge of this particular case. No! You have been here for some time, monsieur, and you have not been idle. Quite the contrary, in fact. Our meeting, for example, was no accident, and I have indulged you this far, but I believe it is high time you either tell me what is going on or let me go to bed."

"Monsieur, I—"

"Please," Mr. Quayle interrupted. "It has been a long day,

Inspector, and I am excruciatingly tired, so I would appreciate it if we could dispense with these games."

Chief Inspector Tallier regarded Quayle for a long moment. "As you wish," he said at last. "No more games."

"Merci." Mr. Quayle steeled himself. "So, I'll ask you again: why am I here?"

Tallier grimaced, but true to his word, he answered.

* * *

"For the past few months," Chief Inspector Tallier began, "I have been on the trail of a particularly dangerous criminal, and I was, before this evening's tragic interruption, on the brink of making an arrest."

"How exciting," Mr. Quayle's tone was dry.

"Oui," Tallier nodded. "Tell me, Monsieur Quayle, are you familiar with La Chimère?"

"No, I don't believe I..." Mr. Quayle frowned, an old, forgotten memory floating to the surface. "Wait a moment! Wasn't there a thief going by that name? Always leaving calling cards and toying with the police? That sort of thing?"

"Précisément."

"But surely that was years ago, wasn't it? Before the War?"

"Oui, but recently La Chimère, or someone using their old nom de guerre, has reemerged and has been making his or her way through Europe stealing everything from gems and diamonds to priceless works of art." Tallier shook his head. "I'm not surprised you haven't heard of it. Thus far, their exploits have been restricted to the Continent, and your English newspapers have been more concerned with matters close to home, non?"

"Quite." Mr. Quayle frowned. "But what does that have to do with—"

"Patience, mon ami," Tallier smiled softly. "Patience. All will be revealed."

Mr. Quayle had his doubts about that. Tallier was being unexpectedly forthcoming thus far, but he suspected the Frenchman would want something in return. Nothing in life was free, least of all information.

"A few months ago," Tallier continued, "we received word that La Chimère was in France, first in Paris—where I became involved—and then later on the Riviera in Treville-sur-Mer."

"So, you followed," Mr. Quayle .

"Mais oui."

"Mm." Mr. Quayle regarded Tallier thoughtfully for a moment. "And is this an official investigation?"

"Official? No, no, no! Officially, I am on les vacances. A gentleman of leisure, non?"

"I see." This was personal, then. Something had happened in Paris, something Tallier did not wish to mention.

"La Chimère has a noted fondness for art," Tallier continued, "and a tendency to target the rich and the powerful. This, naturally, led me to—"

"—the Lady Rosaline."

"Précisément." Tallier grinned. "And I became convinced that La Chimère was planning to steal from her."

"And so?" Mr. Quayle prompted.

"And so, I had a word with Lady Rosaline." Tallier sighed. "She listened quite intently but refused my help in the end."

"Interesting." By all accounts, including Lord Unsworth's, Lady Rosaline had been enormously proud of her collection. So, why would she be so cavalier with its protection? Unless, of course, she had some other reason to keep the police away. "Quite interesting."

"I thought so, too, monsieur," Tallier said. "And now she's dead, and the 'jewel of her collection' is missing."

"Yes," Mr. Quayle said. "And that does point in a rather definitive direction, doesn't it? But don't you think it's time you stopped playing coy with me, Chief Inspector?"

"Coy?"

"You know exactly who La Chimère is, or at least you think you do. Otherwise, you would hardly have been on the 'brink' of an arrest."

"Ah," Tallier shrugged. "You are quite right. There is one particular person, or rather two people, whose passports and movements indicate that they have been present for all of the recent thefts attributed to La Chimère."

"And who might they be?"

Tallier tutted. "Now, who's playing coy, monsieur? Surely you can guess?"

"Of course I can." Mr. Quayle snorted. "The Count and Countess Scarlioni."

"Mais oui. Très bien, monsieur!"

Mr. Quayle had expected as much. "You were reasonably careful," he said, "but you could never quite disguise how closely you were watching them. And I couldn't help but notice that your interest in myself and the Unsworths only developed *after* the Count had befriended Arthur. Initially, I thought it was because of those spy rumors, but, of course, that was when I believed you were with French Intelligence, not the Sûreté."

"Please understand, Monsieur Quayle, that while I enjoyed our little chats enormously, I will not apologize for my duplicity. It was necessary at the time."

"Oh?"

"When I learned that your employer, Lord Unsworth, was known to be a collector of particular and expensive taste, I grew...concerned."

"That the Count was planning to steal from him?" No,

Mr. Quayle thought to himself, that wasn't quite right. "Oh, I see. You thought he might be a buyer!"

"Potentially, oui. And it was not a possibility that I could ignore, not when the Count was so quick to befriend Arthur." Tallier was unapologetic. "For a time, I wondered if Lord Unsworth and the Count had arranged to make contact using His Lordship's nephew as the go-between, but it rapidly became apparent that no one in their right mind would entrust Arthur with such a task."

"Quite." Mr. Quayle stifled a laugh. Tallier was not laughing, however.

"But," he continued, "there was one person Lord Unsworth might have trusted."

"Meaning me."

"Naturellement."

"And what made you change your mind?" Quayle asked. "Or have you?"

"After we first met," Tallier said, "I took the liberty of making a few inquiries and heard some disturbing rumors about your time in Whitehall."

"I'm sure you did." Mr. Quayle held himself utterly still, not allowing himself so much as a single twitch or expression.

"And then, I spoke with a colleague of mine at Scotland Yard, who referred to you as...comment dit-on?...'an interfering little busybody.' He was convinced that you were a Whitehall spook. Is that the word—'spook?' A spy by another name."

Mr. Quayle grunted. He had a good idea who Tallier had been speaking to and what tales he would have been telling.

"Your friend, Wintle, was more discreet," Tallier added, "but they both agreed that while you tend to become involved, you are not the sort of man who would buy or sell stolen goods."

"What a sterling recommendation!" Although, Mr. Quayle

noted, Tallier had not quite answered his initial question. "In any case, I suppose that congratulations are in order."

"Congratulations?" Tallier frowned. "Pourquoi?"

"Well, it does appear as though you've solved the murder, Chief Inspector. And in a rather convincing fashion, I might add. Two thieves, a stolen statuette, and a dead woman, do point in a rather obvious direction. Lady Rosaline must have interrupted them while the Count and Countess were stealing the statuette and was murdered for her trouble. All very neat and tidy, non?"

"Oui," Tallier agreed. "All very neat and tidy."

"So, why are you talking to me rather than them?"

"Ah." Tallier clicked his tongue in frustration. "The Count, you see, refused to demean himself by answering our questions. Instead, he and his wife immediately sailed back to Treville-sur-Mer."

"Sailed?"

"The Count's yacht was moored at Lady Rosaline's private dock."

"I see." Mr. Quayle frowned. "And you let them go?"

"There appears to have been some truth to those rumors we were discussing," Tallier replied. "Count Scarlioni and his wife possess diplomatic immunity, and when my colleagues protested, Scarlioni suggested they contact the Italian ambassador."

"He actually said that?"

"Apparently," Tallier confirmed.

"That was either exceptionally clever of him or exceptionally stupid." Mr. Quayle pursed his lips thoughtfully. "I wonder which it was."

"And then, of course," Chief Inspector Tallier added, "there is the matter of their alibis."

"Alibis?" Mr. Quayle blinked. "As in more than one?"

"Mais oui."

"And are they reliable?"

"I'm afraid I was hoping you could tell me that."

Mr. Quayle had a sudden sinking feeling in his gut. "And how exactly would I know?" he asked, dreading the answer.

"Because," Chief Inspector Tallier explained, "while the Count and Countess may have played cards all evening, most of the other players were less...stationary. Some came earlier. Some joined later. Some stormed out or went to relieve themselves, and so on. Non, mon ami! The only person who was with them from the moment the first hand was dealt until the last was your charge, the Hon. Arthur Druce.

"Of course, it was." Mr. Quayle cursed under his breath.

"And in his statement," Chief Inspector Tallier continued remorselessly, "Monsieur Arthur insists most stridently that amidst all the comings and the goings, neither the Count nor the Countess ever once left the room. But, as you yourself told me, he owes Scarlioni a rather substantial sum of money and might therefore be tempted to...shall we say *mislead* on their behalf? So, I must ask you, Monsieur Quayle, the same question you asked me: is he reliable?"

14

THE JUGE D'INSTRUCTION

"And?" the Juge d'Instruction asked the following morning. "What did he say, this Englishman of yours?"

Chief Inspector Tallier frowned and took a reviving sip of coffee before leaning back with an appreciative sigh. He and M. Jarre were seated by the unlit fireplace in the Judge's office, the table in front of them piled high with all the accompanying paperwork of the case: witness statements, background files, finger and footprint reports, and a set of newly developed photographs from the crime scene, not to mention the freshly brewed coffee pot or the plate of slightly stale biscuits.

"Monsieur Quayle," the Chief Inspector reported, "said that while Arthur Druce could be a fool at times, he was usually an honest fool." He snorted and snatched a biscuit from the plate. He had not eaten since dinner the night before, and his mind required nourishment. "Quayle also added that if Druce was lying, the boy's mother would have him hung, drawn, and quartered. Lady Constance has something of a reputation, I believe, and it's only gotten worse since the...*trouble* with her husband."

"I see." M. Jarre laced his fingers together and adopted the air of a man lost deep in thought. A slender, boney figure who preferred tight collars and sharp creases, Jarre was not as old as he appeared or, indeed, as old as he thought he was. Poor Jarre had lived much of his life impatiently waiting to become a distinguished, elder statesman and had latched onto the first hints of gray in his hair like a drowning man clutching for a raft.

Tallier, who was, in fact, two years the Judge's senior, found the whole thing ridiculous, but the two men had worked together many times over the years, and he respected Jarre's keen eyes and shrewd legal mind.

"That's not quite a yes or a no," M. Jarre pointed out. "He can be quite cagey, this Quayle, non?"

"Oui," Tallier agreed. "Monsieur Quayle was being cautious, I think. He didn't want to commit himself fully until he'd had his own word with Arthur."

"So, you think he's hard at work, untangling your inconvenient alibis for you?"

"Mr. Quayle is an efficient, clever man and, more importantly, he is highly motivated to keep the Unsworth family out of trouble. If he hasn't already extracted the truth from Arthur, I'm sure he will have by this evening." Tallier shrugged and brushed a few stray crumbs from his lap.

"But even if he does," Jarre pushed, "do you really think he'll tell you?"

"Not necessarily," Tallier allowed. "But I don't believe that Monsieur Quayle has lied to me yet. Nor do I believe that he would resort to withholding evidence outright, not unless he had no other choice."

"Mm." Jarre was not convinced. "You know what Duvot and Barras believe?"

"Naturellement." Tallier was far too polite to scoff, but his feelings were obvious at a glance. "They think that Lord Unsworth lured Lady Rosaline away from the party and then either killed her himself or commissioned Monsieur Quayle to do it for him." Tallier shook his head. "Rather fanciful, in my opinion. I doubt Lady Rosaline has ever been lured anywhere in her life."

"I don't believe Duvot and Barras would have put the case against them quite so strongly," M. Jarre said. "But they *are* convinced that Lord Unsworth and his secretary know more than they're saying, and were...surprised when you let the Unsworths go so quickly."

"Oh, they most definitely know more than they're saying." Tallier smiled sharply. "Everyone always does, but the trouble with people like the Unsworths is that the harder you press them, the more they close ranks. No, the trick, I've found, Monsieur Jarre, is to convince them that helping *us* is the best way to help *themselves* and, at present, Monsieur Quayle is our most effective means of persuasion."

"So, he's the lure to bait your trap."

"If it comes to that." Tallier leaned forward. "But, for the moment, I'm merely keeping an eye on him. What I'm more concerned with is—"

"Yes, I know." Jarre unfolded his fingers with a sigh. "Scarlioni. Now, I know you think that Duvot and Barras are jumping to conclusions, but are you quite sure that *you're* not willfully blinding yourself as well, Tallier? Missing the forest for the trees?"

It was a valid point, but Chief Inspector Tallier was having none of it. "A rare and priceless work of art has been stolen. A woman was found murdered in the immediate vicinity, and two known—"

"Suspected," Jarre interrupted.

"—known art thieves were on the premises." This time

Tallier did scoff. "Now, I am prepared to accept that these facts may not all be inextricably linked, sir," he said, "but at least two of them are. I'd bet my life on that."

"But how? Unless Arthur Druce is lying to protect them, after all?"

"They had an alibi in Paris, too," Tallier pointed out. "More than one, in fact, but they were guilty then, and they're guilty now. Count Scarlioni is La Chimère, and so is his wife."

"Let's say you're right," Jarre mused thoughtfully. "Let's say they faked their alibi and somehow slipped away from the card game. What then? Lady Rosaline caught them in the act, so they bludgeoned her to death?" The Juge d'Instruction shook his head. "If I remember rightly, La Chimère has never been particularly violent, not even before the War."

"That is true," Chief Inspector Tallier admitted. "And at this stage, I'm not saying they killed her, and I'm not saying they didn't. All I'm saying is they stole that statuette, and if you let me search Scarlioni's yacht, I'll prove it!"

"You think they managed to smuggle it out?"

"Well, they *were* in an awful hurry to leave last night. Count Scarlioni claimed diplomatic immunity, and he's never been nervous enough to try that before."

"Mmm." The Juge d'Instruction studied Tallier for a moment, choosing his words cautiously. "You need to be careful, Tallier," he warned. "The Prefect called my house this morning, just after he'd had word from the Interior Minister."

"And?"

"Apparently, the Italian Ambassador is paying particular attention to this case, although, thus far, the embassy has made no official inquiries."

The Chief Inspector accepted this piece of intelligence with a nod. "I'm not surprised," he said. "Diplomatic immunity or no, Count Scarlioni's exact status has always been somewhat ambiguous. I suspect he has several friends in high places." Tallier pursed his lips. "Or, perhaps, low places," he said after a moment's thought.

"The Count's title has always been dubious at best," the Judge agreed. "The name Scarlioni appears in neither the *Almanac de Gotha* nor the *Libro d'Oro della Nobiltà Italian,* but he would hardly be the first person to masquerade as a nobleman." Jarre grinned outright. "The Riviera is crawling with nobility of every possible denomination, and I doubt if more than half of them are genuine." He eyed Tallier pointedly. "Most of them are not murderers, though, or thieves for that matter."

"True, but I can't help but wonder who the Count was before he was the Count. It may not matter whether he is a nobleman or a tanner's son in the long run, but it may help me understand him."

"Perhaps." Jarre sighed again. "We've been friends a long time, Tallier, a long, long time, and I trust your judgment. If you say the Count is La Chimère, then the Count is La Chimère. If you say he killed Lady Rosaline, then I believe he killed Lady Rosaline. But as a judge, mon ami, I need more than that. All you've offered me so far are suspicions and conjecture, and without more evidence—any evidence, for that matter—I cannot possibly issue a search warrant for that yacht, not with the Prefect breathing down my neck. And you know that, Tallier."

"Yes, I know."

"So, if you want my advice, I suggest you forget Scarlioni for the time being and focus on the others. I'm sure there are plenty of possibilities apart from Unsworth."

"Oh, yes!" Tallier laughed. "They have all been very eager to point the finger at each other." Before he could elucidate, however, the telephone rang, and M. Jarre rose stiffly from his chair.

"Jarre speaking," he answered with a frown that only

deepened the more he listened. "Yes...yes...I understand. We'll be there shortly."

"Well?" Chief Inspector Tallier asked when the Judge was finished. "What happened?"

"That was Inspector Barras," M. Jarre reported with a confused look on his face. "The Count and Countess just walked in downstairs. Apparently, they want to talk to you."

15

MR. QUAYLE GETS TO WORK

It was a bright, glorious day—not at all the sort of morning that should follow a murder—but Mr. Quayle was not enjoying the sunshine. It could have been raining or snowing, for all the difference it would have made. No! All his thought, his self, his very being was concentrated inward, where neither the feel of the breeze on his face nor the chittering songs of the birds could reach. He was alone with himself and, for the moment, everything else was but an irritant, easily and necessarily ignored.

Sitting out on His Lordship's veranda, Mr. Quayle twirled a pen absently between his fingers as he opened a notebook on his lap. Lord Unsworth had rented the rather large, somewhat dilapidated villa for a song, just one slightly impoverished aristocrat paying another slightly impoverished aristocrat and thereby conspiring to keep poverty and dissolution at bay for another year.

Mr. Quayle had made all the arrangements, of course, at His Lordship's instructions. It had been a simple enough task, although now he wished they had chosen a different village far from Treville-sur-Mer. Then, perhaps, Quayle would not be expected to arrange another murder inquiry. Naturally, it was flattering that His Lordship had such faith in his abilities, but as far as Mr. Quayle was concerned, any success he might have had in the past was entirely down to luck and circumstance, and perhaps, if he allowed himself the compliment, a modicum of common sense—nothing more and nothing less.

Although, it would be a lie to say that he hadn't experienced a jolt of excitement, buried beneath the exasperation and exhaustion, at the prospect of another case. Stumbling into bed at just past one in the morning, he had hardly slept a wink, his mind in an uproar. Even his legs had been restless, full of energy, and eager to begin. But where to start? That was the question which had kept him awake, the question which absorbed him.

Absently, almost without thought, Mr. Quayle leaned over and began to jot down a few ideas in his notebook:

- What was Lady Rosaline so frightened of?
- What to do about Unsworth's letter? Was Lady Rosaline lying?
- Who stole the statuette, and how? And where is it now?
- Who is La Chimère?
- Follow the money. Is there money?
- Who killed Lady Rosaline? Motive, means, opportunity.

A minute or two later, Quayle scowled down at what he'd written. He had hoped that putting his thoughts down on paper would help, but instead, his mind was spiraling out of control, leaping from one possibility to the next without rhyme or reason—disjointed and disorganized. This was not like him at all.

Last time, by virtue of his role as Lord Unsworth's secretary, Quayle had possessed the distinct advantage of knowing the family, the lay of the land, so to speak, and he had been at the center of events. But now he was on the outside peering in, forced to scratch at the surface, which meant everyone would be more far less willing to talk. And with good reason. Mr. Quayle would be the first to admit that he had no official role in the investigation, no business asking questions. But Lord Unsworth had requested his help, and Quayle had agreed, so he would do what he must as soon as he figured out what that was.

There was one way, of course, one obvious chance to burrow his way inside and dig his boots in deep. The trouble was Tallier clearly wanted him to take that path, so Quayle distrusted it on principle. He did not appreciate being led around by the nose or maneuvered into position. Lady Rosaline had been doing that before she died, and now Tallier was attempting to do much the same.

But, still, it *was* a place to start, and when Arthur came bounding onto the veranda, Quayle had no choice but to resign himself to his fate. The universe, it seemed, had spoken.

"Oh, hullo, Quayle!" Arthur exclaimed. "I didn't see you there!" He glanced down at the notebook in Quayle's lap. "I'm sorry. Did you want to be alone? I could—"

"Not at all," Quayle said. "Please, join me."

"I say, that's awfully kind of you." Arthur dragged a chair over to the side where it couldn't be seen from the door and sat down with an audible sigh of satisfaction.

Mr. Quayle tried not to smile as he watched the maneuver. "Hiding from your mother?" he asked.

"God, yes!" Arthur didn't even bother to pretend. "She's

been on the warpath all morning. I mean, did you see her glaring at Fanny over breakfast?"

"Where is Fanny?" Mr. Quayle wondered.

"She slipped out ages ago to see Hollins and those artist friends of hers. Whatshisname? Um—"

"Léger," Mr. Quayle finished, nodding to himself. "Interesting."

That was another way in, he reminded himself, and Fanny could well be the key. Perhaps he wasn't so fenced in after all.

"Now, I don't blame her for sounding the retreat," Arthur said, "but Fanny has rather left me to bear the brunt of it. Mother's been haranguing me for hours, and she keeps twisting my ear. I swear, if she tells me I'm *'just like my father'* one more time, I'll...well...I'll—" Arthur's gust of false bravado faded swiftly. "—I won't do much of anything, will I?" he asked with a sigh. "I never do. Not that the rest of you are any better! Uncle Edward's been avoiding her all morning. He just keeps pacing back and forth. And you, Quayle, you slunk away with that look in your eye."

"What look?"

"The look that says you've been asked to solve a murder again," Arthur answered with a mischievous grin, "and you're not sure whether you're annoyed or secretly pleased."

Mr. Quayle was impressed. That was uncommonly perceptive of Arthur. "I wasn't aware I had a look for that," he said.

Arthur shrugged. "You forget that I was there in London that first time. I've seen you work your magic before, more than anyone when it comes down to it."

"Mmm." Quayle acknowledged the point. "So you have. And does that mean you've learned your lesson? No more climbing out windows?"

"No more climbing out windows," Arthur affirmed, turning away in embarrassment.

"Good. And you will tell me everything this time."

"I *am* telling you everything!" Arthur protested.

"Are you sure?" Mr. Quayle pressed. "You haven't left anything out? About your card game last night? About the Count?"

"The Count!" Arthur shot to his feet. "Why is everyone so interested in the bloody Count?"

"Well," Mr. Quayle explained. "Chief Inspector Tallier is interested because he's been chasing Scarlioni for months and because, although he didn't say as much, I suspect the Count and Countess got the better of him in Paris. And *I* am interested in the Count because he is interested in you, and I don't know why."

"He's a friend, that's all."

"A friend who loaned you almost a thousand pounds?" Mr. Quayle's eyebrows rose meaningfully. "A friend who you've only known for a few weeks? Come now, Arthur, use your brain! I know you're not nearly as silly as all that."

"Well, I have...wondered," Arthur admitted, slinking back down into his chair. "But he and his wife have always been very kind, even when I won last night, which is more than I can say for the other players."

"Is that so?"

"Yes! And I swear the Count couldn't possibly have left the room. We were playing poker all night, and by the last hand he and I were the only ones left in the game."

Mr. Quayle removed his glasses and rubbed the bridge of his nose thoughtfully. "Alright, tell me about this game of yours," he said. "Everything you can remember—every hand, every bet, every fold, and, most importantly, every coming and going."

"It was incredible," Arthur said. "Just incredible! An ace of hearts here, a king of hearts there, and—*voila*—a royal flush! And then a hand or two later, when I was praying desperately for a king of spades, on the last draw—behold—a full house! Incredible! Even when all I could manage was a paltry two-of-a-kind, somehow it was enough. Last night, it was always enough!"

"I see." Mr. Quayle frowned, and the more Arthur spoke, the more frustrated Quayle became, because no matter how he questioned him, Arthur's story never wavered. Not once.

Neither the Count nor the Countess had left the room at any time.

And yet, despite the impossibility, Mr. Quayle was more convinced than ever that Tallier was right. The Count and Countess *were* involved, but for the life of him, Quayle still couldn't see how. It was infuriating! The answer was so obvious it was staring him in the face, but what was it?

It all had to do with that blasted game. He was sure of it. Quayle had seen Arthur play cards before, and he was a perfectly decent poker player, but the Count was a bona fide card sharp. There was no way that Scarlioni had lost by mere happenstance. No! The game must have been rigged in Arthur's favor. But, again, why? There was a piece missing. There had to be.

"Do you know where any of the other players are?" Quayle asked. "This Dabney, for instance?"

"Oh, yes. He's staying at the Hotel Magellan."

"Excellent! I wonder if he'd be willing to have a word."

"Now?" Arthur asked.

"Yes, now." Mr. Quayle rose to his feet and smiled encouragingly. Already he could feel the exhaustion fading, his thoughts quickening. He had spent enough time pondering the questions. Now, it was time to find some answers.

It was time for him to get to work.

16

THE COUNT AND COUNTESS

At a quarter past ten, Count Scarlioni and his wife were ushered arm-in-arm into M. Jarre's office. Both seemed irritatingly fresh and well-groomed, the Count in his sharp, Italian suit and the Countess in her flowing dress. Together they were the picture of modern elegance and style—seemingly more at home on the society pages than in the office of the Juge d'Instruction.

And yet they betrayed no obvious sense of unease as each additional civility, each meaningless banality dripped from their tongues with the kind of effortless charm which suggested, delicately, of course, that they were doing you a favor by even talking to you, that their very presence was a gift. And in a way, Tallier reflected, it was.

Shielded behind diplomatic immunity and protected by powerful friends at the Italian embassy, Scarlioni had managed to wriggle out of questioning last night, and yet here he was, placing himself at Tallier's disposal. It was not a risk the Count would have taken without reason.

"Thank you for coming," M. Jarre said once they had all taken their seats. "It is kind of you to grace us with your presence." Tallier hid a smile at that. No one could twist the knife with such urbane politeness as Jarre. If the Count noticed the subtle jab, however, he gave no sign, and the Countess beside him was so expressionless as to seem carved from marble.

"Before we begin, messieurs," Scarlioni said. "I would like to apologize for my behavior last night. I was unconscionably rude to your officers and, as I would not like you to think me ill-mannered—"

"Ill-mannered?" Chief Inspector Tallier interjected. "Forgive me, Count Scarlioni, but this was not some breach of etiquette. You and your wife fled the scene of a murder investigation and informed my colleagues in no uncertain terms that answering their questions was beneath your dignity."

"I suppose I did say that, didn't I?" the Count smirked.

"You did," Tallier replied. "And when Inspector Barras persisted, you suggested he take up the matter with the Italian Embassy."

The Count winced visibly. "As I said, that was rude of me. But my wife," he explained, "was quite shaken by the murder —such a shocking business—and I thought it best to take her away from that place as soon as possible. For her nerves, you understand."

Countess Scarlioni did not appear even remotely shaken, and Tallier was willing to bet that her nerves were far steadier than her husband's, but he accepted the Count's explanation without protest.

"Of course," Tallier said with exactly as much sincerity as he had received. "And I hope your wife appreciates the loving care and devotion you've shown her but, given recent events, I'm sure you can see why Judge Jarre and I might find your presence this morning a little...curious. Non?"

"Yes, about that...I...uh...I realized I might have made a mistake," the Count said. "And I was worried that our leaving might have given you the wrong impression."

Tallier nodded encouragingly. "And what impression might that be?"

"That we have something to hide."

Taller nodded once in apparent sympathy. "And do you?" he asked.

"Of course not!" The reply was immediate. "We were playing cards all evening! You can ask anyone. All the usual suspects were there: Leger, Carrodus, Dabney, Sir Julius…"

"And don't forget Arthur, darling," the Countess added, breaking her silence.

"Indeed not!" Her husband nodded vigorously. "How could we forget Arthur? He's probably the only one who enjoyed himself last night."

Chief Inspector Tallier stifled a grin. The Count and Countess had just listed out all their alibis in a row and practically dared him to accuse them of anything. Such aplomb! Such daring! He could admire that, although he suspected they were in danger of flying too close to the sun, and was very much looking forward to being there when they fell back down to earth.

"We have asked them," Tallier admitted. "After all, they were perfectly willing to give us their statements last night, although since you're here now, I take it you've reconsidered?"

"Yes," the Count replied graciously. "We are always willing to help the police in every way we can. Isn't that so, darling?"

"Of course." Her smile was almost dazzling enough to distract from her husband's hilariously blatant lie.

"That's very generous of you, monsieur," Tallier said, matching them lie for lie, as he removed a notebook from his jacket. "So, perhaps we could start with this card game of yours? I understand that you provided the chips and playing cards."

"We did," the Count admitted. "My wife and I are inveterate gamblers, you see, and we like to be able to play everywhere we go. A few years ago, I even had a bespoke poker box constructed—polished mahogany, exquisite craftsmanship—so we could bring our chips and cards anywhere. Trains, boats—"

"Parties?"

The Count nodded. "Rosaline insisted, if you must know. She, too, was an enthusiastic player, you see. That's why she moved so close to Monte Carlo, and many of her friends were gamblers as well."

"Were you expecting her to join you last night?"

"Yes. Rosaline usually put in an appearance towards the end of the night, and she usually won too."

"I don't doubt it," Tallier said. "She seemed a formidable woman."

"You met her?"

"Only once, but she made quite an impression."

"She could have that effect, yes," the Count agreed with a smile.

"How well did you know her?"

"I'm not sure anyone knew Lady Rosaline *well*. In truth, we were not much more than acquaintances. Lucia and I were not her usual sort. Neither of us has an artistic bone in our bodies."

"And yet she invited you to her party?"

"Rosaline would invite anyone if she found them interesting, mysterious, or scandalous enough."

"Which did she find you?"

"All three, probably," the Count grinned. "An irresistible combination."

"Are you saying she found you…irresistible?"

"No." The Count laughed. "I think she found me more amusing than anything else, but we shared an opinion of her late husband."

"Captain Lorenzo De Marchi?"

"Ah." The Count shifted uncomfortably. "So you know about De Marchi."

"I know that you are said to have had an altercation with him shortly before his death, and I am curious if Lady Rosaline was involved."

"Not at all," the Count said. "I objected to his politics,"

"And what are your politics, may I ask?"

"I believe my country has become unbearably ugly," the Count replied. "The trains may run like clockwork, but there is no appreciation for beauty, no place left for art or for artists." Tallier wondered if Scarlioni had a specific artist in mind.

"And yet you travel on a diplomatic visa," the Chief Inspector replied, "claim diplomatic immunity, and are of interest to the Italian ambassador. Tell me, does he know of your...artistic leanings?"

"I fail to see how that is relevant, Chief Inspector."

"Relevant?" Tallier shrugged. "Perhaps not, but it is certainly curious, non?"

"Forgive me, Chief Inspector," the Countess said. She had barely spoken thus far, preferring to allow her husband to dominate the conversation, but she had been eyeing Tallier throughout with an increasingly puzzled expression. "But have we met before?"

"What?" The Count frowned, but Tallier only smiled. He had been expecting the question.

"Indeed we have, Countess," the Chief Inspector admitted. "Just recently, in fact, at one of Madame Zorka's little parties in Paris."

"Madame Zorka!" The Count smiled thinnly. "How extraordinary! But then, I suppose she does have the most eclectic taste in guests. Please do forgive me for not recognizing you sooner."

"Not at all." Tallier waved the apology away. "You were quite distracted at the time and, in fairness, I was disguised in a butler's livery."

"How intriguing!" The Countess smiled. "What an exciting life you must lead!"

"It certainly was on that particular occasion."

"Oh?"

"That was another eventful night," Tallier said. "Not unlike last night. No one was murdered, thankfully, but a string of pearls was stolen from around the neck of a Balkan princess."

"Oh, yes!" The Countess did not so much as flinch. "I remember now! That was quite a night, wasn't it, darling?"

"Quite memorable," the Count agreed readily enough. While his control was not as ironclad as his wife's, it was still rather impressive. Even Chief Inspector Tallier, who was watching him with discreetly rapt attention, caught only the faintest flicker of surprise and alarm before the Count's mask was firmly back in place. "Wasn't that the evening you had your disagreement with Major Lapointe's wife, my dear?"

"I do believe it was!" the Countess cried. "You know, I'd quite forgotten about that. Such a dreadful woman, no sense of occasion. But tell us, Chief Inspector, what on earth were you doing there, disguised as a butler, no less?"

Chief Inspector Tallier glanced first at her, then at her husband before speaking. "I wonder if either of you has ever heard of La Chimère?"

"La Chimère?" the Countess frowned in apparent concentration. "I'm sure I've heard that name somewhere recently. Oh, I know!" She turned to her husband with eyebrows raised. "Wasn't there something in the paper, darling?"

"Yes," the Count answered. "He's a gentleman thief, I believe, one of the old school, who has been blazing a trail all over Europe, and—forgive me for saying so, Chief Inspector—making a fool of the police wherever he goes."

"Oui," Tallier agreed, "they've made our lives quite difficult of late. But recently, I received word that this infamous La Chimère was in Paris planning to steal the Princess of Myrtrov's pearls."

"Did you?"

"It was an anonymous letter," Inspector Tallier explained. "But not one we could afford to ignore."

"No, of course not."

"So, I made a few inquiries, a few arrangements, and then, with the princess' permission, I set a little trap on the night of the party."

"My goodness!" the Countess gasped. "You must have been very persuasive!"

"But you didn't catch him, did you?" her husband asked.

"No," Inspector Tallier admitted. "Unfortunately, my prey eluded me and somehow managed to smuggle the pearls out from under my nose."

The Count and Countess both made suitably sympathetic sounds but, as Tallier had hoped, he detected a telltale hint of glee in their eyes.

"The princess must have been furious," Count Scarlioni said. "First, you used her as bait, and then, not only did you fail to catch your quarry, but you also lost her neckless."

Chief Inspector Tallier replied with an ostentatiously gallic shrug. "No one was entirely successful that night," he said. "I took precautions, you see. The stolen pearls were made of glass, while the real ones were kept safely under lock and key. So, Her Highness was actually quite grateful in the end, despite my failure to catch the thief, although the papers were less...generous."

For a brief moment, there was something ugly in the Countess' eyes, but within moments her poker face was firmly back in place. "That's quite a story," she said. "And quite a coincidence."

"Coincidence?"

"Well, I understand there was another theft last night, just like at Madame Zorka's party."

"There was."

"And here we three are again," the Countess pointed out. "As I said, quite a coincidence. Unless! You weren't setting another trap, were you, Inspector?"

Beside her, the Count snorted. "Tell me," he said between suppressed laughs, "Did you brush off your butler's uniform, or were you one of the footmen this time? Wait, don't tell me. I know!" He grinned. "You were in the band, I wager."

"No," Chief Inspector Tallier replied. "I wasn't in the band. So, I suppose that's another bet you would have lost."

"Excuse me?"

"Well, I understand you lost a lot of money last night. Is this so?"

It was the Count's turn to shrug. "I did," he admitted. "But what of it? My luck ran out last night, that's all. It happens, no?"

"Yes," Chief Inspector Tallier agreed with a thin, pointed smile. "It does."

* * *

"WELL, THAT WAS A WASTE OF TIME," M. Jarre exclaimed once the Count and Countess had left. "Why did they bother coming here if all they were going to do was spout lies and evasions? They could have done that last night and saved us some time."

"Oh, I think they had a very definite purpose in mind," Tallier replied as he stood to pour himself a fresh cup of coffee. "They wanted to learn something from us that was worth the risk of coming here."

M. Jarre pondered that with a frown, pausing only to shake his head when Tallier offered to refill his cup. "Do you think they learned what they wanted?" he asked.

"I think so, yes, but I learned something as well."

"From that parade of nonsense?" Jarre was incredulous, but Tallier nodded seriously.

"Not from what they said," he explained, "although they may have made a mistake there too, but rather from how they said it."

"Oh?"

"They're scared," Tallier revealed with a triumphant grin. "They panicked last night, and now they're scrambling to regain their footing. Don't you see? Claiming diplomatic immunity, avoiding questions, and then coming here today—these aren't the moves of someone in control of the game."

"Maybe not, but cornered animals are at their most dangerous," Jarre warned.

"I know," Chief Inspector Tallier said. "But desperate animals make mistakes, and Scarlioni is getting rather desperate indeed. All we need to do is crack his alibi, and then one more lapse, one more slip up, and I'll have him! You see if I don't!"

17

THE FALSE ALIBI

"It's a pleasure to meet you, Mr. Quayle," George Dabney said with an engaging, almost admiring grin. "Arthur here has told me something of your exploits." They were standing in the lobby of the Hotel Magellan while all around them, the tourists and travelers swerved about their business, their voices echoing in half a dozen languages.

Exploits, eh? Mr. Quayle scrutinized the sportsman carefully as they shook hands. Tall, fair, and athletic, Dabney was very much the proper English gentleman—well-tanned and well-muscled—but there was a glint of recklessness lurking in his eyes. Quayle had known quite a few like that during the War. Full of vim and vigor, they were always eager for action, always the first to volunteer, the first to go over the top, and, inevitably, the first to die.

"Arthur exaggerates, I'm sure," Quayle said.

"Not a bit of it!" Arthur protested. "This man," he explained to Dabney, "saved me from the gallows!"

"Well, maybe from your own stupidity," Mr. Quayle muttered under his breath before turning to Dabney. "Has Arthur explained why we wanted to see you?"

"He has indeed," Dabney said. "But, in all honestly, I'm not sure I can be of much help." He led the pair of them over to a quiet corner of the hotel bar, looking over his shoulder from time to time as if to check if anyone was watching, then looking slightly sad when no one was.

"The truth is," he continued once they'd all sat, "I was a... satellite in Rosaline's court, an ornament. You see, she still liked to act the kingmaker, but it wasn't as though the avant-garde was knocking down the door, begging for her blessing. Lately, her circle has shrunken and withered on the vine. Most of Rosaline's pet artists are tired, forgotten old things like Carrodus or *desperate*, forgotten old things like Léger. So, she needed me to provide a touch of youth to the proceedings."

"Did that bother you?" Quayle wondered. "Being an ornament?"

"Not at all! Why should it?" Dabney replied. "I'm not an artist. I never needed *her* to make me a king. Besides, I found her amusing." He smiled softly to himself. "I reckon Rosaline must have been a force to be reckoned with in her day, but my own interests are more... modern." As he spoke, Dabney winked at a gaggle of young flappers at another table who all giggled obligingly.

Mr. Quayle was only partially convinced by the performance, however, but if the dashing sportsman and racecar driver wanted to pretend that he hadn't been half in love with a woman old enough to be his mother, then that was his own affair. Quayle is more interested in the card game. Disappointingly, though, Dabney and Arthur's accounts proved essentially identical. *Infuriatingly so.*

"Tell me," Mr. Quayle said when Dabney was done, "what did you make of the other players?"

"What did I make of them?"

"Yes," Mr. Quayle clarified. "Scarlioni, for example, was he any good?"

"Very good, I should say," Dabney replied, his confusion clearing. "That man's a professional—cold and precise. And I'm fairly certain he was counting cards—"

"—I say! Really?" Arthur was flabbergasted, but Mr. Quayle merely nodded. That accorded with his own assessment of the Count.

"And as for the others, let me see—" Dabney was warming to the topic now. "—Sir Julius is an optimist. He always thinks he can bluff his way out of anything, brazening it out with hope and a prayer." His eyes narrowed in thought. "Carrodus was different, though. He was more conservative, played the odds. A gifted amateur, I'd say."

"And Arthur?"

"Arthur?" Dabney snorted. "Arthur's style hasn't changed since we were boys: haphazard and streaky at best."

"Worked last night," Arthur pointed out mildly, seemingly unmoved by his friend's assessment.

"Mm." Dabney made no further reply, but his expression was tight as though he was holding himself back. That wouldn't do, Mr. Quayle decided. That wouldn't do at all.

"And how *was* Arthur last night?" he asked. "Streaky as usual?"

"Lucky," Dabney replied. "*Very lucky.*"

"I see." Like Mr. Quayle, Dabney was clearly suspicious of Arthur's good fortune but he was too polite to air his doubts with Arthur sitting right there. So be it! "You do realize that there is *one* player you've forgotten," Quayle pointed out instead.

"Is there?" Dabney blinked in confusion. "Who?"

"Why, the Countess, of course."

"The Countess?" Dabney frowned. "No, I didn't forget

about her, but she only played a few hands before tiring of the game."

"I thought you said she never left?"

"She didn't!" Dabney said. "The Countess spent the remainder of the evening either prowling around the room fixing drinks or hovering over her husband's shoulder and making occasional, murmured suggestions."

Mr. Quayle leaned forward in sudden rapt attention. "Then how can you be sure, either of you, that the Countess was there the whole time?"

"Now, just a minute!" Dabney protested.

"Do you really think we would have missed her just strolling out?" Arthur asked. "We're not blind!"

"No, you're not blind. But you, Arthur, were having the luck of your life, and you, Mr. Dabney, were trying to figure out how he was managing it. *All* the players were." Quayle smiled to himself. His thoughts were flying now, so clear and precise he could almost picture the scene. "And I never said she 'just strolled out.' No! The Countess chose her moment well. She waited until you were all at your most distracted, then she seized her chance and slipped away."

"Nonsense!" Dabney said. "That's impossible!" But he didn't sound quite so sure as his words suggested.

"Difficult, yes, but not impossible. You both told me how dark and smokey the room was while you were playing, and as the night wore on, the game absorbed more and more of your attention. Can you truly swear, either of you, that the Countess was absolutely there the entire time? Or did you only *think* she was?"

"No, I-I couldn't swear it, but I—"

"—I don't know," Arthur admitted. "She might have left. She might not have. Honestly, when I got that royal flush, a horde of elephants could have danced the Charleston, and I would have never noticed."

Dabney sighed. "No," he agreed. "I couldn't swear it either. But if you're right, Quayle, she took quite a risk, and that's *me* saying that."

"There was no risk in leaving," Mr. Quayle said. "If anyone saw her, it would have been easy enough to make excuses. No! The real trouble was in coming back and pretending she never left." As well as what she did with the statuette in between, but that was another problem and Mr. Quayle had no desire to confuse the issue.

"Whatever else happened, she was *definitely* there for the final hand," Dabney insisted. "I remember she was quite upset with her husband for losing."

"Is that so?" The anger had been a nice touch, Mr. Quayle thought, a way to ensure everyone noted her presence, but like everything else about the card game, it had been a bluff—an intricately simple piece of misdirection. This was only one piece of the puzzle, of course, and Quayle was far from convinced that the Count and Countess had murdered anyone, but it wasn't a bad start.

Not a bad start at all.

18

PORTRAIT OF A HOUSE IN MOURNING

Fanny was worried about Hollins. He had been acting oddly all morning—barely talking, barely eating, instead staring forlornly into the middle distance for long stretches of time. If she hadn't known better, Fanny would have thought he was grieving, but Hollins had never met Lady Rosaline before last night, when she had seemingly gone out of her way to ignore him. And yet, following her death, the laughing, endearingly earnest Hollins that Fanny knew had been reduced to a sullen, sunken-eyed shadow.

Of course, he was hardly the only one who had been transformed overnight. In death, Lady Rosaline Barrett De Marchi, the Widow of Treville-sur-Mer, had been turned at a stroke from sinner into saint, from Magdalene to Madonna. And Léger himself, who only yesterday had seethed and snarled at the very thought of her, was now hard at work hurriedly rewriting history and perfecting his new role as mourner-in-chief.

Perched on the settee in his usual place, Léger was again holding court, this time over a house in mourning, as blatant lies and half-truths spilled from his tongue like gospel. In

Léger's latest sermon, Lady Rosaline became like a mother to him, with Léger himself cast as the wayward but much-beloved son. Never mind that there was scarcely a decade between them or that Léger's futile attempts at seducing Rosaline were the stuff of legend and mockery.

No one was mocking now, however, and Léger's performance last night had already borne fruit. According to Anne-Marie, Léger had sold three paintings since the murder—one at the party and two this morning—all to discerning patrons and fresh converts to the burgeoning myth of the Widow and her Beloved Artist.

Not that those paintings were particularly good, in Fanny's opinion. Léger's early paintings were all quite classical in form and subject, such that even his flirtations with Impressionism, likely instigated by Lady Rosaline, had never strayed too far from his inclination towards realism. The latest paintings, however, fresh from his studio, were less formal, less precise, as if, free from Lady Rosaline's direction, he had contemplated a shift in style before recoiling. The end result was a hodgepodge, a halfway house neither here nor there, although only Fanny seemed to notice.

Meanwhile, Léger's disciples and adherents had more than doubled since yesterday afternoon. The crowd was jammed into the drawing room, filling every conceivable space from the floor to the sofas to the windowsills, and all were hanging on the Great Artist's every word. It was a sickening display, but Hollins was too distracted to share in Fanny's distaste, and Anne-Marie, who could usually be relied upon to at least roll her eyes, was far more subdued than usual.

Huddled in a corner of the room with Márta and an elderly gentleman with a severe, white beard, who could only be the elusive Herr Darvas, Madame Léger seemed increasingly worried, even moreso when talk turned from her husband's elegiac declarations to the murder and the fate of Lady Rosaline's now orphaned art collection.

It had long been assumed that ownership of the collection would be transferred to the Musée de Saint-Jean le Décapité, but no one knew if Lady Rosaline had actually stipulated that in her will.

"I admit," Herr Darvas confided to the room, "that I am not sure if Raymond will honor his mother's intentions."

From his perch, Léger nodded vigorously. "I've never trusted that boy," he said solemnly. "Even as a child, Raymond had no appreciation for the arts and little love for his mother or his mother's friends. He may have invited us to the memorial tomorrow but, if I were you, Herr Darvas, I would not trust him to do the right thing."

But the right thing for whom, Fanny wondered to herself. For Raymond? For Léger? For Darvas? Or, perhaps, for Anne-Marie and Márta, who were both frowning in ever-deepening concern? No! If Fanny was in Raymond's shoes, she wasn't at all sure she would help Léger either. And as for Herr Darvas, the elderly man appeared courtly and polite, but Fanny found something oddly disquieting about him—a cunning glint in his eyes.

In fact, there was something oddly disquieting about all of them, and as they began to discuss the swirling rumors that Count Scarlioni and the notorious La Chimère were one and the same, a rumor which had emerged that afternoon with uncanny abruptness, Fanny sensed the same brewing, poisoned atmosphere from the night before. Lady Rosaline's death, it seemed, had only made it worse.

Before Fanny could think of prying more closely, however, she was interrupted by a sudden and insistent tapping on the window. The whole room stuttered to a halt, and Léger, who had been mid-diatribe, turned with an angry glare.

There was a man in the garden, peering in through the

window with a sheepishly determined expression, and to Fanny's surprise and alarm, it was Arthur.

"Isn't that your brother?" Madame Léger addressed her from the far side of the room. "Albert? Ambrose?"

"Arthur," Fanny corrected. "And he's my cousin."

"Whoever he is," Márta said, "it would appear that he needs to speak with you urgently."

"If you would excuse me." Fanny rose to her feet. "I should probably see what he wants."

Once outside, Fanny grabbed Arthur by the arm and dragged him along the path to the precipice of the cliff. The last time she had stood here, only yesterday, she had felt at peace, but there was no peace now.

"What are you doing here?" she demanded.

"I needed to see you," he replied, looking far too pleased with himself. And then Arthur uttered perhaps the most terrifying sentence Fanny had ever heard, one which made her blood run cold and her thoughts run for cover.

"Don't worry," Arthur said with what he must have thought was a reassuring grin. "I have an idea!"

***

"Well, what do you think?"

Chief Inspector Tallier clicked his tongue and leaned back in his chair. Throughout Mr. Quayle's explanation, Tallier's expression had changed little, revealing almost nothing of his thoughts. Was this, Mr. Quayle wondered, what it was like talking to him? How disconcerting!

The two men were squeezed into a tiny hole-in-the-wall deep within the bowels of the police station. There was no window and barely enough room for the desk, let alone two people, but the Chief Inspector did not seem overly bothered by his accommodations.

"What do I think," the Frenchman repeated. The cogs and gears were turning visibly yet mysteriously behind his eyes. "Très bien." He nodded to himself before seemingly coming to a decision. "I think that you are probably right, Monsieur Quayle. It is precisely the sort of maneuver that would appeal to them."

"So, you agree." Mr. Quayle eyed Tallier searchingly. "And you don't think it's too fanciful? I mean, surely there are simpler ways to falsify an alibi. Even if half the other players thought Arthur was cheating, hoping that no one would notice the Countess leaving was…risky."

"It was," Tallier agreed. "But, as you say, not so risky as it might have been. And the Count is a gambler, is he not? A professional? He counts the cards, stacks the deck, and then lets the chips fall as they may. Besides…"

"Yes?"

"They've done it before," Tallier revealed. "It's one of the Scarlioni's favorite little tricks. The only difference is that in Paris, their roles were reversed. It was the Countess who made a spectacle of herself while the Count sneaked away unnoticed."

Mr. Quayle scowled. "So, you knew?" he demanded. "In that case, what was the point of having me scrambling about?"

"No, no, mon ami." Tallier shook his head. "I did not know. I merely suspected that the card game and Monsieur Arthur were at the heart of it, that some sleight of hand had been employed, but I did not know how. It took me ages to work it out in Paris, and I had no great confidence that I would be much faster this time. You solved it quite handily, however. My secret weapon, n'est-ce pas?"

Mr. Quayle accepted the not-quite-compliment warily. "So, it's over then?" he asked. "You've got your man, and you can return home to Paris in triumph with laurels on your head?"

"Not exactly." Tallier laughed. "You have explained it to my satisfaction, mon ami, but that is not enough." He shrugged apologetically. "In the end, what proof is it that you have brought me?" he asked. "That Monsieur Druce and Monsieur Dabney now say that they think the Countess *may* have slipped out of the room while their attentions were elsewhere? '*May*,' mon ami, is not a good word. Especially since these very same gentlemen swore last night that the Countess did not leave her husband's side. It is, so to speak, their word against…their word, which, as I'm sure you'll agree, is très difficile."

"It's definitely not ideal," Mr. Quayle allowed. "But what sort of proof did you have in mind?"

"Well, the Bernini itself would be ideal," Tallier replied. "We may know how the Countess managed to steal it, but the question remains: where is the statuette now? And how did they manage to smuggle it out of the villa?"

"I never saw the statuette myself," Mr. Quayle said thoughtfully, "but judging by the size of the pedestal, it is not something you could hide in your coat. Not that Scarlioni was wearing a coat."

"Exactement." Tallier nodded. "But there has been some mention of a poker box, which may—there's that word again—have been big enough to secrete the Bernini. The only trouble is that no one seems to know where it is, including the Count and Countess."

"Oh?"

"They were here earlier this morning, ever so eager to help with our investigation, but I believe what they really wanted was to know if we had the box."

"Which you don't?"

"No. The cards and chips were all in the Billiards Room,

where the players left them, but we haven't found any trace of the box. I have men searching the grounds, of course, but I'm not hopeful."

"Where does that leave us?"

"Us?" The Chief Inspector sent Mr. Quayle an amused, searching glance before shrugging. "Well, if we don't have the box," he said, "and Scarlioni doesn't have the box, then who does?"

"You suspect there is someone else involved? A third member of their little gang?"

"No." Tallier immediately disagreed. "If that were so, then the Count would have known where the box was, or at least who might have it. No, I believe there is something lurking beneath the surface of this affair, something which has only just begun to emerge into view."

Quayle agreed wholeheartedly but had little more than half-formed ideas and inchoate notions to offer. So, he said nothing, and the two men fell into a companionable, ponderous silence for a time, each lost in a world of their own thoughts. And so they might have remained indefinitely if Tallier's phone had not begun to ring.

The shrill noise pierced their shared quiet like a gunshot. Tallier started but answered speedily enough, and Mr. Quayle observed the Chief Inspector's face for any hint or scrap of information, but to no avail.

No doubt aware of the scrutiny, Chief Inspector Tallier turned his chair away, and Mr. Quayle was forced to content himself with a few snatches of clumsily understood French.

"Forgive me, Monsieur Quayle," Chief Inspector Tallier said once he had finished and placed the receiver back down. "But there is some business I must see to."

"Of course." Mr. Quayle stood without protest. "You have a murder to investigate. I understand perfectly."

Tallier eyed him suspiciously but Quayle remained

outwardly innocent, and after a moment, the Chief Inspector bid him farewell, snatching up the telephone to make calls of his own.

Pausing outside in the hallway and dodging as a police constable scrambled past, Quayle took the opportunity to gather his thoughts. Tallier was right to be suspicious. Quayle had not caught everything, but what he had overheard and understood was enough to worry him deeply.

It seemed that Tallier's men had been keeping an eye on last night's guests all day, watching not only the Count and Countess but everyone who had been at the party—every one of interest, at least, including Lord Unsworth and his family. The police had gleaned little from their observations, however. The Count and Countess, for example, had apparently spent the afternoon taking a suspiciously leisurely stroll around Treville-sur-Mer and its environs. But now the Count had disappeared, vanishing on the early evening breeze.

Naturally, Tallier was concerned. His main suspect, the man he had been chasing for months, had just slipped through his fingers yet again, but what worried Quayle the most was another piece of intelligence. While the Count had given the police the slip, the Countess remained in full view and was heading back toward their yacht where apparently, for some god-forsaken reason, Arthur was waiting for her!

Mr. Quayle sighed to himself. Sometimes, just sometimes, he wondered why he even bothered.

19

ARTHUR'S BRILLIANT PLAN

As he crouched behind a box on the dockside, Arthur did his best to appear inconspicuous. He had found the Scarlioni's yacht without much difficulty. All it had taken was a few questions in the right ears, and a few francs slipped discreetly into the right hands. So far, so good! Except, the Count and Countess had not been at home, forcing Arthur to do the one thing he hated more than anything else—wait and wait and wait.

It had been hours since then, and still no sign of his elusive quarry, which had given Arthur all the time he needed to do the second thing he hated more than anything in the world—think. Round and round, his thoughts went, spinning and spinning, until he felt sick and dizzy from the whirl of it. Initially eager to help and boyishly pleased at the chance for another adventure, Arthur now found himself increasingly hesitant.

It had seemed like such a good idea at the time! Fanny hadn't thought so—spoilsport—but Dabney had agreed immediately and had even helped him figure out what he would say and how. The plan was simple enough. Arthur would use his friendship with the Count to inveigle his way on board the yacht and poke around—see what he could find.

Arthur knew from Quayle that the police suspected the Count and Countess of stealing the statuette and possibly even murdering Lady Rosaline, but he knew too that they had no proof. In fact, Arthur himself was the main impediment, the bone caught in the throat of justice, as he had put it to Dabney in an unusually poetic moment.

But what if Arthur could find the proof? Wouldn't that be something? He grinned at the thought, his confidence returning. He realized, of course, that he hadn't made a particularly good showing the previous year and that last night he had somehow managed, although he was still not quite sure how, to drag the family into yet another murder case. But this time, Arthur would to prove to his mother, to Quayle, and to Uncle Edward that he could clean up his own mess.

Peeking over the crate, Arthur was rewarded at last. The Countess had returned! There was no sign of her husband, but after waiting all this time, Arthur was in no mood to delay any longer. Just as he started to rise, however, Mr. Quayle came barreling down the peer and yanked Arthur back.

"What are you doing here?" Arthur asked, blinking at him in shock.

"More to the point," Mr. Quayle replied, "What are *you* doing here?"

"Fanny told you, didn't she?" Arthur mumbled. She had made her feelings about his plan abundantly clear, but he hadn't expected her to run and tattle to Quayle.

"No, she did not." Mr. Quayle's eyes narrowed. "And I expected better from her, but never mind about Fanny. What do you think you're doing? I've only just managed to extract you from this blasted business, and the minute—*the minute*—I turn away, you throw yourself back in head first!"

"Now, wait a moment, Quayle," Arthur protested. "I'm not a complete fool! I have done this sort of thing before, you know. Before we met, I got into all kinds of scrapes on behalf of my friends. Always good in a pinch is Arthur! Always eager to help!" He nodded earnestly. "Why, as you'll recall, I even managed to evade the police last year when they were chasing me!"

"Yes, you did," Mr. Quayle agreed readily, far too readily in Arthur's opinion. "But they still caught you in the end, didn't they?"

"Well, yes, but—"

"And you couldn't evade *me*, could you?"

Arthur stared at his feet as he shifted about uncomfortably. "No, I suppose not," he admitted.

"Ahem!" The two men looked up and found Countess Scarlioni peering down at them over the side of the crate. "Can I help you, gentlemen?" she asked pointedly.

Mr. Quayle reacted with enviable alacrity and was on his feet within moments. Nothing about him suggested that he had been in the least bit surprised by her appearance.

"Contessa." He greeted her with a polite nod as if they were passing acquaintances encountering one another at a garden party rather than near strangers meeting on the docks.

Arthur was far less composed and stumbled upright in a tangle of limbs, making, he was sure, an absolute laughingstock of himself. The Countess, however, did not laugh or sneer or snicker. Instead, she merely stared at them, her gaze demanding answers.

So, Arthur, ever helpful, provided them.

* * *

Mr. Quayle watched in resigned horror as Arthur made what he likely believed to be a passable attempt at subtlety—

less of a bull in a china shop and more a large dog. Weighing his options, however, Quayle chose to remain silent. The Countess was unlikely to respond well to whatever ill-conceived nonsense Arthur had in mind, but any response could be telling at this stage. Perhaps Arthur's tendency to barge in where angels feared to tread might just have its uses after all. *Perhaps*.

"I was hoping to speak to your husband about last night," Arthur said in his most earnest, friendly voice.

The Countess, who had previously treated Arthur with a species of fond bemusement, was now noticeably distant and chilly.

"Unfortunately," she replied, sounding distinctly unapologetic, "the Count is not here at the moment, but then the two of you probably already knew that."

Mr. Quayle was careful not to frown or react in any way when her gaze widened to include him. There was something sly, almost accusing, about her words and manner that he couldn't quite understand.

Arthur, of course, missed the byplay completely. "I don't suppose we could wait on board?" he requested far too innocently, waving his hand towards the yacht moored only a few feet away.

"No. I don't believe that will be possible." The Countess' voice was even colder now, and Mr. Quayle caught more than a few notes of suspicion lurking underneath.

"But, surely..." Arthur attempted to press, unwisely in Quayle's opinion. He was showing his hand too clearly.

"I'm afraid not," the Countess said decisively.

Arthur seemed taken aback by her abruptness but quickly changed tactics. "Then perhaps you know when he might return, Countess?" he asked hopefully, but she only shrugged in response.

"I am not responsible for all my husband's comings and goings," she said.

"Speaking of comings and goings," Arthur said, boldly meeting her eyes. "What of yours last night?"

"My comings and goings?" The Countess frowned. "Why, Arthur, whatever do you mean?"

"What if I were to say that I saw you leave the Billiards Room last night," he replied, struggling to hold back a grin.

Beside him, Mr. Quayle fought the urge to groan and rub his eyes in despair. So, this was Arthur's brilliant plan? It was bold, to be sure, and not without merit. Unlike Quayle, the Countess had no way of knowing whether Arthur was lying or not. But it was still a risk, a terrible, unnecessary risk. If the Countess was involved in the murder, then even hinting at blackmail could prove to be a death sentence. And yet here Arthur was, grinning and enjoying himself, clearly delighted with his own cleverness.

"Please understand," Arthur continued, unaware of the heart attack he was causing beneath Quayle's placid surface, "I'm not accusing you of anything. All I'm saying is that at the time of the murder, you were not quite where you said you were and, as I've already corroborated your story to the police, that puts me in a rather delicate position. You understand? I'm only trying to help."

"Are you blackmailing me?" The Countess gasped theatrically before rewarding Arthur with a brief mocking burst of applause. "If so, then I must say this is, frankly, the most awkward attempt I have ever had the privilege to witness, and I'm sure the Count will be very sorry he missed it."

Arthur straightened in not entirely feigned indignation. He had practiced that speech several times and did not appreciate it being characterized as awkward. The Countess, however, held out a finger to stop him.

"Now, Arthur, let us speak plainly. It does not matter if I

left the room or if you saw me. Nor does it matter if I am lying or if you are. What matters is that you are bluffing."

"I'm not bluffing," Arthur protested, but the Countess shook her head.

"Don't be a fool," she said slowly, as if speaking to a child. "If you were to change your story now, all it would prove is that you are unreliable, and, as you may recall, I do have other witnesses. No! I'm afraid you have no cards to play, my dear, and you may attempt to brazen this out if you so wish, but," she sneered, "we both know you're not a particularly good poker player, are you?"

"He was last night," Mr. Quayle pointed out mildly and was startled by the sudden hostility which erupted in the Countess' eyes.

"Ah!" she cried. "The organ grinder speaks!"

"I beg your pardon?"

"It all becomes clear," she said. "I thought someone had been putting ideas in dear Arthur's head, winding him up and letting him go."

"I'm afraid Arthur's ideas are all his own," Quayle said honestly. "I am merely here as an observer."

"Yes, you are, aren't you?" the Countess agreed. "But what, I wonder, are you here to observe? Earlier, Arthur was quite eager to board the yacht. So tell me, what exactly was he expecting to find?"

"I'm sure I don't know what you mean." It was Mr. Quayle's first lie of the conversation.

"Then perhaps you can explain what you and Arthur were doing hiding behind a crate because, from where I'm standing, it looks as though you were waiting to ambush me, amongst other things."

"Other things?" Mr. Quayle was confused by the comment. Indeed, he was finding the Countess' whole demeanor increasingly puzzling. It was almost as if she was having a different conversation entirely. "I have no idea what you mean," he said.

"Of course not!" The Countess scoffed. "I overlooked you, Mr. Quayle, but I won't make that mistake again. Using Arthur as your catspaw was a nice touch, but now I see you for what you are—a snake in the grass."

Quayle was shocked. He and the Countess had scarcely shared more than a dozen words before now, and as far as he was aware, he had done nothing to provoke her ire. So, what was going on here? What lay behind her sudden attack?

He barely had time to defend himself, however, before they were interrupted by the sudden screech of wheels and tires.

Chief Inspector Tallier and the police had arrived in force.

Confused and increasingly alarmed, Mr. Quayle could only follow, with Arthur in tow, as Tallier swept his way onto the yacht and down into the cabin below. The Chief Inspector seemed distracted, barely acknowledging anyone apart from the Countess, but there was an urgency to his steps and movement that Quayle had not seen before. Something must have happened—something terrible.

As he descended into the yacht, the possibilities swirled ominously in Mr. Quayle's mind. To his surprise, no one had stopped him, although Inspector Barras had spared a moment to glare at him and Arthur. Inspector Duvot was also there, along with an older, stiff-collared gentleman, who Quayle presumed to be Judge Jarre.

When he reached the bottom of the stairs, however, all thoughts of Jarre, Barras, or even Tallier were briefly driven from his mind, and Mr. Quayle realized in an instant why the Countess had been so edgy earlier.

The yacht had been ransacked—chairs and tables upended, books pulled down, mattresses overturned, floorboards capsized, and papers and belongings strewn everywhere. Someone had been looking for something and had been none-to-gentle in their search.

"This is an outrage!" the Countess cried, then pointed an accusing finger straight at Quayle and Arthur. "You did this!" she hissed. "All of you! You've been working together, and I will not stand for it! When my husband hears about this—"

Chief Inspector Tallier coughed delicately. "I'm afraid, Countess Scarlioni," he said, "your husband won't be hearing about anything ever again."

"And why is that?" she demanded.

"Count Scarlioni's body was discovered along the shore about twenty minutes ago," the Chief Inspector answered as gently as he could under the circumstances. "It appears that he has been murdered."

PART III

THE AFTERMATH

20

THE MEMORIAL

Trailing a few steps behind Lord Unsworth and the others as they ascended the stairs to Lady Rosaline's villa—Raymond's villa now—Mr. Quayle took a moment to collect his thoughts. It had been a long night—the latest in what felt like an endless series of long, long nights. The police had questioned him and Arthur sharply but briefly, much to Lord Unsworth and Lady Constance's relief. Ironically, as insulting and degrading as it was for the family to have been spied upon by the French constabulary, it had provided them all with one entirely unanticipated benefit—an unimpeachable alibi for Count Scarlioni's murder.

It was now mid-afternoon on the following day, and Raymond and Vivi were waiting in the entrance hall, again playing host to seemingly all of Treville-sur-Mer and beyond. This time, however, with no Lady Rosaline to hold court, the house felt barren and empty. It was hard to remember that this same room had echoed with music and laughter just over forty-eight hours ago. But then two days could be a lifetime, as Mr. Quayle knew better than most, and judging by the dark circles he could see under Raymond's eyes, their host had learnt the same hard lesson.

Lady Rosaline's funeral had been held that morning—a deliberately and pointedly family affair with only Raymond and Vivi in attendance. Naturally, this had caused no small amount of bitterness amongst Lady Rosaline's horde of self-professed nearest and dearest—Jean-Paul Léger chief among them—and this afternoon's hastily arranged memorial had only slightly mollified their bruised egos.

For his part, Raymond was making no effort to welcome them as he greeted his mother's friends, acquaintances, and various hangers-on with a tortured, surly expression. Not that Quayle could blame him. He suspected that Raymond had only held the memorial in the first place to counter Léger's blatant attempt to seize control of Lady Rosaline's legacy. The in-fighting had already begun, it seemed, although half the guests hadn't even been invited.

Unexpectedly, however, His Lordship *had* been invited, which was strange given that Raymond had made his feelings for Lord Unsworth quite clear the other night. Rude and insolent was how Lady Constance had described him. *Unconscionably rude.*

But when it was Lord Unsworth's turn to offer his condolences, Raymond stepped forward instead, and the whole room seemed to hold its breath. Mr. Quayle was well aware of the rumors that were circulating—vicious half-truths and innuendos—and he could feel the crowd sharpening its knives. If they were hoping for blood, however, they were soon to be disappointed.

"Thank you for coming, Lord Unsworth," Raymond said almost sheepishly. "It would have meant a great deal to my mother."

"I'm not so sure," His Lordship replied. "Despite what

people seem to think, your mother and I hadn't spoken for many years."

"Yes, I know," Raymond replied. "She told me as much, but you're the only person here, I think, who knew her before she was famous, when she was still Rose instead of Rosaline. Actually, now that Father and Weatherford are gone, you might be the only one left in the world."

"Possibly."

Behind them, Vivi coughed, and Raymond cleared his throat. "It has been brought to my attention," he said, "that I may owe you an apology."

Lady Constance snorted, but Lord Unsworth contented himself with raising his eyebrows. Neither of them spoke, however, preferring to let Raymond flounder.

"I thought you were like all the others, you see," he said, "just another desperate old man, panting after my mother's money, but you're the only one who hasn't mentioned my mother's will, not even in passing. It's been the first word out of everyone else's mouth."

"Why would I mention your mother's will?" Lord Unsworth was incredulous.

"Well, quite, but no one else seems to share your reticence." Raymond glared over His Lordship's shoulder. "Least of all, Herr Darvas."

"The curator?"

"Mmm." Raymond nodded. "He and his daughter came slinking over the very next morning. Mother hadn't even been dead twelve hours, and they were already on at me about the will, the collection, what they'd been promised." Raymond snorted. "And look, here he is now!"

Mr. Quayle turned with some interest as the elderly curator and his daughter made their way over, and was even more interested when the young woman, Márta, shared a brief nod with Fanny.

"Herr Darvas," Raymond greeted, shaking the Hungarian's hand solemnly. "So glad you could join us."

"Of course, of course," Herr Darvas murmured his own appropriately sympathetic if a trifle stilted, condolences. "I wonder, Raymond," he said, once the niceties had been observed, if you've had time to—"

"I don't believe you know Lord Unsworth," Raymond interrupted with all the subtlety of a rhinoceros.

"Unsworth?" Herr Darvas stroked his beard thoughtfully. "Ah, yes! I remember!" he cried. "The Unsworth Trove!" The elderly gentleman beamed from behind his beard. "Your Lordship's collection of medieval artifacts is famous. I am no great expert on the period, but—"

"Not at all." Lord Unsworth was far too pleased to mention any previous quibbles.

"Your Lordship is kind," Herr Darvas said, "but I know my limitations. The medieval period and I have a passing acquaintance merely, but it is said that you have your share of treasures, and I know that Professor Thascalos from the University of Bordeaux has always spoken highly of you."

It was Lord Unsworth's turn to be modest. "Thascalos flatters me. I am very familiar with my own family's history. Indeed, I have been writing a volume on the subject for some years now, but outside my narrow field, I am an amateur."

Herr Darvas' answering smile was polite but unconvinced. "I am sure that is not true," he said. "But now, as delightful as it is to talk with you, Lord Unsworth, I have my own collection to attend to, so if you'll excuse me?" He clicked his heels together sharply, and turned, catching Raymond and Vivi just as they had been about to slip away.

"One moment Raymond," Darvas called. "If I may? The museum and I are eager to make arrangements for the movement and storage of your mother's artworks. Preservation is most important, da? And we were hoping—"

"Forgive me, Herr Darvas," Raymond protested. "But the will has not been read yet. My mother's lawyer is still on his way from Paris. He should be here this evening, but until then..."

"Yes, yes!" Darvas waved his hand dismissively. "But your mother's wishes were well-known, and the sooner we can make preparations, the sooner we can be out of your hair, no?"

Watching as Herr Darvas and his daughter led Raymond and Vivi away to a quiet corner, Lady Constance pursed her lips in disgust. She had not been impressed by Raymond's apology but was even less taken by Darvas' rather unseemly eagerness to lay hands on Lady Rosaline's collection.

"But what can one expect from foreigners?" She sneered. "No sense of propriety."

Fanny cleared her throat awkwardly. "Actually, Aunt Constance," she revealed, "there is a feeling amongst Darvas and others that Raymond might withhold the collection out of spite."

Lord Unsworth was unconvinced. "If Rosaline truly did bequeath her collection to Darvas, as she told Constance and I that she would, then there's little Raymond could do about it, spite or no spite. And frankly, he doesn't strike me as being particularly interested in his mother's art. Certainly, not enough to make a fuss over it."

Mr. Quayle nodded. He agreed with His Lordship's assessment, but there was something about Darvas's eagerness, what Lady Constance called his lack of propriety, that had sent Quayle's mind whirring. Herr Darvas had all the appearance of a careful, somber man, not the kind of person who would press a newly bereaved son unnecessarily. But as Lord Unsworth had said, it was doubtful that Raymond would be willing or even able to go against the terms of his mother's will. So, either Lady Rosaline had changed her mind, or...

"Tell me, sir," Mr. Quayle asked, "what is your opinion of Lady Rosaline's collection?"

"My opinion?" Lord Unsworth frowned thoughtfully. "Well, I'm happy to say I know vanishingly little about modern art, but from what I could see of Rosaline's medieval collection, it was...passable enough, for an amateur, that is."

"Passable?"

"Indeed." His Lordship nodded. "This Darvas fellow appears to be quite a knowledgeable fellow. His manners leave something to be desired, of course, but—"

"You're only saying that because he complimented your trove," Fanny teased.

"Ah, yes, well..." Embarrassed, Lord Unsworth rubbed the back of his neck awkwardly.

"But?" Mr. Quayle prompted.

"But there were a few mistakes here and there. Nothing serious, mind you, but it was still surprising."

"What sort of mistakes? Mislabeling?"

"In a way." Lord Unsworth was struggling to explain himself. "Never anything egregious, mind you, but occasionally an object or a tapestry would be attributed to the slightly wrong period or country. They were all easy, even understandable, mistakes to make, hard to notice unless you were an expert."

"I see."

"Why?" Lord Unsworth asked. "You don't think it could have something to do with Rosaline's murder, do you Quayle?"

"No, nothing like that," Mr. Quayle said. "It was just a stray thought, nothing more."

But no one was fooled for a moment. Everyone in the family was beginning to recognize that look in Quayle's eyes.

21

LA CONTESSA

"Why don't we start from the beginning?" Chief Inspector Tallier suggested gently. For the past few hours, he and Jarre had been nestled in the judge's office, questioning the Countess repeatedly, largely to no avail.

"Again?" she asked with an arched eyebrow. "We have been over this six times, Chief Inspector, and I'm not sure what you think you'll learn from a seventh. As I told you, I have no knowledge of my husband's movements after we parted last night, nor do I know who he was meeting or where. He is—*was*—a very secretive man, and he preferred to keep his private affairs private." Then she brightened as if an idea had suddenly occurred to her. "Perhaps you should have a word with Arthur and that Mr. Quayle. They as good as tried to blackmail me earlier. I'm sure I've mentioned that."

"You have," Tallier allowed. "But what of it?"

"Well, maybe they tried to blackmail Francesco first," she theorized. "And when he wouldn't pay, they murdered him." She tilted her head slightly. "Well, not Arthur, perhaps. He's not quite clever enough, but that Quayle is a tricky one."

"We have taken their statements," Chief Inspector Tallier

replied, hiding a frown. They, too, had not been entirely forthcoming in his estimation. "But regardless of whatever they were up to last night, at the moment, it is your story I'm most concerned with."

"My *story?*" Her eyes flashed dangerously. "Are you calling me a liar, Chief Inspector? May I remind you that my husband has just been murdered!"

Judge Jarre steepled his fingers and regarded the Countess with his characteristic stare, halfway between a beleaguered bureaucrat and stern disciplinarian.

"We are not accusing you of anything, Madame La Contessa, but the Chief Inspector and I cannot help but feel as though you have been holding back. And with your husband's unfortunate death, his connections at the Italian Embassy may no longer be willing to help. So, it is in your best interests and ours to—"

"His connections?" The Countess laughed outright—a loud, braying sound that erupted spontaneously from her chest. "Francesco had no connections at the embassy," she revealed. "He was a nobody, a butcher's boy from the south who bought himself a second-hand title and polished up his hand-me-down manners. No, Judge Jarre, I'm afraid that I'm the one with friends at the embassy."

The Judge did not so much as blink, however. "It does not matter," he said with a shrug. "Your friends, his friends, either way, they have abandoned you."

"I beg your pardon?"

"I spoke with the Italian Ambassador personally an hour or two ago," Jarre revealed. "And he is no longer interested in helping you, madame. Murder is a very different matter from theft, n'est-ce pas?"

"I thought you weren't accusing me of anything," the Countess replied. "But that sounded perilously close to an accusation."

"Not at all," Jarre said, lying through his teeth. "But you must realize how this looks. Wives have been known to kill their husbands, after all."

"And thieves," Chief Inspector Tallier added, "have been known to fall out."

"Thieves." The Countess' lips thinned. "I presume you're referring to Arthur's claims last night, but can you truly rely on the word of a would-be blackmailer who changes his story so easily? Hardly what I'd call proof."

"You were there in Paris," Tallier pointed out.

"So were a great many other people, including you, Chief Inspector," she replied coolly. "Now, there's a thought! Perhaps *you* are La Chimère, Chief Inspector, chasing yourself around the country."

"That would be clever of me," Tallier allowed, "but you're still deflecting, madame."

The Countess leaned back, examining him, as Jarre stilled beside him, forgotten but still watching. Tallier could practically see her gauging the angles, carefully weighing her options one by one.

Yesterday, when the Count and Countess had invited themselves over and sat in this very office, Tallier had realized that the Countess was the more formidable of the pair, and nothing since then had altered his opinion. She had held her own for several hours thus far against two highly experienced interrogators and had made only a handful of minor mistakes. And, more importantly, she had not cried, not once either this morning or last night, not even a single tear.

One might be forgiven for thinking her unmoved, perhaps suspiciously so, but every once in a while, Tallier caught her sharpening knives behind her eyes. No, as far as he could tell, the Countess wasn't unmoved, but neither was she heartbroken at the loss of her beloved husband. Instead, she was angry, seething with a terrifying, vengeful, all-consuming rage.

"Whatever else you may think of us," she said, "the Count and I are not now nor have we ever been La Chimère." She shook her head. "Now, you may believe me or not. That is your choice. But it is the truth."

Chief Inspector Tallier did not reply, did not so much as blink, but to his great surprise, he thought that he might believe her after all. And that changed everything.

"As for my husband, I loved him dearly, which again, you may choose to believe or not at your own discretion, but I was never blind to his faults." She smirked. "And he did not lack for enemies."

"Did you have anyone particular in mind?" Jarre asked.

"I do," the Countess replied baldly. "Jean-Paul Léger."

"Léger?" Jarre frowned. "Why?"

"Because my husband and Madame Léger have been having an affair for months now," she replied matter-of-factly. "Ann-Marie was one of many, you understand, and they were all much the same—usually slightly older, desperately unhappy, and, of course, fabulously wealthy."

"I see." Tallier hesitated. The Countess had been discussing her husband's affairs lightly as if they were merely discussing the weather, but this was still a delicate topic. "Earlier," he said, "I asked Raymond if the Count and his mother—"

"No." The Countess shook her head vehemently. "He tried his luck, of course, but Rosaline just laughed in his face. She found him amusing, I think, and predictable. Madame Léger proved more receptive, however."

"He told you this?" Tallier asked.

"Oh, yes, Chief Inspector." The Countess grinned in fond, malicious remembrance. "It amused Francisco to toy with his conquests, and it amused me to watch. It was one of our little games."

And what were their other games, Chief Inspector Tallier

wondered but did not ask. Instead, he tilted his head questioningly at Jarre and received a nod in confirmation.

"If you would excuse us for a moment?" Tallier asked.

The Countess shrugged and dismissed them with a wave of her hand as if the office was her abode and they were her guests.

Withdrawing to the other side of the room, near the window, Tallier and Jarre huddled together in hushed consultation.

"She's right," Jarre admitted. "As much as I would prefer to arrest her and be done with it, we have no hard evidence linking the Countess to either of the murders or even to those thefts of yours. She may be La Chimèrie, but—"

"Perhaps." Tallier was no longer sure.

"You believed her?" Jarre peered up at him questioningly. "I'm surprised."

"I still think that she and the Count are responsible for the stolen Bernini and for the recent thefts in Paris," Tallier said, "but it does not necessarily follow that they are La Chimèrie."

"You are suggesting that there is another thief out there?"

"Mais oui." Tallier nodded darkly. "And they've been stringing me along, whoever they are. Those anonymous letters," he explained when he caught Jarre's questioning glance. "Someone purposely led me right to the Count and Countess."

Jarre pursed his lips in understanding. "In either case, unless we find something to charge her with, we have no authority to hold her, diplomatic immunity or no."

"We have no choice but to release her," Tallier agreed. "But I'm more concerned about who searched the yacht while the Count and Countess were away and, perhaps more importantly, what they were looking for. The missing Bernini or something else?"

"And then there are Messrs. Druce and Quayle," Jarre added.

Tallier frowned. "I don't believe for a moment that they were attempting to blackmail the Countess, but they are involved somehow. That whole family is, but how deeply remains to be seen."

"So, what now?"

"Now," the Chief Inspector said, "I take a closer look at Monsieur et Madame Léger."

22

THE WIDOW'S LEGACY

It soon became apparent that Lady Rosaline's memorial would be a somber, strained affair, a far cry from the noisy, boisterous celebration she would have wanted. In life, the Widow of Treville-sur-Mer had been a creature of excess, filling every room with noise and laughter and directing her friends and favorites as though they were actors on a stage. But with her death, the curtain had fallen, and the music had come to a halt, leaving those left behind to drift aimlessly from room to room without script or direction, forced to improvise their lines and, indeed, their lives.

It was a pathetic, sorry sight—a reminder of how much influence Lady Rosaline had wielded over those who knew her and how swiftly that influence had faded into dust. This was not, Mr. Quayle realized, a celebration, but rather the final nail in her coffin, and he wondered if Raymond had planned it that way.

Wandering along the edges of the gathering, Mr. Quayle slipped quietly from room to room, listening, observing, and ever-so-delicately snooping, but to his surprise, he found the task unusually difficult. Quayle had always possessed a gift for unobtrusiveness, for fading into the woodwork. As a boy, he had often unintentionally startled friends and family alike with his mere presence, and afterwards, the army had made good use of his talents, as had the Ministry, at times.

But today, whichever room he entered, Quayle soon found himself the target of wary, suspicious eyes, and hushed whispers followed in his wake. He had become suddenly and inconveniently notorious, at least amongst Lady Rosaline's nearest and dearest.

There were no secrets in Treville-sur-Mer, and Mr. Quayle was known to be the man who had discovered Lady Rosaline's body and who, some whispered none-too-quietly, had likely murdered her at Lord Unsworth's behest.

Raymond's rather public apology in the foyer had helped dispel some of those rumors, but only some. Raymond was not held in exceptionally high regard, so his word did not count for nearly as much as it might have, and Lord Unsworth and his family did make for extremely convenient scapegoats.

Interestingly, Jean-Paul Léger seemed to be adapting the best to the new circumstances, but then, Mr. Quayle reflected, the artist had lived outside Lady Rosaline's influence once before, albeit without much success, and her death had freed him to remake himself at last.

He was still the same jealous, bitter man, of course, and judging by the still visible tremors in his hands and the vague squinting in his eyes, Léger had not resumed drinking. But in the absence of any other strong voices, people were turning to him, some reluctantly and others in relief—any port in a storm.

Raymond, meanwhile, was all but forgotten, his place as host and chief mourner supplanted, and was glaring at Léger with violence in his eyes while Vivi murmured soothingly in his ear. Although, from her expression, Vivi was nearly as angry as her husband, and they were not the only ones.

Madame Léger had formed a worried trinity in the corner with Márta and Herr Darvas, and the three of them were whispering furiously, far too low for Mr. Quayle to hear. And Sir Julius, who, with the death of Sir Weatherford, had lost two patrons in a matter of months, had escaped into the gardens and was drowning his sorrows in seemingly endless glasses of champagne. No one was more upset, however, than Carrodus. He and Léger had come to blows the other night, and the writer looked increasingly keen for another round.

Having finished his largely fruitless wanderings, Mr. Quayle returned to Lord Unsworth and the others near the window.

"Mr. Hollins not joining you?" Mr. Quayle asked as he slid next to Fanny.

"Quayle!" she cried, startled. "Where did you—" Fanny cleared her throat and darted a quick, sullen glance towards her aunt and uncle. "No," she replied, "he's not."

"It's for the best, dear," Lady Constance interjected in what she probably believed was a sympathetic tone. "He's just like all the other strays you used to drag home, feckless and highly unsuitable."

"I'm not sure this is the time, Connie," Lord Unsworth tried, but she was not to be dissuaded.

"I heard that Sir Alistair Dabney's son was around here somewhere," continued Lady Constance, ignoring her brother. "Now, he would be a far more—"

"Dabney?" Fanny was incredulous. "George Dabney? He's a buffoon, Aunt Constance. The only thing he cares about are his precious bloody automobiles! Always dashing about racing trains and crashing cars! No, thank you. Besides," she said. "I'm quite capable of making my own choices."

"Are you, indeed?" Lady Constance snorted. "Well, we all know how well that turned out last time."

"Steady on, Connie!" Lord Unsworth said.

"I hardly think you should be casting that particular stone, Aunt Constance."

"Fanny!"

"What did you say to me, young lady?" Lady Constance's eyes narrowed further still, her voice razor-sharp, a warning to all who heard it—here there be dragons.

Fanny boldly met her aunt's gaze, if only for a moment, before quickly turning away. "I apologize," she said. "That was uncalled for."

"Mmm." Lady Constance's stare did not waver, but slowly she nodded, if not in forgiveness, then in understanding.

"That was brave of you," Mr. Quayle said quietly.

"It was foolish," Fanny corrected. "And I'm not even sure Hollins is worth the trouble it will cause."

"Is that why you came separately?"

"No," Fanny shook her head. "He wasn't invited. And, while I'll never admit as much to Aunt Constance, I'm glad to be free of him for a few hours or so. He's been moping and brooding ever since Lady Rosaline was murdered. If he was here, I daresay he'd be crying into the canapés."

"Oh?" Mr. Quayle nodded over her shoulder to where a fresh-faced Hollins was speaking with Sir Julius.

"I don't understand." Fanny blinked. "What is he doing here?"

"What, indeed?" Perhaps Mr. Hollins warranted a closer look after all.

"If I might have your attention, s'il vous plaît!" Léger cried, his voice a horse bray, easily cutting through the uneasy murmurs and rumblings of the crowd. "S'il vous plaît!"

The old artist stumbled forward and then turned to squint at the slowly assembling crowd with a somber, beatific expression on his face, as if welcoming them to *his* house, *his* party. Behind him, a bay of great French doors opened onto the gardens, where the afternoon sun beat down, casting strange shadows amongst the fountains and hedges.

"Merci," he said. "Merci. This is a sad time, n'est-ce pas? The world has lost one of its guiding lights, a doyenne of the stage, a patron of the arts cruelly torn from us. But I think it is important that we, those of us who knew her best, remember her life and not her death. And in that spirit, I would like to say a few words about the Lady Rosaline Barrett Di Marchi I knew." Léger almost seemed to be holding back a sob. If this was a performance, Mr. Quayle thought, then Léger was an unexpected master. "Rosaline was a kind and wonderful woman. A forgiving woman..."

As he spoke, more than a few eyes, Quayle's among them, turned towards Raymond and Vivi, trying to gauge their response, but it was Carrodus who interrupted.

"How dare you!" the old playwright spat. "How dare you stand there and pretend that she forgave you? You're nothing but a fraud and a sham! Rosaline gave you everything. She made you who you are, and in return, you spat in her face. You defied her and defamed her! And I cannot just stand by and—"

"That's enough!" Raymond interjected with more force than anyone had thought possible. "That's enough, both of you!" He glared first at Léger, then at Carrodus, before turning on the crowd itself. "I won't have it! My mother is dead, do you understand? She was murdered, beaten to death, and her prize possession stolen. That is not something to be celebrated or memorialized. Or fought over. I invited you here because I felt I had no choice, but I will not allow one of my mother's sycophants, let alone one who betrayed her, sprout this nonsense."

"Thank you," Carrodus nodded.

"You're no better." Raymond sneered. "Hoarding mother's old letters and papers like they were the crown jewels and helping her rewrite history. No, I won't have it! I'm sick and tired of everyone treating her like some sort of paragon. My mother was no saint, and you all know it. And you two are definitely no apostles."

"Darling," Vivi said softly, placing a soothing hand on his arm. "Please."

"No," he snapped. "It's time people stopped lying and started telling the truth—"

"I couldn't agree more."

As one, the whole room turned to find Chief Inspector Tallier standing apologetically in the doorway. "Forgive me for intruding," he said into the sudden silence, "but I was hoping to have a word with Monsieur Léger."

"Me?" Léger frowned in Tallier's general direction. "Pourquoi?"

"I just have a few minor questions," the Chief Inspector explained. "Nothing more."

That was a lie. Mr. Quayle could feel his heart beating viciously in his chest. Tallier had found something or knew something.

"Of course." Raymond grinned, looking happier than Mr. Quayle had ever seen him. "Please, Chief Inspector, my house is at your disposal. By all means, ask Léger your questions."

* * *

IF THE GATHERING had been uneasy before, Léger's departure with the police in tow threatened to ignite a full-blown panic. Riot and mutiny were in the air, although it remained as aimless as before, with no one quite sure who or what they should be mutinying against.

Carrodus had immediately stormed out in a huff, wiping

back tears, and Raymond had followed suit not long after, fleeing upstairs to take refuge in the family's private wing and leaving poor Vivi to handle the fallout. That was twice now that Raymond had retreated rather than face the horde. But, Mr. Quayle noted, he had also twice proved himself willing to confront Léger on a more personal level. The first time had been in defense of Vivi, a perfectly understandable motive, but this afternoon's outburst was more complicated.

In the fight over Lady Rosaline's legacy, Raymond, it seemed, was determined to preserve his mother's reputation, or rather one particular aspect of it. Whereas Léger and Carrodus were attempting to legitimize, even canonize, Lady Rosaline and merely disagreed over who had the right to do so, Raymond was oddly insistent on reminding the world that his mother had been more sinner than saint. It was a curious position for Raymond to take, given his palpable distaste for his mother's ill-repute. Grief, perhaps, or something more?

Unfortunately, with Raymond sulking upstairs, Léger snatched away by the police, and Carrodus departed for parts unknown, Mr. Quayle was left with a different puzzle entirely. Mr. Hollins. And he was not the only one interested in the young man.

"What are you doing here?" Fanny demanded, ignoring Lady Constance's cries as she charged over to Hollins' side. Mr. Quayle followed a few steps behind. He had questions of his own but judged that the young man was far more likely to respond to Fanny's exhortations.

Mr. Hollins grimaced but still managed to greet her with a wane smile. The poor man looked exhausted, with dark circles under his eyes and a pinched, almost hunted, expression on his face. "I thought I should pay my respects," he explained. "I felt it was the least I could do."

"But why?" Fanny wanted to know. "I know you hoped she

might fund your play, but the woman practically ignored you. So, why do you care?"

Hollins hesitated. It was brief, lasting only for a moment, but it was enough to send Mr. Quayle's mind racing.

"Ahem." Sir Julius Markham-Smythe had been listening silently from Hollins' side, but now he took it upon himself to rescue the beleaguered young man. "Excuse me," he said, "but you must be the Hon. Frances Statham, yes?"

"Everyone calls me Fanny."

"Well, it is a pleasure to meet you, an absolute pleasure. Your young man here has told me so much about you."

"Has he?" Her eyes narrowed dangerously.

"All good, I promise," Sir Julius soothed with a grin. "And the gentleman hovering behind you must be the infamous Mr. Quayle."

"Infamous, am I?" Quayle asked, accepting Sir Julius' handshake with a slanted smile.

"Oh, unquestionably!" Sir Julius exclaimed. "I shall tell you in confidence, sir, that half the people in this room are convinced that you murdered Rosaline."

"And the other half?"

"They *hope* you did because it would mean they could stop suspecting each other."

"And you?" Mr. Quayle pressed, suddenly curious. "What do you think?"

"Oh, I have no opinion," Sir Julius replied, holding his hands up in mock surrender. "I just hope that if you are the killer, you'll leave me well enough alone."

Mr. Quayle smirked. It was impossible not to be at least partially charmed by Sir Julius' teasing.

"You know Mr. Hollins quite well, I take it?" he asked.

"Quite well," Sir Julius agreed with a laugh. "Joseph used to be my editor on the *London Chronicle* before he found God, by which I mean Lenin and Marx, and ran off to join the theater."

"That's not quite how it happened," Hollins protested, glaring at Sir Julius in embarrassment.

"Maybe not." Sir Julius shrugged. "But that's how Weatherford described it."

"Weatherford? You mean Lord Clarence Weatherford?"

"Of course!" Sir Julius nodded. "Clarence was my publisher, my employer, and my friend for over a decade. That's how I first met Joseph. Clarence was his guardian, you see."

"I didn't know that!" Fanny exclaimed and turned to Hollins with a frown. "You told me you lost your guardian recently, but I had no idea it was Lord Weatherford."

Hollins shrugged. "I don't like to talk about it," he said. "And besides, it hardly seemed important at the time."

Mr. Quayle could not help but note that there seemed to be quite a bit that Hollins didn't want to discuss.

"I understand that Lord Weatherford and Lady Rosaline were quite close," he said, eyeing Hollins carefully, and was rewarded with the barest of flinches. There was a story there, all right.

"Indeed," Sir Julius agreed. "As far as I could tell, Clarence was Rosaline's only true friend."

"I see." Mr. Quayle glanced at Hollins, who was now deep in conversation with Fanny. *Curiouser and curiouser*.

"Weatherford was the only one willing to risk publishing Rosaline's memoirs," Sir Julius said, pulling Quayle from his thoughts.

"Her memoirs?"

"Oh, yes." Sir Julius nodded. "Although I suspect the risk was not as great as Clarence suggested. Scandal sells, after all, and Rosaline's life was nothing if not scandalous. Of course, there were plenty of people, mostly her old partners in crime, who were not looking forward to publication, but I reckon Clarence and Rosaline were going to be making money hand over fist. And Carrodus, of course."

"Carrodus? Oh, I see! Raymond did say he was helping her 'rewrite history,' didn't he?"

"Just so." Sir Julius grinned. "From award-winning playwright to a glorified amanuensis, quite a step down for him, I daresay."

"Interesting," Mr. Quayle murmured. "I wonder what will happen to her memoirs now?"

"Depends on Raymond, I suppose," Sir Julius replied, surprising Quayle, who hadn't intended to speak his thoughts aloud. "Until today, I would have wagered good money that he would have burned them and scattered the ashes."

"But now?"

Sir Julius grinned slyly. "Whoever has Rosaline's memoirs would be able to control her legacy, and that would be one way to outmaneuver Léger once and for all." Mr. Quayle was surprised. That had been perilously close to his own views on the matter. "I know people think me a fool, Mr. Quayle," Sir Julius said. "And they're not altogether wrong. I drink too much. I talk too much, and I bet too much. But you're not the only one who knows how to use his eyes."

"I never thought I was," Mr. Quayle said, although he was not quite able to contain his surprise.

Sir Julius was right, though. Lady Rosaline's memoirs could prove a potent weapon and, finished or unfinished, they could not be ignored. But where were they? Carrodus, apparently, was in possession of many of her old papers and letters, including Lord Unsworth's, perhaps, so he was the most likely custodian, especially if, as Sir Julius and Raymond had implied, Carrodus had been doing more than helping Lady Rosaline compose her memoirs.

Mr. Quayle frowned. In the brewing war over her legacy,

Lady Rosaline's memoirs, her art collection, and even her funeral had all become battlegrounds for Raymond, Carrodus, and Léger to snap and fight over like vultures pecking at her remains. But was any of it enough to kill over?

That was the question.

23

LISTENING AT KEYHOLES

"Please, have a seat, monsieur," Chief Inspector Tallier said, gesturing with one hand towards the billiard's table still laden, two days later, with the remnants of that final, fateful card game. In his other hand, Tallier held a beaten, black leather briefcase, which he quickly deposited on the table, and then he stood and waited. Patience was a virtue that Tallier had painstakingly taught himself over the years, and he was rewarded when, after a brief hesitation, Léger shuffled over and sat down.

To Tallier's eyes, the older man was clearly on edge, his nerves afire with thwarted anger and simmering violence. There was no doubt in Tallier's mind that Léger had been on the brink of fighting both Carrodus and Raymond, and all told, the Chief Inspector wasn't sure who would have won.

"Would you care for a drink?" he asked but did not stop to wait for the answer, pouring Léger a stiff brandy from the cabinet along the far wall.

"Merci." Léger accepted the glass eager but did not drink. "But if I may ask, Inspector, what is all this about? I've told you everything I know."

"Perhaps," Tallier allowed with a disarming, if not quite believing, smile. "But first, would you care to tell me what that was all about back there? Raymond does not seem to care for you or Carrodus much, does he?"

"Raymond is a bitter, vicious little..." Léger bit back a curse, then started again. "He's never cared for his mother's friends or his mother's reputation," he said, visibly controlling his temper. "But now, all of a sudden, he wants to tell her story, to make sure we don't forget who Rosaline really was? How would he know?"

"Well, he is her son, after all," Tallier pointed out.

"Pfui!" Léger dismissed Tallier's comment with a contemptuous wave. "Raymond abandoned her years ago. They'd barely spoken for nearly a decade, until he turned up last Christmas."

"Abandoned." Tallier tapped his lip thoughtfully. "That's an interesting choice of word, considering..."

"Considering what?" Léger glared up at Tallier with bloodshed in his eyes.

"Forgive me for saying so, Monsieur Léger," the Chief Inspector replied with an unapologetic shrug, "but Raymond is not the only one to have abandoned Lady Rosaline, only to return years later. Nor is he the only one confused, shall we say, by your recent change in attitude towards his mother."

"I'm not sure what you mean." That was a lie, and they both knew it.

"When I arrived earlier," Tallier continued, "I believe I overheard you referring to Lady Rosaline as a 'guiding light' and a 'kind and wonderful woman', or words to that effect."

"And?" Léger crossed his arms defiantly. "What of it?" he demanded.

"Nothing in and of itself, but they are strange words to describe a woman you recently accused of 'sabotaging' your career, n'est-ce pas?"

"That was just a minor disagreement between friends," Léger protested, draining his glass in a single gulp.

Tallier eyed the empty glass for a second and then retrieved the entire decanter, placing it in front of Léger with a thud.

"A minor disagreement, you say?"

"That's right." Léger did not bother to thank the Chief Inspector this time and simply poured himself another glass, downed it, and then poured himself a third.

"In that case, I'm sure you won't mind having a look at these." From his briefcase, the Chief Inspector retrieved a rather thick, overstuffed folder and placed three newspaper clippings down on the table one by one.

"I'm afraid, Chief Inspector," Léger said, patting his pockets, "that I appear to have misplaced my glasses."

"Not to worry," Tallier replied. "Allow me to explain. They are all interviews from your last showing in Paris. In this one," he said, tapping the first on the left, "you refer to Lady Rosaline as 'a parasite who has spent her life leaching from her betters' and here—" he indicated the second, "you call her 'a petticoat tyrant whose reign of terror must be brought to a swift and long-overdue end' and you end this last one with: 'Viva la Revolución!' and suggest she be 'introduced to Madame Guillotine.' If this is a minor disagreement, monsieur, I would not like to see what you consider a deadly feud."

"Perhaps my words were a little...overzealous, Chief Inspector," Léger admitted. "But that is my nature. I am an artist, n'est ce pas? And as an artist, I am given to bouts of violent, creative passion. That is not a crime."

"Very well, then let us speak of your passion." Chief Inspector Tallier pulled back a chair with a screech and calmly sat down. "It has gotten you into some trouble over the years, has it not? Your file here is impressively thick and details a long and storied history of barroom brawls, petty feuds, illegal duels, one or two minor stabbings, and—" Tallier flipped briskly through the file. "—Ah, here we are," he said, tapping the appropriate report with a triumphant finger. "It says you once bit a man's ear off in a fit of...creative passion. Apparently, the man looked at your wife the wrong way."

Léger scowled. The decanter next to him was more than half empty now, but still he poured himself another glass. "That was all a long time ago," he protested dismissing his spotted history with a shaky wave of his hand. "I'm a changed man."

"Not all that long ago," Tallier pointed out. "You may not have stabbed or bitten anyone lately, but the most recent incident was only three months ago, was it not? So, you see my dilemma. You have a temper, Monsieur Léger, and while you have been suspiciously eager to recast your relationship with Lady Rosaline as one of love and friendship, you, in fact, blamed her for the failure of your career. And as for Count Scarlioni—"

"Yes?"

"Perhaps," Tallier delicately suggested, "the Count also looked at your wife the wrong way, and you had another bout of...creative passion."

"How dare you!" Jean-Paul Léger slammed his hands on the table hard enough to rattle the glasses and drew angrily to his feet. "I will not be insulted like this! That man never touched my wife, and if you say he did—"

"Sit down," Chief Inspector Tallier interrupted coldly. "We're not finished."

Léger reeled back as if slapped and momentarily looked as if he would strike Tallier, but something in the Chief Inspector's eyes stopped him. And, after a moment, Léger obeyed.

"Excellent." Chief Inspector Tallier smiled. "Shall we continue?"

* * *

Mr. Quayle was sitting alone, far away from the hustle and noise of the other guests and the doubting glares that accompanied his newfound notoriety. Having made his excuses and effected his escape, the secretary-cum-sleuth had found a small wooden bench nestled in the shadow of the house. Behind him loomed Lady Rosaline's villa in all its glory, an architectural hodgepodge of styles and excess, painted orange and purple in the late afternoon sun. But beneath the all ephemera, the bones and foundations of the old convent remained visible, but only if one knew where to look.

Mr. Quayle was not looking, however. Instead, his head was bent, and his eyes were fixed firmly on his lap where he was turning his spectacles over and over in his hand, faster and faster in time with his thoughts. Snatches of conversation echoed through his mind while pieces of the puzzle wandered boldly into view before scurrying away the moment he took note.

This case was tied in knots and untangling them was only half the challenge. Some were related to each other or followed from each other, but did any of them lead where he wanted to go? There had been two murders already, perhaps even three. And that was a thought worth pondering—*Weatherford*. His death had set all this in motion, at least so far as Quayle was concerned. After all, it was only in his absence that Unsworth and, consequently, Quayle himself had become involved.

"There you are!" Fanny called, emerging from the bushes with a triumphant smile. "I was looking for you."

It was a measure of how distracted he had become that Quayle hadn't heard her approach and a measure of how on edge he was that the normally self-possessed man visibly started.

"Are you alright?" Fanny asked.

"Perfectly alright, thank you." Mr. Quayle started to rise, but Fanny waved him back down. "You surprised me, that's all," he said. "I thought you and Mr. Hollins—"

"Mr. Hollins," Fanny interrupted, "has left for the evening, although fled might be more accurate. Aunt Constance kept glaring at him from across the room."

"I see."

"Actually, it was Hollins I wanted to talk to you about."

"Yes?"

Fanny didn't answer right away, however. Instead, sitting down beside him, she stared into the distance, collecting her thoughts.

"He's been acting oddly," she said finally. "Ever since Lady Rosaline was murdered, it's as if he's a changed man, and I'm beginning to have doubts."

"Doubts?" Mr. Quayle probed lightly, and after a moment's hesitation, Fanny turned to meet his eyes.

"Suspicions," she clarified.

Mr. Quayle tilted his head slightly and considered the young woman before him. She was outwardly calm, but it was a jagged, frantic sort of calm that spoke volumes of her inner torment. "What sort of suspicions?" he asked. "Are you suggesting that he might have killed Lady Rosaline? Or Scarlioni?"

Fanny laughed mirthlessly. "Truthfully, Quayle, I'm not sure what I'm suggesting. I used to be quite confident in my judgment. Aunt Constance and all the rest could sneer at my friends all they wanted, but I knew in my heart that they were wrong and I was right. These days, though, I'm finding it difficult to trust my instincts."

Mr. Quayle thought about saying something, about offering a few trite words of comfort, but that wasn't what

Fanny needed. She wanted answers, and he wasn't sure he could give them—not yet.

"So," Fanny said, gazing at Quayle with far too much faith and trust. "I was hoping you might have an opinion."

"That's very flattering of you," Mr. Quayle replied with a modest shrug. "But, I'm hardly an infallible judge of character myself, and, strictly speaking, it is not my place to have opinions about your...gentlemen friends."

"But that's what you do, isn't it?" Fanny waved her hand vaguely. "Solve mysteries, listen at keyholes…"

"I'll have you know that I have never listened through a keyhole in my life!" Quayle protested in mock indignation, and was pleased to see a faint smile whisper across her face.

"Well, wherever you listen from," she said, "you no doubt have your fingers in all manner of pies by now."

"I'm not sure if that is an insult or a compliment."

"Whichever you please." Fanny shrugged. "So long as you don't try to tell me you haven't been spying on Mr. Hollins."

"Spying is such an unfortunate word. I may have made a few perfectly reasonable inquiries, but I would hardly call that spying."

"Wouldn't you?"

"Mmm." Mr. Quayle acknowledged her point with a nod. "But that being said, you would still be better placed to account for his recent behavior than I, although he does seem to know more than he's saying, perhaps a great deal more, considering Lord Weatherford turns out to have been his guardian."

"Yes, that was a shock," Fanny agreed. "And raises all sorts of questions in my mind. Starting with why he needed me to wheedle him an invitation in the first place. If Hollins was so desperate to meet Lady Rosaline and ingratiate himself into her circle, why didn't he just mention his guardian's name? Surely, she would have welcomed him with open arms?"

"That's an excellent question," Mr. Quayle said. "Perhaps you should ask him."

"I did." Fanny sighed, looking every inch her eighteen years. "But he wouldn't answer. Instead, he just...ran away." She shook her head angrily. "I suppose that was for the best. Anything he said would have been a lie anyway."

Mr. Quayle hesitated for a moment, then took the plunge. "Fanny, I know you've been lied to," he said. "I know you were hurt deeply, and I'm not suggesting for a moment that you forgive or forget, but it does not necessarily follow that everything is a lie. You have a fine, sharp mind, Fanny. You just have to remember how to trust yourself again. And always keep your eyes and ears open."

"I have been," Fanny replied. "And I've watched you with Sir Julius and others—asking questions, poking around, investigating. I know everyone around here seems to think you and Uncle Edward had something to do with Lady Rosaline's death, but the police appear to have moved on, just as you said they would. And now that you've rescued Arthur from last night's foolishness, as far as I can see, you have no reason to involve yourself."

"Do you have a point?"

"I have a question," Fanny corrected.

"Yes?" Mr. Quayle turned to give her his full attention. "What is it?"

"Just how close were Uncle Edward and Lady Rosaline back in the day?"

"Again, I'd say that would be a question for Lord Unsworth, not me."

"Because you don't know?" Fanny pressed. "Or because it's not your place to say?"

"Both." Even as he answered, however, Quayle was straining to listen. There were voices on the air, raised voices coming from inside the house.

"You're deflecting," Fanny said. "You know I could never ask Uncle Edward. He would be so...awkward, and I—"

"Shhh." Mr. Quayle put a finger to his lips to silence her and then, with the same finger, indicated the window to their right. Fanny frowned, offended, but then she, too, heard the voices.

Rising slowly, Mr. Quayle crept along the wall, gesturing for Fanny to follow. The two of them must have made for a peculiar sight, stepping through the flowers and grass and crouching beneath a window.

"So, you don't listen at keyholes, but windows are fine," Fanny murmured but subsided at Quayle's scowl. He was concentrating with all his might, trying to hear and, more importantly, understand what was being said.

There were two of them inside, a man and a woman, and they were both speaking in French, a language in which Quayle was largely fluent, but inconveniently rusty.

"It's been over an hour since the police failed to arrest you," the woman said, and beside Quayle, Fanny gaped in shock.

"That's Anne-Marie!" she said.

"I know," he mouthed back, holding back a sigh. He never would have imagined that Arthur would prove the stealthier of the cousins.

"Where have you been?" Madame Léger asked.

"Around." Her husband was slurring and clearly drunk. "Here and there. You should be careful, though, my dear. Y-y-you almost sounded disappointed."

"Not at all, darling," Madame Léger replied unconvincingly. "But I am grateful for the Chief Inspector's intervention. It spared us your speech."

"Damnit, Anne! Why must you be so..."

"Yes?" Madame Léger tone was sharp as a dagger. "Tell me, Jean-Paul, what am I?"

There was silence, and then Léger took a deep breath, audible even from afar. "You haven't been particularly helpful lately," he said. "In fact, ever since Rosaline died, you've been incredibly...unsupportive."

Madame Léger's answering laugh required no translation. "Unhelpful?" she repeated. "Unsupportive? Me? When have I ever not supported you, Jean-Paul? Hmm? When? You have no idea what I have done, what I have sacrificed for you. I have mended your shirts, sewn your buttons, entertained your guests, and looked the other way time and time again as you chased after one skirt or another. And what have you done for me in return, apart from complain and drink your troubles away?"

"How dare you! I-I—"

"So," she continued, ignoring his sputtering protests, "you will forgive me, Jean-Paul, if I do not wish to hear you sing that woman's praises as if you were the favored son. It's laughable and clearly desperate. Little wonder no one else wanted to hear it either."

"That's not fair," Léger said. "I might be...ignoring parts of our history, but we were close to Rosaline once, and might have been so again, if she hadn't been murdered. All I've done is focus on the good times, that's all. And I haven't done too badly out of it, either, have I?"

"You mean those paintings you've been selling these past few days?" Madame Léger scoffed. "How many is it now? Four? Five?"

"Six." Léger sounded positively smug to Quayle's ears. "I sold another one here at the memorial."

"Congratulations! That's more than you've sold all year. Of course, they're hardly your finest work, but the pickings are slim these days."

"People have been quite complimentary," Léger countered.

"Have they now?"

"Yes. So, clearly, those fools in Paris had no idea what they were talking about!"

"Even so," Madame Léger said, "you needed Rosaline to sell them for you. Still holding your hand from beyond the grave."

There was an aborted cry, followed by the sound of glass shattering. Fanny started to rise, but Mr. Quayle shook his head firmly. That had been a cry of rage, not pain, and there were no further sounds of a struggle.

"Temper, temper," Madame Léger said at length, sounding more amused than anything. "Now look what you've done! Raymond was unhappy with you before, but this..." She tutted mockingly.

"Why should I care what Raymond thinks? He has no right! No right!"

"And you do?" she pressed. "Did you truly believe Rosaline didn't know you were spitting poison behind her back? Half your little acolytes were scurrying back to her every week to report everything you'd said—, every little insult and slur. Face it, Jean-Paul, you've always needed Rosaline more than she ever needed you. Not even her death could change that."

"I am the greatest artist of my generation!" Léger shouted loud enough to send nearby birds scattering in the garden.

"Just because Rosaline called you that doesn't make it so, darling. You might have been the anointed one, but she had other artists in her collection, remember?"

Léger's voice fell. "Of course, I remember, but—"

"Never mind!" Her tone brokered no argument. "Just tell me what the police wanted with you."

"Apparently, Chief Inspector Tallier finds my praise for Rosaline as suspicious as you do."

"Does he?" Madame Léger chuckled. "How insightful of him."

"He also suggested that I might have murdered Count Scarlioni because he was having an affair with you."

Silence filled the room. Mr. Quayle shuffled closer to the window, straining to listen, but there was nothing to hear.

"And what did you say to that?" Madame Léger asked at length.

"I denied it, of course," Léger replied. "Said the very idea of you and Scarlioni was insulting."

"So you lied."

Fanny gasped. She was fluent enough in French to have understood that much, at least. Unfortunately, her response had been loud enough to bring both Légers to the window. Quayle and Fanny pressed themselves against the stone wall, struggling not to breathe or utter a single sound, but after an interminably long moment, they were safe. First, Léger and then his wife retreated into the room, their suspicions, if they had any, assuaged.

"Tell me," Madame Léger continued. "If he knows about the affair and your troubles with Rosaline, why didn't Tallier arrest you?"

"I have an alibi for her death, remember? I was nowhere near Rosaline when she was killed."

"Weren't you?"

"What's that supposed to mean?" Léger demanded.

"Well," his wife said in a false, bright voice, "I was just wondering. After you made a fool of yourself with Vivi that night, where exactly did you go?"

"Where did *you*?" Léger snapped in response. "When I returned to the garden, you were nowhere to be seen. So, where were you, Anne?" Madame Léger did not answer. "That's what I thought. Try not to ask questions you wouldn't want to answer yourself."

"I'll remember that."

Léger sighed. "Anne?" he asked softly, so softly, in fact, that Quayle barely heard him. "W-why him? Why Scarlioni?"

"Why not?"

"He was a liar, a thief, and a charlatan! Surely, you could—"

"Oh, Jean-Paul!" There was a bitter smile in Madame Léger's voice. "If I had any trouble with liars or thieves, I never would have married you in the first place." And with that, there came the sound footsteps, or rather heels, clacking on the stone floor, followed by a door slamming irrevocably shut.

Slowly, carefully, Mr. Quayle and Fanny inched their way back the way they'd come, only straightening when they were far enough out of sight.

"So," Fanny said. "The Count was having an affair with Anne-Marie." Her eyes were wide, and she was clearly having difficulties believing or even grasping the concept.

"Apparently." Although, as far as Mr. Quayle was concerned, that was not necessarily the most crucial part of the conversation. Before he could say as much, however, they both turned, distracted by the stench and sight of smoke wafting on the breeze. It was Carrodus' cottage, nestled a little way down the hill but still firmly on the villa's grounds.

And it was burning!

24

THE BURNING

Mr. Quayle careened down through the garden towards Carrodus' cottage at breakneck speed, trampling flower beds, swerving around hedges, and sometimes stumbling to catch his footing. The hill was quite steep in places, and the garden paths were not designed for the swiftest routes. In one corner of his mind, Quayle was dimly aware of Fanny running a few steps behind, almost matching his pace despite her less-than-practical shoes. While in another corner, a single thought was thrumming like a bell, urgent and all-consuming. Carrodus' cottage held the repository of Lady Rosaline's letters, her correspondence, and perhaps even the draft of her memoirs. Her life's story and most intimate thoughts were all there, spilled onto ink and paper—and paper *burned*.

Quayle had little time for such considerations, however. Charging forward with his head bent and vision narrowed, he was more a creature of muscle memory and instinct than thought. His senses were sharp and his breathing heavy as he leapt over a small wooden fence and came to rest just outside the cottage.

The inferno lay before him, spewing great plumes of thick, black smoke and flame, which wafted to and fro according to the whims of the evening breeze, carrying the pungent stench of fire and ash. Embers danced like fireflies in the air, and the terrible heat of the flames lashed against Quayle's face, nearly driving him back a step. It had been some years since he had confronted such destruction and Quayle had never thought to do so again.

As he circled cautiously around the outskirts of the fire, Quayle came at last to the back of the house, where a window opened onto the crackling, burning remains of a study or library. And, peering closer through the dust, ash, and flame, he caught glimpses of the ruin within—bookshelves overturned, boxes aflame, beams crashing down from the ceiling, and a man lying prone and motionless beside the fireplace. It was Carrodus.

If there had been time to think, Mr. Quayle might, perhaps, have hesitated, but instead, he leapt into action. Holding a pocket handkerchief to his nose and mouth and knowing full well that it would not be enough, he charged into the inferno.

Flames and smoke immediately pressed against him from all sides, choking and burning, but still, he stumbled doggedly onwards, coughing and sputtering all the while. It was not a particularly large room, but that made little difference, as Quayle could barely see more than an inch or so in front of him, and the terrain itself was treacherous.

Every step was a thousand miles, beset by dangers and certain death. It was like being back in the trenches again, forced into the fires of no man's land. Three times during the War, Quayle had taken part in a massive, all-out charge. Three times he had clambered over the top and hurtled himself through that blighted landscape of barbed wire, mud, and death, assaulting the German lines and the German shells armed only with an officer's revolver. This time, though, Quayle had no one else to blame. He had sent himself into the slaughter.

Mr. Quayle stumbled once, twice, careening through the charred, overturned remains of a table and chairs before regaining his footing. A few more steps and he almost overshot, nearly tripping over Carrodus' legs. The man did not so much as twitch or groan, remaining as still and motionless as before.

A sudden clattering, crashing noise erupted from above him, and Quayle flinched, certain that the ceiling was about to collapse, that he and Carrodus were both as good as dead.

But there was no crash, no flaming, fatal wooden beams. Instead, a figure emerged out of the haze and smoke, silhouetted against the blaze, and it took Quayle half a second to recognize Tallier.

There was no time or air to waste on words. The two men each took one of Carrodus' prone arms, and together they half carried, half dragged him back the way they had come. The return journey felt even longer and more fraught, but there were two of them this time, and eventually they emerged from the maelstrom into the fresh evening air.

Able to breathe again at last, Quayle and Tallier gently lowered Carrodus to the ground and then collapsed on either side of him. Both men were coughing and breathing heavily, and Mr. Quayle slowly became aware of Fanny hovering over his shoulder and shouting urgently in his ear.

It took a considerable act of will to force Fanny's words to make sense. For a moment, it had been as if she were speaking gibberish, as if she and the world itself were far, far away, but with a crashing jolt, Mr. Quayle came barreling back to himself. His heart was thundering in his chest, and his lungs felt heavy and clogged.

"Can you hear me, Quayle?" Fanny asked. "Are you hurt?"

Mr. Quayle blinked blearily up at her. "Hurt?" he repeated. "No, I don't think so."

"Are you sure?" Her face was furrowed in alarm. "You have blood on your hands."

Quayle glanced down, and sure enough, his hands were covered in blood. A quick inventory, however, revealed no injuries that he could see, but then he turned his attention to Carrodus. The old playwright was alive. That was the first thing Quayle noticed. For once, he hadn't been too late. But the back of Carrodus' head was bloody.

This was no accident, Mr. Quayle realized, confirming a suspicion that he'd barely had time to form. Carrodus had been bashed over the head and left to burn. Someone had tried to murder him!

Mr. Quayle glanced at Tallier and the Chief Inspector nodded slowly.

"Tonight," Tallier said breathlessly. "Once this is all taken care of, I think it's time you and I had a proper conversation, don't you, Monsieur Quayle?"

Mr. Quayle agreed wholeheartedly, but before he could say as much, he was interrupted by a sudden fit of coughing.

Tonight then.

LATER THAT EVENING, a little after six o'clock, Chief Inspector Tallier presented himself as agreed at the Unsworth's rented villa and was ushered into the study where Mr. Quayle and His Lordship were waiting for him. Lord Unsworth had remained largely uninvolved in Quayle's investigation thus far, preferring to stay at a distance and leave such matters in his secretary's capable hands. Mr. Quayle had prevailed upon him, however, so now he was involving himself. There was no choice.

If Tallier was surprised by Lord Unsworth's presence, he made no outward sign. Still smelling of smoke and ash, the Frenchman exhaustedly fumbled his way through the usual greetings and pleasantries.

"How is Carrodus?" Mr. Quayle asked, biting back a cough as the three men sat. He, too, had not fully recovered from his brush with fire and death, although, unlike the Chief Inspector, Quayle had managed to arrange both a change of clothes and a bath.

"Alive," Tallier replied. "But his doctors cannot say for how long. If he survives the night, there is a good chance, but if he does not..." Tallier shrugged helplessly.

"Another murder," Lord Unsworth said with a sigh, revealing a deep, bitterly amused well of frustration. "That would make three...*again*."

"Three that we know of, sir," Mr. Quayle said. "There could be others."

"*Others?*" His Lordship was distinctly displeased. "Please understand, Quayle, that I am not blaming you, but the carnage is starting to become a tad excessive."

"I don't disagree."

Chief Inspector Tallier's gaze had narrowed sharply, almost suspiciously, at the suggestion of a fourth potential murder, but, displaying the sly patience which made him so dangerous in Quayle's opinion, the Chief Inspector chose not to pry for now. It was a forbearance that Quayle did not expect to last.

"Monsieur Carrodus was struck on the back of the head," he reported. "Unlike the others, however, this time, our murderer did not quite finish the job. Rushed, perhaps, or else he had other things on his mind."

"The fire?"

"Just so," Tallier nodded. "Curiously, Carrodus himself was

in the midst of burning some of Lady Rosaline's papers when he was attacked."

"Was he indeed?" Lord Unsworth snorted. "Rosaline told me she'd given him the papers for safekeeping."

"Perhaps this was safekeeping," Mr. Quayle suggested. "I take it, however, that Carrodus' activities did not cause the fire."

"No," Tallier said. "Someone deliberately set the house ablaze."

"I see." Mr. Quayle was not surprised. "Well, hopefully, Carrodus will be able to shed some light on the situation, should he come round."

"Speaking of shedding light on the situation, monsieur," Tallier replied, placing a singed, blackened envelope on the table, "would you have a look at this, s'il te plaît? You as well, Lord Unsworth, if you would be so kind?"

"What is it?" Lord Unsworth asked, although, like Quayle, he must have had his suspicions.

"As I said," Tallier replied, his eyes flickering from one to the other. "Carrodus had in his possession the preponderance of Lady Rosaline's papers, and while most of them were burnt beyond all recognition, some, such as this one, survived largely intact." The Chief Inspector leaned forward. "It purports to be a letter from one of her admirers dated some thirty years ago—a letter from *you,* Lord Unsworth."

"Ah." His Lordship accepted the revelation calmly. "I'm not sure what you would have me say, Chief Inspector," he said.

"The truth."

"Is that all?" Lord Unsworth sounded oddly wistful for a moment. "May I?" He reached out to take the letter, but Tallier held up a hand to stop him.

"I'm afraid not, Lord Unsworth," he said, sounding genuinely apologetic. "It is evidence, n'est-ce pas?"

"Evidence?" His Lordship straightened and gathered his wounded dignity and outrage around him like a cloak. "So, you believe I killed her, after all? Over what, this letter? Don't be ridiculous!"

"Not necessarily." Tallier remained placid in the face of Lord Unsworth's simmering wrath. "I will admit, though, that I have been puzzled over the nature and depth of your family's involvement in her murder. There was your nephew and his closeness to the Count and Countess, your niece and her relationship with the Légers, and, of course, Monsieur Quayle here, who seemed to be tripping over another body every time I turned my back, non?"

"I only tripped over one body!" Mr. Quayle protested, quite reasonably in his opinion, but Tallier was unimpressed by the technicality.

"But despite all that," he continued, "I have always believed that your conversation with Lady Rosaline, Lord Unsworth, was the most significant. And now that I have this letter, much is explained."

"Have you read it?" Lord Unsworth asked.

"Oui." Chief Inspector Tallier's reply was even and unyielding. "It was my duty."

"And what you read," His Lordship asked, "was it worth killing over?"

Tallier shook his head. "I would not have thought so," he said. "Inconvenient, oui, considering the scrutiny of a murder investigation, and embarrassing, no doubt, for a man of your position and circumstance, but no, Lord Unsworth, there was nothing in there I would have thought worthy of murder."

"And yet?"

Chief Inspector Tallier smirked slightly. "Your Monsieur Quayle may have the luxury of acting solely upon what he believes or thinks, but unfortunately, I do not. Judge Jarre has already questioned my leniency regarding you, and is of the opinion that I should have interrogated you sooner and more vigorously. The very fact that we are having this conversation in your charming villa and not at the offices of the Sûreté in Treville-sur-Mer is a gesture of my esteem and respect. But I will have answers, Lord Unsworth, and I will have the truth."

His Lordship glanced at Mr. Quayle, but his loyal, efficient secretary made no comment. It was Lord Unsworth's decision.

"Very well," His Lordship said at last. "Very well."

Lord Unsworth was a brave man in his own fashion, and once the decision was made, he did not flinch or turn away. In a clear, dry voice, as if he was lecturing on ancient family history, detailing events that had taken place centuries rather than days ago, he explained everything—Lady Rosaline's request, his refusal, and his guilt. And he explained, too, Lady Constance's suspicions.

"My sister believes that Rosaline only mentioned the letter in a subtle attempt to blackmail me, while Quayle has cannily refused to say what he thinks. But surely Rosaline did not need the money?"

"Perhaps," Chief Inspector Tallier replied when Lord Unsworth had finished. "Perhaps not. The nature of Lady Rosaline's finances is something else I have been puzzling over, but in either case, you should have told me all this sooner."

"It was not your business," Lord Unsworth said plainly. "And as far as I'm concerned, it still isn't, but Mr. Quayle believes we can trust you, and I bow to his judgment in these matters."

"Eh bien, thank goodness for Monsieur Quayle!" Tallier bestowed upon him a wry, thankful smile, which Quayle returned briefly. "But now, monsieur," the Chief Inspector said, "you spoke earlier of a fourth murder, did you not?"

"A possible murder, Chief Inspector," Mr. Quayle replied.

"But yes, it is difficult to ignore that there was another, earlier death in Lady Rosaline's circle, one which led directly in many ways to our current predicament."

"Weatherford," Chief Inspector Tallier deduced, having followed Quayle's chain of logic with ease.

"Precisely."

"But he died of natural causes."

"Did he?" Mr. Quayle was not so sure. "I would not like to tell you your business, Chief Inspector, but I would suggest looking into the circumstances of his death."

"Would you?" The two men stared at each other for a long moment until, at last, a tired grin pulled at the edges of Tallier's mouth. "As it happens," he revealed, "I already have."

Mr. Quayle tried not to let his surprise show. "You have?"

"Oui." The Chief Inspector's grin widened as he reached into his briefcase. "I have his file here. Of course, you realize, monsieur," he said, "that allowing you to read this would be most unorthodox."

"I appreciate that," Mr. Quayle replied, "but, if I may, Chief Inspector, your entire investigation has been nothing if not unorthodox. After all, officially, you are still on les vacances, are you not? And as for your gestures of esteem and respect," Mr. Quayle smirked, "let us not pretend. You have long suspected that Lord Unsworth was holding something back, but you calculated, quite rightly, that you would catch more flies with honey. This is hardly the time to start being orthodox, Chief Inspector, n'est-ce pas?"

"Touché, mon ami." Tallier acknowledged Quayle's point with a wry tilt of the head, completely unembarrassed to have his machinations exposed. "Touché."

"In the meantime," Mr. Quayle suggested as he reached for the file. "I suggest you ask for His Lordship's opinion on Lady Rosaline's collection."

"Her collection? Why?"

Mr. Quayle did not answer, however, and was quickly engrossed, reading through the thin, somewhat sparse material in quiet, contemplative silence. He was dimly aware, as he thumbed through the notes, of His Lordship lighting his pipe beside him and offering Tallier his theories and opinions regarding the medieval artifacts in Lady Rosaline's collection. Lord Unsworth did not go so far as to call them frauds or fakes, but he did not have to. Tallier's mind was as swift as Quayle's—swifter in some respects.

At last, having digested the contents of the police and doctor's reports, Quayle threw the file and his spectacles onto the table and rubbed his eyes tiredly.

"Well," he said, "that certainly seems quite straightforward, although the telegram in Weatherford's pocket is interesting."

"At the very least, it corroborates Your Lordship's story," Tallier agreed, nodding to Lord Unsworth, "but not much more. We still have no idea what was worrying Lady Rosaline so deeply." He sighed. "As you saw, the doctor found no evidence of foul play, but he was not looking for any. Lord Weatherford had a fragile heart and a bad habit of ignoring medical advice. Nothing suspicious or untoward there..."

"But surely," Lord Unsworth interjected, "there are all manner of poisons that could mimic a heart attack? I am no expert, but—"

"Indeed," Tallier agreed. "Foxglove, for one. But I'm afraid, Lord Unsworth, the trouble, in this case, is not method or motive but opportunity. If, as you suggest, Lord Weatherford was poisoned, then there must, therefore, be a poisoner, n'est-ce pas? And, unfortunately, everyone connected to Lady Rosaline's murder has an alibi for Lord Weatherford's death."

"Everyone?" Mr. Quayle repeated darkly.

"Mais oui," Chief Inspector Tallier said unhappily. "Every

single one. Apart from Vivi, who was on board the northbound Blue Train to Paris, and Monsieur Hollins, who was in England, the rest were all here on the Riviera. The Count and Countess Scarlioni were both in Monte Carlo, as was Sir Julius. Jean-Paul Léger and his wife were hosting their regular soiree. Carrodus, Herr Darvas, and his daughter, Márta were all seen in and about Treville-sur-Mer, and Monsieur Dabney was stopped for joyriding along the coast."

"And Raymond?" Mr. Quayle asked.

"Monsieur Raymond drove his wife to the train station the previous evening and then stopped at a café for a bite to eat, avoiding his mother, no doubt. But there is no way he, or any of them, for that matter, could have been on the Riviera on Wednesday evening and somehow aboard the Blue Train from Paris the following afternoon. The only one—the only one—who could have possibly done it is Vivi, and only if she immediately switched trains. But we know, and I have checked, that she did not. C'est impossible!"

"So it would appear." Mr. Quayle frowned as a thought struck him. "So it would appear, Chief Inspector. But I wonder..."

PART IV

THE FINAL PIECES OF THE PUZZLE

25

THE POINT OF NO RETURN

Arthur glared down at the map in increasing frustration. The bloody thing was in French! Of course, it was! After all, they were in France, weren't they? What other language would it be in? Arthur cursed himself for his stupidity and, upon reflection, also lobbed a few silent curses at his Cambridge tutors for their criminal negligence. He could, courtesy of a classical education, conjugate Latin and Greek until his brains fell out, but his grasp of modern French was non-existent.

Although, Arthur supposed, he didn't really *need* to read French in order to navigate. All that mattered was whether or not he could pinpoint their location on the map—to the nearest village or two—and find their way to Paris. As long as he could sound out the words and match the French on the road signs to the French on the map, they should be fine. And, indeed, they might have been if not for George Dabney and his infernal, bloody driving.

Arthur had no idea how anyone was supposed to get their bearings when the countryside and all its accompanying signposts and markers were little more than a nauseating blur glimpsed, if they were glimpsed at all, for only a brief second in the rearview mirror. Arthur had always thought of himself as something of an adventurer, and he had been quite excited when Mr. Quayle suggested that he could help test out a little theory for him, and even moreso when they had enlisted Dabney's aide. *A proper adventure! A chance to prove himself and atone for his earlier mistakes!*

But now, after several hours, more than a few near-death experiences, and half a dozen run-ins with various locals, Arthur could say for true and certain that he was not enjoying himself in any way, shape, or form. In fact, he felt rather sick.

Dabney, by contrast, was clearly having the time of his life! Mr. Quayle had given him an excuse to prove his daredevil driving bona fides, and Dabney was taking full advantage. His second attempt to race the Blue Train to Paris would not end like the first. Sir Julius and Raymond may have won the original bet, but Dabney would have the final laugh, if it was the last thing he did. No one would stop him now, and this time, he was helping to catch a killer! What a riot!

Suddenly, Arthur was forced, and not for the first time, to cling desperately onto the sideboard for dear life, as Dabney careened at breakneck speed down yet another bend in the road. An unfortunate farmer with his cart in tow was forced to dash precipitously out of the way and shouted a litany of invectives after them, which Arthur did not need to speak French to understand.

Having escaped near certain death and made an enemy for life, Dabney threw back his head and laughed—a joyous, maddened sound—and Arthur could only stare. Dabney had always been a trifle mad, even when they were at school, but he seemed to have gotten worse.

Gagging slightly and trying not to tremble, poor Arthur turned his attention back to the map. It wouldn't help any, of course, but at least it would keep his eyes off the road and his impending death. If they survived this, Arthur thought to himself, his mother was going to kill him.

And then she was going to kill Mr. Quayle.

* * *

"Are you quite sure about this?" His Lordship asked, although it struck Quayle as less of a question and more of a plea for reassurance.

Lord Unsworth had remained largely silent last night as Quayle and Tallier shared their nascent thoughts and plans, but now His Lordship's qualms were showing. And rightfully so. Mr. Quayle's primary purpose, his raison d'etre, had always been to keep the Unsworth family out of the fray—a difficult task at the best of times—but what he was proposing now was the precise opposite.

"I am moderately confident, sir." Mr. Quayle's sense of duty and honor mandated the qualifier. "And I promise I will do my utmost to keep them safe."

"Mmm." They were standing in Lord Unsworth's study, the morning sun almost unearthly bright through the window, while outside, the air was once more alive with birdsong. Altogether it promised to be yet another glorious day, like something from a dream. But appearances can be deceptive, and thus far, their sojourn on the Riviera had been more of a nightmare than anything else.

"It's not that I don't trust your judgment, Quayle," His Lordship said. "After all, you've seldom steered us wrong in the past, but is it necessary to involve my niece and nephew?"

"Necessary? Perhaps not, but with respect, sir," Mr. Quayle pointed out, "they already are involved."

"Even Fanny?"

"*Especially* Fanny, I'm afraid," Mr. Quayle replied gently, knowing full well the impact his words would have. Fanny was and always had been His Lordship's favorite, the daughter he never had. "If I'm right, she may be in for quite a shock before all of this is over, although how much of one remains to be seen."

Lord Unsworth pondered that statement for a moment, examining it from all angles before nodding. "Yes," he agreed sadly. "I suppose so. And Arthur?"

"Quite frankly, Your Lordship, if we had left him to his own devices, Arthur was liable to have gone charging off on some harebrained scheme of his own...*again*."

"True enough." Lord Unsworth sighed, and the two men shared a look of shared exasperation.

"At least this way," Mr. Quayle reassured him, "we have some semblance of an idea of where he is and what he's doing."

"Connie won't be pleased," Lord Unsworth warned. "About any of this."

"No," Mr. Quayle allowed. "She won't be. But not to worry, sir. This time I'll handle Lady Constance."

"Will you, indeed? As I recall, there was a time not so long ago when my sister utterly despised you."

"Her Ladyship and I have come to ...an understanding," Mr. Quayle explained. "And I'm sure I'll be able to calm her fears...eventually." He shrugged, displaying a confidence in his soothing powers that he did not quite feel. "Either way, there are a few questions I've been meaning to ask her."

"Oh?" Lord Unsworth raised his eyebrows, unable to hide his curiosity. "What about?"

"About the past, sir," Mr. Quayle said. "About Lady Rosaline."

"But I've told you everything I can remember about those days," His Lordship protested. "Everything of importance, at least."

"Yes, you have."

Lord Unsworth blinked in shock. "You're not suggesting that Connie has been keeping secrets, are you? That she knows more than she's saying?"

"I rather suspect, sir, that your sister always knows more than she's saying."

"Hah!" His Lordship laughed, but any trace of humor soon faded away, leaving only a lingering, all-consuming worry. "You might be right at that," he murmured. "Yes, I think you might be right." The two men met each other's eyes for a long, solemn moment. They both knew that His Lordship hadn't merely been talking about Lady Constance.

"If you wish, sir, I can still stop all this now," Mr. Quayle said quietly, his voice barely above a whisper. "We're no longer suspects, no longer involved unless we choose to be, and, if you give the word, we can still walk away and leave this matter to the police. But this is our last chance, sir. Arthur's joyride is one thing, but we're about to cross the Rubicon, and once those wheels have been set in motion, there will be no turning back. So, if you have any—"

"No." Lord Unsworth shook his head. "I thank you for the offer, Quayle, but in a way, I crossed this particular Rubicon almost thirty years ago, and I intend to see it through to the end."

Mr. Quayle nodded. "Then, if you will excuse me, Your Lordship," he said. "I must be on my way. I have a very busy day ahead of me. In fact, I daresay we all do."

* * *

If Chief Inspector Tallier was at all deterred by the prospect of the long day ahead, he gave no sign. Indeed, he had a palpable, almost criminal, spring in his step as he bounded up the stairs to ring the doorbell at the Villa Barrett De Marchi. His unfortunate colleagues were far less jaunty, having slaved through the night to no apparent purpose, and were none the wiser as to their superior's cheerfulness. And, watching from the corner of his eye as Inspector Barras desperately tried to hide his scowl and Duvot surreptitiously rubbed the sleep from his eyes, the Chief Inspector was in no hurry to enlighten them. It was too soon for that and, besides, it was the final member of their little band who had the most cause for complaint, and not a single word had passed her lips.

Professor Antoinette Thascalos from the University of Bordeaux was an eminent art historian, appraiser, and sometime police consultant who had done Tallier the inestimable favor of abandoning her work, her students, and her much overdue grading to leap onto the overnight train to follow a hunch. No matter how this turned out, Tallier owed the sleep-deprived academic a rather large and expensive dinner.

A moment later, Genevieve Montague Barrett answered the door and blearily ushered them inside, eyeing Professor Thascalos curiously.

"Please forgive the early hour, Madame Barrett," Chief Inspector Tallier said. "You know Inspectors Duvot and Barras, I believe, but allow me to introduce Professor Thascalos, who has kindly agreed to assist us this morning."

"Professor," Madame Barrett greeted. "I'm sure I've heard your name before, although I wasn't expecting a, uh..." She coughed to cover her embarrassment. "Perhaps you know Herr Darvas, madame le professeur?"

"Oui," Thascalos replied, graciously ignoring Vivi's little faux paus. "Herr Darvas and I have crossed swords many times, both within and without the hallowed halls of academia."

"I see."

"Excusez-moi," Chief Inspector Tallier interjected. "But

we were hoping, madame, to have a word with you and your husband, if this is convenient."

"Oh, of course." She rubbed her face tiredly. "If you could wait here a moment, Chief Inspector, I'll go and fetch Raymond, although I'm not sure how much help he'll be in his present state. That wretched lawyer of his only left an hour or so ago. They spent most of the night going over Rosaline's will."

"Did they?" Tallier's interest was piqued. "There were no surprises, were there?"

"Not with the will itself, no," she replied. "The only surprise there was that she named Carrodus as her executor, although Raymond may be forced to act in his stead." Madame Barrett hesitated. "Have you had any word about him?"

"Monsieur Carrodus is still alive," Tallier said. "But given the damage, there's no telling when, or *if*, he'll ever wake, madame."

"Such a tragedy," she sighed. "But forgive me, Chief Inspector, I'd better go find Raymond."

"What's going on here?" her husband demanded, emerging from the doorway to the West Wing. "Vivi?"

"Ah, Monsieur Barrett!" Tallier turned with a smile. "So good of you to join us. I understand that there have been some...difficulties with your mother's estate?"

Raymond frowned. "I'm not entirely sure that's any of your business, Chief Inspector."

"At the moment, monsieur, *everything* is my business. You wish to catch the murderer, non?"

"Yes, of course. Forgive me, Chief Inspector. It has been a long night." Raymond rubbed his forehead wearily. "As expected," he said, "I have inherited the villa and much of the estate, apart from Carrodus' cottage, of course, along with all of my mother's debts, which were far more extensive than I realized."

"And the collection?"

"No surprises there." Raymond sneered. "My mother's artwork is to be donated to the museum just as soon as the arrangements can be made. Herr Darvas should be thrilled. He has been pestering me about it for days."

"Has he? Well, as it happens, the collection is why we have come. "If you wouldn't mind, Professor Thascalos here would like to have a little look around."

"At the artwork?"

"Mais oui."

"Of course." Raymond and Vivi glanced at each other, puzzled. "Be our guests."

"Merci." Tallier nodded to the professor, who headed towards the East Wing with Inspectors Duvot and Barras in tow. "And in the meantime, while the professor goes about her work, I wondered if the three of us might have a word or two of our own?"

Chief Inspector Tallier accompanied his request with his most disarming grin, as Raymond and Vivi led him toward the study. In truth, Tallier was no less tired than any of the others, but his exhaustion was purely of the body, while his mind was as alive and sharp as ever, like a hound that had scented blood on the wind. This was going to be a good day. He could feel it.

26

THE PRODIGAL DAUGHTER

"Forgive me, Chief Inspector, but did I hear you rightly? You're not seriously suggesting that my mother's collection, her pride and joy, is nothing more than an assortment of fakes and forgeries?"

They had all retired to the upstairs sitting room, where Tallier had first met the couple, and the Chief Inspector could already see the first few minor alterations. Someone had made a passable attempt at dusting, and the remaining paintings and quite a few of the photographs which had rested on the mantlepiece had been removed. The shape of things to come, no doubt.

"I am not suggesting anything at the moment, monsieur," Tallier replied. "It is a possibility, merely, but a possibility one must explore, n'est-ce pas?"

"Of course." Raymond and Vivi were sitting together on the settee, regarding the Chief Inspector with near identical expressions of earnest surprise, although Raymond was not entirely displeased at the prospect of his mother's posthumous embarrassment, not if the sly grin tugging at the corner of his lips was any indication.

"But I mean, it's incredible!" Raymond turned to his wife, still unable to contain his shock. "To think that she could..." he frowned suddenly as a new thought occurred to him. "Mind you, Chief Inspector," he said, "for all that she prided herself on her ability to recite the history and provenance of every item in her collection, I'm not sure that Mother could actually tell the difference between a genuine and a fake. She could speak the lingo, you understand, but I don't know if she ever had the eye."

"Hmm." Tallier nodded. "Something to keep in mind, but even if she had known, your mother would hardly be the only woman in your life keeping secrets."

Raymond reared back, completely bewildered by the sudden shift in conversation. "And what, precisely, is that supposed to mean?" he asked.

Tallier had chosen his moment and his tone with great care, slipping the knife in so quietly and in such a matter-of-fact manner that it had taken Raymond a moment or two to realize what had been said. His wife, Vivi, however, was far more attentive, and even as Raymond flailed and made an abortive attempt at outrage, Vivi was visibly and defiantly steeling herself for what was to come.

"Your wife, monsieur," Tallier explained with gentle remorselessness, "has also been hiding something from us. Have you not, madame?"

"I'm sure I don't know what you mean, Chief Inspector." It was a reflexive denial, and judging by her face, Vivi did not honestly expect to be believed, but she was determined to make the Chief Inspector work for the truth. As it happened, Tallier was only too happy to oblige.

"It has been a long night for all of us," he began, slipping into that lilting, story-telling mode where he was at his most dangerous. "Even my wife."

"Your wife?" Vivi and Raymond exchanged incredulous glances. Whatever they had been expecting, it was not that.

"Mais oui," Tallier nodded proudly. "She has been busy all night going through her old playbills, and I received a telephone call from her just before I left the station confirming my suspicions."

"And what suspicions would those be?"

"Ever since we first met, Madame Barrett, I have been sure that I recognized you from somewhere. Your voice and your mannerisms were all familiar to me, and now I know why. Indeed, I have seen you perform many times. For you, madame, like your mother-in-law before you, were an actress magnifique!"

"You're very kind," Vivi replied darkly, clearly not enjoying the comparison.

"And like your mother-in-law," Tallier continued, "you chose for yourself a stage name: Genevieve Desrosiers."

"That is hardly a crime, Chief Inspector."

"Indeed, it is not. But in an old interview with a theater magazine—my wife, you see, was an avid theatergoer and a collector par excellence—you revealed that your true name was Genevieve Marchant."

"So? What of it?" Raymond interjected. "If you're accusing my wife—"

"Raymond!" She squeezed his hand tightly and silenced him with a shake of her head. "Let the Chief Inspector speak."

"Merci." Tallier was watching their interplay closely. As he had suspected, Vivi was the cooler, more calculated of the two. She would not wriggle on the hook. "Now, as you say, there is no crime, no great mystery in changing your name for the stage. It is a time-honored practice, n'est-ce pas? But Marchant, now that is a name I have heard before in connection with Lady

Rosaline." He turned the full weight of his attention to Vivi. "There was a Christophe Marchant, was there not?" he asked. "Who threw himself in front of the Blue Train some years ago, reportedly because Lady Rosaline had ended their affair?"

"Yes." Vivi's lips were pressed into a thin, angry line. "There was."

"Your father, I believe."

"Yes," she snarled.

Tallier nodded. "Forgive me, but why did you not mention this at the start?"

Vivi snorted. "Raymond and I thought it might make me a suspect," she explained.

"That may be so," Tallier pointed out gently, "but you must realize that keeping it a secret was hardly the best way to appear innocent."

"Indeed." Vivi scowled. "I suppose you want the whole story?"

"It would be for the best, I think, madame."

"For whom," she muttered, then waved her hand impatiently when Tallier leaned forward to urge her. "Yes, yes!" she said. "I'll tell you."

But it was nearly a minute before she spoke again. For his part, however, Chief Inspector Tallier was content to wait and watch.

"The rumors were true," Vivi said finally, her voice coming as if from a long, long way away. "I was a child at the time, but I still remember it quite well. My father fell in love with Lady Rosaline like so many before him, and like so many before him, he spent all his wealth and savings buying her presents—jewels and furs, trinkets and stockings. While my mother and I starved, he lavished Lady Rosaline with everything he could afford and more. Always more!"

Her face was trembling with anger, and there was a noticeable tremor in her voice, one which Tallier thought he recognized from her well-regarded turn as Lady Macbeth.

"And then," Vivi continued, dripping with renewed scorn, "when Rosaline abandoned him, my father—my dear, darling father—threw himself in front of the train rather than face his family."

"I'm sorry."

"Why? It's not your fault. You're not to blame."

"And who is to blame?" Tallier asked.

"Rosaline, of course!" Vivi growled. "That's what you want me to say, isn't it?"

"Only if it's true."

"Of course, it's true!" she snapped. "I've blamed Rosaline all my life. That's why I sought Raymond out. That's why I married him, in hopes of getting close to Rosaline and having my revenge." She laughed. "But instead, I found them hopelessly estranged. What a joke!"

"And that's why you proposed a reconciliation."

"Precisely." She shrugged. "It took some doing, of course, since, ironically, hating his mother was something Raymond and I shared, but in the end, I convinced him to attempt a reconciliation."

"And she was receptive?"

"Eventually," Raymond supplied.

"I see." Tallier's eyes flickered for a moment, trying and failing to pierce Raymond's expression. He did not seem surprised by his wife's revelations. In fact, he did not seem much of anything at all. For once, Raymond was the more inscrutable of the pair.

"And so, once this reconciliation had been achieved, you had her in your grasp," Tallier asked, turning his attention back to Vivi. "What then?"

"I confronted her, of course."

"When was this?"

"The night she died." Vivi shook her head. "And as it turned out, for all my plotting and planning, Rosaline already knew exactly who I was. Not that she apologized."

"Is that so?"

"Oh, yes, Chief Inspector. She told me that she'd never asked my father for the jewels or furs. That she'd never slept with him or encouraged his attentions in any way. His actions, she said, were his own, and if he 'couldn't handle the strain,' then that was hardly her fault, was it?"

"This was not, perhaps, the reaction you were hoping for?"

"Of course not!" Vivi sat bolt upright. "And the worst of it was that she was happy I had married Raymond. Happy! That was supposed to be my revenge, and she was happy."

"Did she say why?"

"Yes." Vivi deflated slightly. "Rosaline said that he deserved to have at least one person in his life who loved him." And with that, Vivi turned to look at her husband for the first time since she'd begun. There was such a strange, angry sort of tenderness in her gaze that Tallier had to fight the urge to turn away. "I suppose," she said, almost wonderingly, "that was the moment when I realized for myself that I really do love him."

Raymond's face crumpled at that, and the Chief Inspector awkwardly cleared his throat. "This is all very touching," he said. "But it does give you a most convincing motive to kill Lady Rosaline."

"Yes," Vivi agreed. "But not the others. I barely knew Carrodus, and I never even spoke to the Count. Let alone, Weatherford!"

"Mais oui." Chief Inspector Tallier acknowledged. "Then let us speak instead about the night of Lady Rosaline's murder."

"I've told you all about that."

"Oui, you have, madame," Tallier agreed. "But that was before you admitted to confronting the woman you blamed for your father's death on that very night. So tell me, s'il vous plait, when exactly did you confront your mother-in-law?"

"Ah, well, you see...um..." she glanced at her husband, momentarily at a loss for words. "I, uh..."

"It was not, perhaps, sometime after your little incident with Monsieur Léger in the garden?" Chief Inspector Tallier offered helpfully. "When you claimed that you and Monsieur Raymond were here in this very room and never left?"

"Perhaps," Vivi admitted once it was clear that there was no point in denying it. "I mean, yes. Oui. We did come up here like we said, but after a few minutes I went to find her."

"Where did you go?"

"Downstairs to the collection."

"To the room with the Bernini?"

"No!" Vivi shook her head. "No, no! It was in one of those infernal courtyards."

"And did you see anyone while you were there?" Tallier asked.

"You mean, did anyone see me?" Vivi asked. "In other words, do I have an alibi?"

"I mean both," the Chief Inspector answered. "So, did you?"

Vivi glanced at Raymond for a moment, then nodded. "Yes!" she cried. "Yes, I remember now! I did see someone, Chief Inspector. It was that lecherous old fool Léger!"

"Was it?" Tallier's voice was deliberately skeptical. "And what was he doing there?"

"I don't know. Perhaps you should ask him. But he didn't want to be seen, I can tell you that much. He kept skulking about in the dark, ducking out of sight."

"Did he? And you're sure..."

"Excusez-moi, Chief Inspector!"

Tallier turned to find Professor Thascalos bursting excitedly into the room, followed by Duvot and Barras at a more sedate pace.

"Ah, Professor!" Tallier greeted. "You've found something, I take it?"

"Certainement!" Thascalos was practically vibrating in place. "I've barely started, but I've already identified four fraudulent pieces. Four!" She grinned, looking suddenly half her age.

"So it's true," Raymond murmured. "Mother's collection really is a fraud!" This time there was no mistaking the smile on his face.

"It would appear so, monsieur," Tallier said, his thoughts racing far ahead. Mr. Quayle and Lord Unsworth had been right about the collection after all. So, perhaps, Quayle had been right about other things as well. Only one way to find out!

The Chief Inspector leapt to his feet. "Thank you for your assistance, Madame et Monsieur Barrett," he said. "Inspector Duvot here will assist you in amending your statements while Barras and I have a little chat with Monsieur Léger. I believe it is high time he answered a few more questions."

27

A QUIET LITTLE REVENGE

Meanwhile, unaware that one of his theories had been proven true in such dramatic fashion, Mr. Quayle was perched on a sofa in Madame Léger's sitting room, attempting to prove another. Beside him, Fanny was exhibiting a queer mixture of embarrassment and determination. She was far too well-bred not to feel ashamed at imposing on her friendship with Anne-Marie Léger or at wheedling her way inside under what might uncharitably be considered false pretenses. But she had been eager to help from the start, and it was not in her nature to turn back now.

"I'm afraid my husband is not with us at the moment," Madame Léger said as she offered Quayle a freshly poured cup of tea.

"Not to worry." Mr. Quayle accepted the cup with a polite smile. "I'm sure he is a very busy man, and, if I may, Madame Léger, I am actually quite glad of the opportunity to speak with you first."

"Ah." She nodded as if confirming something to herself. "Then it is Jean-Paul you wish to speak of."

"I'm afraid so."

"What has he done now?" Madame Léger sighed. "He hasn't gotten himself into a fight, has he? Don't tell me he attacked that cousin of yours, Fanny? Arthur, is it?"

"No." Fanny shook her head. "He hasn't attacked Arthur."

"Merde!" Madame Léger leaned forward in alarm. "Not Lord Unsworth! You have to understand that he's been out most nights, drowning his grief at one of the local bars, and when he drinks, Jean-Paul can become...belligerent. Comprenez vous? He doesn't always know what he's doing or what he's saying—"

"Please don't worry, madame," Mr. Quayle interrupted gently. "As far as I know, your husband has not assaulted anyone, at least not anyone in my employer's family."

"I see." Madame Léger frowned. "Then what, precisely, did you wish to discuss, may I ask?"

"I'm sorry." Madame Léger had been looking right at Quayle, but it was Fanny who answered. "I'm so sorry, Anne-Marie," she repeated. "I didn't mean to pry, but after Lady Rosaline's funeral, Mr. Quayle and I were in the gardens, and we couldn't help but—"

"Ah, you were eavesdropping," Madame Léger finished. "Spying on me and my husband."

"In fairness, Madame Léger, you and your husband were speaking rather loudly at the time," Mr. Quayle said, coming to Fanny's rescue. "It would have been difficult *not* to overhear."

"Yes," she agreed with great reluctance. "I suppose that's true. Now, I don't know what you two think you overheard, but—"

"You can trust me," Fanny said. "I promise."

"Can I?" Madame Léger was skeptical. "And what about your Mr. Quayle here?"

"My family and I have found him to be a great friend, someone who can be very useful in a crisis and very discreet."

"And you think I am in need of such discretion?"

"I don't know," Fanny replied honestly. "Only you can say for certain, Anne-Marie."

"Hmm." Madame Léger hesitated, studying Mr. Quayle almost as carefully as he studied her in return, but only for a moment. And then, with a deep breath, she took the plunge. "So be it," she said at last. "I suppose it is something of a relief to have this all out in the open. I must admit that playing the devoted wife has been rather exhausting these past few years."

Fanny nodded in understanding. "But why the Count?" she asked. "Of all people, why him?"

"Any number of reasons, my dear. Because he was there, because he offered, because it seemed like a good idea at the time..." Madame Léger laughed. "Oh, I won't say that I wasn't flattered by his attentions," she added, "but I never had any illusions about Scarlioni. He was a charmer, an adulterer, and a lout, who was clearly pursuing me for some peculiar motive of his own, but I didn't mind. Why should I? After all, I've been married to Jean-Paul—the original lout—for nearly twenty years. At least Scarlioni deigned to pay me some attention!"

"Besides," Mr. Quayle suggested, "you had a particular motive of your own, didn't you?"

"Of course!" Now that she had begun her story, Madame Léger was being refreshingly, disarmingly candid about the whole affair. "Originally, Scarlioni was to be my quiet little revenge, my chance to give Jean-Paul a taste of his own medicine. Let *him* squirm and rage for a change. Let *him* see me consorting with another man, and a *younger man* at that," she grinned proudly.

"From what I've seen of your husband," Mr. Quayle agreed, "that would certainly hurt him the most."

"You mean because he can't help but pant and skulk after every young woman who crosses his path?"

"That is not, perhaps, how I would have phrased it," Mr. Quayle said, fumbling slightly. "However—"

"That's because you are still walking on eggshells, monsieur," Madame Léger said. "Because, like everyone else, you do not wish to upset me, as if I do not know the man I married. That is why you have kept quiet, is it not, Fanny?"

"Me?"

"Mais oui. You are beautiful, young, and English. I cannot believe that my husband did not make advances at least once."

Fanny looked even more embarrassed than when they'd sat down. "In the beginning," Fanny admitted, unable to meet Madame Léger's eyes, "he made a special effort to tell me all about his paintings and sculptures…"

"Talking to a beautiful woman about himself," Madame Léger said scornfully. "I'm sure he'd never been happier."

Fanny grimaced. "But, Anne-Marie, I swear—"

"—you never gave him the time of day," Madame Léger finished for her. "And you hurried away as fast as you could, leaving him to stare after you in wounded confusion." She shook her head, and for a moment, Mr. Quayle thought she seemed desperately sad before the bitterness returned in full force. "Of course, you did, my dear!" Madame Léger exclaimed. "Everyone always does! Not like in the old days. My husband prefers youth, you see, but youth does not prefer him back."

"And so, it would hurt your husband all the more when the dangerous young Count Scarlioni paid court to his wife, the woman who he had, forgive me, madame, abandoned in his pursuit of youth."

"Exactement." Madame Léger favored him with an approving, if sad smile. "You *do* understand, don't you, Monsieur Quayle?"

"Oui, madame, I understand." Mr. Quayle sipped his tea, eyeing her closely over the rim of his spectacles before dropping a single word carefully but deliberately into the conversation as though lobbing a stone into a pond and watching for ripples. "*Originally*," he said.

"Excusez-moi?"

"Earlier," Mr. Quayle said, "you said that Scarlioni was *originally* your quiet little revenge. A word which suggests that he became something more over time."

"You are quick, monsieur! I did not fall in love with him, if that is what you mean."

"I wasn't suggesting you had."

"No, you weren't, were you?" Madame Léger said almost to herself. "The truth is that it wasn't Scarlioni who became something more, but he did plant the seeds for a different kind of revenge."

"What do you mean?" Fanny asked, unable to help herself.

"He encouraged me to start painting and sculpting again," Madame Léger explained. "I hadn't picked up a brush in years, not since..."

"Yes?" Mr. Quayle asked once it was clear that she wasn't going to continue of her own volition.

"Oh, I'm sure Márta's told Fanny here all about my sordid past. She does so enjoy being righteous on my behalf."

"She said you had been a successful artist," Fanny said.

"A thriving artist," Madame Léger said. "All my dreams were about to come true. I was going to be the greatest artist of my generation, you know, with Rosaline as my backer, my patroness, and my dearest friend." She scoffed. "That dream barely lasted a summer before I met Jean-Paul and introduced him to Rosaline. Everything changed after that, and as the years passed, I painted less and less. Jean-Paul would broker no rival, least of all in his own home, and he knew—he *always* knew—that I was better than him." She sat up straight, erect, and proud. "And I still am," she declared defiantly. "Especially now."

"Oui," Mr. Quayle agreed. "I understand that his last showing was an utter disaster."

"Not entirely," Madame Léger corrected. "There were one or two pieces that showed...promise. But that's not the point."

"And what is the point?"

"The point, Monsieur Quayle, is that over the years, I have allowed my artistic talents to atrophy and wither on the vine, but Count Scarlioni's encouragement breathed new life into me. After decades spent sleepwalking, I was awake at last!" Madame Léger shed whole years with her smile. "And I was grateful to him for that," she added, "but when he ended things a few months ago, I didn't waste so much as a single tear. I didn't need him anymore, you see, not when I had my easel. Painting for myself, I soon found, was a much better revenge."

"I see." Mr. Quayle did not doubt for a moment that Madame Léger had told the absolute truth, and yet there was something about her story that gnawed at him, as if an answer had just strolled idly into view, if only he was clever enough to see it. "Tell me," he asked, "did your husband know about the affair?"

"I'm not sure." Madame Léger shrugged. "I made no effort to hide it, of course. I even did my best to flaunt on occasion, but Jean-Paul has never been the most perceptive of men, and he was distracted at the time—first by his little feud with Rosaline and then by his pathetic attempts to crawl back into her good graces. For anything more, you'd have to ask him."

"Ah." Mr. Quayle thought he understood Madame Léger completely now and found that he liked her enormously—this stifled, bitter woman who, as her twilight years approached, was finally effecting her escape and her revenge. But was painting and sculpting truly enough to assuage the anger he sensed swelling behind her sly smiles?

She may have started small with a fleeting little affair—barely more than a fling—albeit one which had been carefully chosen to hurt but, by her own account, she had rapidly advanced to a more artistically fulfilling form of revenge. Was she capable of escalating still further, Mr. Quayle wondered, and what form might that take? He covered a delighted smile behind another sip of tea. What a fine puzzle Madame Léger had turned out to be!

"It appears, Monsieur Quayle," she said, tilting her head to the right, "that you will have the opportunity to ask him your questions, after all."

"Oh?"

"Do you hear that?" She raised a wry, dainty finger, and it was Mr. Quayle's turn to tilt his head, followed shortly by a confused Fanny. A moment later, Mr. Quayle heard the stumbling sound of heavy footsteps and muffled curses coming from outside. "That's Jean-Paul," Madame Léger revealed, "deigning to make an appearance."

And so the three of them, Mr. Quayle, Madame Léger, and Fanny, sat in awkward silence and listened as Jean-Paul Léger, once renowned as the greatest artist of his generation, fumbled and rattled with his keys before belatedly staggering in through the front door with a wallop.

"Anne?" he called. "Anne-Marie?"

"In here," she replied, favoring Mr. Quayle and Fanny with a quick, mischievous smirk, and a few moments later, Léger stumbled into the room smelling of wine and liquors and sporting haggard circles under his eyes.

"Ah, there you are!" The artist frowned blearily at the unexpected gathering. "Fanny!" he smiled somewhat unsteadily. "How good of you to—" Suddenly, his eyes narrowed, and he charged forward a few stumbling steps to glare belatedly down at Mr. Quayle. "Who the hell are you?" he demanded.

"Good morning, monsieur," Mr. Quayle replied, rising easily to his feet, utterly unaffected by Léger's belligerent, hungover attempt at intimidation. "We actually met a few days ago, if you recall. You and your wife were kind enough to invite me, and I am a great admirer—"

On any other day, in any other week, the blatant flattery would probably have worked wonders, but today Léger was too worried, too on edge.

"What do you want?" he snapped.

Mr. Quayle remained unmoved by the older man's tone, even when Léger took a few threatening steps forward. The artist was taller and broader but also far older and unsteady on his feet. And his hands, Mr. Quayle noted, were shaking.

"Fanny and I were just having a rather enlightening conversation with Madame Léger," Quayle answered. "And I was hoping that you and I could have the same opportunity before the police arrived, but that doesn't seem likely now."

Léger blinked at him in blank incomprehension. "What are you talking about? What police?" And then, with exquisite timing, the doorbell chose that precise moment to ring.

"That will be Chief Inspector Tallier, I imagine," Mr. Quayle announced. "Along with a warrant to search the house...and the studio, of course." As he spoke, Quayle eyed both Légers closely but was rewarded for his efforts with only confusion and blankness, respectively.

"A warrant?" Léger was too puzzled to be angry anymore. "Anne-Marie, what is he talking about?"

But Anne-Marie shook her head, and no matter how they pleaded, Mr. Quayle refused to say anything further. Instead, he merely sat there, sipping his tea and watching while the doorbell rang again.

And again.

28

THE ARTIST'S STUDIO

Chief Inspector Tallier watched as Barras and his handpicked men went about their search of the Légers' cottage. Every square inch, every painting, every sketch, every maquette, every single piece of furniture was meticulously examined, photographed, and recorded in a maelstrom of official, organized chaos. Although bracing themselves against the onslaught, the Légers, Tallier noted, were not presenting a particularly united front at the moment.

Jean-Paul Léger was standing apart from the others in a corner of his own, glaring at the proceedings with a kind of wounded anger, as if unable to comprehend the sheer effrontery occurring around him. His life's work, his pride and glory, was being manhandled before his eyes, its importance reduced to a few lines in a policeman's inventory.

Anne-Marie, meanwhile, had stationed herself on the far side of the room—as far, in fact, as possible—with young Fanny for company, and she appeared to be, in her own subtle way, enjoying her husband's humiliation.

"You and Lord Unsworth were right, mon ami," Tallier whispered to Mr. Quayle as the Englishman moved to join him. "We did find several forgeries in Lady Rosaline's collection."

"How many?" Mr. Quayle asked softly.

"Professor Thascalos had identified four by the time I left, but she seemed confident that she would find more soon enough."

"Four already?" Far from pleased, as Tallier might have expected, Mr. Quayle almost sounded surprised by the number, but quickly turned thoughtful. "I wonder…"

"Oui?" Tallier prompted, but Quayle merely shook his head.

"Just a passing thought," he said with a dismissive wave. "But what about Vivi Montague Barrett? Did you catch your little actress?"

"Mais oui." Chief Inspector Tallier nodded contentedly. "She admitted everything…eventually."

"Capital! So, *you* were right as well, Chief Inspector," Mr. Quayle noted. "The prodigal daughter did come to wreak her revenge!"

"Revenge, oui," Tallier replied. "But not, I think, murder."

Mr. Quayle sent him a quick, searching look. "Are you sure?" he asked. "She had the motive and, I presume, the opportunity?"

"Oui." The Chief Inspector inclined his head reluctantly. "She has amended her statement. It turns out she did leave Raymond in the drawing room for a time when she went to confront her mother-in-law. This means your Lord Unsworth is no longer the last person to have seen Lady Rosaline alive."

Mr. Quayle's eyes narrowed. "I thought you'd removed His Lordship from suspicion."

"I did." Tallier shrugged. "But now I have the proof! And she told to me something else most interesting."

"And what would that be?"

"Madame Barrett believes that she saw Monsieur Léger in

the villa while she was speaking with Rosaline, and she thinks he was taking great pains not to be seen."

"Does she?" Tallier could practically hear the gears turning behind the Englishman's eyes. It was almost like looking in a mirror. "And do you believe her?"

"I believe it is *possible*, but in this case, as I think you know, nothing it is certain, mon ami. Although where before, all was in shadow, we have begun at last to shine some light here and there, non?"

"Mm. And in the interest of shining lights into dark places," Mr. Quayle said, "I have sent a telegram to Inspector Wintle back in England. It's a long shot, but hopefully, I'll hear back before too long."

"Another of your passing thoughts?" A few days ago, the question might have been accompanied by an irritated bite to his words, but today the Chief Inspector favored Quayle with a fond, approving smile. They were moving in lockstep now, even if one or both of them was still keeping a surprise or three up their sleeve.

"Perhaps." Mr. Quayle nodded. "But until I've heard back, I would prefer to keep my own counsel. It's much easier to keep this newfound reputation of mine when no one ever hears about my mistakes."

"The luxury of the amateur," Tallier said, but again there was nothing but friendship in his voice.

"We've finished with the house, sir," Inspector Barras interrupted, eyeing Quayle disapprovingly. "All that remains is the workshop."

"Ah, oui!" This was the crux of the matter, and Tallier felt a renewed sense of purpose pulsing through his veins. "Then, by all means, Inspector, let us search the workshop!"

* * *

LÉGER'S WORKSHOP AND STUDIO, it soon emerged, was located in an oddly cube-shaped outbuilding some ways from the house. An eyesore painted white with large windows and tightly drawn curtains, it proclaimed its eccentricities for all to see, and it was also, crucially, kept heavily locked and bolted at all times. Only Léger himself had a key, and he did not, the great artist assured Tallier, allow anyone else inside—not the maid, not the charwoman, and most assuredly not his wife.

Chief Inspector Tallier turned an appraising glance to the woman in question. Madame Léger, still accompanied closely by Fanny, had followed the police and her husband over to the studio. Mr. Quayle, Tallier noted, had joined them as well and was regarding the proceedings with a keen, almost palpable interest.

"No, Chief Inspector," Madame Léger confirmed, answering Tallier's unspoken question, "my husband has never permitted me a key. Indeed, I have seldom been inside. Only Rosaline was afforded that privilege—rarely at first, and then not at all." Madame Léger was utterly stone-faced as she spoke, which in itself was as much a tell as anything. "Jean-Paul," she continued, "has always been very protective, very secretive, about his works-in-progress. Although, as Fanny here can attest, once he's finished a piece, he is all too eager to discuss his process in depth."

Tallier accepted her explanation with a nod, although inwardly, his eyebrows were raised. Clearly, there was no love lost between husband and wife.

"Monsieur Léger," he said, holding out his hand. "The key, s'il vous plait."

The great artist was reluctant, of course, but the Chief Inspector was unyielding. This was not the time to coddle Léger's artistic sensibilities, if that's all they were, and bowing to the inevitable with a grumble, Léger produced the key.

"Merci." Tallier accepted it with a grateful half-smile as if there had been no difficulties whatsoever. "If you would be so kind as to do the honors, Inspector," he said, handing the all-important key over to Barras.

Inspector Barras set about his task with brisk efficiency, pushing the door open and ushering the men inside. Despite the overt strangeness of its outsides, the interior of Léger's studio was disappointingly conventional. Inside, they found several half-finished paintings and sketches, some of which were quite good, in Tallier's humble layman's opinion.

"Sir!" Barras called, and Tallier abandoned his thoughts, galvanized by the sense of urgency in the Inspector's voice.

Barras was standing by one of the windows, gazing down at a rather tall mound covered in a white cloth. And then, with a dramatic flair of his own, the Inspector pulled the covering aside, revealing a statuette sitting innocently on Léger's workbench, glinting prettily in the morning sun. It was, of course, the missing Bernini.

At last!

The responses were as immediate as they were varied. Barras, for one, was utterly triumphant and turned to grace Tallier with an approving look for the first time in their short acquaintance. Meanwhile, from somewhere behind them, Fanny let out an audible gasp, and a quick glance confirmed that although Madame Léger had remained silent, her face had paled considerably.

And as for Léger himself—

"What?" the artist cried, staring at the statuette in horror. "I don't...I don't understand...what is *that* doing here?"

"My question exactly, monsieur," Inspector Barras replied sharply. "I am arresting you on suspicion of theft, murder—"

"Murder?" Léger cried. "You can't think that I...that I—"

Jean-Paul Léger broke off suddenly, jerking his head first this way and then that, searching desperately for allies, but found only suspicion and disbelief. No one, it seemed, particularly not his wife, believed him for a moment. "Anne?" he tried, pleading to his wife. "Anne-Marie, please! You don't really think I killed Rosaline, do you?"

But Madame Léger said nothing and would not even look her husband in the eye. It was, Chief Inspector Tallier thought, a rather sad scene, although to his eye, Léger looked more confused than anything as he was led roughly away. Judging by his expression, Mr. Quayle had noticed it too, and the two men shared a long, suspicious look.

Interesting, the Chief Inspector thought to himself. Very interesting.

***

"Why did you say that?" Fanny asked once the police were gone. Having dragged the so-called man of the house away in chains, the various officers of the law had not lingered for much longer, leaving the house in a state of some confusion and disarray.

Madame Léger, who had been standing in one of the few untouched corners, staring around blankly, turned and blinked at her.

"Excusez-moi?" she asked.

"The Chief Inspector," Fanny explained. "You told him that your husband was the only one with a key to the workshop."

"That's right."

"But I saw you," Fanny insisted. "That afternoon before the party, I saw you coming from the workshop."

"Ridiculous! You must have been mistaken," Madame Léger snapped, perhaps a trifle too quickly. "I might have been coming from that direction, but..." She sighed, suddenly remembering herself. "I'm sorry, Fanny," she said. "I didn't mean to shout. The truth is I barely know what I'm saying. I could have believed almost anything of my husband, but the thought that he murdered Rosaline..." She grimaced. "He must have hated her so much!"

"Would you like us to contact one of your friends?" Mr. Quayle interrupted. "Márta perhaps? Or Herr Darvas? After all, I'm sure they'll be pleased to know how well their little plan has turned out."

"I beg your pardon?"

"Please, Madame Léger, let us not play any more games. For the past few days, you and Márta have been doing everything in your power to point the finger at Monsieur Léger. It was deftly done, of course, and it even had me fooled for a time. But it was all just a little too convenient. That conversation Fanny and I overheard in the garden, and now the stolen statuette—the coup de grâce. One touch too many, in my opinion."

"Forgive me, Monsieur Quayle, but I don't—"

"Of course, you do," Mr. Quayle replied. "And, of course, Fanny saw you coming from the studio because, for all your protestations to the contrary, your husband is not and never has been the only one with a key to the workshop, has he? How could he be? After all, it's your workshop, too, is it not?"

29

CONFRONTATIONS AND REVELATIONS

In the end, they did not call Márta or Herr Darvas. Instead, at Mr. Quayle's insistence, the three of them—Madame Léger, Fanny, and Quayle himself—alighted in a taxi to the Darvas' hotel in Treville-sur-Mer. It was to be an unannounced visit, again at Mr. Quayle's insistence.

Arriving at the hotel, however, they quickly discovered that Márta and Herr Darvas were not alone. The Countess Scarlioni, impeccably dressed and ferociously armed with an ivory-handled pistol, had made herself at home in the Darvas' rather plush room and was holding its occupants at gunpoint when Mr. Quayle and the others slipped inside.

There was a moment of pure confusion. Fanny let out a startled cry while Madame Léger recoiled and made an abortive lunge for the door. Márta, who had been sitting by her father, leapt up violently as if to help her, although what she meant to do beyond providing another target was unclear.

"Don't move!" the Countess cried, brandishing her weapon with great determination but, to Mr. Quayle's eyes, very little practice. "Nobody move!"

Silence. Stillness.

Only Herr Darvas remained unaffected by the chaos around him. He had been sitting calmly when Mr. Quayle and company arrived, and he had remained sitting calmly throughout, as if such things were an everyday occurrence not worthy of his attention.

Mr. Quayle admired the man's composure. He himself had been startled by the Countess' presence and by the gun, but now that the threat of violence had faded for the moment, he was, actually, quite pleased. Having everyone all together would simplify matters enormously—or complicate them.

"Countess Scarlioni," he said with a slight bow. "It is a pleasure to see you again."

"You!" the Countess spat. "I remember you. The organ grinder who sent Arthur to blackmail me."

Mr. Quayle sighed. "Yes, I can see why you might think me responsible for that, but it was not my idea. Arthur was acting entirely on his own, half-baked initiative."

"Even if I believed you, Signore Quayle, you've still been interfering for days, sticking your nose in where it's not wanted. And now you're here interfering yet again, and I will not have it!"

In a few angry steps, she was standing right in front of him, aiming her pistol straight at his chest. Quayle did not so much as blink, however, and never took his eyes from her own. "I apologize for the intrusion," he said. "I can see that you were in the middle of something, but would you please stop waving that pistol of yours around? You might hurt someone."

"Perhaps that's the idea."

"No," Mr. Quayle replied calmly. "You may be a thief, Countess Scarlioni, but you're not a killer."

"Are you sure about that?"

"Quite sure. No one here is a killer."

"Now I know you're a fool," the Countess replied. "Or

else you're lying. My husband received an anonymous letter on the day he died, summoning him to a secret meeting. Now, it's taken me a while, but I've finally worked out who sent it and why."

"Have you? Excellent!" Mr. Quayle grinned. "That was one of the questions I hoped you could answer."

The Countess' lips thinned, but she was no longer looking at Quayle. Her ire had shifted to Márta and her father. "The Italian ambassador is an old friend of mine," Countess Scarlioni said, "and he has been keeping a close eye on the investigation for me. This morning he informed me that the police had requisitioned an art historian and forgery expert and had booked her on the overnight train from Paris. Why would they do that, I wondered, unless they were expecting to find something?"

"Why, indeed?" Mr. Quayle murmured, but his mind was pondering another question: did Chief Inspector Tallier know his investigation had been compromised to this degree? If the Countess knew this much, what else might she know? And even more concerning, who else had eyes and ears in the Sûreté?

"Apparently," the Countess continued, "the police are interested in Lady Rosaline's collection. And if there are forgeries in there, then it is no great difficulty working out who might be responsible. After all, unlike the police, I know for a fact that while my husband and I are guilty of several high society robberies, we are *not* La Chimère. And more to the point, I know that before my husband's untimely death, he was closing in on the real culprits."

"Interesting. But why bother?" Mr. Quayle asked.

"Because someone tipped the police off about our Paris theft, and that same someone informed Chief Inspector Tallier that we were on the Riviera. One ill turn deserves another..."

"No honor amongst thieves, then?" Mr. Quayle smirked. "It appears that you and I have arrived on much the same errand, and while I cannot promise you all the answers, I can make a stab at some of them, if you'll indulge me."

"Oh, very well!" Reluctantly, the Countess allowed Quayle and Fanny to take their seats and even more reluctantly ushered Madame Léger to the sofa with Márta and Herr Darvas. "If you insist."

"Thank you. Are we all sitting comfortably?" Mr. Quayle asked with an ironic twist to his lips.

"Yes, yes, get on with it," the Countess demanded, waving her revolver at him.

"As you wish." Despite his words, however, Mr. Quayle did not speak immediately, his eyes instead roving over the gathering appraisingly. "Currently," he said, "the police believe, as they were meant to believe, that Monsieur Jean-Paul Léger is responsible for the forgeries they've discovered in and amongst Lady Rosaline's collection."

"*Meant* to believe?" Fanny frowned. "Are you suggesting that he's innocent?"

"Let's not get ahead of ourselves, Fanny," Mr. Quayle replied gently. "Léger is, of course, the most logical suspect. After all, who could possibly forge so many masterpieces other than the man recognized as one of France's greatest living artists, a man, moreover, who is known to despise Rosaline? Except!" Mr. Quayle held up a single finger. "There is one small problem with this theory. Monsieur Léger is not quite the artist he once was. Indeed, he is not much of an artist at all, is he? Not anymore."

"What do you mean?" Fanny turned to her friend, Anne-Marie, for an explanation, but Madame Léger did not respond. She was too busy glaring at Quayle, although her anger was nothing compared to Márta's. That young woman had violence on her mind, and if she had possessed the pistol instead of Countess Scarlioni, Mr. Quayle feared that he would have been found with a bullet in his head.

"Léger's hands tremble," Quayle answered Fanny when it was clear no one else was in the mood to volunteer an explanation. "We've all seen it, I'm sure, and assumed it was from the drink, but they tremble even when he's sober. It must be difficult to paint or sculpt when you can't trust your hands or, worse, your eyes."

"His eyes?" This time it was the Countess who asked, leaning forward, engrossed despite herself. "You mean that odious man is going blind?"

"Indeed," Mr. Quayle confirmed. "Or am I mistaken, Madame Léger?"

Too startled to lie, Anne-Marie could only stare and nod in shock. "How on earth did you know that?" she asked.

"Ah! It was a guess," Mr. Quayle admitted. "But an informed one. Your husband blamed Lady Rosaline for the failure of that last disastrous showing in Paris," he explained, "but that was not the whole truth. You see, I have read some of the reviews, and, as far as I can tell, there was no shortage of ladies and gentlemen of the press eager for him to succeed. Not entirely on his own merits, of course, but for the drama of Lady Rosaline's tame artist breaking his chains at last." Mr. Quayle chuckled. "Their verdict, however, was all much the same—disappointment. His brushwork was unsteady, not the characteristic sharp lines he was known for, and the images themselves lacked the usual verisimilitude. The paintings were more impressionistic. One reviewer used the term *myopic*, which I found unintentionally suggestive, and theorized that Léger might have taken a belated, late-career turn toward impressionism."

Mr. Quayle glanced around. Everyone, even the Countess, was hanging on his every word, although Herr Darvas was making a good show of nonchalance. The old Hungarian's mind was racing, gauging the angles. Like Quayle, Darvas was thinking three or four steps ahead. A dangerous man, Quayle realized, and the one he most needed to talk.

"Fanny informed me, however, that Monsieur Léger's views on impressionism were regressive and vitriolic at best, and that such a turn was highly unlikely. No!" Mr. Quayle's voice rang out like a shot. "I propose that there is a far more likely explanation. Jean-Paul Léger was, as he had always done, painting what he saw precisely as he saw it, providing a realistic depiction of a world quite literally slipping away from him. But if I'm right, how to explain his more recent paintings, the ones he's been selling these past few days?"

"Well?" Márta demanded. "If you're so clever, how do you explain it?"

Mr. Quayle smiled dangerously. "I simply remembered what you yourself have been so keen to remind us, Fräulein: that there is *another* artist living under the Léger's roof, one with equal, if less celebrated, talents. Someone who could complete her husband's unfinished works, perhaps even improve upon them."

"Was that supposed to be a compliment, monsieur?" Madame Léger asked. "If so, then it is in poor taste."

"Perhaps," Mr. Quayle said. "But it is true, nonetheless. You have taken great pains, madame, to insist that you only recently started painting again. You claimed that the Count encouraged you, but—"

"Hah!" Countess Scarlioni laughed. "Encouraged you? He was using you!"

"I know that," Madame Léger snapped. "I'm not a fool!"

"No, Madame Léger, you're not a fool. But you have been painting again for quite some time now, and you've become rather good at mimicking your husband's style."

"I may not be a fool in your estimation, Monsieur Quayle,

but you must think my husband a very great one indeed not to have noticed."

"On the contrary, madame, it is you who thinks your husband a very great fool, and in this, at least, you are right." Mr. Quayle shrugged. "I'll admit that I wasn't sure, at first, how much he knew or suspected, but then I saw his face the other day while people were complimenting his latest work. That was not the face of a man swallowing his pride, and that's when I knew for sure. Monsieur Léger had no idea that you had been...*touching up* his pieces, and he still doesn't, unless I miss my guess."

Mr. Quayle almost felt sorry for the misanthropic old artist. His hour of vindication had come, and he was being praised, at last, solely on his own merits, unaware that those merits were, in fact, his wife's. That would be a bitter pill to swallow, but after all the years of misery Jean-Paul had subjected her to, Mr. Quayle could not find it in himself to begrudge Anne-Marie Léger her little revenge. Jean-Paul had robbed her of her identity as an artist, and now, in a manner of speaking, she had returned the favor. Justice was seldom so pleasingly symmetrical.

"I suppose he wouldn't be able to see the difference anymore between his work and yours," Quayle resumed, "not unless he was looking closely. And I doubt he is aware that you have been making use of his studio. Why would he be? After all, he spends all his time away, and, besides, you have been exquisitely careful, madame."

Mr. Quayle took a deep breath. He had been on reasonably steady ground thus far, but now it was time to take a leap and play his final card. Much depended upon how the others reacted.

"Of course, Madame Léger," Mr. Quayle said, "if you can mimic one style, then why not mimic another? And another? And another? If you cannot be acknowledged as one of the greatest artists of your generation, why not get paid to be its greatest forger?"

Madame Léger scoffed. "Are you suggesting that I somehow forged Rosaline's entire collection without my husband noticing? Don't be absurd!"

"Not at all," Mr. Quayle assured her. "That, as you say, would be absurd. No! Given the number of forgeries involved, I'd estimate that it likely took dozens of artists, each doing a few pieces here and there. But you are responsible for some of them, encouraged and recruited, no doubt, by your good friend Márta."

"Ah!" Márta sneered. "I was wondering where I came in!"

"Don't worry." Mr. Quayle was unperturbed by her scorn. "I hadn't forgotten you, either of you. You see, the problem for you and your father is that even if the police continue to believe that Léger is the forger, sooner or later, they're going to ask themselves how he managed to steal and replace so many paintings." He glanced over at Darvas, but hidden behind his beard, the old man was inscrutable. His daughter less so.

"It's absurd, really," Mr. Quayle continued. "Even the Countess managed to work it out. And once the police do, it's only a matter of time before they realize that there's only one person who could have organized a theft and forgery ring on this scale. The same person who, since the beginning, has been eager—desperate even—to take custody of the collection."

Mr. Quayle leaned back and folded his hands calmly in his lap. He had said what needed to be said. The gauntlet had been thrown. All that remained was to see whether or not Darvas would pick it up. The Hungarian would be taking a risk either way, but Quayle had already taken a risk himself in showing his cards so soon, and he hoped his display of trust would play a part in Darvas' calculations.

A RATHER DASTARDLY DEATH

Immediately, Márta and her father erupted into a hushed, urgent conversation in their native German. The words flew swift and fast, almost too quick to catch. Márta was unconvinced, of course. She had been glaring daggers at Mr. Quayle since he arrived and had only grown more incensed with each word out of his mouth, but Herr Darvas was calmer and more deliberate.

After over a minute of this frantic back and forth, while the others just sat and watched, Mr. Quayle cleared his throat delicately. "If I might interject," he said. "I feel that I ought to mention that I *am* somewhat fluent in German—a souvenir from the War, much like my barely passable French."

Márta's mouth dropped open in surprised, angry suspicion, unappeased by Mr. Quayle's disarmingly innocent smile, but Herr Darvas recovered himself almost instantly.

"Bravo, Herr Quayle," he said. "Bravo! You are, indeed, a most clever young man."

It was an unnecessary piece of flattery, offered more as a test than anything else, and Quayle waved it aside easily. He would not be distracted by such trifles, not when his object was in sight.

Herr Darvas accepted Quayle's response in the spirit it had been given and granted Quayle a nod of appreciation as though from a past master to a promising student. "I applaud your ingenuity, sir," he said. "But I see no reason why I should speak with you. As I have already explained to the Countess when she burst in here waving her pistol around, I am not a man to be moved by threats."

"I assure you, Herr Darvas, that I mean you and your daughter no harm, and I have no intention of threatening you."

Márta laughed bitterly at that and opened her mouth to denounce Quayle, but her father waved her into silence, and she reluctantly obeyed.

"You claim that you mean us no harm, Herr Quayle," he said. "But you have spent the past fifteen minutes wielding your knowledge and your suspicions like a knife, slicing hither and thither to see who bleeds. So, tell me, please, how am I to trust such a man?"

"Because," Mr. Quayle replied, "I am not interested in the thefts or the forgeries, and never have been. To the police, they are important, but to me, they are purely incidental. All I care about are the murders, and I believe that you and your daughter can help in that regard."

"And if we do?" Herr Darvas wondered. "What then?"

"Then, I, in turn, will help you," Mr. Quayle said, spreading his hands wide, "as much as I am able without, of course, breaking any laws."

"Of course," Herr Darvas agreed.

"So, do we have a deal?"

"Da." Herr Darvas nodded reluctantly. "We have a deal."

30

LA CHIMÈRE

Despite his agreement, Herr Darvas was in no immediate hurry to begin his story. Either unaware or deliberately uncaring of his captive audience—one of whom was still armed with a pistol—he made a show of patting his pockets before removing and then slowly and methodically lighting his pipe.

Watching the routine, Mr. Quayle fought the urge to grin. Darvas was a clever old fox and was using his time wisely—picking and choosing his truths. Guile and tactics. Quayle doubted he would learn anything from the Hungarian that Darvas did not intend to reveal, but that could be useful in and of itself, and thankfully Márta was far less careful.

After nearly a minute, Darvas completed his preparations and began to explain, at least in part, his role in events. "As you suspected," he said in a dry, academic voice, as if he was addressing a conference of his peers, "I did, indeed, facilitate the various thefts and forgeries surrounding Lady Rosaline's estate. It was a simple enough scheme once it was put into place but, as I am sure you can appreciate, Mr. Quayle, the devil is in the details."

"That has been my experience as well," Quayle agreed.

"Genuine masterpieces were loaned to my museum," Darvas explained, "and, occasionally, a few forgeries were returned in their place. Márta used her gallery connections to locate artists and clients, and I arranged a few discreet auctions."

"As you say," Mr. Quayle replied, "a simple enough plan, provided one remains cautious and doesn't become too greedy. And yet there seems to have been more than the *occasional* forgery slipped into the collection. Indeed, the numbers involved strike me as being distinctly incautious, not to say reckless, which I find curious, Herr Darvas, since you do not appear to be an incautious man."

"Certainly not!" Herr Darvas was visibly affronted by the notion. "I consider myself a man of prudence and temperance in all things. That is how I have survived and thrived as long as I have. But you see, contrary to all appearances, I am neither the organizer nor the instigator of this particular scheme. Like so many of us, I merely played my part."

"I see." Mr. Quayle was pleased as another piece slotted into place.

"What's that supposed to mean?" Countess Scarlioni demanded. "If you weren't in charge, then who?" She was not the only one desperate for an answer. Fanny was leaning forward, hanging on every word, and Madame Léger could not entirely hide her curiosity. Mr. Quayle glanced from them to Darvas pointedly. It was the Hungarian's revelation to share.

"Why, it was Lady Rosaline, of course," Darvas answered. "Who else could it be?"

"What?"

"But why would Rosaline—"

"She needed money desperately," Darvas replied, cutting through Fanny and the Countess' protests. "But when I offered to help sell a few pieces of her collection, she refused absolutely. There was nothing, Rosaline told me, that she treasured more than her reputation."

"Her reputation?" the Countess asked. "What reputation? She was a...well...far be it for me to speak ill of the dead, but we all know what Rosaline was."

"Just so." Herr Darvas nodded. "Just so. We all knew her reputation: Lady Rosaline Barrett De Marchi—the Widow of Treville-sur-Mer—known far and wide for her scandals, her wealth, and her art. But take away the wealth and the art, and all that remains is the *scandal*. After all, while a wealthy, eccentric, cultured widow with a scandalous past is allowed to be a figure of romance, a *poor* widow with that same past is just another old whore—an actress who married above her station. And that is what she feared above all else: to be reduced to her scandals, to be diminished."

"But she still needed the money," Mr. Quayle prompted. "I understand her debts were extensive."

"Do you?" Herr Darvas puffed on his pipe thoughtfully. "I wonder how you came to that understanding?" Mr. Quayle offered a minute shrug in place of an answer. Darvas was more than clever enough to guess. "Oh, yes," he said. "Rosaline needed the money all right. So, in the end, after much deliberation, she made a counteroffer. Rosaline had decided to sell her collection, after all, but only on the condition that no one knew. As far as the world at large was concerned, she was to remain as rich and her collection as vast as ever. And, to my surprise, it worked!"

The Countess, Fanny, and, surprisingly, Madam Léger were all visibly shocked by this revelation, but Mr. Quayle remained unperturbed.

"Thank you, Herr Darvas, for your honesty," he said with a grateful nod. Not that Mr. Quayle believed for a moment that Darvas had shared all he knew or guessed. "Your story explains a great deal, but not how Lady Rosaline's Bernini statuette was stolen or how it found its way into the Léger's studio. Although this, no doubt, is where our captor, Countess Scarlioni, reenters the narrative."

All eyes turn to the Countess, who glared defiantly at all and sundry before relenting ever so slightly. "How do I know I can trust you?" she asked.

"You don't," he replied honestly. "None of us do, but may I remind you, Countess, that you are the only one here with a gun."

"Mmm." The Countess bit her lip, wavering for a moment, but she was not by nature an indecisive person. "Yes, alright," she relented. "Of course, we stole the statuette! But we never murdered anyone I swear."

"I never said you did," Mr. Quayle replied. "But I'm sure we're all agog to hear how you managed to steal the statuette out from under everyone's noses."

"Haven't you worked that out?" the Countess sneered.

"Mostly." Quayle was unruffled by her hostility. "But I'm less clear on what happened afterwards."

The Countess sighed. "It all started so well," she said, each word a lament. "Our opening moves ran like clockwork. First, we carefully cultivated our alibis, befriending Arthur and the others. Then, that night, when everyone was at their most distracted, I slipped out of the Billiards Room and made my way to the statuette. Lady Rosaline had proudly shown it to us during an earlier visit. We gambled, correctly, that when the time came, no one would pay any attention to me, not when Arthur, of all people, was having such a run of luck at cards. It was a risk, of course, but—"

"You had done it before," Mr. Quayle finished, "in Paris, I believe."

"And in Stockholm, Prague, and Vienna," the Countess admitted. "With minor variations each time. We were nearly caught in Prague, but after that we learned to pick our witnesses with greater care. No one saw me leave that night; no one saw me return, and no one saw me secrete the statuette into a hidden compartment in the poker box, designed for just such a purpose."

"Bravo!" Mr. Quayle applauded. "You succeeded brilliantly, and no one was any the wiser. But what happened then, Countess?"

"Then it all went wrong," she answered. "You found Rosaline's body, and then, suddenly, the police were *everywhere*. In the chaos, we were forced to improvise and had no choice but to leave the box, hoping it wouldn't be noticed. But when we returned, it had disappeared along with the statuette inside." She winced. "I'm ashamed to say we panicked, Francesco more than me, and fled, claiming diplomatic immunity. That was a mistake, I realized soon enough, but there was no turning back. We were trapped." She shook her head in disgust. "But I swear we have no idea who took the box or how the statuette ended up in the Léger's studio. Is that what you said?"

"Yes. The police found it less than an hour ago, but I would like to return, if I may, to the night of the murder. Never mind how you managed to get there. When you stole the statuette, was there any sign of Lady Rosaline?"

"No. There was no one there. The room was deserted."

"But you were not quite as unseen as you believed, were you? That's what brought you here. An anonymous letter, you said? A blackmail letter, perhaps? And a summons to a secret meeting from which your husband never returned."

"Yes," the Countess spat. "Sent by *her*." She pointed her gun like an accusing finger directly at Márta.

"I didn't kill him," that unfortunate young woman protested. "I didn't kill anyone!"

"But you *did* see the Countess that night." It was not a

question. "And you *did* attempt to blackmail her and the Count."

Mr. Quayle's gaze was as unerring as the gun. Herr Darvas had been a match for him, but Márta was another matter. Strong and bitter and so very angry, she had not yet learned the art of subtlety, of being inscrutable when needed. Glancing at her father, she received a short, decisive nod, along with a pointed stare. She was being tested, Mr. Quayle thought, to see if she could handle herself under pressure and if she, too, could pick her truths with care.

"Yes," Márta admitted. "I saw the Countess that night."

"*We* saw the Countess," Madame Léger corrected. "Both of us did."

"Anne!" Márta protested.

"It's alright," Madame Léger insisted. "Monsieur Quayle and I understand each other quite well, I think, and I have no doubt that he'll learn the truth eventually by hook or by crook. At least this way, it'll be over quicker."

"Merci, madame."

"Please, don't thank me, monsieur," Madame Léger said. "As I said, I just want this to be over." She looked tired and drained. Her morning had been quite eventful already, full of ups and downs, and she was approaching the end of her rope.

"After my husband made a fool of himself in front of everyone," Madame Léger said, her bitterness sharp even in her exhaustion, "I went inside and found some dark corner of the collection where I could be alone to compose myself. After a while, don't ask me how long, Márta found me and convinced me to hold my head up and return to the party. As you can imagine, that took some persuading, but I do have some practice in maintaining my dignity."

"On the way back, though," Márta said, taking up the story, "we heard voices coming from one of the courtyards—angry voices."

"Did you recognize them?"

"One of them was Rosaline. I'm sure of that." Márta frowned. "But the other..."

"Was it a man or a woman?"

"It was Vivi," Madame Léger said, and there was no room for doubt in her voice. "I'm sure of it. I couldn't hear the words, but she was furious."

"I see."

"We weren't the only ones listening," Márta added. "He was there too."

"He?"

"My husband," Madame Léger said. "Jean-Paul was lurking there in the dark. I doubt he saw us, but we saw him."

"So what did you do?"

"*Do?*" Madame Léger snorted. "What could we do? I had no desire to interrupt Vivi and Rosaline's little tête-à-tête and even less desire to see my husband. So, we made our escape. Luckily, the collection was dark, and we were able to creep away unnoticed, and that was when we saw you." She turned to the Countess. "It was no more than a glimpse, but Márta and I both realized that you were carrying something unusually large under one arm, and I had the distinct sense that you did not want to be seen. We wouldn't have thought much of it—at least *I* wouldn't have—and we would never have followed you, except we were all heading for the main part of the house, and Rosaline's collection can be something of a maze even in broad daylight."

Mr. Quayle agreed. He had experienced that firsthand and was still annoyed with himself for losing his way that night. Much would have been different if he had only been in the Billiards Room at the right time.

"And when did you realize what she was carrying?"

"Once we left the collection and entered the West Wing,"

Márta explained. "That's when we knew for sure that she had Rosaline's Bernini under her arm."

"The pride and joy of the collection, stolen from under everyone's nose!" Madame Léger grinned. "And only we knew where it was!"

"Did you see her put it in the box?"

"Oh yes!" Impossibly, Madame Léger's grin seemed to stretch wider still. "The room was dark and smokey inside, but we had a good view from the doorway, and the Countess was too preoccupied with avoiding the poker players to take any notice of us."

Mr. Quayle spared Countess Scarlioni a glance. She looked furious and deeply embarrassed that she had been followed and spied upon so easily. The very same focus and distraction she had relied upon had blinded her as well.

"And then after the body was discovered," Quayle said, "you saw your chance, but how did you sneak the box off the grounds?"

"We didn't," Márta replied. "All we did was move it into the garden when no one was looking."

"I see. But why move it in the first place?"

Márta shrugged. "I didn't have a definitive plan at the time, but I reasoned that if the police found the box, then the Count and Countess would be arrested for theft and possibly murder. But if the police didn't find the box, I would be in an excellent position to make the Count suffer for hurting my friend." She reached over and took Madame Léger's hand protectively. "The next day, my father and I went to visit Raymond and offer our condolences. He was... not receptive, but our visit allowed me to retrieve the box from the garden."

"Mm." Mr. Quayle's eyes narrowed thoughtfully. "And were you aware of your daughter's activities, Herr Darvas?"

"No," Darvas replied evenly. "Márta did not inform me

until that morning when she produced the box from behind one of the hedges. She knew full well that I would not have approved." He shook his head, rather like a schoolmaster who has been forced to give low marks to a prized student. "I thought I had taught her better than to allow her personal feelings to affect business, but once the box and the statuette were in our possession, we could not return them to the police without answering some awkward questions."

"So instead, you made the best of a bad situation and hid the statuette, disposing of the box as soon as possible."

"Just so." Herr Darvas nodded.

"And that is when you found something, is it not?" Mr. Quayle asked. "A document of some kind, perhaps, or a letter?"

"Da!" Darvas nodded appreciatively. Unlike his flattery earlier, this time, Mr. Quayle thought the Hungarian's admiration was genuine. "When we were unpacking the statuette, we discovered a letter hidden in the base. You are aware, Mr. Quayle, of Lady Rosaline's habit of secreting documents in amongst her collection—behind paintings or in pedestals?"

"It has been mentioned, yes."

"Then you will understand why I was not particularly surprised by my discovery, and at the time, I had no reason to guess at the letter's deadly importance. It was only after the Count was murdered that I began to wonder. But how did *you* guess?"

"Before I found the body," Mr. Quayle said, "the first thing I noticed was that all the paintings in that room were askew. I wasn't sure why until I learned they were Lady Rosaline's favorite hiding places. So, someone had been looking for something that night, but had they found it? There was no way of knowing, not until Arthur told me of the state of the Scarlioni's yacht. Someone had assumed, as the police had, that the Count and Countess were in possession of the statuette and had ransacked the place looking for it, again to no avail. Leaving aside who was doing the searching—there were too many possibilities, including some of the people in this room—I was more concerned with the *what*. What were they so desperate to find?"

As he spoke, Quayle removed his glasses and began to gesture from time to time to emphasize a point. "I considered the possibility of a new will or a birth certificate, but a letter seemed the most likely. I knew that Lady Rosaline was in the habit of keeping all of her correspondence going back decades, and given her reputation, some of those letters must have contained information worth keeping secret. But worth killing over? That was another matter entirely."

Quayle returned his glasses to their proper perch and turned his attention to Márta. "Now," he said, leaning forward eagerly. "Earlier, you said that you wished to make the Count suffer for hurting your friend. How precisely did you intend to do that?"

"Precisely?" Márta blinked. "I didn't have a precise plan, not in the beginning. At first, I considered selling the Bernini back to him." Her lips twitched in a secret little smile so swift that Quayle almost missed it. "The irony of them purchasing their own stolen merchandise appealed to me."

"You little—" The Countess descended on Márta in a sudden fury with gun in hand. She had been embarrassed earlier, but now she was utterly enraged.

Márta, however, had come to the same conclusion as Quayle: that the Countess' pistol was more of a prop than a threat. So, she met the assault boldly, and within moments, the two women were locked in a struggle, exchanging blows and kicks, while the others looked on in shock.

One particularly fierce swipe jolted the Countess back and sent the gun flying across the room. Herr Darvas was on his feet instantly, but Mr. Quayle was faster.

"Excuse me," he said, plucking the pistol from the floor. "If I might have your attention, please?" His voice sliced neatly through the fracas before him, and Mr. Quayle waited patiently for the cries and blows to subside. "Excellent," he said once he had everyone's attention. "If you would all kindly your seats. Márta? Madame La Contessa?"

Mr. Quayle did not need to wave or brandish the pistol. That he was holding it was enough, and slowly, with great reluctance, the two combatants sat back down.

That done, Quayle popped open the chamber and carefully unloaded the revolver, handing the bullets with deliberate nonchalance to Fanny for safekeeping.

"Now, as you were saying?"

Shaken, Márta slowly resumed her story, admitting that before she could put her scheme into action, the Count had been found murdered.

"That put an end to all my plans," she said. "But then I thought of a better use for the statuette. Never mind the Count! Anne-Marie and I could finally deal with her husband once and for all!"

"So, you decided to frame him."

"It was perfect!" Márta said. "The police would have their murderer and their forger all rolled into one, and no one would take another look at the rest of us."

She looked so incredibly pleased with herself and with her own cunning, but Mr. Quayle was not nearly as impressed.

"It was, certainly, an inspired bit of improvisation," he allowed, "but hardly perfect. Indeed, if you hadn't tried so hard to make everyone suspect Léger, I might have overlooked you until it was too late."

Herr Darvas grunted in agreement. "*This*," he told his daughter, "is exactly why you don't mix personal with business. It makes you sloppy and leaves too many obvious motives lying around."

"And there are quite a few motives, aren't there?" Mr. Quayle asked.

"Meaning?"

"Well, Herr Darvas, you had your own plans for the statuette, I believe. Plans which nearly came to fruition."

"And what plans would those be?" The Hungarian was not giving an inch.

"I imagine they involved setting a little trap for the Count and Countess," Mr. Quayle said. "They were circling closer and closer, sniffing around your business for months. And then the Count started befriending Madame Léger, one of your prized forgers and one of the few who could name both you and your daughter personally. Hence the anonymous letters to the police and hence Lady Rosaline's sudden change of heart. Initially, she resisted Chief Inspector Tallier's overtures and with good reason. Her halls were full of forgeries, after all, but I imagine you persuaded her, Herr Darvas, to help set the bait of your trap. Tell me, Countess Scarlioni, why the Bernini? Her Ladyship's collection has quite a few objects that would have been easier to remove."

"One of our clients contacted us," the Countess said in growing realization, "and requested it specifically."

"There, you see!" Mr. Quayle spread his hands. "It all falls into place. And you must have been quite pleased that night, Márta, to catch the Countess in the act. Was that truly a coincidence, I wonder, or were you waiting to ambush her?" No one answered, but Quayle merely shrugged. "In either case," he said, "you had them in your grasp, and then you pushed. Such a shame."

"Do you have a point, Mr. Quayle?" Herr Darvas asked.

"Not as such. I'm merely crossing my t's and dotting my i's," he answered. "As I said earlier, the thefts are not, strictly speaking, my concern. However, I would very much like to see that letter you found, if I may?"

Herr Darvas was silent for a moment, stroking his beard in quiet contemplation. "I should like some assurances first," he said. "What exactly are you planning to do with the letter once you have it?"

"That rather depends on the content," Mr. Quayle replied. "But should it prove relevant, in all likelihood, the police would have to be informed."

"I see."

"May I remind you, Herr Darvas, that while I am working with the police and not for them, I will not withhold evidence, not in a murder inquiry. On the other hand, if you swear to me, Herr Darvas, that the letter fell from the base of the statuette, then that is what I will tell the police, and if they should take that to mean that I found it, then I will do nothing to correct them. Will that suffice?"

"It will."

"They may have other questions, however," Mr. Quayle warned.

Darvas waved his hand dismissively. "I have been in this business for over half a century, Mr. Quayle, and I have been questioned many times over the years but never arrested. Once upon a time, I was even known as La Chimère, although these days I have other people to do the heavy lifting—a veritable army, in fact. Gentlemen thieves and cat burglars like the Count and Countess here are shooting stars, flashes in the pan, but I am a professional. And I did so hope that my daughter would be one as well."

"Father!"

Herr Darvas ignored his daughter and slipped his hand into his left breast pocket. "Here you are," he said.

Mr. Quayle accepted the letter with a grateful smile, and as he read, he began, at long last, to understand. Poor Hollins, he thought to himself. These past few weeks must have been torture for him.

And poor, poor Fanny. What a choice she would have to make.

* * *

Mr. Quayle was wrong, however. In the end, there was no choice, not for Fanny. She read the letter carefully twice over with barely a flicker of emotion, aware all the while of the others watching her. Only Quayle knew Fanny well enough to notice the slight tightening of her back or the barest, tell-tale paleness in her face, but he kept such observations to himself.

When she was finished, Fanny handed the letter back to him, and then, with her head held high, she took her leave and did not look back. Her feet carried her, as if in a dream, along the corridor, down the three flights of stairs, and through the lobby, not stopping until she was outside the hotel.

The sun was shining brightly, and the streets of Treville-sur-Mer were alive with clamor and noise of cars and horses, street vendors, and passersby. It was a veritable, vibrant cacophony, but Fanny, trapped in her own little world, heard none of it. For her, there was nothing but the thundering in her heart and in her thoughts.

The letter itself might have been vaguely worded, but its meaning was abundantly clear. Many years ago, on the eve of her first marriage, a child had been born out of wedlock, and in her desperation, Lady Rosaline had turned to Lord Weatherford. He had somehow managed to spirit the child away and had solemnly promised to see to the newborn's safety and education.

Fanny was no one's fool, and she could connect the pieces as easily as Quayle no doubt had. Knowing what they knew of Weatherford's domestic arrangements, that newborn child could only be Hollins, Weatherford's protegee and ward.

Of course it was Hollins! Fanny cursed herself for her stupidity, for allowing herself to be tricked a second time. Joe had been trying so hard for months to worm his way into Lady Rosaline's circle and had been so pathetically grateful when Fanny herself had invited him as her guest. She should have known that there was something wrong there and then, but she had excused his behavior, even defended him to Aunt Constance. After all, the other artists, writers, and various hangers-on were all equally desperate for Lady Rosaline's attention and favor. Why should Hollins be any different?

And yet—

Fanny scowled, unable to shake the dire certainty that she should have known better. Hollins had acted so strangely after Lady Rosaline died, oddly shaken by the death of a woman he barely knew. But was that because she was his mother or because he had killed her himself?

Fanny couldn't be sure, but there had undoubtedly been a string of deaths surrounding Hollins of late. First, his guardian, Lord Weatherford, died soon after they quarreled, and then his presumed mother was murdered after she'd rejected and ignored him. Too many coincidences! Too many deaths! And Fanny was done making excuses.

Behind her, Mr. Quayle coughed. Fanny had no idea how long he had been standing there, but she was grateful for his forbearance.

"What do you want me to do?" he asked. This morning alone, she had seen him be by turns both gentle and cajoling, and harsh and demanding, but here and now, he was utterly stone-faced, divulging not even the minutest hint as to his own thoughts on the matter.

"Call the police," Fanny replied without hesitation.

"Are you quite certain?" Mr. Quayle asked. "You know what that will involve, and once we—"

"Call the police," Fanny repeated. "He lied to me and used

me to get close to Lady Rosaline. For that, I want him to suffer. I want to see him destroyed." There was no hesitation in her voice, no kindness.

"Very well." Mr. Quayle nodded. His eyes were hooded and his face unreadable, but at that moment, Fanny reminded him of no one so much as Lady Constance at her most vengeful. The family resemblance was sudden and startling. "I shall do my best," he said and meant it.

31

THE FINAL PIECE OF THE PUZZLE

Mr. Quayle was as good as his word, and despite any lingering, gnawing doubts, he had immediately contacted Chief Inspector Tallier and set the wheels of justice—or, perhaps, vengeance—in motion. Almost everyone, it seemed, suddenly shared in Fanny's utter conviction that Hollins was guilty. The letter, of course, was highly suggestive, as was the unavoidable fact that Hollins had kept his relationship with Lady Rosaline secret. But it was Fanny's testimony, her seething, unyielding certainty, which had ultimately swayed Tallier and the others.

Clutching her uncle's hand for support, she had unleashed a torrent of accusations, suspicions, and self-recriminations, as if determined to find evidence of guilt in Hollins' every move, every word, and every breath. Mr. Quayle understood, of course. Major Eatwell had betrayed her, so she had deliberately sought out his opposite in Hollins, and now he too had proved himself a liar at best and a murderer at worst. And in her present state, Fanny was all too ready to believe the worst.

Mr. Quayle was not so sure, however. Hollins was

undoubtedly a fool and a liar and was clearly involved in this business up to his neck, but there were still too many questions left unanswered. Fanny might be allowing her emotions to cloud her judgment, but he had no such difficulty, and it soon emerged that he was not the only one with doubts.

M. Jarre, the Juge d'Instruction, arrived later than the others and missed Fanny's bravura performance. Stiff, correct, and highly unimpressed, Jarre was clearly under a great deal of pressure to solve the case as quickly as possible and had no desire to indulge in any digressions or doubts.

"This is nothing more than a wild goose chase!" the Juge d'Instruction declared. "This Englishman of yours," he said, indicating Quayle with a sharp, accusing finger, "has you chasing down rabbit holes and making a fool of yourself. We can't even say for sure that Lord Weatherford *was* murdered! The medical examiner found no evidence of foul play of any kind."

"Because he wasn't looking for any, sir," Tallier murmured.

"And as for the rest of it?" Jarre said, ignoring him. "False identities? Illegitimate sons? Hidden letters?" The Judge shook his head. "Overromanticized claptrap! And even if—*if* —Monsieur Quayle is right about Hollins' identity, we have Léger in custody."

Tallier frowned, and Jarre pulled him aside, having been reminded of their audience. Fanny had retreated to her room soon after she gave her statement, and Lord Unsworth had followed after to provide what comfort he could, but Mr. Quayle was still there in the drawing room, eyeing the proceedings with interest.

"You've done good work, Tallier," Jarre said in a voice not quite low enough to escape Quayle's sharp ears. "Efficient, quick work. So, don't start making this any more complicated than it already is. Léger is our man, I'm sure of it. He has a temper and a long history of violence and petty brawling, able to intimidate men less than half his age. *Means*. Léger blamed Lady Rosaline for ruining his career and hated Count Scarlioni for having an affair with his wife. *Motive*. And he was seen in the villa stalking Lady Rosaline on the night of her murder. *Opportunity*. Everything else is a distraction."

"The forgeries—"

"—Are a distraction," Jarre declared. "I know you came out here to catch your little thief—La Chimère—but this is a murder investigation, and I have the Minister breathing down my neck, so unless you have any solid evidence to the contrary, please do me a favor and focus on the task at hand."

"I'm not saying that Léger isn't a person of interest or that he doesn't have a strong motive," Tallier protested. "All I'm saying is that we cannot ignore the recent revelations about Hollins. There are still too many unanswered questions. Surely, you must see that?"

"And we'll deal with them," Jarre replied evenly. "I promise. We'll even find this Hollins and ring some answers from him, but like it or not, the statuette was found in Léger's studio."

Listening, Mr. Quayle applauded Márta and Madame Léger. Their plan had been slapdash and faulty from the start, yet it appeared to have worked perfectly. Twice Quayle had opened his mouth to interject, and twice he had held his tongue. He had made Herr Darvas a promise, and the time had not yet come to break it. Besides, he had no evidence to offer, solid or otherwise, only concerns and doubts, which were only growing.

It seemed that every time Quayle peeled back another layer or revealed another secret, it simply led to another blind alley. Even when he had bestirred himself at last, all it had done was bring Fanny pain and send the police careening off after someone who might yet prove innocent. There were other irons in the fire, of course, but Quayle felt as if he'd been trailing behind for this entire case, groping and stumbling in the dark. Perhaps, he thought to himself, it was time to have a word with Lady Constance.

* * *

SLIPPING AWAY, Mr. Quayle found Lady Constance sitting on the veranda, knitting quietly and enjoying the fresh ocean breeze and the spellbinding view. Below, the waters were sparkling in the late afternoon sun as ships and yachts meandered about offshore, and birds swooped and dived overhead. Distracted first by his duties and then by the murders, Mr. Quayle had not been able to enjoy the beauty of the Riviera, but he took a moment to do so now, and for a minute or two Mr. Quayle and Lady Constance shared a companionable silence.

"Have they finished, then?" Lady Constance asked.

"I'm afraid not," Mr. Quayle said. "The police are still trying to decide whether they favor Léger or Hollins."

"The artist or the communist." Lady Constance scoffed. "They appear to be spoilt for choice."

"Indeed."

Lady Constance indicated the seat next to her with an imperiously gracious wave of her hand, and Mr. Quayle sat down with an appreciative nod. "And who do you favor?" she asked. "You must have some idea by now."

Quayle grimaced. "It's difficult to say..."

"Ah!" Lady Constance raised her eyebrows and favored Quayle with an appraising look. "Neither of them. Well, well, well. You think they're innocent, don't you?"

"Even if I did, there's no way of proving it."

"Spare me the diplomatic shillyshallying, Quayle," Lady Constance said. "You're not in Whitehall anymore. The truth is that you have doubts. I can see them written all over your face. And yet knowing that he might be innocent, you still allowed Fanny to turn in her young man."

"I am, of course, sympathetic to Fanny's distress, but the police did have the right to know, and Fanny did have the right to tell them." Mr. Quayle shrugged. "It was *her* decision, and I'm not even sure it was the wrong one."

"Oh, very honorable!" Lady Constance did not quite sneer this time. "But I know you better than that. You play the part of the diplomatic, efficient, honorable young man quite well, but you and I have spent the past few months working side by side to destroy my lousy cheat of a husband, so I know how your mind works. No, I can see the truth, even if you're hiding it from yourself."

"What truth is that, Lady Constance?"

"You're using Hollins as bait."

Mr. Quayle frowned and started to apologize, but Lady Constance shook her head.

"There's no need to apologize," she said. "Beneath your overdeveloped sense of duty and honor, Quayle, you're really nothing more than a clever, ruthless little bastard, and as far as I'm concerned, that's the only good reason for keeping you around. This family needs someone like you guarding the gates."

"I'm not sure I've ever been so insulted or so flattered in my life," he said.

"More diplomatic nonsense."

Caught, Mr. Quayle could only shake his head. "As it happens," he said once he'd recovered, "there was something else I wanted to discuss with you."

"Naturally." Lady Constance was unimpressed. "I didn't think you'd wandered onto the veranda by accident. But first, there's something I'd like to ask you."

"Your Ladyship?"

"I don't suppose you could tell me my son's whereabouts, could you?"

Mr. Quayle consulted his watch and made a quick mental calculation. "Arthur should be somewhere on the outskirts of Paris by now," he answered. "Assuming all has gone well."

"So, you've roped him into your little schemes as well. I thought as much."

"With respect, Lady Constance, he roped himself. And, as I explained to His Lordship, I thought this was the best way to keep him out of trouble."

"While allowing him to feel useful," she allowed an almost imperceptible smile.

"Exactly." Mr. Quayle nodded. "Although, I must point out that he is, in fact, being quite useful."

"If you say so." Lady Constance was unconvinced but didn't press any further. "And now, what was it you wished to speak of?"

"Ah, yes." Mr. Quayle chose his words with care. "I wondered if you could share a little of what you remember—"

"—About Rosaline?"

"For a start." Quayle nodded. "And about Lord Weatherford."

"And my brother?" she asked. It was a test, but Quayle was ready for her.

"Only if you deem it necessary," he replied. "But what I'm most interested in is the truth about General Alexander Montague Barrett."

Lady Constance placed her knitting needles on her lap with the sharp ends pointing towards Quayle. "What makes you think I know anything about General Montague Barrett?" she demanded, but her protest was merely pro forma, and Mr. Quayle was matter-of-fact in his reply.

"Whenever the General's name has been mentioned," he said, "you have been quick with a sneer and a pointed comment. Indeed, I've come to the opinion that you may have despised him even more than you did Rosaline, or are my eyes playing tricks on me?"

"No." Lady Constance shook her head. "They're not. Rest assured, Mr. Quayle, that you have been as infuriatingly perceptive as ever." Her gaze, usually stern and fierce, turned suddenly wistful, but no less unforgiving. "As far as I'm concerned," she said, "Alexander Montague Barrett was nothing more than a philanderer and a rogue, and no matter what that son of his, Raymond, insists, the general and his wife were both as bad as each other."

"And what makes you say that?"

"It's not my story," she replied, "and I never knew the half of it, but..."

And as Lady Constance began to explain the bits and pieces she remembered, the fragments of gossip and hearsay nearly thirty years old, Mr. Quayle's face slowly split into a genuine, if politely subtle, grin.

At last.

All the pieces fit at last. Until now, Quayle had only suspected, but now he knew for certain who had killed Lady Rosaline and the Count, who had attacked Carrodus, and even before all that, who had murdered Lord Weatherford. And he thought he knew why. The only trouble was that Mr. Quayle was still unsure if it was actually possible.

For that, he still needed Arthur.

32

AN UNFORTUNATE FAMILY RESEMBLANCE

They had done it! They had actually done it! They had beaten the Blue Train! Arthur could barely believe his eyes, but as Dabney slammed on the brakes and the Rover Light Six came to a halt across the street from the Gare du Nord train station, he could only laugh and grin, and rub his tired, red-rimmed eyes.

It had been touch-and-go most of the way, not only because of the seemingly endless near-death experiences—Arthur had lost count at twenty or thereabouts—but because of the country roads and river crossings. A heavy fog had descended as they approached Paris, and thanks to Arthur's utter failure as a navigator and his inability to read a map properly in any language, they had gotten lost twice along the way. But it had been Paris itself that saved them in the end, just as Dabney had predicted months earlier.

All the time they had lost, the mistakes they'd made, were washed away. While the Blue Train had wasted forty-five wonderous minutes circling around the outskirts of the city, Arthur and Dabney had driven straight through the heart of the metropole to arrive at the station with twenty minutes to spare.

Dabney himself was simply ecstatic with joy, whooping and hollering his triumph for all to hear. More than a few passersby were glaring at them, but Arthur paid them no heed. He and Dabney had earned their moment after spending nearly twenty-four hours on the road without food or sleep.

Belatedly, Arthur remembered that they hadn't been racing the train for a laugh. Their errand was in deadly earnest. He needed to find a phone and contact Quayle. The man had been right! By the skin of his teeth, but right all the same!

"Excusez-moi?"

Arthur blinked and found a pair of French policemen glaring down at him and Dabney. "Oui?" he asked blearily.

"May we see your papers, s'il vous plaît?"

"My...my papers?" Arthur frowned and patted his pockets absently as his mind struggled to understand what was happening. "Why do you need to see my papers?"

"There have been reports, monsieur," one of the policemen replied, "of two Englishmen driving recklessly and with great haste from Treville-sur-Mer."

"And we just received word," the other added, "that a suspected murderer, one Monsieur Joseph Hollins, has disappeared from that same town and is on the run. And so, again, if you would please hand over your papers?"

It was a command, and Arthur was thrilled to obey. This time the countrywide manhunt wasn't after him at all. How marvelous! Except—

"I appear to have left my papers in Treville-sur-Mer," he said. "But my name is Arthur Druce, and this is George Dabney. We're actually assisting in that very murder investigation, so if you would just let us—"

But try as he might, the policemen wouldn't believe him, and the more Arthur tried to explain, the more suspicious they became until they finally arrested him and Dabney and dragged them away in handcuffs, while behind them, the Blue Train pulled into the station.

* * *

"What is the meaning of this?" Lady Constance demanded. "How dare you arrest my son?"

Her Ladyship was in full fury, angrier than she had been in months. Not since her husband's betrayal and the rage and vengeance which followed afterwards had Mr. Quayle seen her quite so incensed. Her voice echoed through the drawing room, gathering steam as it reverberated off the high ceilings, and sent Chief Inspector Tallier and Judge Jarre both scrambling back under the onslaught. Her gaze was worse, though. Piercing and unblinkingly sharp, she skewered both men, demanding answers. And Quayle could see the moment they realized that she was truly a force to be reckoned with. Tallier had dealt with her before, but only in a brief, minor capacity. Now, she was on the warpath.

There was a brief, silent argument, which Tallier won, leaving M. Jarre, the renowned jurist and magistrate, to face the angry Englishwoman alone.

"We apologize, Lady Constance," he said, holding out his hands placatingly. "The Paris police mistook him for this Monsieur Hollins, but—"

"My son looks nothing like him!" Lady Constance interjected. "Bloody foreigners! Why can't they tell a proper Englishman from that...that...Communist!"

Wincing, Mr. Quayle removed his glasses and rubbed the bridge of his nose awkwardly. The irony of Lady Constance, herself a foreigner in a foreign land and one, moreover, who regularly failed to distinguish the French from the Italians, the Spanish, or any of a dozen other nationalities, accusing Jarre of being unable to tell two Englishmen apart was not lost on Quayle.

"As I said," the Judge tried again, "we do apologize for the mistake. However, your son and this Monsieur Dabney were acting most suspiciously, and during their drive from Treville-sur-Mer to Paris, they committed a number of traffic violations and misdemeanors and angered quite a few of our rural citizens."

"Even so, I—"

"More importantly," M. Jarre continued in perhaps the bravest moment of his life, "they both claimed to be acting on Monsieur Quayle's instructions and were supposedly," he sighed "helping to solve a murder. God save us from amateurs!" He turned to his colleague. "Did you know anything about this, Chief Inspector?" he asked.

"Non." Tallier glanced at Quayle but shook his head. "Not a thing."

"Then, Monsieur Quayle," the Judge said, "I invite you to explain yourself."

"Well, you see." Mr. Quayle cleared his throat. "It's all straightforward. Arthur and Dabney have been attempting to solve a little mystery for me."

"That's not their concern," Jarre replied. "And neither is it yours."

"Perhaps not strictly speaking," Mr. Quayle admitted. "But the family have made it their concern, and therefore it is, in fact, mine. So tell me, before they were arrested, had Arthur and Dabney managed to beat the Blue Train to Paris? This is important."

"What does that have to do with anything?" Jarre demanded, but behind him, Chief Inspector Tallier was frowning thoughtfully.

"Earlier this year," Quayle explained, "for a bet, Dabney attempted to race the Blue Train to Paris. A fact which everyone in Lady Rosaline's circle was well-aware of—"

"Of course, they are! It was in all the newspapers," Jarre revealed.

"Was it?" Mr. Quayle fiddled with his glasses for a moment, turning them over in his hands as he thought. "In any case, Dabney's little escapade started giving me ideas, just as they must have given someone else ideas."

"Nonsense! Another wild goose chase," M. Jarre muttered in disgust. But at the same time, Tallier stepped forward with a question on his lips.

"What ideas?" he asked.

"I've been trying to work out if and how it might be possible for someone to have been in Treville-sur-Mer during the afternoon when the Blue Train arrived and yet somehow on the following morning contrive to catch the very same Blue Train in Paris going in the opposite direction."

"You think they might have done what Dabney failed to do? Drive all night and outpace the train?"

"Possibly. So, I ask again: before Arthur and Dabney were arrested, did they beat the train?"

"Oui," Chief Inspector Tallier nodded. "They were arrested at the station."

"Mmm." Mr. Quayle leaned back in satisfaction. "Excellent!"

"You think you know who it is, don't you?" Tallier asked. "You let me chase after Léger while all the time you had someone else in mind. But who?"

"Ahem." Before the Chief Inspector could finish the question, however, he was interrupted by a delicately polite little cough.

Lord Unsworth's butler, Perkins, was standing unobtrusively in the doorway. "Forgive me, gentlemen," he said. "But a telegram has arrived for you, Mr. Quayle. From England."

"Excellent!" Quayle all but leapt across the room, accepted the telegram, and hurriedly read through the missive. It was from Inspector Wintle of the Thornburgh Constabulary, who had kindly made some inquiries on Quayle's behalf.

Well, well, well. Calmly folding the telegram and placing it in his pocket, Mr. Quayle smiled. Now, at last, he had all the pieces in his possession. His mood, however, was not to last.

Perkins had remained at his side throughout and was regarding Quayle with an ominously worried expression.

"What is it, Perkins?" Quayle asked. "Is there something else?"

"Well, sir," the butler replied. "A letter arrived for Miss Fanny about twenty minutes ago."

"Oh? Who from?"

"I'm not sure, but I believe it was from the gentleman you've been looking for."

"Mr. Hollins?" Mr. Quayle stared at Perkins growing alarm. "Has Fanny seen the letter?"

"Her maid took it up a few minutes ago," Perkins replied.

"I see."

It was at that moment that Lord Unsworth came charging into the room in a state of high agitation.

"I only left her for a few minutes," he announced. "Just a few minutes."

"What are you talking about, Eddy?" Lady Constance demanded. "Left who?"

A lead weight pressed down on Mr. Quayle's stomach. *She wouldn't have, would she?* Surely, Fanny had enough of a head on her shoulders not to—

"It's Fanny," His Lordship said. "I only stepped away for a

few minutes, and when I returned, her room was empty, and the window was open."

Mr. Quayle clenched his eyelids tight as a pounding headache erupted behind his eyes. Sometimes, just sometimes, the Unsworth family resemblance was unfortunately and inconveniently strong.

"Forgive me, Your Lordship, but you don't mean that she—"

"I'm afraid so." Lord Unsworth looked utterly stricken. "It appears that Fanny has decided to emulate Arthur and abscond out the window. But I don't understand where she could have possibly gone."

"To see Hollins," Mr. Quayle replied. "No doubt, to hear his side of the story. And I'm afraid that means she's now in great danger."

PART V

OLD SINS, LONG SHADOWS

33

ONE LAST CHANCE

Slipping on board the northbound Blue Train a little after 7:30, Fanny found Hollins in the salon car, exactly where his note said he would be, wearing a waiter's uniform and a patently ridiculous false moustache. He looked quite the character, like something out of one of his more absurd plays. His French, however, was excellent, as was his accent—Swiss by the sound of it.

"Quite the disguise, eh?" he whispered as he came to her table, looking far too pleased with himself for a liar and a murderer.

"The uniform suits you," Fanny hissed. "Although, I doubt that mustache would fool anyone for long."

"You'd be surprised," Hollins said, and a quick glance around the carriage revealed several bearded and mustachioed concoctions, all waxed and shaped to within an inch of their lives. "I was a waiter on this train for almost a year," he explained. "One of my first jobs after I quit the newspaper, and as you can see, I still have a few friends on board who were willing to help."

"But I wonder if they know they're helping a murderer?" Fanny said.

Hollins' eyes widened. "Keep your voice down! Do you want to see me hang?"

"I haven't decided yet."

"But you came," Hollins stared at her like a lost child. "I thought you—"

"I know what you thought," Fanny said sharply. "But I will not be taken advantage of, nor will I be taken for granted. I am here because I decided, against my own better judgment, to give you a chance—one chance—to prove your innocence. I felt I owed you that much. But if you fail to convince me, I won't hesitate to turn you in to the police. I've already done it once today, and I will do so again. Do you understand me?"

Hollins stared into her face for a long, interminable moment, searching for any sign that she might relent, for even the slightest crack in her armor, but Fanny met his eyes coldly, as immutable and impassive as stone.

"Yes," he said at last. "I understand."

"Good, then I suggest we find somewhere a little more private."

"Cabin number 7 is usually kept empty," Hollins revealed. "And the porter is an old friend."

"Very well."

* * *

THE CABIN WAS PLUSH with wooden paneling, all the latest innovations and resplendent in the warm glow of the electric lamps, but Fanny ignored the luxury. At that moment, all that mattered was Hollins.

"Well?" she demanded. "Are you going to say anything?"

"Yes," Hollins replied. "Yes, of course."

And so, he began to talk, stumbling awkwardly over his

words and watching all the while to see if anything he said was having the slightest effect. It was a pathetic, desperate sight, but Fanny remained utterly unmoved. She had learned from the best.

"I suppose it all starts with Lord Weatherford. He raised me as his ward, you know, and I—" Hollins sighed and rubbed his forehead tiredly. "Forgive me, I've told you all this," he said. "I don't know why I—"

"Actually," Fanny pointed out in a tone not only reminiscent of her uncle's fussy exactitude but also steeped, almost dripping, with her aunt's chilliest disdain, "I believe it was Sir Julius who mentioned it."

Hollins grimaced. "Yes, I was keeping that rather quiet, wasn't I?"

"It's hardly the only thing you've been keeping quiet."

"No," Hollins agreed, "it isn't."

Impatient, Fanny raised her eyebrows pointedly, silently commanding him to continue, and after half a minute or so, Hollins obeyed.

"Weatherford made for a...distant guardian," he said. "And I spent my childhood being moved around from school to school. One in England, one in France, another in Switzerland..."

"Is this relevant?" Fanny demanded so abruptly that Hollins could only blink in shock. Aunt Constance would have been proud.

"No, I-I suppose not..." Hollins stared at her like a wounded bird with such a strange look of betrayal on his face, as if, despite everything, he couldn't quite believe that she would speak to him like this. But that only made her angrier. How dare he expect sympathy? She was the one who had been betrayed, not him.

"I never knew who my parents were," Hollins said, hastily resuming his story. Whatever he had seen in her eyes, Hollins appeared to have received the message loud and clear. "No one would ever tell me. Oh, there were rumors, of course, that Weatherford was my father, but he would never say anything one way or the other. It took me years to work up the courage to ask him directly." Hollins looked utterly defeated. "Even then, he still wouldn't tell me."

"Your falling out!" Fanny realized. "So, that's why you ran."

"Yes." Hollins folded in on himself, shying away from Fanny's gaze. "That's why I ran away," he said. "But I did more than that. I destroyed his dream. He had plans for me, you see. High hopes and high expectations! Everyone knew he was grooming me to take over the *London Chronicle*, but that was only the beginning. He wanted me to enter politics one day and maybe become an MP for some godforsaken corner of the country. The old man had it all mapped out. So instead, I threw his job back in his face, fled to the Continent, and became a socialist."

"Just to spite him?"

Hollins nodded shakily, but there was a perverse sort of pride lurking in the corner of his eyes. "Just to spite him," he agreed.

This was a side to Hollins that Fanny had never seen before, never even glimpsed, and it gave meaning to the pitiful earnestness of his play and, indeed, of his politics. It did not, however, mean that he was innocent or that she forgave him.

"I was still convinced that Weatherford was my father, even if the old bastard wouldn't admit it, and I already suspected that Lady Rosaline was my mother."

"Did you? Why?"

"Oh, that was no great secret!" Hollins barked a short humorless laugh. "Weatherford's devotion to her was legendary in certain circles, and there was always someone willing to whisper the choicest rumors in my ear."

"Gossip and innuendo?" Fanny was disappointed. "That was your reasoning?"

"Part of it," he admitted. "And then there were the letters."

"Letters?" Fanny couldn't resist the jolt of surprised excitement that tore through her. "What letters?"

"Rosaline's letters," Hollins explained. "Weatherford kept all of them going back decades. I'd found them when I was still a child on one of my rare visits to the estate, and I devoured them in secret. They were both quite cagey, of course, and I was rather young at the time, but I understood enough. More than enough." He sighed. "There was one letter, however, that I could never get my hands on, one that I was sure would finally make everything clear. The smoking gun, if you will. I knew it existed, because I'd seen it, but Weatherford didn't keep it with the others. Instead, he had it with him at all times, like a talisman. I would see him, occasionally, when he thought no one was looking, reading and re-reading the blasted thing with tears in his eyes."

"Did you tell him all this?" Fanny asked. "When you confronted him, did you tell him that you'd read the letters?"

"I did more than that," Hollins said proudly. "I quoted bloody passages at him, but still, he wouldn't tell me the truth. He called me a 'foolish boy' and said I understood nothing. That's when I demanded to read the letter, the one he kept hidden." Hollins closed his eyes and shuddered. "I've never seen him so angry. Sometimes I think he would have disowned me for that, if I hadn't all but disowned myself."

"So, what did you do then?"

"This and that." Hollins shrugged. "I was a porter for a while, waited tables in Paris, and I even had a job on the Blue Train for a time."

"And wrote your play?"

"Yes. I wrote a few articles for a socialist journal, one I

knew Weatherford would see, and the editor put me in touch with an avant-garde theater troupe. We toured Europe for a year or two, and, yes, I wrote my play. You see, Fanny, I've never lied to you about who I am or what I've been doing. I just...didn't tell you everything."

"That *is* lying," Fanny snapped before taking a few deep breaths to calm herself. "So, how did you end up here in Treville-sur-Mer, nipping at your mother's heels?"

"I wasn't—" Hollins caught himself at the last minute, brought up short by the look in her eyes. Fanny was in no mood for prevarication or excuses. "There were rumors," he said, "about Lady Rosaline's memoirs. Even in my self-imposed exile amongst the communists and rabble-rousers, I made sure to keep an eye on my parents, and if she was willing to talk, I thought, maybe Weatherford would be as well. So, I returned to England and went to confront him one last time, but I was too late. He had just left for London, summoned to France by who else but Lady Rosaline."

"He died en route," Fanny said.

"Yes, I know." Hollins sighed deeply. "I was there."

"You were there?" Fanny was incredulous. "On the train?"

"I'd just missed him at the hall, so I hurried to London myself. Some of my friends were still working on the Blue Train, and they smuggled me on board as one of the waiters. I didn't really have a plan, but I thought—I hoped—that once we reached Treville-sur-Mer, I could confront both my parents at once. But then Weatherford, he...he...started choking and..." Hollins shuddered. "It was horrible."

"So you were in the dining car when he died?" Fanny gaped at him in shock.

"I'm the one who served him his soup." Hollins shook his head darkly. "His last meal."

"I see." Fanny's lips tightened in a thin, suspicious line. "I don't suppose you have any proof of your claims?"

"I do!" Hollins reached into his pocket eagerly, and Fanny flinched, half expecting him to produce a knife or a gun. Instead, it was an old, yellowing letter, and a startled gasp escaped Fanny's lips.

"Is that—"

"Rosaline's letter to Weatherford?" Hollins nodded. "The very same."

"How did you come by that?"

"I took it from his pocket."

"When he died?" Fanny stared at Hollins, aghast. "You stole it from your dying father's pocket?"

"I did." There was no remorse on Hollins' face. "I held his hand while he died and did what I could to comfort him, but then I took what was mine. I had to, you see. I had to know the truth!"

"And did you find what you were looking for?"

"Mostly. You can read it if you like," Hollins said, but Fanny shook her head. She had read Weatherford's letter this afternoon, and judging by Hollins' reaction, Rosaline's reply had been just as careful—not quite the smoking gun Hollins had hoped.

"What I don't understand," she said, "is what you've been doing in Treville-sur-Mer all this time. You had the letter. Why not confront your mother?"

"You think I didn't try?" Hollins almost wailed in despair. "That's all I did for over a month! I tried and tried, but I couldn't get close to her, not until you invited me. I thought all my prayers had been answered, but she looked right through me, and then she was gone."

"She wasn't just gone," Fanny pointed out, "she was murdered."

"Yes, murdered." Hollins grimaced. "And that's when I began to wonder: what if Weatherford had been murdered as well?"

"And still you kept silent?"

"I didn't know what else to do. What if I was next?"

"Mmm." Given her recent taste in men, Fanny found that she could no longer trust her judgment. She *wanted* to believe Hollins, but that only made her suspect him all the more. "That's quite a story, Joseph," she said, making no effort to hide her skepticism. "By your own admission, you had every reason and opportunity to kill Lord Weatherford and Lady Rosaline."

"No! Fanny, I swear—"

But whatever Hollins was going to swear was lost when the carriage door slid open, and who should enter but Raymond Montague Barrett?

"I'm not interrupting anything, am I?" he asked with faux politeness, brandishing a revolver in his hand. As he spoke, the train, at last, accompanied by billows of smoke and screeching wheels, pulled out of the station, and resumed its journey northward towards Paris.

Exactly on schedule.

34

OLD SINS, LONG SHADOWS

Fanny watched Raymond closely as the train hurtled down the French countryside, unable to quite believe her eyes. In her desperation to never be tricked or blinded again, all Fanny had managed to do was to trick and blind herself. She had been so sure that Hollins was guilty. So sure! And yet, the evidence was sitting right in front of her eyes, laughing at her. And he *was* laughing. That was the worst of it. No, not just laughing! Gloating.

Raymond, it seemed, was his mother's son, after all, and he was relishing the chance to take center stage himself, albeit in front of a captive audience, and crow over his victory like a pantomime villain in one of his mother's less successful plays.

Having immediately snatched the letter from Hollins' hand, Raymond was now holding Fanny and Hollins at gunpoint and in his proprietary glee, Fanny caught a shadow of Lady Rosaline's pride in her collection and her reputation. But while the mother had collected art and scandal, the son appeared to collect murders.

"And then, of course, there was Lord Weatherford!"

Raymond said with a self-satisfied smile. "His was the first but far and away the hardest murder to arrange. It was almost like a magic trick."

He paused expectantly, as if waiting for his audience to gasp and ask how he'd managed it. Hollins was in no mood to play along, but Fanny was only too happy to oblige.

"So, how *did* you do it, Raymond?" she asked, keenly aware that every minute Raymond remained talking was another minute he wasn't committing murder.

Raymond puffed up smugly in his seat. Although the wry glint in his eye suggested that he knew what she was about, he couldn't quite resist the chance to preen. In fairness, Fanny supposed, it was likely that he'd seldom had the opportunity, not with Lady Rosaline for a mother.

"First," Raymond began, "I made sure I was seen in Treville-sur-Mer that evening, having dinner in some middling little café. That was crucial. Even if the police suspected murder and even if they somehow connected Weatherford to me, I had the perfect alibi. I was on the other side of the country! How could I have possibly murdered him?"

"And how did you?" Fanny prompted.

"I waited until the Blue Train had left Treville-sur-Mer," Raymond explained, "and then I drove all through the night and into the morning. I kept to the back roads and did my best not to raise any alarms."

"You drove all the way to Paris?" Hollins asked incredulously. "Overnight?"

"It wasn't nearly as difficult as it sounds." He shrugged in a pantomime of modesty. "In fairness, it was George Dabney who first gave me the idea. One night while we were playing cards, he boasted about his ridiculous plan to race the train, so I wagered that he couldn't. There was no great plan about it. I just wanted to wipe the smirk off his face. But then..." Raymond shook his head. "I couldn't believe it! He'd almost done it—*would have* done it if not for those bloody policemen!"

"So you decided you could do better," Fanny said. "That you could succeed where a racecar driver had failed."

"An amateur racecar driver," Raymond corrected. "But yes, I did. Dabney was doing it for a lark, a bet, but I would be in deadly earnest. I knew from his telegram to my mother when Weatherford would be arriving in France and what train he would be on. From there, it was a simply matter of logistics and timing."

"What if the police had caught you?"

"While I was racing to Paris?" Raymond laughed. "Easy! I'd say that I was trying to embarrass my dear friend Dabney and succeed where he'd failed. The police would have rolled their eyes, muttered something impolite under their breath, and then let me off with the same slap on the wrist they gave him. No harm, no foul! All I'd have to do was find another way to…dispose of Weatherford."

"But you weren't caught."

"No, not even close! I was lucky. It was a clear, bright night, and the roads were all but empty, at least the ones I chose. And once in Paris, I parked my car in a friend's garage and boarded the southbound train under an assumed name. After that, all it took was a little drop of poison in poor Weatherford's soup. Not that it was easy to arrange, mind you, but that night everything was going my way. It was glorious!" Raymond's face fell. "Or at least it was, until I learned about that damn letter."

"Letters," Fanny pointed out. "There are two of them."

"Yes, I know." Raymond patted his pocket and favored Hollins with a slight nod. "You were ahead of me there," he admitted. "It wasn't until I confronted my mother that I even knew they existed, and I've been searching for them ever since."

"Killing for them, you mean," Fanny said coldly. "And futilely, as it turns out."

"Futilely?" Raymond smirked. "I've just recovered one from your young man here. I'd hardly call that futile."

"You may have recovered *one* letter, Mr. Barrett," she said. "But the police have the other one."

"How do you know that?"

"Why, I gave it to them myself."

"*You* did?" Fanny's answering smile was as smug as any Raymond had given. "Where was it?" he demanded. "I've looked for that blasted thing everywhere!"

"Where Lady Rosaline put it, of course," Fanny replied. "In the base of the statuette."

"Obviously." Raymond was not impressed. "I worked that much out ages ago. Mother thought she was so clever with her little riddles, but she never tired of saying that she and Mary Magdalene kept each other's secrets. What I want to know is: *where was the bloody statuette?*"

"Herr Darvas and his daughter *acquired* it, shall we say, under somewhat convoluted circumstances."

"Hah!" Raymond's laugh promised violence. "That sly old bastard! You're telling me that he's had it all this time and never said a word? Not even to try his hand at blackmail?"

Fanny nodded, taking vicious and well-earned amusement from his rage. "Herr Darvas was, I believe, far too prudent to blackmail a potential murderer. Besides, he had his own troubles."

"This is all very interesting," Hollins interjected. He had been listening so quietly as Raymond preened and Fanny bantered that she had almost forgotten he was there. "Tell me," he demanded with a sudden bout of courage. "How could you do it? How could you kill Weatherford? How could you kill our mother—"

"*Our* mother?" Raymond blinked in confusion for a

moment before his face split into the broadest, most gleefully vicious grin Fanny had ever encountered. "Oh, I see," he said. "You still haven't figured it out, have you, *brother?*"

"What do you mean? Figured what out?" Hollins glanced at Fanny, but she was as much in the dark as he was.

"Well, well, well." If anything, Raymond's grin only widened. "I suppose I can't blame you. I, myself, only discovered the truth by accident."

"What truth?"

The sound Raymond made in answer was less a laugh than a strange, broken screech. "You asked me how I could kill our mother," he said. "Well, it was quite simple. I smashed her head in with her beloved Bernini, the pride of her collection. And, I must say, I found it enormously satisfying. Although not, I think, as satisfying as killing you will be, *brother*."

"Wait!" Fanny cried, but it was no use. Raymond lifted his pistol, aimed, and a moment later, a gunshot rang out in the carriage.

And another. And another.

35

MR. QUAYLE EXPLAINS

They were all gathered on board the Blue Train in the dining car where, in a sense, it had all begun. Mr. Quayle absently noted the fresh flowers arrayed on every table and the handwritten menus placed at the ready, all sadly abandoned. The passengers and diners had been evacuated nearly half an hour ago, released into the wild to tell their stories and spread their gossip. Indeed, the poor, overworked spokesman for the Paris-Lyon-Méditerranée Railway Company, who had so nimbly swept Lord Weatherford's death under the carpet, would, Mr. Quayle feared, be unable to wave this evening's events away quite so quickly. Not now that the sumptuous, carpeted halls of Le Train Bleu, that temple of steam-powered luxury, had been desecrated, tainted, perhaps forever, by murder and death. And it was all *his* fault.

For all his protestations of modesty, of being a secretary and not a detective, secretly in his heart of hearts, Mr. Quayle had believed himself to be really quite good at this. Despite his supposed cleverness and vaunted efficiency, however, in the end, he had resorted to setting a trap and had allowed

Fanny to place herself in danger. If only he had been quicker, sharper, more alert, then all this might have been avoided.

If only.

Lord Unsworth and Lady Constance were seated on one side of the dining car, while Tallier and Jarre were on the other, with poor Mr. Hollins hovering awkwardly in the middle. And then, of course, there was the murderer himself, seething in his chair and flanked by Inspectors Duvot and Barras.

"You shot me," Raymond repeated for what must have been the hundredth time, blinking up at Fanny's triumphant visage in wounded bewilderment.

"Of course I did," she replied. "And fair is fair, you tried to shoot me first. Well, me *and* Hollins."

"Yes, but...you...how did you...?" His voice trailed off into a sudden grunt of pain, and as a police medic tended none too gently to the bullet wound in his leg, Fanny did not bother trying to hide her smirk.

"Did you really believe I wouldn't take precautions?" she asked. "I'm not a fool."

And with that she flounced with a palpable spring in her step over to the waiting arms of her family.

"It was rather clever of you," Mr. Quayle told her. "Taking the gun from my coat pocket before you left."

Fanny brightened. "I thought I would be better safe than sorry. When you gave me the bullets from Countess Scarlioni's gun for safekeeping, I saw you put the pistol in your coat pocket, so when I slipped away to see Hollins, I made a little detour to your room and took the liberty of borrowing it. When Raymond raised his gun to shoot Hollins, I fired first. It was as simple as that." Fanny shrugged, the very picture of false modesty. "I may not have the greatest aim in the world," she admitted, "but that was hardly necessary in such close quarters."

Mr. Quayle sighed. Fanny was positively pleased with herself, and rightfully so. She had apprehended a murderer, after all. But Quayle could not escape the feeling that she and the Unsworths had only averted tragedy by the skin of their teeth.

"Excuse-moi!" Chief Inspector Tallier cried. "Mesdames et Messieurs, if I might have your attention. There are, I think, still one or two questions that need to be answered, non? Monsieur Raymond Montague Barrett, would you care to explain yourself, s'il vous plaît?"

Raymond said nothing, merely glaring at all and sundry and pouting like a child who'd just lost his favorite game.

"Very well," Tallier said. "Then, perhaps, Monsieur Quayle here would oblige us by answering them."

"Me?"

"Bien sûr," Tallier nodded. "It was *you* who first suspected Raymond, n'est-ce pas?"

"I suppose so, but..." Quayle glanced around the dining car at the sea of expectant faces and one angry, bitter glare. "Well, if you insist, Chief Inspector," he said, rising wearily to his feet.

Removing his glasses, Mr. Quayle rubbed the bridge of his nose and took a moment to organize his thoughts.

"Since the start," he said, "Raymond has always struck me as the most likely suspect. Oh, he had an alibi for his mother's murder, of course! But it was shaky at best, and like the Scarlioni's pantomime with Arthur, it always felt somehow too perfect and yet not quite perfect enough. And later, no one seemed to know where he was when the Count was killed or when Carrodus was attacked. But even if I was right, Raymond had despised his mother for much of his life. So why kill her now?" Mr. Quayle shook his head. "I was still grasping in the dark, scrabbling for a motive, and there were so many motives: the theft, the collection, spurned lovers, old enemies, even the memoirs. So, I returned to the beginning, or at least *my* beginning. The very first question I ever asked myself about Lady Rosaline."

"Which was?" Lord Unsworth.

"The same question we were all asking ourselves, sir," Mr. Quayle explained. "What did she want with the family? Why was she so determined to approach you?"

"Those mysterious incidents she'd been experiencing," His Lordship realized. "Rosaline was convinced that someone was opening her letters, moving objects around on her desk, and even disturbing the paintings. So she turned to me, probably because there was no one else she could trust." He shook his head. "Or rather, she turned to *you*."

"Precisely," Mr. Quayle nodded. "And so, I applied myself to that original mystery, to the problem Lady Rosaline had wanted me to solve, and it immediately became clear that whoever it was, they were searching for something in particular. Lady Rosaline had told Lord Unsworth that she kept all of her correspondence going back decades. Could that have been what they were after? Her forthcoming memoirs had certainly ruffled a few feathers, and we soon discovered that she was attempting to blackmail a great many people. Was someone trying to take the bullets from her gun? Or were they intent on stopping publication?" Mr. Quayle grimaced. "Again, there were too many motives, too many possibilities, so I turned my attention from the *why* to the *who*."

"You mean, who had the opportunity to rifle through her papers?" Fanny asked.

"Exactly." Quayle offered her an encouraging smile. "Obviously, it had to be someone with access to the villa. Raymond and Vivi were both staying there, bringing Raymond firmly back into the picture, but Carrodus was also close at hand. He had a cottage on the estate, and even Léger only lived a few minutes away." Mr. Quayle shrugged apologetically. "And then there was Mr. Hollins, who was trying so hard to get close to Lady Rosaline and who later demonstrated his ability to sneak onto the grounds. The trouble with keeping one's friends close and one's enemies closer is that they are pressed together in easy reach. But in focusing on the incidents, I remembered something that His Lordship had told me quite early on."

"Did you?" Lord Unsworth straightened in his chair. "What was it I said?"

"Regarding Lady Rosaline," Mr. Quayle replied. "You told me, sir, that she had only approached you for help in Lord Weatherford's absence."

"That's right," His Lordship agreed. "She and Weatherford remained close until the end, whereas I hadn't spoken to Rosaline for decades. If he hadn't passed away, she would have turned to him in a heartbeat."

"And that made me wonder," Mr. Quayle said. "What if she *had* turned to him, after all? And sure enough, when Chief Inspector Tallier allowed me a peek at the police report, I discovered that Lady Rosaline had sent Weatherford a telegram summoning him to Treville-sur-Mer. His death had not been considered suspicious at the time, but now, with recent events in mind, it was a possibility that I could not ignore."

Mr. Quayle shook his head. "If Weatherford *had* been murdered, however, then Raymond was suddenly, irrevocably in the clear. After all, he had been seen by multiple witnesses in Treville-sur-Mer on that Wednesday evening. He even dropped his wife off at the station, so she could catch the *northbound* train to Paris and was seen eating at a local café nearly an hour later. How, then, could he possibly have been on board the *southbound* train *from* Paris the following afternoon? It was an impossibility." He nodded sharply to Raymond, one professional acknowledging another. "And yet, something about Raymond was still troubling me, and I realized there was one—*just one*—possible way he might have managed to reach Paris in time."

"Hence the car race," Chief Inspector Tallier noted. "I see. So, that's why you had Dabney and Arthur racing against the clock."

"Yes, although I had no great faith in how it would turn out," Mr. Quayle admitted. "I was beginning to turn my attention in other directions."

"Hollins?"

"Eventually." Mr. Quayle scowled. He did not like being fooled, even briefly. "Certainly, once Fanny and I had discovered the letter and learned of his true parentage, Hollins became a person of considerable interest, but what was his motive?"

"Revenge," M. Jarre suggested. "Punishing her for abandoning him."

"That was one possibility," Mr. Quayle agreed, politely ignoring just how dismissive Jarre had been of Hollins as a suspect only hours before. Indeed, dismissive of anyone who wasn't Jean-Paul Léger. "But I had seen Hollins at the Léger's house the day after the murder and spoken to him briefly at the memorial. He did not strike me as guilty but as grieving. Besides, Hollins' existence provided me with something I had lacked all along: a motive for Raymond."

"Hmm." Chief Inspector Tallier tapped his lip thoughtfully. "I think I understand the shape of what you are suggesting, mon ami, and I admit that it all seems perfectly reasonable on the face of it. You believe that Raymond has been killing to keep his mother's dirtiest little secret safe and to prevent anyone, least of all the man himself, from discovering Hollins' true parentage."

"That was the general idea, yes."

All eyes turned to Raymond, who shrunk back for a moment before raising his head high, unabashed and proud.

"Hmm." Tallier's eyes narrowed. "But given Lady Rosaline's reputation, an illegitimate son is hardly surprising, non? Indeed, it's almost expected, n'est-ce pas? And from what I have seen of him, Raymond has taken a somewhat knowing attitude to his mother's reputation. In fact, when Léger attempted to canonize Lady Rosaline, wasn't it Raymond who reminded everyone of her scandals?"

"Yes, it was," Mr. Quayle acknowledged. "And that, too, was interesting to me. Raymond, it seemed, was simultaneously repulsed by and yet heavily invested in his mother's reputation. Why would that be, I wondered. Why would Raymond, of all people, be so keen to remind everyone of his mother's scandals? Surely that would be counterproductive if he was trying to keep his bastard half-brother a secret? No! I was missing something, a vital piece of the puzzle. I could see where it might fit but not how or what."

Quayle glanced around the dining car, thrilled by the feeling of having them all hanging on his every word. He was enjoying himself, he realized, all doubt and guilt momentarily forgotten. *This* was his stage.

"And then," he said, "an idea occurred to me so outrageous and yet so obvious that everything, at last, began to make sense. Not all at once, mind you, but slowly, piece by piece."

"What idea?" Tallier asked. Quayle could practically see the Chief Inspector's mind whirring, and it wouldn't be long before the Frenchman overtook him.

"We all know Lady Rosaline's reputation," Mr. Quayle said. "The Scandalous Widow of Treville-sur-Mer with her three husbands and a thousand lovers. But—" he gestured sharply with his glasses, stabbing the air for emphasis, "the more we peer behind the curtain, the more it all rings oddly hollow. She may have spent her life surrounded by a horde of admirers, but were any of them ever truly more than that?"

"What do you mean?" Lord Unsworth asked with a frown.

"Well." Mr. Quayle hesitated. They were on potentially dangerous, not to mention embarrassing, ground now. "Despite his best efforts, and his claims to the contrary, Léger was never her lover. Indeed, Lady Rosaline does not appear to have taken *any* of her supposed lovers to bed—not Carrodus or Sir Julius or Lord Weatherford." There was another name on that list, of course, and they all knew it, but no one, least of all Quayle, was willing to mention Lord Unsworth.

His Lordship deliberately met Mr. Quayle's eyes and acknowledged his discretion with a slight nod and the barest hint of a smile, which Quayle returned.

"Even poor Vivi's father," he resumed, "who killed himself for love of Rosaline, was kept forever at a distance."

"And so?" Tallier prompted, although he must have had some inkling of where Quayle was headed.

"So," Mr. Quayle continued, "what if they *all* were? What if Lady Rosaline kept *everyone* at a distance, and her scandalous reputation was just that—a reputation. One as carefully cultivated as her status as an art collector and ultimately just as fraudulent. What if Lady Rosaline's truest, deepest, darkest secret was that she was and always had been *loyal?*"

"Loyal?" Lady Constance erupted into sudden but not entirely disbelieving laughter. "You can't be serious, Quayle!" she exclaimed.

"I am." Mr. Quayle did not retreat a single inch. "And once I'd realized that, much of what had been puzzling me about Lady Rosaline was suddenly clear. But where did that leave Hollins?" Mr. Quayle shrugged modestly. "In fact, it was you, Lady Constance, who filled in that last missing piece for me."

"Did I?" Lady Constance's eyes narrowed, but within

seconds her face had cleared in perfect understanding. "Oh, I see!" she nodded to herself, satisfied. "Of course."

"Forgive me, Mr. Hollins," Quayle said, turning to the forlorn young man, "this will not be easy for you to hear."

"Easy?" Hollins stared up at him incredulously. "My brother—"

"*Half*-brother," Raymond interjected, unable to help himself.

"My brother," Hollins continued doggedly, "tried to murder me less than an hour ago, and just before that, Fanny all but accused me of murder. None of this, Mr. Quayle, has been remotely easy."

It was a fair point and only made Quayle's role even harder. "I understand," he said. "And I am sorry, but, despite what we all believed, Lady Rosaline is not your mother. Indeed, for the purposes of this investigation, your mother is largely beside the point. The real question is: who was your *father*?"

"My father?" Hollins repeated in a small, broken voice. "Weatherford, surely?"

"No, I'm afraid not."

"Then who?" Hollins demanded. The poor man looked as though he was about to cry. "Tell me, please. Who was my father?"

He had asked Quayle, but it was Lady Constance who answered.

"Your father, Mr. Hollins," she said, her voice like a pronouncement of doom, "was General Alexander Montague Barrett."

36

CONFESSIONS

No one spoke. They scarcely even breathed as Lady Constance's revelation echoed throughout the dining car. All was silence. All was still. And then, Raymond began to laugh. It was the same screeching, broken laugh as before, only this time, there was a vicious, vengeful edge to it. He had failed to kill Hollins, but here and now, Raymond could still hurt him.

"How does it feel?" Raymond asked, his voice dripping with scorn. "How does it feel to have your whole world, everything you thought you knew, twisted and mutilated? Tell me, *brother*, how does it feel?"

The words rang out like gunshots, and Hollins fell back under the assault. All of a sudden, the man of words, the would-be playwright, was unable to speak or think. Watching him shudder and almost crawl into his seat, Mr. Quayle thought he could understand, at least in part, the maelstrom in Hollins' mind. Quayle, himself, had experienced it once before, been shaken to his very foundations, and he was genuinely sorry to have placed Hollins in this position. But Raymond was a bitter, spiteful creature, and if the urge to lash out caused him to loosen his tongue, then so be it. Besides, Hollins deserved the chance to confront his brother face to face, to hear the truth.

"Stop it!" Fanny cried, leaning forward to rest a comforting hand on Hollins' arm. "Give him a moment, please!"

"Why?" Raymond demanded, turning to her with a violent tilt of his head. "No one gave *me* a moment. All I had was my father's stupid valet, Cummings. Once that man started, he wouldn't stop! He just wouldn't stop!" Raymond balled his hand into a fist and pounded his leg—once, twice for emphasis, then winced in pain. "I had to sit there at his bedside and listen as he tore my world apart. So my brother Joseph here can bloody well sit and listen too!"

"How did you find out?" Quayle interjected. "About Hollins? About your father?"

"Haven't you worked that out? You seem to know everything else."

"Hardly everything," Mr. Quayle demurred. "Although, I imagine it had something to do with your mother's memoirs."

"Bravo!" Raymond sneered. "The clever Mr. Quayle!"

Unmoved by Raymond's scorn, Quayle simply waited. Some men needed to shout, but he seldom did.

"Vivi and I were living in Paris, you see," Raymond said, looking anywhere but at Quayle, "when I suddenly began to hear rumors about my mother's memoirs, usually from old, worried friends desperate for reassurance. Not that I had any reassurances to give." He shrugged. "Initially, of course, I was unconcerned by the whole business. I had built a life for myself outside my mother's shadow, away from the shame of her past, and nothing she had said or done could possibly hurt me anymore. Or so I thought. But then, quite by chance, I ran into a friend of my father who pointed out that it wasn't just my mother's indiscretions that she could share with the world. According to him, my father had a few secrets of his own, and she knew where the bodies were buried, so to speak."

"And you believed him?" Mr. Quayle asked. "Just like that?"

"Not at first," Raymond replied. "Not for some months, in fact, but as the rumors swirled louder and louder, I found that I couldn't ignore the possibility."

"So you went to confront her at the villa?"

"Absolutely not!" Raymond was aghast. "I went to England to see the only man living who might know the truth —my father's old valet and former army batman, Cummings. He was dying by the time I tracked him down, not surprising, considering he was already quite old when I was a boy, but he confirmed what I'd feared. There *were* skeletons in my father's cupboard."

"Not quite the paragon you'd thought, then?" That was Fanny, the words slipping through her teeth almost before she realized. Her impudence was rewarded with a terrifying glare, but even as Lord Unsworth wrapped a protective arm around her, she leaned forward to meet Raymond's gaze unflinchingly. Only one of them had been shot that night, and it wasn't her.

"Before he married my mother," Raymond continued, his sudden burst of ire sputtering, "Father had an affair with one of her actress friends and got the foolish girl pregnant. So, before she agreed to marry him, my mother, of all people, made him agree to help her friend and, more importantly, *the child*."

"Me." Hollins was spellbound, a peculiar mix of disgust and desperation playing across his face.

"You!" Raymond spat.

"W-w-what happened to her?" Hollins asked slowly, the

words forced from between sobbing breaths. "What happened to my mother?"

"She died in childbirth," Raymond answered savagely. "But *my* mother took it upon herself to ensure that you were properly looked after." Raymond scoffed. "Mother even allowed the world to think that she was the one who had been unfaithful, who had given birth to a child out of wedlock. Although Mother already had something of a reputation, so I doubt it was that much of a sacrifice." He scowled, unable to hide the wounded, childlike bewilderment at the heart of his bitterness. "Even so," he added, "it was more consideration than she ever showed me or my father."

Mr. Quayle was not altogether surprised. From what he'd heard, General Alexander Montague Barrett did not sound as though he'd earned much consideration.

"But that wasn't enough for him," Raymond continued. "Oh, no! After decades of silence, of keeping my father's secrets, all of a sudden, that fool, Cummings, couldn't keep his damned mouth shut! I had to hear about my father's parade of mistresses. And, worse, he wouldn't stop praising my mother. It was all 'Lady Rosaline this' and 'Lady Rosaline that.' In Cummings' telling, she was a model of bloody virtue. My mother, the *faithful*, uncomplaining wife! Have you ever heard such nonsense?"

"Except it wasn't nonsense, was it?" Mr. Quayle pointed out, but Raymond ignored him.

"All my life," he said, "I've idolized my father. He was a hero, a soldier, a righteous man and, most of all, he was everything my mother was not. And this...this...this wizened old servant dared besmirch his memory? To lie to me, the General's own son? No!" Raymond jerked his head from side to side, each movement visceral, almost violent enough to crack his neck. "No!" he repeated. "I couldn't have that! Nothing could be allowed to tarnish my father's reputation! Nothing! And I couldn't have people finding out about you." He nodded to Hollins, who was staring at him in dawning horror. "So, I..."

"Killed him," Hollins realized. "He could have told me so much, and you killed him."

"Smothered him with a pillow," Raymond said, looking quite satisfied with himself. He had been aiming for nonchalance, but there was a vindictiveness in his eyes and in the corners of his mouth. "The man was dying anyway."

"How did you find me?" Hollins asked, and Mr. Quayle was pleased to see him straightening his back and controlling the tremble in his voice.

"Cummings couldn't remember which of Mother's endless admirers had taken you in," Raymond replied, "but I knew that even all those years ago, Lord Weatherford was the only one she would have trusted with something like this, the only one who would have agreed. And once I learned of Weatherford's ward, it was not difficult to fill in the pieces. Weatherford was always my mother's closest friend, and most damning of all, you were just about the right age."

"So, what then?" asked Hollins.

"I returned to France and feigned a reconciliation with my mother. Vivi had been pushing me to do it for ages—a chance for her to confront the woman who had driven her father to suicide—but I'd resisted. Now, though, at long last, I obliged her. Mother was so pleased! But all I wanted was to find and destroy any evidence of my father's infidelity—letters, birth certificates, anything!"

"So, Quayle was right," Fanny breathed, unable to help herself. "You were the cause of all those odd disturbances we heard about. The objects being moved, the paintings disturbed, even her correspondence not being where she left it. That was all you, searching."

"Quite right," Raymond sneered. "I was not quite as subtle as I'd hoped, and Mother started getting worried. I don't know if she ever fully suspected me, but she began taking precautions. First, she moved her archives to Carrodus' house for safekeeping, and then she summoned Lord Weatherford to France." He grinned. "That was a godsend. The perfect opportunity! Weatherford had been a recluse for years, running his businesses by telegram and phone, but he couldn't resist my mother's call. So I killed him before he could arrive, and on the night of the party, I finally confronted my mother outright. Let's just say it did not go well," he finished with a menacing glare.

"And you did all this," Mr. Quayle said, carefully reentering the conversation, "to protect your father's reputation? A man who had been dead for decades?"

"Reputation is everything," Raymond replied. "I learned that from my mother."

"And there was nothing else, no other reason?"

Raymond's eyes narrowed. "What do you know?" he demanded.

Mr. Quayle was triumphant. "Earlier this evening," he revealed, "I received a telegram from my old friend, Inspector Wintle, which confirmed my suspicions."

"Ah!" Chief Inspector Tallier called from the other side of the room. "I was wondering if you were ever going to mention that."

"All in good time," Mr. Quayle . "Inspector Wintle informed me that when General Alexander Montague Barrett made his will, he was unforgivingly exact, or vague, I suppose, depending on your point of view, and left everything he owned, all his wealth and his estate in its entirety to his *eldest son*."

"Damn you!" Raymond hissed.

"Now," Mr. Quayle continued, "when he wrote his will, the General's eldest was his son by a previous marriage, but that unfortunate young man died in an aeroplane accident, leaving Raymond as the sole heir. But if Hollins, who is, I believe, almost exactly a year older, could prove that he was the General's son, then—"

"Wait!" Hollins frowned. "You mean that I'm...that I..."

"As far as the law is concerned," Mr. Quayle said, "illegitimate or not, you are General Alexander Montague Barrett's sole heir."

"Ah, I see." Chief Inspector Tallier clicked his tongue, his expression halfway between annoyance and admiration, as he glared at Raymond.

"What?" Mr. Quayle asked, noticing his expression. "What is it, Chief Inspector?"

"The first time we met," the Chief Inspector said, "Monsieur Raymond Barrett told me everything I needed to know. He insisted that he had no reason to kill for *his mother's* money, and I believed him. But he never said anything about his father's."

"No," Mr. Quayle said, turning to Raymond with a victorious smile. "He wouldn't, would he?"

37

LOOSE ENDS AND FOND FAREWELLS

Mr. Quayle glanced around the platform at Treville-sur-Mer. The late afternoon sun was starting to sink towards the horizon, and he could hear the babble of voices as a throng of passengers embarked onto the Blue Train, the Unsworths among them. The porters had just finished collecting their luggage, and Quayle could see His Lordship huddled a few feet away with Lady Constance and Arthur, the three of them resolutely not watching as Fanny and her young man, Hollins, were exchanging words further down the platform.

Almost a week had passed since Raymond's arrest—the blink of an eye and a lifetime all in one—and in that week, life on the Riviera had entered into a kind of reverie, as if the Unsworths were all sleepwalking through their days. Before, the Riviera had been the dream, but now the sun, the sea, the sky, and all the rest hardly registered. Now it was the Unsworths themselves who were the dream—walking shades and echoes, stumbling through their days in a blind stupor.

Arthur, newly released from prison, had returned from Paris in high spirits only to discover that Fanny had nearly died and, worse, that she had stolen his thunder. If anyone, he thought, should have the chance to chase a murderer down the length of the Blue Train, it should have been *him*. Naturally, Lady Constance had not taken kindly to that remark and had hauled her son away from the breakfast table by his ear, leaving the others to eat in awkward silence, accompanied by the distant sounds of a mother happily haranguing her son.

Two days later, also at breakfast, His Lordship announced that the family would be returning to England. He had decided, and rightfully so in Mr. Quayle's opinion, that the family's sojourn on the Riviera had been a complete and unmitigated disaster. They had come to escape the shadow of one murder case only to wander straight into another, and if that was to be their life, then Lord Unsworth was determined to endure it from the comfort of his own home and his own library.

Therefore, bags packed and travel arrangements made, the Unsworth family was now loitering on the platform, ready to board the Blue Train one last time.

"Ah, Monsieur Quayle! I hoped I might find you here!" Mr. Quayle turned with a smile to find Chief Inspector Tallier weaving his way toward him through the crowd.

"I wasn't sure you'd come," Mr. Quayle greeted the Frenchman.

"But, of course, mon ami! If nothing else, I had to share with you the news."

"Oh?"

"Monsieur Carrodus," Tallier revealed. "He is awake!"

"That is good news." Mr. Quayle nodded to himself. "Fanny will be relieved. She was fond of him, I think. But is he talking?"

"Not yet," Tallier said. "But the doctors tell me it will not be long."

"And Raymond?" Mr. Quayle asked. "Or am I not permitted to inquire?"

Tallier waved his hand dismissively. "Monsieur Raymond will make a full recovery," he said. "His lawyers, they make the noise, but your Mademoiselle Fanny did not hit anything vital."

"She might be less relieved by that," Mr. Quayle murmured.

"Oui, c'est possible," Tallier grinned in acknowledgment. "Unfortunately, since the train, he has become far less cooperative."

"Oh?"

"Raymond continues to profess his wife's innocence. She may have lied for him at the party and played an important role in his Blue Train pantomime, but according to Raymond, Vivi knew nothing, absolutely nothing."

"I see." Mr. Quayle sounded about as convinced as Tallier looked. "And do you believe him?"

"Pas du tout," the Chief Inspector shook his head. "But as Jarre has pointed out to me more than once these past few days, it is not what we *believe* that matters. It is what we can *prove* and, alas, we have no concrete evidence to implicate Vivi in any of it. However, it is hard not to notice that she seems to have gotten what she wanted after all. With Lady Rosaline dead and her family destroyed, Vivi's vengeance is complete."

"Even if you're right," Mr. Quayle said, "I wonder if Vivi still considers it a victory. You said she came to love Raymond, yes?"

Tallier considered the question for a moment, then nodded firmly. "Oui," he confirmed. "I would say she does."

"And if he's still lying for her, I'd say he loves her back." Mr. Quayle chuckled. "How strange."

"L'amour," Tallier said softly. "But Raymond is hardly the

only one lying," he pointed out. "Even you have not been entirely honest with me."

"I beg your pardon?"

"Come now, mon ami! Did you really think I believed your ridiculous little story about Lady Rosaline's letter accidentally falling out of the statuette?"

"But it did," Mr. Quayle protested in all honesty.

"Oui, of that, I have no doubt," Tallier replied. "I'm quite sure that it was hidden precisely where you said it was, but as for who really found it..." Tallier narrowed his eyes. "I suppose legally I would be well within my rights to have you arrested for withholding evidence, but in the circumstances, that would be a tad ungrateful, n'est-ce pas?"

"I'm hardly likely to disagree," Mr. Quayle replied with a wry smirk. "Not when I'm sure you have a pretty shrewd idea who it might have been."

"But, of course!" Tallier grinned. "That is not so difficult, mon ami, but finding them, encouraging them to talk? That is another matter. Countess Scarlioni has holed herself up at the Italian Embassy, no doubt hoping to ride out the storm, and as for—" Tallier broke off suddenly to tip his hat at someone passing behind Quayle. "Madame Léger," he greeted. "This is a surprise."

Mr. Quayle turned, and sure enough, there was Anne-Marie Léger dressed in her finest with her luggage in one hand and a determined expression on her face.

"Chief Inspector," she greeted, her eyes darting to Quayle. "Monsieur."

Mr. Quayle inclined his head in greeting. The two had not spoken since the hotel room. Indeed, as far as he was aware, none of them had spoken to either himself or Fanny. Too many bridges had been burnt.

"I understand that you have released my husband, Chief Inspector," Madame Léger said. Although she was speaking to Tallier, her gaze remained fixed on Quayle's face as if searching or accusing.

"Oui, madame," Tallier replied, feigning not to notice the interplay. "There was nothing we could hold him on, although I admit we are still investigating how Lady Rosaline's statuette came to be in your studio."

"My husband's studio," she corrected.

"As you say." Chief Inspector Tallier shrugged as if it was of no consequence and instead pointed to her luggage. "You are leaving Treville-sur-Mer?" he asked.

"I have family in Paris," Madame Léger explained. "No matter what happens now, I can no longer stay with that man. Jean-Paul and I are through, and I feel that it is long past time I lived my own life, in Paris perhaps, or Venice, or..."

Tallier cleared his throat delicately. "I would appreciate it, madame," he said, "if you were to remain in France, preferably in Paris, for the time being."

"Pourquoi?"

"Because, Madame Léger, there are still some questions I may need you to answer. Par exemple, were you aware that your good friend, Márta, and her father, Herr Darvas, have both disappeared overnight? Their hotel room is empty, and they have removed a substantial sum of money from their bank accounts, as well as, I understand, from the endowment at the Musée de Saint-Jean le Décapité. I don't suppose you know anything about that, madame?"

Madame Léger did not. Indeed, she quickly, and not altogether convincingly, professed herself to be shocked and appalled before making her excuses and quietly taking her leave.

"You're just letting her walk away?"

"Not at all, mon ami," the Chief Inspector said. "I have men following her even as we speak, and we already have eyes on her family in Paris."

"You believe Herr Darvas will contact her?"

"Or Márta." Tallier smiled sharply. "Madame Léger knows too much, I think, to be left to her own devices. If this Herr Darvas is who I think he is—"

"And who is that?"

"La Chimère, of course," Chief Inspector Tallier replied. "L'original! And if I am correct, as I see from your blank expression that I am, then Herr Darvas is a professional, and he will not like to leave the loose ends lying about."

"He is quite careful, I think," Mr. Quayle warned. "A cautious man."

"Naturellement." Tallier was undeterred. "But his daughter less so, non? And Madame Léger is not the professional. She will make mistakes. They *all* will, sooner or later." The owlish little Frenchman had never looked more dangerous. "I may have been wrong about the Count and Countess, but now that I know the truth, I promise you that I will catch La Chimère in the end."

"Of that, M. Tallier, I have no doubt," Mr. Quayle said. "I have nothing but faith in you."

"Merci," Chief Inspector Tallier replied with a broad smile. "It has been a pleasure, mon ami. If you are ever in Paris, it would be my honor to show you around, and I am sure my wife, she would love to meet you."

"That's kind of you." Mr. Quayle reached out, and the two men shook hands farewell. As they did so, however, Mr. Quayle felt Tallier slip something into his pocket—something old and crinkly and ever so slightly singed. It felt rather like a letter.

"Very kind," Mr. Quayle repeated and meant it.

"Au revoir, Monsieur Quayle," M. Tallier said. "Au revoir."

And then the owlish little man was gone, disappearing back into the crowd with a whistle on his lips.

38

THE ROAD NOT TAKEN

"Are you sure you're alright?" Fanny asked. She and Hollins were standing slightly apart from the others, having been granted a veneer of privacy on the crowded platform. Poor Hollins had always seemed vaguely lost to her, but now, cleared of all charges, he had somehow gotten worse.

"I'm not sure what I am," he admitted. "It's so strange. After a lifetime of searching, I have the answers I've been looking for, if not the answers I expected." He snorted. "I was convinced Lady Rosaline was my mother and Weatherford my father. So convinced!"

"It was an easy mistake to make in the circumstances," Fanny replied. She had made it herself, after all.

"I know." Hollins nodded. "But I'm still unsure how I feel about it all. My mother, my true mother, died when I was born. I don't even know her name."

"Celia," Fanny supplied, happy to be of some help. "Celia Ward."

"But how did you—?"

"My Aunt Constance," Fanny explained, "can be a font of information when the mood strikes her. She knew your father, the General, briefly many years ago, and her mind is a repository of scandals."

"I see." Hollins looked briefly hopeful. "I don't suppose she would—"

"—I highly doubt it," Fanny said, glancing over her shoulder. Arthur was helping his mother up onto the train, like the dutiful son he was when sufficiently bullied. As if aware of her gaze, Aunt Constance turned and eyed Fanny and Hollins sharply. But after a moment or so, her face softened ever so slightly, although most people would not have recognized it as such. Acknowledging it for the peace offering it was, Fanny smiled in thanks. "Although, perhaps," she said, "Aunt Constance might be willing to write you a letter, but I wouldn't expect much more than that. I doubt her stories will be...favorable."

"She gave me my mother's name," Hollins replied. "Which is more than I've ever known. So, anything, anything at all, would be a blessing, no matter what it is. After all, as far as newfound relatives go, I doubt anyone could be quite as bad as Raymond."

"Well, he *did* try to murder you," Fanny said. "Not to mention me."

"Yes, and I'm awfully sorry about that. It's no easy thing learning that you have a half-brother at the same moment he tries to kill you for money you never even knew you had."

Fanny paused a moment. "Has there been any word?"

"I'll be meeting with the Montague Barret Family lawyer later this week," Hollins revealed. "But given the precise wording of the will, it seems likely that I shall be coming into a small fortune, whatever Raymond hasn't already spent, at least."

"Congratulations." Fanny had never personally needed to worry about money in her life, but she understood, intellectually, that it could be quite debilitating to be without.

"Thank you." Hollins shook his head. "I've never had money of my own," he said. "Before I cut ties, Weatherford provided me with a generous stipend, of course, but it never felt as though it was my money—not really. But now?" There was that look again. Lost and adrift, Hollins had never seemed so uncertain. "I'm not quite sure what to do with it all," he revealed. "Give it to the poor? Donate it to the Socialist Party? Buy myself a theater and start a company? Or, perhaps, a theatrical magazine? I just...I don't know."

"Well," Fanny said with a smile. "It's your money, Joeseph. Your decision."

"Yes, well..." Hollins shifted awkwardly, and Fanny felt a sudden premonition trickle through her thoughts and down into her stomach. "Actually," Hollins said, "I was rather hoping it could be *our* decision."

Fanny raised her eyebrows. "Are you asking me to marry you, Mr. Hollins?"

"Yes, I...I suppose I am."

"Well, that's very flattering," she said. "And I'm quite fond of you—"

"*But?*" Hollins prompted. It was the first time in their acquaintance that he had ever interrupted her.

"But," Fanny continued with an apologetic little smile, "I have no intention of marrying you. I am genuinely sorry that I suspected you of murder, but the plain fact of the matter is that you did lie to me, Joseph, and you kept secrets from me. And if I've learned nothing else from recent events, it's that I could never permit that in a husband. Not ever." She placed a consoling, rueful hand on his arm. "I am sorry," she said.

"No," Hollins sighed, "you're not, and I was a fool to ask." He shrugged. "But then, I've been a fool about quite a bit lately, haven't I?"

"We both have, I think," Fanny agreed. "But I hope that despite everything, we can still part as friends."

"Of course," Hollins said, swallowing his dismay and his pride. "You saved my life, Fanny, and I'll never forget that. *Never*."

He held out his hand, and Fanny shook it firmly and then, after a slight hesitation, placed a single chaste kiss on his cheek.

"Goodbye," she whispered softly but without regret. "Goodbye."

* * *

With a jolt and a mournful cry of the engine, the Blue Train lurched into motion and departed, at long last, from the station. His Lordship was sitting alone by the window, watching as Treville-sur-Mer receded from view, lost behind the hills and trees, a soon-to-be distant memory, or so he hoped.

Lord Unsworth had never considered himself a man given to regret. He had devoted himself to his estate, his collection, his family, and his books, and he had been content to do so. He still felt the loss of his son keenly, of course, like a wound that refused to fully heal, but that was not a regret as such. It was a tragedy, yes, but also a source of pride. Teddy had given his life for King and Country, as many of their ancestors had done before him going back to the days of William the Conqueror, and there was solace in that and strength. Besides, Lord Unsworth thought, he still had Fanny.

His darling girl had nearly gotten herself killed in a stunt worthy of her cousin, and the thought of it still sent his heart rattling in his chest. That would have broken him, utterly and finally, but thankfully, all was well that ended well. His Lordship only hoped that Fanny didn't have too many regrets of her own.

He was sure that boy, Hollins, had proposed. Lord

Unsworth had not seen him produce a ring or bend down on one knee, but he was certain, nonetheless, just as he was certain of Fanny's answer. Connie would be pleased, naturally. She had not liked the socialist even before he was a suspected murderer, and his innocence had not altered her opinion in the slightest. Lord Unsworth laughed to himself. As if he had been any less disapproving!

He had always thought that Fanny and Hollins were ill-suited, almost as ill-suited as he and Lady Rosaline had been all those years ago. It had taken His Lordship a long time to accept that, but it appeared that his niece was wiser in such matters than he had ever been, although if so, it was a wisdom dearly bought.

"Your Lordship?" There was a knock on the cabin door, and Lord Unsworth took a second to compose himself.

"Enter," he called, and the door slid open immediately to admit his secretary's bespectacled form.

"You wished to speak with me, Your Lordship?" Mr. Quayle asked, folding his arms behind him and standing at attention, almost as if facing a firing squad. The secretary had been like that all week—diffident, apologetic, and oozing guilt. He had even tried to tender his resignation, as if Lord Unsworth had any intention of letting the man go. Quayle was a part of the family in his own particular way.

"Yes." Lord Unsworth nodded to the seat across from him. "Please, sit, Mr. Quayle."

"Thank you, sir."

"It was unfair of me to ask you to solve Rosaline's murder and insist that you become involved."

"Sir, I—"

His Lordship held up a hand hand to silence him. "It has not escaped my notice, Mr. Quayle, that this is the *second* time I have asked you to solve a murder on my behalf and the second time you have succeeded beyond my wildest expectations. I understand your feelings, but you are not responsible for my niece's actions, or my nephew's, for that matter."

"You asked me to keep them safe, sir," Quayle protested. "And I failed."

"You've twice done the impossible, Mr. Quayle," Lord Unsworth replied, "but that does not make you a miracle worker. Fanny is a woman grown, as much as it pains me to say it, and her mistakes must be her own. Now, this is my word, and it is final. There will be no resignation. In fact, I fear we will soon need your services more than ever. I thought we could escape to the Riviera, but instead, we are worse off than we began."

Mr. Quayle frowned. "There have been a few...murmurings in the press," he admitted. "And I imagine they will only increase once we're back in England."

"Two murders in one year!" Lord Unsworth was aghast. "Well, two cases. I'm not even sure how many bodies there've been..."

"Six, sir," Mr. Quayle offered helpfully. "Thankfully, Carrodus is recovering, or else it would have been seven."

"Six murders!" His Lordship exclaimed, then sighed and ran his fingers nervously through his hair. "Connie was right. This *is* starting to become a habit."

"Hopefully not, sir." But even Quayle's perfectly neutral expression could not entirely hide his doubts.

"At least you were able to find Rosaline's killer," Lord Unsworth said. "It is, I admit, a cold comfort, but a comfort, nonetheless. It's strange," he mused. "She was an impossible dream, for more reasons than one, but now that she's dead, I..." He fell silent. In truth, he was not quite sure what he wanted to say or what he even meant. "You understand, don't you, Quayle?" he asked.

"Yes, sir," Mr. Quayle replied in a distant, faraway voice. "I understand all about impossible dreams." And then, without another word, Mr. Quayle reached into his pocket and removed a yellowing, slightly singed envelope from his pocket. On the front, it read in familiar handwriting: "To Rosaline."

Lord Unsworth blinked, unable to believe his eyes. Quayle, it seemed, had performed yet another miracle. "Is that my letter?" he asked, dumbfounded.

"Yes, sir," Mr. Quayle nodded. "The police recovered it from Carrodus' house."

"But, surely this is...evidence."

"A great deal of evidence was lost in the fire, sir," Quayle replied. "Who's to say that your letter was not one of them? Not I and not, as it turns out, Chief Inspector Tallier."

"I see." Lord Unsworth's eyes never left the envelope.

"Do you want it, sir?" Mr. Quayle asked.

Did he? Lord Unsworth frowned thoughtfully. Ever since Rosaline had first mentioned it in passing, His Lordship had struggled to remember what he'd written. Lovestruck nonsense, of course. And a poem that should never, ever see the light of day. But those recollections were just vagaries. When it came down to it, no matter how he tried, His Lordship could not recollect a single line of the poem, let alone the rest of it. All lost in the mists of time. And, perhaps, it was better that way.

"No," Lord Unsworth finally answered. "I don't believe I do."

Mr. Quayle accepted his decision without surprise or comment. "Then what would you have me do with it?"

"I believe you said that a great deal of evidence was lost in a fire," His Lordship said. "Perhaps the police are simply confused about *which* fire."

"Sir." Mr. Quayle nodded; his instructions understood. "Will that be all, Your Lordship?"

"Yes, thank you, Quayle."

Lord Unsworth turned back to the window, although his mind was far away and long ago, and he did not notice when Mr. Quayle silently took his leave, any more than he noticed the sea and the sky alight with the purples, oranges, and reds of the setting sun.

"No regrets," he said to himself, alone in his cabin, and idly wondered if it was a lie and if that even mattered.

* * *

FOR HIS PART, Mr. Quayle returned to his own, much smaller berth, one he shared with Lord Unsworth's butler, Perkins. The letter had a strange weight in his pocket, and he was aware of it crinkling and rustling every time he moved. There would be a chance to burn it soon enough, but until then, Mr. Quayle was the custodian of the final tangible piece of a long-ago love—a love that nearly thirty years later had still been strong enough to motivate His Lordship in avenging Lady Rosaline, although not quite so strong as to live forever. Lord Unsworth's quest for justice had been the last ember, unexpectedly reignited by Rosaline's death, but that was all over now. Or was it?

His Lordship had spoken of impossible dreams, and for a moment, Quayle had been transported back to the mud and trenches. He had seen again in his mind's eye all those men and boys who had died in their thousands while he himself survived. And he had thought too of all the roads that could never be traveled, of the nurse in Saint-Domnin who had tended his wounds, and, as always, he had thought of Teddy.

With a heavy sigh, Mr. Quayle abandoned his musings, burying them deep in his mind. He had his instructions, after all. The rest was ancient history.

Settling into his seat, Quayle yawned and nodded to Perkins. It had been a long, long week, and he was tired—so very, very tired. In the end, he had never found the time to wander through the streets of Treville-sur-Mer or to visit the markets and towns. Nor had he managed to lose himself in the olive groves and oleander trees, practice his French, or do any of the dozens of things he had imagined. Instead, he had given a murdered woman justice and, more importantly, had kept the family safe. And now, at long last, he could rest.

Within moments of closing his eyes, Mr. Quayle was fast asleep and his dreams, if he had any, were all his own.

THE END

ABOUT THE AUTHOR

Anthony Slayton is a self-confessed Anglophile, at least when it comes to murder and death. Author of the *Mr. Quayle Mysteries*, he is a life-long mystery aficionado—the more bodies, the better! In his spare time, he can probably be found walking in the park or binge-watching one mystery series or another (possibly just rewatching Poirot and Midsomer Murders for the umpteenth time). You can visit him at...

anthonyslayton.com

Made in the USA
Monee, IL
15 October 2023